DEATH IN DISGUISE

Dressed in the grimy overalls and shapeless cap of a maintenance man, swinging a lantern and whistling an old railroad ditty, Lt. Ryne Lanark started down a stretch of track not far from the main station downtown. High above him, on the bridges that crossed Chicago River, the city's traffic flowed by. But down here, in the grease-blackened domain of the train engine, it was like another world.

The warehouse loomed ahead, just as the message said it would. As an overall wearing railman, Lanark ambled closer. It was time to make his move.

Just when he was within fifteen feet of the building, it suddenly erupted in an explosion of flames, throwing him to the ground, shards of glass and pieces of wood flying around him. Slowly, he got to his feet. He was shook up—but he knew he was okay.

He also knew that he now had his own personal vendetta: to find the bastard who had set him up for death, if it was the last damn thing he ever did!

BLOCKBUSTER FICTION FROM PINNACLE BOOKS!

THE FINAL VOYAGE OF THE S.S.N. SKATE   (17-157, $3.95)
by Stephen Cassell
The "leper" of the U.S. Pacific Fleet, SSN 578 nuclear attack sub
SKATE, has one final mission to perform—an impossible act of
piracy that will pit the underwater deathtrap and its inexperienced
crew against the combined might of the Soviet Navy's finest!

QUEENS GATE RECKONING   (17-164, $3.95)
by Lewis Purdue
Only a wounded CIA operative and a defecting Soviet ballerina
stand in the way of a vast consortium of treason that speeds toward the hour of mankind's ultimate reckoning! From the best-
selling author of THE LINZ TESTAMENT.

FAREWELL TO RUSSIA   (17-165, $4.50)
by Richard Hugo
A KGB agent must race against time to infiltrate the confines of
U.S. nuclear technology after a terrifying accident threatens to
unleash unmitigated devastation!

THE NICODEMUS CODE   (17-133, $3.95)
by Graham N. Smith and Donna Smith
A two-thousand-year-old parchment has been unearthed, un-
leashing a terrifying conspiracy unlike any the world has previously known, one that threatens the life of the Pope himself, and
the ultimate destruction of Christianity!

*Available wherever paperbacks are sold, or order direct from the
Publisher. Send cover price plus 50¢ per copy for mailing and
handling to Pinnacle Books, Dept.17-239, 475 Park Avenue
South, New York, N.Y. 10016. Residents of New York, New Jer-
sey and Pennsylvania must include sales tax. DO NOT SEND
CASH.*

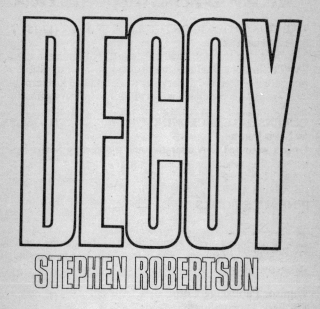

DECOY

STEPHEN ROBERTSON

PINNACLE BOOKS
WINDSOR PUBLISHING CORP.

PINNACLE BOOKS

are published by

Windsor Publishing Corp.
475 Park Avenue South
New York, NY 10016

First printing: June, 1989

Printed in the United States of America

PROLOGUE

It ran *through* her ears, through the spirals, like the blood, going *whoosh-around, whoosh-around, whoosh-around* inside the larger noise that was a continual dull *thrum: thrum-thrum, thrum-thrum-thrum-thrum.*

The sound thundered through her being like that of a roller coaster at top speed. It rang in her ears.

And then she heard no more.

Nor did she feel the incision made across her eyelids after he closed them, first a slit down and then across, leaving a bloody cross at each eye. Another cut was made at the nose, same configuration, drawing more blood but not enough. He dipped his brush into a cup of his own blood, which had been brought to him, and added a bit more here.

With the scalpel he next cut a twisting, curling line on each cheek. Satisfied, he cocked his head to one side, felt the approval well up from deep within him and all around him, and then plunged the scalpel into the throat, severing the jugular.

A crooked, roving tear was made across the throat,

radiating from the jugular on each side. Once more there was not enough blood, so he used a brush, a larger one this time, tamping at the line of the wound with it, watching it drop, slowly dry and coagulate along the line, sending rivulets all about.

He was done.

The others could do what they wished with her now, but his work was finished, save for disposing of the remains.

The details for disposal evolved with each of the girls, the third now on the table in the clinic. The sound of the machine she'd been hooked up to fell silent, and the feeling inside him was like that of a lover sated.

Voices in the room told him the others were anxious to put a mark on their dead member. He backed away. They moved in with crude knives, razors, scissors, whatever they'd found or brought. In the meantime, he saw to the preparation of the girl's blood in properly measured units, with the approximate mix of plasma, knowing he must stretch it as far as possible. It was a very rich and heady mixture, both pure and exact, to be fed on later, privately.

There was some commotion among the others. One of the boys didn't want to mark the dead girl. The others, including the girls, goaded him into it and when he did they all laughed good-naturedly, dazedly. And stupidly they went off to the sex room adjoining the clinic to lay naked with one another, please one another without fear of harm. The sacrifice was over.

He owned the body now, as he owned the blood. With the blood he controlled his life and the lives of others. With the sacrifices he measured out life and death. It was a god-like feeling he would never tire of.

He wanted to shout it to the world, but for now at least, it must remain his secret, and any member of the sect who showed signs of weakness, overt moral compunction against his wishes, any who refused the simple taking of a few pints of their own rich blood when he called for it, then they must be terminated—but not before the blood was strained, purified and packaged.

He began the pleasant task of packaging it now, taking each pliable bag into the storage locker off the clinic, filling his blood bank to overflowing. Soon he would have to get workmen to come in to install a new freezer, make more room for the blood.

ONE

Lieutenant Ryne Lanark ran, stumbling over the ill-fitting, clownish shoes he wore, a pair of open-toed, dog-bitten fake leathers with worn souls. The long dark cotton coat flapped around and about him like an ancient moth-eaten cape. His floppy fedora flew away with the strong Chicago gusts, revealing a fine head of dark hair. His three-day growth of stubble was ready to graduate to beard status. He hadn't slept in a comfortable bed for twenty hours, pulling double-duty in a stakeout for the Lincoln Park Phantom thief. He'd had no luck whatsoever, and the feeling now was bad, as he raced headlong toward the sounds of sirens and lights several blocks south of his decoy position. He shouted into the microphone beneath his lapel for his partner, but Skully had either fallen asleep or was indisposed some other way. Most likely with a hooker. The man was a serious police asshole. Lanark had known all along he couldn't trust him for backup, and in fact Skully might be listening in just for laughs. Lanark had lost partners in the past. Word about the 26th

Precinct had marked him a dangerous man, and Skully, if anything, wasn't about to get himself into any tight spots with a dangerous man.

"Skully, come in, damn it!" He gave it a last effort before stopping at the already-erected police barricade to flash his badge and enter the scene of what appeared to be a major crime. He saw Al Riordan in the thick of it and went toward the burly, barrel-shaped detective. Riordan was in charge of the Upscale Slasher killings and it sadly appeared there was a newly discovered victim, a pretty little rich girl no doubt.

The press, the public, the commissioner and the mayor's office would be breathing down Riordan's neck before dawn. The effects of the case were showing on him. His eyes were dark circles, his hair was visibly thinning and graying as if overnight, his nerves were shot, skin drawn and pale. The man was a walking zombie these days, Lanark thought. So why shouldn't he welcome help from Lanark? Why was he making it so hard for Lanark to throw in with the investigative unit which had, after all, been calling for additional help in this precinct and the adjoining one?

"What've you got, Riordan?"

Albert Riordan looked up from the pad he jotted notes on, paused his pen and stared back at Lanark, not recognizing him at first. He regarded Lanark with a queer squint, his nose sniffing like a bassett hound. "You stink," he finally answered. "What've you been drinking?"

"I don't drink it, I just douse myself with it."

Morris Fabia, Riordan's partner, said, "Next time try lighter fluid." Fabia lit up a cigarette and began to puff. "Jeeze, what trash heap you been sleeping in, Lanark?"

"I was in the park, a block down—"

"See anything unusual come or go?"

"No, not so's anyone would notice."

"Treadmarks on the grass indicate a truck or van. See anything like that?"

"Must've seen a hundred vans go by, more."

"In the last few hours?"

"Lots of traffic moving along here, man. What's happened? What's brought you out?"

"Predawn jogger, big, heavy-muscled guy over there found a dead girl in the bushes." Riordan said.

The three detectives stood on the sidewalk fronting the park not a block from the zoo, and Fabia made a crack about how fitting a location it was for Ryne's monkey business. Ryne Lanark spit out the soggy, unlit but wet cigar stub he held in his teeth and it hit Fabia in his sweaty little ferret cheek.

"Goddamnit, Riordan, can't you for once leave this wooden head home in his case? Give me a straight answer. You going to—"

Fabia grabbed Ryne by the collar, Riordan grabbed hold of Fabia, dropping his notepad and pen all in one reaction. "Back off, back off!" shouted Riordan. "Surprised at you, Morris."

The men parted, Lanark's near royal blue eyes fixing Fabia with an icy stare. By comparison, Albert Riordan was calm and collected. Nothing to get heated up about, was Riordan's watchword, but Ryne knew that, like most of the other cops in the precinct, Riordan didn't care for Lanark. It was one reason Lanark worked alone, usually undercover, or on a case that

11

called for a gutsy decoy man. Lanark had gone through several partners. Two were dead, one was in a wheelchair for life, a fourth asked for and got a transfer. None of them worked out. Lanark had been left with no partner, which suited him, and an exaggerated reputation as a dangerous, loose cannon in the department. As far as Lanark was concerned it was an undeserved reputation, but now that it was hoisted upon him, he was finding that he rather liked the fit.

"I got enough goddamn trouble here without you, Lanark, so if you don't mind, move your ass on out," Riordan told him now, the cool set of gray eyes examining him closely.

"It's another *glove*, isn't it? Another white glove," Lanark said, pulling away from Riordan. Both men were ranked Lieutenant detectives, but Lanark was behind Riordan by a classification called second. As a first lieutenant, beefy, big jawed Albert Riordan could throw his weight around if he liked, and usually he liked it just fine.

"I want in, Riordan . . . I think I could help," said Lanark, not in a pleading way, but in a matter of fact way. Uniformed cops standing about drew in to hear what they could between the two detectives. If they had had time they would have taken bets on Riordan's reaction.

"You want to see the dead girl, don't you, Lanark? That's why you came all this way, climbed outa' the sewer and came all this way . . . All right, she's on the other side of the viaduct back of the trees."

Lincoln Park wound along the lake shore here like a Chinese dragon, or a maze on a game board, and Lanark stepped into it, out of the light thrown from the

12

pole under which Riordan stood. Riordan could be a real ass, Ryne thought, as he approached the group of cops with the macabre duty of watching over the corpse until the coroner and the medic team might arrive.

"Same m.o.?," asked Ryne, approaching the uniforms when suddenly Ryne realized that one of the cops was going through the girl's purse. "Hey, asshole, that's not to be touched."

"Just back out of here, Lanark," said the cop with the purse in his large hands, burliest of the three. It was Ryne's temporary partner, Joe Skully. One of the other cops put a restraining hand out to Lanark.

The third cop said in a nasal whisper, "We share four ways, Skully, what's the difference?"

"You goddamned vultures," Ryne said evenly.

Skully said, *"He's* different, real queer."

Skully was thumbing through the money, quite a thick wad. The victim was rich, like earlier victims who'd died with a white glove stuffed in their wounded throats and a second jammed into disfigured vaginas. "This broad was loaded," Skully was telling the others, trying to ignore Ryne, when he was hit hard with a flying drop-kick from Lanark. Lanark was on an incline and he used it for a second lunge at the bigger man. Racing at Skully, Lanark saw a staggering form stepping over the spilled contents of the purse. Skully was also being showered with the money, bills winging about like UFO kites. Lanark's body block threw Skully further off balance, and he went to one knee, dropping the two or three bills he'd managed to hold tight to. But Joe Skully was not easily dissuaded, or pushed around. He grabbed Lanark by the throat with both hands before Lanark was off the ground.

Squeezing off Lanark's air supply! Would Lanark's throat burst beneath the crushing hands before asphyxiation set in? Lanark saw a dull haze come over his eyes and settle there. Falling, rolling about the night-blanketed grass, the two men were locked in battle, Lanark's own grip a ferocious vise on Skully's throat until Lanark instinctively brought his knee up at just the right moment.

Searing pain shot through Skully's brain from his testicles, making him let go and scream. It was a spine-chilling scream, a banshee wail of pain, the man slumping over, moaning, cursing Lanark.

"Sonofamotherscrewing fuck!"

Lanark, standing, gasping for air, nonetheless kicked out with a viscious blow to the other man's jaw, sending him sprawling into the lagoon they had come upon. Skully lay half in and half out of the water. Lanark grabbed him by the hair and forced his face into the water, holding it there as the big man fought, trembled, shivered. Lanark was effectively drowning the man, calling him the single word cops used for all forms of low life.

"Asshole! You, stink, Skully!"

Riordan and Fabia had run down the slope after the fighting men, just behind the other uniforms who each had a hand on Lanark, desperately trying to pry him loose from Skully.

Fabia snatched out his weapon TV-cop style and placed the muzzle into Lanark's cheek until it hurt and said, "Let him go, Lanark! Now!"

Lanark eased his hold on Skully and was dragged off the other man. He crawled and slumped in the grass at a distance, hearing Skully's gasp for air and his choking. Another few minutes and he'd have drowned the scavenging bastard.

"Jesus! Christ, Lanark, you psycho!" screamed Riordan in his ear as loud as he could where Ryne now lay, his hands and face wet from the splashing water. "You get the hell out of here, Lanark, now! You got me?"

Lanark, exhausted, angry with himself, got up to his knees, while the other cops were telling Riordan that Skully'd been jumped by Ryne without provocation and that Skully was holding a lady's purse in his hand which he had found and was preparing to bring to Riordan when Lanark exploded.

"That true, Lanark?" Riordan asked, turning to where Lanark had been. He now saw Lanark was back up the slope and kneeling over the body of the mur-dered girl.

"Get the bastard out of here, now!" ordered Rior-dan.

"Let me do it," said Fabia, his weapon still drawn.

"Put your gun away," ordered Riordan. "You men, get Lanark on his feet and away from the crime scene." Riordan looked up the slope again at Lanark who was slowly rocking on his knees to some music he alone heard. Riordan had looked at the man's record, had given him the benefit of the doubt when he had asked to be assigned to the special task force investigating the killer they were beginning to refer to as "The Glove," and Riordan might've called him up if the fool had gone through proper channels, bided his time, but now this.

Something screwed up about that guy, Al Riordan

15

told himself, and we'd all be better off if he wound up like his partners.

Deceased.

Bureau-ese for "murdered," Ryne thought as he did a quick study of the dead girl, hardly out of her teens, if that. Nose slits, eye cuts, cheeks slashed.

Long, slender legs. Raven dark hair, long and disheveled now. Large eyes, the lids in mascara, a blue or green, hard to say with the poor light here. A bit heavy on the makeup for Lanark's liking. Skin was chalky from it about the cheekbones, the rouge giving too much away. Maybe a tease, certainly no more than that. Lithe fingers, tiny wrists, no rope burns.

Then he forced himself to look at the throat wound, the glove gag and the nasty jagged red line. Coroner was likely to find that, like the other two before her, the wound was not jagged at all, but as neat a slice as any power tool might make. The jagged appearance came from the coagulated blood about the wound.

Son of a bitch got in close and comfortable to administer that wound, without binding the girl. She knew her attacker. At least long enough to allow him in close. Coroner would also find semen in her vagina. Her killer made love to her before he cut her throat, stuffed the glove down to her larynx and finally slashed away at her private parts.

On one of the victims, the flesh was cleaved from the breasts as well.

Lanark didn't know if he had the nerve to look beneath the blanket, which had been hastily thrown over the nude form, to view the remainder of the killer's

16

butchery. Instead, he rocked slowly and solemnly over her, saying a silent prayer for her and others like her, others like his mother and his sister . . .

Lanark felt their hands on him like a sudden electric shock, the cops ordered by Riordan to move him out. It was a good excuse to look no more on the deceased, the murdered. Besides, he'd seen enough, enough to tell him he wanted more than ever to be the man to find "The Glove" so that he could blow his head off with his .357 Magnum.

He saw that the deceased, Molle Pitfield, someone had called her, was not much older than his sister had been when she died in a similar, even more brutal fashion. Whoever this pervert with the white kid gloves was, a butler or a dentist, a man who fancied himself the "Pink Panther" of homicide, Ryne wanted a piece of him; actually he wanted more than a piece.

But now it was a certainty he would be effectively kept from the case. Riordan would see to that. Yet, he knew, down deep, the fault was his own.

TWO

Thirteen wasn't exactly Lanark's lucky number, it just followed him wherever he went like a stray dog begging; a constant reminder, a ghost that could neither be walked away from nor fully recognized, or even fathomed. But here it was again, now the number of his new precinct, a precinct plagued with a reputation for cops on the take, cops on the edge, and cops who couldn't cut it on the street. Precinct 13 was a dumping ground for the city's defective cops, and Lanark's uncontrollable temper had landed him square in the middle of it.

His rage at Skully's skimming money off a dead woman had cost him dearly, much more than it had the bastard criminal. No one else came forward on his behalf. No one else knew a damned thing about what really had gone down, and those who did were keeping silent. Maybe he'd go after Olsen or Neil if he thought it'd do any good, but they were hardly more than rookies, just trying to get by in a department run on rules made by guys like Skully. Riordan had listened with some attentive interest to Ryne's side of the story for a moment or two, but there was no way to prove it.

The Captain came down hard this time, real hard.

Ryne didn't lose his rank, but he was fined and he was effectively "demoted" in real terms. Precinct 13 . . . filled with departmental rejects, people who had crumpled under the pressures of police work in one form or another. House of alcoholics, druggies, rabbits and men like Ryne Lanark, men whose murderous rage often took such hold of them they could not control their own free-wheeling impulse to right the wrongs of the world with a single gunshot to the head.

Once before, he had been torn and dragged from a man he nearly killed with his fists, a filthy pimp who had enraged him by beating one of his women senseless in an alleyway. Lanark had meted out an ancient justice on that occasion, giving the man the beating of his life. It had taken his partner at the time and two other cops ten minutes to pry loose the hold he had on the jackal.

He had seen shrinks after his family had been killed and had openly talked about how the hatred inside him had festered. But no more, not since his decision to join the police academy, had he ever spoken of that nightmare. The academy was never told. The department hadn't a clue. The shrinks he had been sent to on more than one occasion by his superiors didn't know. Only his uncle and a few close friends knew, some of the guys that hung out at his bar. A handful were other cops, but they'd been friends first, co-workers second, and he trusted them to keep his secrets, as they had done all this time.

Had the force known that he was the same Lanark whose parents and sister were murdered, his reasons for joining the force would have automatically been thrown into question, studied and analyzed under a too-bright light. The intensity of the light would reveal him as little better than a killer himself, a man bent on revenge. A man who swore an oath to one day locate and execute the men responsible for the New Year's Eve massacre of his entire family.

Like "The Glove," these killers used knives, too.

Lanark had known for years now that he likely would never again be completely on keel, not so long as he remembered the ghosts of his past. *Thirteen.* It had been the thirteenth hour of the last day of the year 1983 that he lost his family to gutter rats. Police reports, dry and insensitive process papers, had branded their words on his brain nonetheless, words like 'deceased." The report he forced them to allow him to see read like a turgid death knoll, speaking of the incident as if it had occurred in another time and place:

Four-fifteen (family disturbance, possible weapon fired) at 211 Aberdeen; 1:55 A.M. call from neighbor logged. Response time, 2:03 A.M. Three deceased found on premises, Lucky 13th Pub, proprietor, wife and daughter. One witness, caller, Mrs. Thomas Janklow—friend of the family. Witness's account foggy; party was in full swing at Pub an hour earlier. Closing was 1:30 A.M.

Proprietor, male, white 5′7½″, late 50s–early 60s, died of gunshot wound to temple; had been bound and gagged. Female, late 50s, 5′4″, wife, died of multiple slash wounds. Female, mid-20s, 5′9″, daughter, also dead of knife wounds sustained.

It had occurred in the tavern, his father's pub. Lanark pictured every detail of the little place, a corner drinking hole for locals on the near North Side, displaced hillbillies most of them. Two A.M. and the cops were on the scene. Far too late. The gun shots were the payoff, the finish, and the killers had fled.

9One boarder's tale was a horror story of rape and mutilation. She'd been asleep upstairs when she heard the odd noises she had first dismissed as a drunken quarrel. Then she went to investigate. What she saw so terrified her, she went into a daze and sat staring through a crack in the door for fifteen, possibly twenty minutes before she finally telephoned, but it was already far too late. They used knives on Lanark's mother and sister. His unconscious father, tied and gagged, was then shot to death, two bullets to the temple, in execution fashion.

Lanark's career as an actor ended then, and his career as a policeman began.

The name of his father's Irish pub was *The Lucky 13th.* Tom Lanark, a hearty sixty-two, had been a veteran of World War II, his proud unit, the Thirteenth Infantry, had been part of the famous *Rifle Company K* which had spent four years in Europe at the front. It all ended in an old man's being victimized, his family brutalized by four armed punks out for jollies on New Year's Eve.

Ryne thought of his beautiful older sister who had given him the courage to leave home; he thought, too, of his strong, caring mother. Each time he did so, he could not get past the images of horror their bodies presented at the morgue.

He blamed every directionless, air-headed druggie on the Chicago streets. He blamed the cops. He blamed himself. And he was filled with venom, anger and frustration. And every working day on the force he put out feelers, ever in search of those who had gone free and were likely committing the same crime over today.

Any reports of crimes even remotely similar and Lanark wanted a piece of it, to the annoyance of everyone around him, from dispatchers to top brass.

Only one thing was sure: from the moment he learned of the terrible incident, his career as an actor was over. He had just gotten word from his agent that NBC liked his characterization of Pete Zant for a pilot film that was sure to lead into a weekly program about big city crime fighters on the order of the *Untouchables*. Zant, a modern-day Eliot Ness, fought the drug syndicate the way Ness fought Capone and Frank Nitty and Bugs Moran. No music videos or fashion shows, just tough cops fighting tough evil. Production schedule was set, writers had scripts waiting, filming was to begin by the Ides of March when Lanark's phone rang. It was Bill Leinbaugh, his agent, telling him of the tragedy back home in Chicago.

He pondered Bill Leinbaugh for a moment. The man was a lot like his father. A World War II vet, in the business of providing for his family ever since, a treasure of stories and secrets behind everything he said. Leinbaugh was understanding, but he was also angry and upset with Lanark's decision to return to Chicago

22

and walk away from the Zant role, a role that could make up for the years of struggle. But he also understood Lanark's position, and finally accepted it, even if he himself was cut out of the big-grossing deal that finally came about with another actor, not of Leinbaugh's stable.

For a while Ryne wandered Chicago's near North Side streets at night, alone, inviting trouble to strike him. He armed himself and seriously looked for anyone who might look the part of the killers who had destroyed his family, the family he had planned to bestow so much on once he became famous and rich in Hollywood. Soon he was frequenting the filthiest areas of the city. Sleeping by day, he became a vampire of sorts, seeking blood, seeking revenge, but a month passed with no results, and then two. His thirst for revenge going unsatisfied, the rage built up in him like additional muscle, hardening him.

To keep his muscles hard, he began again at the neighborhood gym where boxers and weightlifters worked out. Some of the weights were older than he was. There wasn't an aerobics class or a Nautilus in the place. The gym floor was the real thing, no fabricated walls either. But even here the cost was high. Money grew tight, scarce; and he was going to lose the tavern unless he changed his destructive behavior.

Frustrated beyond words, obsessive as he was, he finally sat himself down and decided to straighten himself out long enough to organize his efforts to full potential. He was first and foremost an actor, but returning to the glitz and make-believe world of film making seemed out of the question. Still, as Ryne Lanark, he had failed miserably to learn anything of value about the killers who had gotten away with murdering the three people in the world he loved most. He knew he must somehow find and destroy the killers, even if it meant going to prison himself, but he also knew he must now use his head, draw on his acting abilities. He knew also that he must reopen *The Lucky 13th*, hire a manager, and recoup loses already accrued.

Ryne didn't have to think too hard to know who he could trust to manage affairs at the pub. He knew just the man to manage the place, his uncle Jack Tebo. Tebo had seen him through the funeral, a real brick of a man, and he loved the tavern. This settled, with all the payments for the lapsed liquor license and a thousand other incidentals Jack Tebo alone seemed to understand, Ryne finally set in motion his larger plan, to obtain a license to hunt and kill the kind of vermin infesting Chicago that had destroyed his family.

He had seen, spoken with and pretended to be one of them himself, going among them, in his two-month long search for the killers he wanted. He knew he could be more effective with a badge. He knew he had to become a cop. Undercover, with a badge, he would be free to locate and destroy any and all gutter scum that dared come his way. Drawing pay for it seemed like icing.

His father's gun collection was his now, and he cleaned every piece, including his army-issue rifles, even the one he carried across Europe, from the Ruhr to the Rhine. In the little apartment room above the tavern where Ryne now lived with his Uncle Jack, he spent hours with the guns. In the back of his mind he knew that one reason he stayed, one reason he re-opened the bar, was the off-chance they would one day return, and Ryne felt more than a twinge of guilt that he had placed Jack Tebo in harm's way. But there was nothing he could do for it. His hatred drove him now.

Added to his arsenal, Ryne began to collect more modern machinery, a .357 Magnum, and a fully automatic Uzi which, with a single squeeze of the trigger, emptied the magazine in seconds. His mind made up, Lanark entered the Chicago Police Academy at the age of thirty-two, during the spring of 1984. That had been some five years now. His anger, bitterness and frustration still commingled inside, still teemed with a life of their own. His reasons for joining the force were purely personal, but despite this fact, he'd gone from a uniformed cop to plainclothes detective and undercover specialist quickly. Given his natural talent and ability as an actor, he was recognized and prized by the department, until his venomous nature surfaced.

Now he was on the outs with departmental brass, ostensibly for bringing down the press with shouts of police brutality. All over a street pimp who had brutalized a prostitute to the point where she now lay in a coma at St. Stephen's.

Ryne's career was put on hold, too. The 13th precinct was a purgatory.

Ryne took in the place at a glance, one of the old station houses built about the turn of the century in the style of a bank of that era. Squat, square, fortress feel to the place, some five, maybe six stories if you counted the rooftop. Every window covered in bars save for administration, where the bars were removed to accommodate air-conditioning units. Every window was large, like a cyclop's eye, arched over the top with a Romanesque brow.

Inside: dirty, loud, cramped, busy, phones like so many bees. It wasn't quite the purgatory others made it out to be. But it was yellow and mahogany brown, reminding Lanark of the aged high school corridors he knew at Wells High on Ashland and Augusta, a million years ago.

He was confronted by an enormous desk where a sergeant was clipping papers together and mumbling to himself behind a set of bars. The front desk took up most of the entire hallway. Lanark cleared his throat and instantly the sergeant put up a hand for him to hold on, an auto-response to anyone standing before his desk, Ryne reasoned.

"Officer Lanark, reporting, Sergeant," Ryne announced to the precinct sergeant, a huge man who looked at him over a pair of glasses, and replied in a sharp, militaristic fashion.

"Right, got you here, from the 24th, aren't you?" Not waiting for a reply, he said, "Come 'round here, and I'll show you where you'll be parking it."

Lanark followed the hefty man into the more spacious squad room. "Park it in the last desk on the right, Samuels's old place. Might be some of his junk still in the drawers . . . guess you can box it up if you like and leave it with me."

The 24th wasn't Ryne's old precinct, but he let it slide to ask the more interesting question: "Why can't Samuels box it up himself?"

The enormous sergeant glared at Lanark. "Didn't you hear?"

"No, Sergeant, I didn't hear anything."

"Samuels shot himself through the ear. He's too dead to box shit."

Lanark felt instantly foolish and realized the beehive noise and activity of the precinct had come to a low-level hum as others stared at the newcomer.

"Sorry . . . sorry," Ryne said, feeling it was a lame reply.

"Collection box is on the file cabinet over there, and the casket's at Dunn's on Ogden at Humbolt."

"Got it."

"Hey, Lanark," said the tough, Irish sergeant, "Captain Wood likes to see every new man first thing, so . . ."

He pointed the direction.

Lanark nodded, feeling the eyes of the others in the precinct on him. "Right, right," Lanark read the sergeant's name tag: *Sergeant O'Hurley.*

But Lanark was stopped by another man before he got to the Captain's office. "You the Lanark beat the shit out of that pimp and got busted to here, aren't you?"

"Guess that'd be me, yeah."

"Pimps are a dime a dozen, man. You want to go at it with a real bad guy next time, then maybe they won't fry you." The man's smile was lopsided, even snarly, and Lanark thought it a natural, or perhaps habitual snarl, not intended for him personally, or specifically.

The story sent out on Lanark through official channels had dredged up the pimp. So far, few people knew of the incident with Skully. "This particular pimp irked me."

"Irked you," he repeated, laughing. "Hear that,

27

guys?'' he asked the others. 'I like this guy. My name's Milt, Milt—''

''Know-it-all!' shouted another man to finish Milt's name.

"Wiemer, Milton Wiemer."

"What kind of Captain we got behind the door?" asked Lanark.

"Asshole, but a fair one, kinda okay as brass goes. Been sitting behind a desk too long, you know?"

"How long you been in the precinct, Milt?"

"Too long, a year longer than Samuels."

"Why'd Samuels do it?"

"Why does any man do it? Hell, you asking me?"

Lanark nodded, understanding, and started for the door that read *Captain Paul L. Wood,* thinking how Milt smelled of booze. A glance at the clock told him it was not quite eight A.M. yet. Milt, the only friendly greeting he was likely to get, was the resident drunk.

He rapped at the door and heard a grunt from within that he took to mean come in. Wood was a wide-shouldered, heavy-set man with dark features and a brooding scowl that seemed less of a scowl as he regarded the new face that entered his small, cluttered office.

"You're Lanark?"

"Yes, sir."

"Been reading your file, Lanark. Lots of quarrels and lots of trouble, head-bashing shit on the street. Says you got a temper problem. That right? Not here, it ain't right. This kinda' crap'll get your badge pulled, you savvy?" He didn't leave Lanark space to answer his twenty questions, just raced onward with what was a half-prepared, half-impromptu speech. "Shrink reports got you listed as possible psycho-cop, if you don't check out first like . . . like . . ."

"I'm not suicidal, sir."

"No, just *homicidal.*"

"When it's called for!"

"Don't raise your godamned voice to me, mister, not here, ever! I got a squad room full of dinks and rejects out there who already question my ability to lead a department. I don't need you, Lanark, and I don't appreciate your being hoisted on me like Jimmy Cagney fresh out of Sing-Sing."

"White Heat, seen the film a dozen times. I don't really act like mad Cagney, do I? Lanark started to object, but Wood, ignoring the hopelessly angry expression, charged ahead with what he wanted to say.

"Hell, Lanark, in all my years I've never seen a jacket like yours. Five years on the force, rising to your present rank over the back of others, promising as hell, and yet continually in trouble."

"Goes hand in hand with the territory."

"Shut up and listen."

"All right, so I'm listening," Lanark said, taking a chair across from Wood, meeting him eyeball to eyeball. But Wood was unhappy with this arrangement and he got up, flipping Lanark's file closed, beginning to pace like a caged animal, first this way and then the next, saying nothing, allowing Lanark to sit like a docile child for as long as he could get away with it. Lanark got a square look now at the man's height, build and posture. He was hefty, a good girth, likely from too much beer, a good 280 pounds, Lanark's trained eye told him, and tall enough to play ball with the Bulls. In a moment, the big man exploded again. "You want to tell me what gives? Shrinks have filled out reports on you like you were some kind of whacko we ought to be taking off the street, not putting *on* the street, but none of it reads right. All this horseshit about a violent, uncontrollable rage, but no information as to *why*. Who's it directed at? How'd it come about? You're a mystery, Lanark, and I don't like a mystery—not here, not under my command.''

"Do better with drunks, men on the take?"

"Hell yes, I do. I know what makes those guys out there tick,'' he pointed to the door. "You, you're like a walking time bomb, and I swear, you go off under my command, and you'll regret the day you met me, mister! You got that?'

"I think it's clear enough. Can I go now?"

This enraged Wood, his eyes dilating, his teeth grinding. He, too, had a problem holding onto his temper. "I'm no psychoanalyst, Lanark, but I'm a good judge of character. You ought to get help . . . real professional help, not some police shrink quack who gets his knowledge from *Detective* magazine. Either that, or a good, off-duty beating.''

The veiled threat was not so veiled. Lanark turned to follow the other man's tiger-like movement behind him, half expecting blows to rain down on him. "I'm game, if it comes to that.'' And he was game, always a spoiler for a fight, ever since the incident at his father's pub, for whether he won or lost a fight, the beating was cathartic; a payback in a sense, for not having been there with his family, for not having saved them, for not having died alongside them. Ironic that he should not have died with them. All his life he was the one left out, a part of the family, but always *apart* from them as well . . . and now it appeared this family truth would continue on into eternity. "I'm game . . ." he repeated. "Hell, I'm game every time I work a decoy operation."

"Trust me, kid, you don't want to be game meat for Paul Wood."

Lanark stood and turned to face the other man, about to explode, his fists clenched, his broad jaw set. "This your standard procedure, Captain, or is this welcoming a special spiel just for me?"

"There aren't too many guys in that squad room out there who haven't been game for me, at one time or another, and not one of the jackoffs has thanked me for it. But they're not the problem, you are."

The man literally ruled with an iron fist! Lanark could like him if he'd go easier on the tonsils.

"I do my job as best I can, sir. Shrinks don't have to be on the street, and they don't see the—"

"Bullshit, bullshit, Lanark. I don't want to hear that crap here. You got something bothering you, makes you reckless and wild, stuck deep inside you! Well, get it out, now, *yesterday!* Talk to me if you won't talk to someone else. I'm your goddamned daddy here, your Mother Superior and your best friend all rolled into one. Hell, *nobody* wants to work with you, 'cause you've gotten partners wounded. So you're bound and determined to show everybody you're a bloody mean-spirited self-righteous scum-hating spoiled cop! So you don't play unless you make the rules, right? Am I right so far? You're a loner, and a cop who is a loner is a dangerous item."

"I do my job with dedication, sir . . . sometimes I'm just too dedicated about it."

"Your *dedication*, as you call it, has gotten you here, under my thumb; it's put one partner in a wheel-chair—"

"That wasn't my—"

"Shut up! It's gotten two other partners dead."

"Joey Swan got himself killed and the report will verify that!"

"A report you filled out."

"You Swan's uncle or something? The guy was stupid and reckless! He didn't need *me* to get himself killed, he did fine on his own."

"*Here*—now—you play by *my* rules, you got that? And that means you put a lid on your problem or you're facing an end to your once promising career as a cop." Wood stepped away from the face-off, returning to his desk chair, and Ryne realized he had been maneuvered back into the same posture and position as when he entered. He also felt that Wood had purposefully manipulated him, pulling an argument from him. Maybe the guy was more psychoanalyst than he let on. *Probably took a night course at UC extension.* Now he thinks he knows it all. "Yes, *sir,* sir!" Lanark replied to the Captain snidely as he slumped back into the chair, his eyes returning to Wood's.

"You think I won't kick your ass in the alley out back—"

Ryne thought of Jim Arness playing Matt Dillon on *Gunsmoke,* doing exactly that to prisoners he particularly disliked.

"—then I'll kick it off the force! Try me."

But Lanark only half heard the Captain's final remarks, his attention suddenly taken away, his ear turned toward the closed door. It was too quiet out in

32

the squad room. At first, he pictured all the burn-outs atop one another trying desperately to get an ear to the door to overhear the commotion Wood had put up. But that didn't compute. Guys like Wiemer, they didn't need to weasel up to a door to get the low-down. Guys like him heard the speeches so often they could repeat each one verbatim in a drunken stupor, or asleep. Then why so quiet on the other side of the door?

"You hear something funny, Captain?"

"What? What's funny? Something strike you as funny?" Wood was confused by the sudden, curious question. "You trying to be *funny*, Lanark?"

Lanark got to his feet and went toward the door, cocking an ear. "No, *listen* . . . squad room . . . it's . . . too quiet."

Wood considered this and got on his intercom but could get no answer from Sergeant O'Hurley. "What the hell gives?" The only noise outside was the ringing of the unmanned telephones.

Wood got up and started for the door, but Ryne stopped him. "Careful."

Wood snatched open the door, pulling free of Lanark, and the instant he did so a bullet splintered the door inches from his head. Lanark, unseen by the gunman, opened a window and was on the fire escape, making his way to ground level. Someone had walked into the station with one of those damned .25-caliber handguns, cheap imitation weapons that could explode in the gunman's hand, or blow a hole through some-body—easily purchased, easily concealed. Someone with a beef, reasoned Lanark as he made his way down. But the sound of the gunshot was powerful, perhaps

33

too powerful to be a .25; maybe it was an even dumber scenario inside the squad room: a cop had gotten careless with his weapon, a .38 most likely. A suspect, somebody on his way to holding perhaps, or on his way to interrogation, had lifted the gun, resulting in a standoff. By now, he likely had a hostage collared as well. Stupid place to make a play, a hostage-taking inside a police precinct. Guy could be on something, or simply loony. Either way, he was deadly.

Ryne Lanark rushed down the spindly fire escape steps. Clanking underfoot. Sunlight in his eyes. Traffic and street noise all around. It reminded him of an exercise at the police academy, not the situation, but the purpose. Rush into a situation and determine, from all the variables and strange faces, in a fraction of a second *who* was the gunman, was he or she going to fire, what you must do: decide, fire and pray you got the killer before he got you. Often more than one bystander, or a hostage, was killed by the officer's hand, and even more often, in the second you realized your mistake, you were dead as well, a pinpoint of red light indicating where the bullet had entered your chest. At the academy there was a saying, *a recruit died a thousand deaths*.

All artificial reality, training for crisis on simulators, but the Big Mother ($37,000 Firearms Training System, or FATS) simulator was tough to take. In fact, even hard-boiled beat cops were being returned to the academy to re-tool their reflexes against what the recruits called *Gunfight at the PC Corral*. The simulation was so exacting and demanding that seasoned veterans came out in a cold sweat. The simulator confronted the recruit with life-size villains, some of whom looked like grocery-shopping middle-Americans, while others were Black, Hispanic and just ugly bag people and winos. Often, an innocent Black was blown away while a Caucasian female or a guy in white collar and tie put six bullets into the trainee.

One of the most difficult to judge was the routine family squabble, a four-fifteen gone sour, when someone pulled a weapon; or the equally routine pulling over of an automobile, stepping up to the window and reacting to someone who has either a gun or a license in his or her purse. Another scenario was the armed robbery. Alarm is set off. Two men race from the liquor store. One turns at you with a gun in his hand. You fire. You've just killed the store manager. Same scene comes at you again the following try-out. You withhold your fire. You're dead. The store manager's inside this time, and one of the two holdup men has just killed you.

Each event had multiple possibilities and endings. In a split second the trainee must decide whether to shoot, using a standard service revolver that fired blanks, along with a laser beam. The laser beam would paint bullet holes on the video screen, and, if you were good, on the image of the culprit. The simulator then froze the action, rated the wisdom of your decision, *your cop's instinct*—Ryne had always thought—and the *accuracy* of the shot. For often, if the shot only wounded a man, the FATS image fired from a prone position and could as well kill you in the end. While in the darkened room, faced with full-size people not eight feet away who are sometimes trying to kill you, your heart pounded, blood

35

raced and you were keyed as high as the brain would go, prepared for anything, including your own very possible death. It was, for all its artificiality, as close as the failing recruit would ever get to a real-life situation, like the one Lanark was now engaged in.

This was no academy exercise from which he could walk away if the bad guy used him for a target. No electronic laser zap guns here. Still, the computer gunfights, for all the days and days of frustration and the feeling of inadequacy at having been beaten multiple times by a frigging machine, seeing those lights blip up the score again and again as: *Good Judgment—Hits: 0, Misses: 3,* and looking down at his reaction time at 0.396 seconds had its sobering effect on Lanark now as it had then. Not until he switched the score in his favor 3 to 0 did he leave the PC Corral a walking, talking live cop. Others didn't get as proficient at it, and many couldn't cope, finally dropping out of the academy after they had made it in all other arenas.

Lanark finally reached the last rung in the escape ladder. He now put his weight on the end and rode it to within a few feet of the cement ground, dropping to a crouch just outside a set of windows that looked in on the squad room, but nobody inside, empty. What had happened? What was going to happen? How soon? His every nerve was alive with sensation, his mind racing far ahead of his legs, when he knocked over a cardboard house in his pursuit, beneath which was a sleeping wino without a care in the world save trying to resemble the rest of the trash in the place where he slept, below the precinct building. Lanark kicked hard the old man's legs in his race for the front of the building.

He then raced down the length of the alley and came tearing around the corner, instantly recoiling when the bullet sent his way took out a chunk of stone from the squat, boulder-like precinct building.

"Damn," he cursed himself for not having gone easy around that final turn, giving his position away. He had barely a glance at the man holding Sergeant O'Hurley at gunpoint, maybe 0.396 seconds. The computer would've hit him, but thankfully, his enemy was as human as he, and therefore prone to the same mistakes, the same indecision.

Lanark had seen a short man with unkempt, dirty hair, a braid on one side, definitely Spanish, his eyes turned in his head like an animal cornered or a kid on a brain-cooking crack trip. He also saw that old O'Hurley formed an enormous human shield for the gunman. The gun was a service revolver, a snub-nosed .38, most likely lifted from Wiemer or another negligent cop, maybe O'Hurley himself.

Lanark heard the druggie scream, a familiar high-pitched whine, a plea yet defiant, entwined and resonant, the new chorus of the slums. "I'm tellin' you bastards, the fat pig, he gets it!"

The other cops were closer, the gunman holding them at bay on their own front steps. A crowd had begun to gather at what was hardly a safe distance, some shouting for the man to fire, repeating the word *fire, fire,* in a sicko's version of a mantra.

At the same time Wood was calling to the gunman like the white angel on his shoulder with the opposite advice, "Don't fire . . . don't fire . . . don't do it . . ."

Lanark would like to have weighed his options but he realized he didn't have any.

"A step closer and he gets it!"

"You're surrounded, Hernando, and there's no way we're letting you go free!" shouted Captain Wood from the steps.

Lanark raced back down the alley to where the drunken bum—*a "street person" they were called now*—lay in a heap of cardboard boxes. He hustled the man up and tore off his hat and coat to the old man's whimpering complaints and handed him his sports coat. "The pants, the pants!" Lanark shouted. In less than a minute Lanark had become a hobo, and with gun holstered, and bourbon bottle in hand, he stumbled out into dangerous territory, keeping the rat-chewed brim of the floppy hat low over his dirt-blackened face, and singing, *"What I Did For Love"* drunkenly off-key. It was a calculated risk that could get him killed.

"Get outa' here! Get away!" He heard Hernando shout at him.

He blindly stumbled about, wheeling.

He heard cops shouting for him to get clear of the danger zone. Then someone had hold of him, twisting his left arm. It was a young woman who had grabbed him by the arm and almost caught him in an armlock before their eyes met and she realized he was no ordinary street derelict. To make it look good, Lanark cussed her out and pushed her roughly back to the rear of a car where she'd been keeping her own cover. It looked not at all staged, likely because it hadn't been. She played right along, warning him of danger. She was tall and lithe and pretty in a sunshine-girl fashion, her uniform snug-fitting, to show off a perfect shape. *She must have made one hell of a girl scout cookie salesman. Anytime,* he thought, wondering about her, but he knew Big Mother would by now have cut him to ribbons, and that he truly didn't have time for a single such distraction as a beautiful blonde.

"Your shoes," she whispered.

He had hoped no one would notice, but he'd be damned if he was going to give up a brand new pair of Italian leathers to a street person in an alley. Hopefully, she was the only one to notice. In any event it signaled the moment: bourbon bottle flies skyward when he lets loose a boozy, hysterical laugh while Lanark's gun whips out of its holster and rests instantly against Hernando's head—all before the bottle explodes on the sidewalk.

"Go ahead, Hernando," he growled, his teeth clenched. "Shoot him and you're dead before he is! Go on, fire, fire, fire! You little shit!"

"I'll kill him, goddamnit!" threatened Hernando, a kid with thick, curly hair and a deep, brown complexion.

"We got lots of sergeants in the force, kid," said Lanark, calmly. "He can be replaced, but what about your mother? He goes, and I'm going to look up your mother and guess where this gun goes next? With you in the hereafter watching from Hell! How you going to replace Momma, boy?"

"I ain't got no mother! And this sonofabitch is dead!"

"Go ahead, blow him away, do it, *do it!*" Lanark's shout deep into the kid's ear made him jump involuntarily but Lanark's weapon only went up and down with him.

"Lanark! Lanark!" he heard Wood shouting at him.

"Go on, big shot, pull it, and I swear I pull mine, too!"

"Jesus," moaned the sergeant, looking faint, sweating and trembling.

Hernando swallowed hard, a good sign, thought Lanark. The young tough eased his finger from his gun, not liking the cold feel of the barrel at his temple. Lanark went on speaking, his own finger drawing back the trigger as he did so, making everyone think that Hernando's brains would momentarily be splattered Jello-like all over the street. "They say when a bullet goes through your brain you feel it! Like a jolt in the electric chair, same sensation as when you're executed, kid! You want I should execute you?"

Hernando dropped the gun and collapsed to his knees. Lanark saw that his hands were cuffed in front of him, and yet he'd gotten hold of someone's service revolver inside the precinct. Some jerk had gotten careless, and when Ryne kicked away the gun and looked in the direction of Captain Wood, he saw Milt Wiemer race out to take hold of the .38. It had been Milt's mistake.

"You're just lucky, kid," Milt said to Hernando, "this guy's known around here as a killer cop. He might've blowed your goddamned head off."

"Wiemer, you asshole," said Lanark, snatching the gun from the other man. "Can't you keep possession of your own damned weapon?"

"Hey, go easy," said one of Wiemer's friends. "Coulda' happened to anyone, hot-shot."

"Go easy, hell," replied Lanark, staring in Wood's direction.

"Get this punk to Holding!" cried Wood, going to the sarge, asking after him.

"I'm okay, Captain, okay," said O'Hurley shakily. "Thought for a minute I might be catching up with Samuels, but now, I'm okay . . . okay . . ."

"You ought to break Wiemer's goddamned neck, Sarge," Lanark told the big man as others cleared out.

"Maybe I will."

"I'll take care of Milton Wiemer and discipline in this precinct, Lanark."

Lanark and Wood stared long into one another's eyes before Lanark said, "Sure, you take care of discipline, Captain, if that's what this boils down to, you take care of it."

"Watch your mouth with the captain," warned O'Hurley.

Lanark shook his head at the other two men, amazed and confused somewhat at their reaction. After all, he had just saved O'Hurley's big behind, hadn't he? "You two do what you think is best with Wiemer. But if he ever puts me in jeopardy through his stupidity. . . ."

"Wiemer'll get his," Wood said evenly.

"That was some play," said a female voice behind Lanark, making him turn to face the young, dark-eyed officer who had helped him pull it off.

"My Romeo to your Juliet would be better," he suggested.

She smirked automatically. "Not likely."

"Why not?"

"I don't particularly like tragedies."

"Then you, pretty cop, are in the wrong line of work."

"Oh, but I do like drama," she countered and said to Wood. "Captain, sorry I'm late."

"Keyes?"

"Yes, sir."

"In my office, please, Lanark here knows the way."

"Be delighted, but then, Captain, if you and I are finished with the formalities, Captain . . . can I get to work now?"

"Lanark, what you did . . . it was a nice piece of police work. And no, we're not finished talking. We were interrupted, and I'd like to start over."

"Dressed as I am?"

"Stench and all."

THREE

Stench and all was how he met Officer Shannon Keyes, a Sergeant Lieutenant, First Class (which he mentally agreed to). This time their meeting was, with the exception of his baggy clown outfit, done with all the formality Wood could bring to bear. He seemed ill-at-ease with Shannon in his office, a jumpiness behind his words. The first pretty woman he'd ever had in his inner sanctum, no doubt. Or was there more to it than that? Lanark, unlike Wood, did like a mystery, especially when the mystery was a beautiful woman. Cop or no, she was a feminine creature that, given the right moves, Lanark could enjoy getting to know. He had never slept with another cop before, and the fantasy had its appeal.

Captain Wood had been expecting her along with his miscreant cop, Lanark, when the shooting started. She was a second-year cop, top honors at the academy, and according to Wood, top scorer on the FATS simulator. This gained an approving stare from Lanark.

"You got Big Mother at the PC Corral, really?"

She almost blushed but somehow controlled this with a firm-set jaw, biting her lower lip in a pout and nodding. "I did, sir, Lieutenant."

"How many times out did it take you?"

"Perfect score on my fourth go at it."

Lanark's face visibly dropped. "That's . . ." he wanted to say impossible, ". . . impossibly great . . . how?"

"Got an early start," she tried to explain when Wood broke up the banter between them.

Only two years out of the academy, one spent on patrol duty, the other in Burglary, and now she was, Wood explained, bumped up to undercover work in plainclothes. "Want to explain the uniform, Officer Keyes?" asked Wood, "Since you haven't had need of it for—"

"I was told I'd be put back on beat work here, Captain. Isn't that so?"

"Jesus, what a bunch of screw-ups we got around here lately—sorry . . . didn't mean you two . . . the paperwork guys got you down for plainclothes work, undercover, to be partnered at my discretion."

"Really? I mean, really, sir?" she was ecstatic. "That's what I've been working toward, but . . . but I was told—"

"Yeah, well, forget what you were told."

She drew herself in, something deep within smoldering, Lanark thought. He knew the signs. Sudden rigidness even in the pores of the skin. Face taut. Jaw erect. Eyes slightly closed to hide half the pupils. What was it? he wondered. Would he ever have a chance to know? Not likely.

She'd moved up either by happenstance or some

other quirky way, through the department in meteoric fashion, even faster than Ryne had. Could her academy scores have had that much to do with it? Wood read her sheet, and for the first time today Lanark knew what was going on. Wood, in his own fashion, was not only introducing the two new precinct people to one another, but he was also pairing them. The idea sent Ryne deep within himself, searching for something to say to put a stop to it. He didn't want the responsibility for a young and inexperienced cop on his hands, not again, and certainly not a female.

His eyes began to roll with the thought of it, the enormity of training another partner who, very likely, he would lose one way or another. He'd planned to ask Wood, in due time, to be allowed to continue working alone the way he liked it, and now this . . . *a woman* barely out of the academy. How she got as far as she had, as fast as she had made him now suddenly wonder. Suspicious, actually. No one moved up that fast without a good, or a very bad reason. From experience, Lanark knew it had nothing to do with ability with a firearm, or field smarts, or the number of collars she'd made. She was a climber . . . only question was, how far had she crawled before she began her climb?

Still, she had shown some sharp responses in the incident outside the building.

As an undercover cop she was an untested commodity, and Wood made this painfully clear to her in Lanark's presence. Then he began to rattle off a list of Lanark's collars and accomplishments when Keyes interrupted him to say that she had heard of Lanark's reputation and knew of his record.

"Then you understand my reasoning in pairing the two of you?"

"I understand quite well," she said evenly, a sidelong glance at Lanark, both of them standing, the way Wood liked, before his desk.

"As Lt. Lanark's partner, Officer Keyes," said Wood, looking for her reaction, "you will, I'm certain, fast become a tested commodity. Lots of field work out there."

"I'm ready for it, sir."

"Well, I'm not," muttered Lanark.

"Then get your butt ready for it!"

"Yes, sir . . . but if it doesn't—"

"Make it work out!"

"We'll try," said Shannon, giving Lanark a dark stare.

Her voice, now that she was his partner, suddenly sounded superior instead of refined and sonorous, Ryne thought.

"Division likes the idea." Lanark knew it was the Captain's own. "Division thinks maybe with a woman you won't be quite so gung-ho, Lanark, like what I just saw out there."

"That was a good piece of police work, sir," said Shannon suddenly. "I mean, I thought so, sir."

"That, Officer Keyes, was reckless endangerment. Sergeant O'Hurley might've been killed as a result of Lanark's attempt at *aggression therapy* on the goddamned street."

A curvaceous, dark-eyed brunette, long-legged, pretty but not so pretty as to get in the way, Lanark liked her assessment of his handling of Hernando. But the idea of a woman—*any* woman—as his partner bothered him. She might have the effect the department wanted, she might well slow him down, make him more or less *cautious*. But he didn't care for the word, or the plans of Captain Wood.

But this time, he kept it to himself.

Lanark had never worked with a female partner before, and just walking out into the squad room with her made him feel instantly awkward. "Not at all sure about this," he muttered just loud enough for her to hear, as he walked toward the desk so recently vacated by the cop who'd taken his own life. She took the bait like a marlin.

"Fuck you, Lieutenant, because I'm not altogether gratified either, having you foisted on me."

He shoved open some of the desk drawers, wooden and sticking. He banged around the desk to locate what it was that might be missing. She took up a desk pushed against his. "Just gonna' have to get along, partner, for Captain Wood's sake, *at least here*. You want to can that kind of talk? Besides, it's not becoming to a lady."

"That's what gets you the most, isn't it, Lanark, the fact that I'm a woman."

"I refuse to answer on the grounds that—"

"Stuff it, or answer the question!"

"No," he tried to deny it. "Not entirely true, Keyes. It's just that . . . well, it's no secret, I just don't do well with partners, *any* partners. One of these days, everybody'll just know that, and I'll be allowed to work the most effective way I know."

"On your own?"

"On my own."

"Everybody needs somebody, Lieutenant."

Milt Wiemer harped up and shouted across the room at them. "Hey, hey, you kids sound like godamn newlyweds."

Lanark only frowned, saying nothing. He knew that any bellyaching on the matter would only make a bad situation worse.

"Newlyweds!" said Shannon. "Not even close!"

Awkward, too, Lanark thought, looking across at her big eyes now, because he had to talk to a partner he couldn't comfortably swear around, couldn't be himself with, couldn't so much as belch without saying a pardon. She'd followed him out of the Captain's office on his heels like a shadow, and he thought she'd continue the puppy-dog posture the rest of the week, when suddenly she was in his face, speaking in bitter whisper.

"Thanks for your vote of confidence in front of my new captain, Lanark," she said with a low growl.

"Not to mention it," he replied, "ever again."

"It's not as if you were exactly my first choice or anything."

"You had no choice, no more'n me. Why am I even discussing it?" He looked up to see Sergeant O'Hurley, still a bit greenish, ambling their way with a stack of file folders. "What the hell is this, Sarge?"

O'Hurley unceremoniously dumped the paper between their two abutting desks, saying, "Yours to enjoy." He started away as Lanark and Shannon exchanged a look, Lanark pushing the files toward her side of the two desks, she pushing back.

"Oh, and by the way, Lieutenant," O'Hurley momentarily stopped the paper tug of war. "I want to thank you sincerely for what you did out front—both of you, really. If I'd been in your place, I hope I would have done the same thing, Lieutenant—"

"Forget it."

"No, I'll never forget it," he said solemnly, "not so long as I live. Your just happening to come on at the 13th today saved my life. But I've got to tell you, Lieutenant, if I'd had a gun when you started yelling at that kid to blow my head away, I'd have fried your aaah . . . behind." Even O'Hurley deferred to the female presence.

"Ass . . . the word's ass," she said, angry at the tiptoeing around her. "Please, all of you, don't stand on ceremony on my account."

"Don't worry, partner. The pedestal crumbled long ago," said Lanark.

She half-smiled, half-smirked, "All I could ask, and please, call me Shannon."

"Ryne," he answered after some hesitation.

"Short for?'

"Nothing, just Ryne."

"Just wondering."

"What's all that paper O'Hurley ⌐ found for you?"

"Us!" she corrected him. "Files . . . some previous cases left by Samuels."

"Who the hell was Samuels's partner?"

They both looked around the room for an answer. In one corner three men sat gabbing, one was Wiemer. The other two were paired as partners this shift, Temple and Gowan. Temple was a thick man all around, including his limbs, down to his fingers, his cheeks pudgy red from too much drink, red splotches coloring his nose as well. He and Wiemer must spend a lot of time together. Gowan was a serious-eyed, quiet man who dressed like a school teacher. Finally, Weimer piped up that he had been Samuels's partner, but now he was working with a guy named Udele.

Lanark wondered where this guy Udele was now, but he decided it was none of his business.

Two other detectives, Max Yoshikani and Jeffrey Blum, walked over and asked Lanark if they might not shake his hand, each in his way telling him they felt he had done a great job just outside the precinct doors. Jeff, laughing, asked Lanark if he hadn't paid all the principal actors and set the whole thing up to make himself look good in front of Wood.

Lanark blanched a bit at the word "actors," but then realized young Jeff was using a stock line. "Yeah, cost me a bundle too, but it wasn't Wood I was trying to impress," said Lanark, "it was my new partner here, Shannon, Shannon Keyes."

The backhanded introduction worked on Shannon, who exchanged greetings with Jeff and Max.

"How does a Japanese guy get a name like Max, Max?" asked Lanark.

The smiling eyes of the man grew larger, "Oh, didn't I tell you? I'm not Japanese, I'm a Japanese robot cop, a robocop. M.A.X. stands for Multifaceted Armored Killerguy . . ."

"He's good with jujitsu," added Jeff Blum.

"That right?" asked Lanark. "We'll have to see just how good, won't we, Shannon? How 'bout the gym on Division Street at—"

"YMCA?" asked Max.

"If that suits you."

"Tomorrow night, say eight?"

"I'll be there."

"Sounds like fun," said Shannon, "seeing you get your teeth kicked in."

"Oh, you going to be there?"

"I may, for laughs."

"Plenty of room for you on the mat," said Max to Shannon.

"Just try and get me there," she came right back at him.

"Might be worth the effort."

"So, Wiemer, what about these old files? Want to take them off the new recruits' hands?" asked Lanark. "I mean, they are your responsibility, right?"

"Not mine . . . still carrying mine," said Wiemer, sauntering about the place. Lanark could see he'd been here for so long he actually felt the squad room, the whole building, was his. "Those were some of Samuels's unsolved cases . . . things he . . . he just wouldn't sock away, wouldn't let go for nothing . . . hung up on them. Told him to deep-six the whole lot. Every damned one of them goes back two, maybe three years, some *more!* Guy was off his nut."

"This is going to be a real picnic, working with a hot dog, a ninja, and a drunk," Shannon spoke across to Lanark when the others stepped away, seeing Captain Wood come through his door and march through to the Sergeant's desk in a huff about something.

"Hot dog, isn't that term a little dated?"

"So is male chauvinist pig, but if the shoe fits . . . and while I'm on the subject—"

"So long as we're up front with one another, Keyes," he cut her off.

Wood reentered and shouted at them both to return to his office. They looked at each, she shrugging.

"United we stand," he said, "come on."

Captain Wood softened. As luck would have it, Paul Wood had once been an undercover cop himself, he told them, almost buddy-buddy fashion, but not quite. And without admitting it in so many words, he in fact liked both what he had witnessed on the street moments before, and the impressive number of collars listed in Lanark's file.

"Not everything in your jacket's bad, Lanark, and while you're at the 13th it's going to get better, isn't it?" He didn't expect an answer, nor did he wait for one. "From time to time, Lanark, when you need help, an additional partner," he slowed, "I'm going to be that man."

"You, Captain?"

"Unless you want Wiemer, or one of those other losers out there."

"Yes, sir."

"For now, you work with Officer Keyes. When and *if* you get something, you report directly to me. If you need help or backup on a stakeout, *whatever,* you come to me."

"Tired of riding a desk, sir?"

"You could say that, yeah.'

Lanark reached across and took the Captain's hand. He liked the firm shake and there was something in Wood's eye, a sheen that hadn't been there before, like something was suddenly awakened inside him, some forgotten or lost feeling. "I have something I want you two to go after, Lanark."

"Anything for the cause."

"Between normal duties assigned by myself and routed through O'Hurley, I'd like you to find out what you can about a guy named Sorentino, Tavalez Sorentino."

"Drugs?"

"Drugs, prostitution, rackets, all suspected, nothing proven. On the D.A.'s hit list."

"Big time, huh?"

"Thinks he is. Any way that you can, nail the bastard. He's screwed up more lives than any hundred gang punks like Hernando out there."

"I'll start right in on it, Captain." He looked at Shannon. "I mean, we'll start on it, sir."

"Better," she said.

"And Lanark, one more thing."

"Sir?"

"I'm too old and set in my ways for a lot of shit falling on me from above. You get my drift?"

"Toilets are upstairs, sir?"

Wood watched Lanark's stony face for a smile but he saw none, whereas Shannon Keyes was fighting back a laugh. "Funny, Lanark. I don't want anything disturbing me! And I'm not going to allow you to bring down the hammer on me. Anything goes foul out there with this night-stick mentality of yours, it'll be your ass, not mine! Get control of it, mister, or you'll never get free of this precinct, okay? You're down now as a rogue, a wild-hair in the buttocks of the force. It would be an easy matter to pluck you right out altogether."

"On top of everything else, Captain, you're a poet?"

"Get the hell out of here and go to work."

"Captain, what about the White Glove murders?"

A series of deaths involving the high-rent district had been on the books for some time now. Both the Mayor's office and the Governor's office were highly emotional about the deaths since they involved debutantes from the richest families in and around Chicago. One of the young women found dead by the White-Glove Killer was Mattie Pullman, great-granddaughter to the famous Pullman who made his fortune on the sweat and backs of many an immigrant family. Another was the heir apparent to the Paige fortune. All of the women, three now, had been gruesomely disfigured by a perverted and sick mind. The killer had relieved himself inside each victim, then relieved his long since dead victims of all distinctive features, with a surgical, or carving knife—no one was quite sure. First the nose and eyes were slit, just thin lines. Then the mouth was enlarged, blood making it appear a gaping hole. Breasts and uterus followed in some cases, but not all. Throat wound, the coroner reported, was the deadly one. Once finished, the killer left a single red rose and a once white, now blood-red glove in the victim's mouth and uterus.

Wood, irritated, asked, "Well, what about them?"

"The 13th touches on that area, according to the precinct map, and—"

"That's right, Captain," agreed Shannon.

"Division's got it."

"But—"

"Forget it, Lanark, we've been warned off it."

"Warned off? Shit, Captain—"

"Lanark!"

54

"Captain, if the deaths are occurring within the boundaries of your precinct, whether Division has it or not, if something's not done soon it'll be your ass, not Division's."

"This some kind of obsession with you, Lanark, or what?"

"I don't care to see women murdered and mutilated, sir."

"Nobody does!"

"Somebody does!"

"You know what I mean."

"Answer's still no?"

"Answer is still, no! Outta here, now!"[8]

FOUR

"Where do we start?" Shannon asked when Lanark slumped wearily into the desk chair which almost toppled him over.

He swore at the chair, and then said, "You familiarize yourself with the precinct, there—" he pointed to a map on the wall beside them depicting the streets, parks, schools, points of interest, bisecting highways, cemeteries, municipal buildings, railroad tracks, elevated tracks, roads under construction, dead-end streets, plazas and squares, residential areas and commercial. "Get to know every inch of it. Could save your life someday."

"All right, then what?"

"Telephone book."

"What about it?"

"Call the local utilities people. Identify yourself. See if Sorentino pays his bills on time."

"Then?"

"Then check out every other Sorentino in the book

against a precinct address. *We all need somebody to leeeeean on,*" he tried to carry the tune but failed.

"Sorentino's relatives?"

"Assuming his is a "family business . . .""

"And? So?"

"Relatives are a prime source of information about a man, *if* approached correctly."

"Is that right?"

"You bet your . . . *badge* that's right."

"Look, Lanark, you don't have to watch your language on my account."

"Hey, if it makes me feel better, I'll watch my language, okay? Okay?"

"Okay."

He dove into the bottom of the desk in search of a Chicago phone book. "This may take some time, kid, but be thorough," he told her when he flipped to and through the S's, until he hit upon the six pages of Sorentinos. "Narrow the names down to people in the precinct, that'd be his most likely deputies—family. Some are going to be no use . . . just coincidence. Use the precinct map, if you don't know all the streets. Good study habits could make life easier later."

"What about you? Aren't you interested in knowing every alleyway and—"

"I grew up in this area. I know it like the back of my hand. You take this time, Shannon. It's necessary. Me, I'll be in the field, see what some old contacts know about Tavalez Sorentino."

She sat there as he pushed the thick white pages over to her desk, without another word. He was sticking her with desk duty. Her anger was clearly visible. Lanark sharpened a pencil and gave her a note pad and said,

"Besides, you're in uniform, patrolwoman. That wouldn't work so well in undercover."

"Hold on, Lanark, this busy work could be done by any clerk, fed into the computer for match-up—"

"Good idea. Go to it."

He was leaving. She caught him at the Sergeant's desk. "Where'll we meet, later, I mean?"

"Your place, or mine, you mean?" he said with a smile that was calculated. "Tomorrow, Keyes, right here, second shift, remember, three to one A.M. better than graveyard. See you then."

"But suppose I need to contact you?"

"Very dangerous to even try. Could get me killed. No beepers where I'm going."

"You've got a radio in your car, don't you?"

"Police band, yeah . . . code is Sugar."

"Sugar?"

"Dispatch likes to call me Sugar. They know not to call me direct. It's used in connection with any other vehicle number, the dispatcher ending with a sultry Sugar."

"Clever, even if it is misleading."

"Whatever works, which you should now be about."

She swallowed hard before saying, "You're not going to stonewall me, Lanark, or turn me into your goddamned secretary."

"Hey, what I ordered you to do, Sergeant Lieutenant, is get me a list of possible relatives on Sorentino so we got some shake-downs, and that's standard detective work. Lot of what detectives do, *Detective,* is secretarial in nature. You can't live with that, then talk to the captain."

Wood peered out his door and watched Lanark leave his partner standing in the hall.

Shannon Keyes looked back at her desk, returned and stared at the phone book. To hell with it, she told herself, getting on the phone and calling upstairs to the computer people. "Yes," she said, identifying herself by name and badge number. "Want you to run a cross-check on Chicagoans with the name of Sorentino living within the confines of precinct 13. Can you do that?"

"Yes, but it will take a little time." It was a mild, calm, female voice.

"How much time?"

"It's a matter of getting on the system. Once your request is put through, no time at all, but—"

"How much time are we talking here, a day, two, three?"

"Can get back to you tomorrow with that information, Detective."

Shannon liked the sound of the word as it applied to her. She did a quick mental calculation and realized she could not do the same work in less time today. It was nearing the end of her first day's shift anyway. Tomorrow, according to Wood, she'd be on second watch. That would give the computer people plenty of time. "Okay, that'll be fine. I'll show him," she muttered, thinking of Lanark.

"Detective?"

"Oh, sorry . . . that'll be just fine. Will you contact me in the squad room when it's ready?"

"Will do."

Shannon was hanging up when she heard Wiemer whining something about the fact that pantyhose gave him hives and that there was evidence nylon contrib-

59

uted to crotch irritation. "Why not get the new hot-shot, or better yet, why not the broad Keyes?"

Then Shannon saw Captain Wood and the others were staring in her direction. "Forget it," said Captain Wood, "she's too green. We don't start people on rape cases."

"But she's a woman," said Wiemer. "She's just what the doctor ordered."

"What is it, Captain?"

"Got a creep doing a dirty business up and down Logan Square area between train and bus stops," he said, "two women seriously injured, both raped first."

"I want it," she said instantly.

"Wiemer's been working a stakeout and wearing a dress, but it just makes him look less attractive than he already is."

The other men laughed.

"Well, am I attractive enough?"

"You'll be pulling a double-shift, if you say yes."

"I already have."

"Better let Lanark know."

"Sugar? Sure, if he's near a radio . . ."

"We'll get in touch with him. You go home, get a change of clothes."

"Yes, sir, Captain." She was excited over the new opportunities opening up to her, but a sidelong glance at the precinct map depicting the Logan Square area told her it would take days, maybe weeks, before she would be completely familiar with the lay of the land and the territorial boundaries of the precinct. Something told her that Lanark wasn't going to like it, her jumping in with both feet this way. All the more reason to do it, she told herself firmly.

* * *

What Lanark most needed and wanted was a van, a battered old van with an interior like no other, filled with high-tech, crime fighting equipment and props and disguises. That was the dream.

The reality was he lived with a battered old '71 Javelin without enough trunk space for all of his much needed paraphernalia. Most of his work was done in semi-filthy clothes like the wino's baggy trousers, held up by suspenders, and the torn coat, but quite often—and on the spur of the moment— he needed to change into yet another character. For this, the trunk of the old car was his office. It held makeup kits, wardrobe, props and hats, and additional guns.

He had gone into the alley back of the station house to retrieve his own clothes from the wino, but as might be expected, the drunk was long gone. He'd submit a bill to Wood tomorrow. For now, the outfit might need a little touch up, but it could do service again. He located a favorite hat and then studied himself in the mirror that dangled from the inside of the trunk. He had pulled the car into a vacant lot, back of *Armand's Italian House* restaurant. He'd been told by an informant that Sorentino often transacted business lunches here. A few moments before, a man had gone into the place pulling a young girl with him. The girl seemed opposed to the place for better reason than the quality of the food. Lanark wondered if he could possibly get to her, find out what her problem was. He'd only got a glimpse as he cruised by, but the long, dark hair seemed spiked on end from fear, or anger, or both. The man tugging her could be a small-time pimp, playing up to Sorentino, offering him one of his girls for payment on a bill. Or it could simply be a patron of the restaurant who had a rebellious kid on his hands. She hadn't been dressed like a kid, however. Still, with the Madonna madness among teeny-boppers these days, it was a great deal harder to make such distinctions than a few years back.

It just didn't smell right, no more so than the stench coming from the so-called Italian kitchen. Smell was greasy, Greek, rank with something other than Ragu. After fifteen minutes of poking about the rear garbage dump and windows, one man came out waving a meat cleaver at Lanark. He was in a chef's hat, but he was hardly Italian. In fact, he was decidely Oriental and from the wizened look of him, Lanark guessed Vietnamese.

"You go, get out of heeeeaaa!" he shouted.

"I'm going . . . going . . . gone," Lanark said boozily, raising his prop whiskey bottle to the man's eyes. "But what's-at stink so bad here?"

"Go 'way, now! Boss man say go!" The cleaver was raised.

Lanark felt a wave of revulsion come over him—he wanted to take the cleaver and ram it down the jerk's throat—but he had to remain calm at this juncture. "I do work for you, you savvy? Take garbage out of here for . . . for two dollars?" The greasy chef looked like a Viet Cong colonel.

"We got garbage man . . . don't need garbage picker."

"One dollar . . . get rid of the smell for you before some inspector comes 'long and sees this."

"Awl-light, awl-light, for one dollar, you take what

you want. But get owta' heeeeeaaa, now, tank you very much.'' He stripped off a dollar bill for Lanark's *whiskey guzzler* and then returned inside.

That was easy, Lanark said to himself, helping himself to several fly-ridden trash bags and waddling off with them, rounding the corner, taking it all to his car and plunking them in the back seat, since he hadn't room in the trunk.

Lanark then weighed his options. Should he push it, take his ruse a step further, or hope for another day? He pulled out his wallet. Folded neatly behind the clip of his badge was a crumpled dollar bill. He'd used this same ploy before. He wondered if it would work on Tavalez Sorentino. Snatching out the counterfeit bill, he pushed it deep in his pocket and placed the good bill given him by the kitchen man into his wallet—*his tip,* he mused, for taking away the trash.

He decided to return to the restaurant, but this time he'd go through the front door, create a real disturbance.

He affected the walk, a kind of ambling limp with a sometime weave, not to be overdone. Mumbling to himself, the mumbling becoming more serious as he went, until it was an angry, guttural thing, he located the doors of the establishment. He burst inside, complaining at the top of his lungs, an outraged sot, waving the phony bill in one hand, cursing the man who'd stuck him with it. All the while, Lanark's trained eye took in the lay of the place, the number of people inside, particularly those surrounding Sorentino, and he managed a good look at the tall, angular, dark-skinned man who sat high in his booth with a smirk for a smile, oversized ears, a spiked nose, eyes too close together.

"Armand, Armand," he called out, clearly in control here. "Get this trash out on the street, now!"

The bum wheeled and stumbled toward and into Sorentino's table, a bodyguard lunging forward and jamming a gun into his face.

"Peter!" shouted Sorentino, "Put it away!"

The thug did as instructed but held Lanark by the coat collar. Lanark saw that the girl opposite Sorentino was agitated, and hardly more than sixteen or seventeen years of age. Moments before, Sorentino had been haggling with a man about a price, reaching across and jabbing his hand into her mouth, like a horse trader buying a mare.

Lanark swiped out at the man who had hold of him, the dollar bill still clenched in his fist, he knocked over a wineglass that sent dark burgundy all over Sorentino, who jumped up screaming.

"Sonofabitch! Can't you get this gutter rat out of here, Peter!"

"Lemme go! Lemme go!" shouted Lanark, tearing away. "Geek in the kitchen stole from me! Give me a phony bill! Look at it! Look at it! Fake shit!"

Peter had Lanark by the back of the neck now, in a vise that could snap his spine, but Sorentino, snatching the bill from him, said, "Let him go, Peter. *Let him go!*" Then he turned to Lanark, looking closely at him. The beard hid his features along with the thick, gray brows, smudge marks and carefully applied makeup. Lanark's acting career had taught him well in this regard. "You say someone here gave you this?" He was examining the bill more closely than he examined Lanark.

"Damned straight."

"I do a lot of my own business here, sir," Sorentino

said to the old wino. "You may have discovered something of great importance here. Armand," he continued, "can you explain this?" He handed the bill to the rotund, nervous owner of the place.

"I . . . I have no idea, Mr. Sorentino . . . this man comes in here . . . accuses us . . . you can't seriously think—"

Lanark knew what Sorentino meant by a lot of business being done at the place. He routinely laundered his money here. If someone were replacing it with counterfeit bills, it could ruin his reputation up and down the line of "commerce."

"Mister," moaned Lanark's bum, pleading now, "I ain't got much . . . it ain't right . . . taking advantage of a man down on his luck . . ."

The dark-eyed, dark-haired girl, seeing that no one was watching her, slipped quietly from the booth where Sorentino had been pawing her, and disappeared out the back. Sorentino was studying the bill under the light. It was a phony, one of a wad of bad bills that Lanark used on occasion, a wad he had lifted from a bust. The wad was now part of the junk pile in his trunk, one of his props.

"This man is correct, Armand. Who gave you this, who?" Sorentino was furious. He suspected, as Lanark knew he would, that Armand was skimming.

"Oriental guy," muttered Lanark, "with the chef's hat on. Paid me for taking some of the garbage away."

"Get him out here! I want to talk to this man," shouted Sorentino, who, standing now, could pass for a Spanish Abraham Lincoln. He was raw-boned, high cheeked, his muscles sinewy. He also gave the feel of a practiced mortician.

"You," he said to Lanark, "here . . . here's for your trouble, and anyone in the neighborhood asks, you got it from Tavalez Sorentino." He handed the bum a twenty-dollar bill.

Lanark stared at it, choked, tried to say "thank you," but couldn't, not through the unmanly tears. He just shook his head and ambled out, leaving Armand in a bad way. He'd stirred the ant's nest up without giving himself away. So far, so good.

Now he wanted to dig into that trash.

He went a circuitous route back to the car, being certain he was not followed, before he pulled off the wig and hat, got in and drove toward home, taking Milwaukee Avenue. There, in the back yard, he'd pick through the trash, see what evidentiary information might come of it. Trash was always a long shot, but sometimes the most surprising things jumped out at you, and Ryne had learned in this business that one man's trash was another's gold. He only wished that Keyes was with him to enjoy this part of the "secretarial" side of it all. As he drove for home, he wondered how she was doing with the map and book.

"Sugar . . ." he thought he heard the code word for him come over. Better check in, he thought, but then his eyes were caught by the darting figure of a small woman, girl, really, as she ducked into a stairwell. It was the girl that had been in Sorentino's grasp. He wondered if he dared reveal himself to her, take her into his confidence, try to get her to open up. If he could, maybe they could close down Sorentino sooner. The more he learned and saw of this greaseball, the more he detested the bastard.

He pulled over the car, some eight blocks now from

the restaurant. The girl had gotten far, but not far enough. Sorentino could have her in an hour. She had no place to hide.

Lanark donned the hat again and went into the doorway where she'd disappeared. He had one eye closed against the sun, seeing the doorway was black, and as he entered it, he opened his closed eye and shut the other one. This precaution kept him from the momentary blindness that came when a man stepped from an intensely bright sun to a blackened room. He used it every time he walked into a bar on a day like today.

He read the mailboxes. No female names. A Tony Sorrel—coincidence? he wondered. Or was Sorrel an *aka* for Sorentino. If so, Lanark may've hit the jackpot.

Just then, however, someone was coming straight for the doorway, the guy named Peter, Sorentino's bodyguard. Lanark could see out clearly but *he* could not see in. Lanark rang Tony Sorrel's bell, not expecting an answer, but as a warning to the girl. The bell would act as an alarm, giving her time to escape to a safer place, he thought.

Lanark waited for the other man to step into the black hallway and the instant he did, he leveled a balled-up fist to the man's jaw. Peter went down like a loose bag of potatoes, out cold. When Lanark looked up to the first flight of stairs, hearing noises, he saw the barrel of a gun and leaped back against the wall to a loud bang. The wall opposite him exploded. Tony Sorrel carried a Magnum.

"Police!" shouted Lanark, "Hold your fire!"

But he was speaking to an empty hallway. The couple was on the run. Lanark went out to where the bodyguard lay moaning. He got the man to his feet, taking his weapon from him, and he forced him up the stairs ahead of him, using him as a human shield and making him keep his eyes straight ahead. Lanark didn't want to be recognized.

Each step they took Lanark called out the word police. But this didn't do anymore than cause locks to be bolted on all sides. Once they reached the first landing, Ryne pushed his captive through the one open door which he assumed was Sorrel's.

It was a dingy, one-room apartment, the toilet at the end of the hall. There was a bed, a bureau and a chair and table. Lanark placed the chair at the man's hind end and told him to sit. "I ain't done nothing, not a damned thing," Peter protested, starting to turn.

"Sit down!"

"Hey, you . . . it's you . . . the bum!"

"I said shut up and sit down, Pete!" Lanark cocked his weapon and this had the desired effect on the big goon.

"Whataya' want from me?"

Lanark tied the man's hands and placed a blindfold across his eyes. He didn't want him to get a close look at him. "Who's this guy Sorrel? What's he to Sorentino?"

"Tony's a prick."

"That doesn't exactly answer my question."

"Hey, you really a cop?"

"No, I lied."

"Then who're you?"

"I'm asking the questions, Pete, and we'll sit here all night if need be. We can do it easy and slow, or we can do it fast. How do you like your pain? You ever get cut so you bleed from the gut real slow? I mean, like it takes hours to die? I know how to do that, Pete."

He let the thought take hold of the big man.

"Now, who's Sorrel and what's his connection to Sorentino?"

"He's . . . he's the boss's kid."

"His son?"

"Yes!"

"And the girl?"

"She ain't nothing, just trash."

"She must be something to Tony."

"Kid's stupid. Living in this shit pile when—"

"They're married, aren't they?"

"She'd sell Tony out in a minute. She's a whore. But the kid, he's too stupid to know it."

"Think I get the picture, Pete. Good night."

With a quick, swift downward motion of his gun butt, Lanark put Pete to sleep. The dull crack of it made even Lanark wince. He then went about the room looking for clues that might help him locate Tony and his woman. It had been a buy-out at the restaurant that Lanark had been witness to, Sorrentino trying to purchase the girl's allegiance. She does what he says and she's paid royally, and Tony is once again his boy, simple as that . . . or was it? Lanark knew he could not trust his eyes alone.

A run-through of the few drawers here told him little. A few snapshots of Tony and the girl, the best one of which he kept. He pulled the bed out, looking beneath into shoe boxes. Nothing. He looked between the mattresses and behind the mirror, for anything taped beneath. Nothing. Then he struck paydirt of a sort, a check stub from the U.S. Navy. Tony was in the Navy.

A pattern was emerging, a young man trying to escape his past, his father, but quite unable to do so, changes his name, joins the Navy, not necessarily in that order. Falls in love with a girl, but she's not what the father wants for his son. Even villainous bastards like Sorentino, running drugs and turning out prostitutes, had problems with fatherhood.

Lanark found an envelope from the Department of the Navy. The kid could be located through them, but it might be faster if Lanark could find someone in the building hiding them. If he could only make them believe he wanted to help them. He weighed his options, and the next hour was spent knocking on doors, trying to get a lead on Tony Sorrel. Nothing doing. The building was filled with aged down-and-outs, frightened zombies, many of them. Most of them didn't know what Lanark wanted, no matter how he put it. Some didn't believe he was a cop, despite the badge he flashed. Others had never heard of a Tony Sorrel, or knew of Mrs. Sorrel, or that anyone was living in the apartment at the end, or that today was the first of May.

Lanark left the building the same way he entered, one eye closed to the sudden onset of the sun. When he came out onto the street a bag lady was making off with one of the trash bags that had been in his car.

"Stop! Police!" he shouted after the old woman who turned on him and started throwing scraps and leavings from the bag at him.

"Lady, lady! You want to go to jail?"

The woman took a last swipe at him with a bone, just missing when Lanark ducked, and then she dropped the bag and ambled away amid curses muttered to herself.

The bone caught Lanark's attention. It was an odd bone for a restaurant to be discarding. Definitely not chicken, but neither was it ham. Something in between?

He tied off the trash bag again, trying to beat back the odor. He returned to his car. From there he headed homeward, the watch almost over anyway. Tomorrow would begin the later hours with the second watch. For now, his best bet was the garbage.

He'd get a beer and the elbow-length gloves and get right at it. Maybe Tebo would give him a hand if things were slow in the bar. Maybe Tebo knew what kind of bone it was that the old lady had thrown at him. T-bone? No, that wasn't it, he told himself.

He thought of Sorrel and the girl, alone and running. He thought of his first impressions of Sorentino. The man could be dangerous. He wondered what would have happened to the girl if he hadn't intervened with the phony story and bill, and if the kid had said *no* to his overtures, which, to Lanark's way of thinking, had leaned toward sex as much as anything else. Knowing Sorentino's type, Lanark guessed at a blackmail attempt. Get the girl in a compromising position any way that you can, take photos, threaten, payoff and she disappears. But why so much trouble, unless Sorentino himself didn't want the girl harmed physically?

It was times like this, when brainstorming was needed, that he most missed a partner. But he wasn't quite ready to accept Shannon Keyes as a partner.

Chicago was bathing in humidity tonight, the air so

still a man felt it as he walked through it, both clinging to and resisting him. The sun had been burning down on the pavement all day long and now it sat like a ball of fire in the west, just holding, maintaining, as if it wanted to get a last dig in, or not leave at all tonight. The stillness, the heat and humidity masked a metallic, bloodlike odor with it. The smell of impending rain, the hope and prayer for it, or the real thing, he wondered. At any rate, for now, the heat only added to the fetid smell in Lanark's car. He could expect a complete ribbing from Jack Tebo on arriving at the bar with his three trash bags.

Shadows were lengthening, even if the process was imperceptible, and as he drove he hit light, dark, light and dark again in a pattern created by the city buildings. The pattern reflected both his mood and his life, he thought. How suddenly his own life had gone from light to dark. How his relationships with friends, even Tebo, had changed, mutated actually. He no longer "related." Not to anyone or anything, save his desire for revenge. A case like the one he was working was fodder for his innermost emotions, feeding his hatred. Guys like Tavalez Sorentino put drugs on the streets for guys like the murdering vermin that had mutilated his sister and destroyed his parents.

His hatred had changed with time, as all things must. It was no longer the fiery growth that consumed his bowels every waking moment, and left him shivering in a pool of sweat each morning. That sweet fire around which he knelt and breathed in angry smoke, stoking the building rage, while not entirely consumed, now smoldered beneath the surface, volcano-like. Seething, churning, the fire had made of his insides a viper pit

72

where the snake of hatred was ever hungry for revenge, and so lived on there, vigilant, swarming below the skin in a lake of bile.

Lanark's rage remained the cause and effect of the vicious circle of pain and loneliness, the inability to be content, to find simple happiness like other men; to find any sort of relief other than the occasional binge he indulged himself. As for giving and taking love, such emotions had remained beyond his grasp even with the most caring people.

When Sybil had left him, he'd tried to feel the loss. As great as it was, as much as she meant to him, he could not find the feelings, feelings lost to him with the death of his parents, feelings he'd buried with them. His inability to display and to accept love, that was the cause of his breakup with Sybil Shanley. He knew this and yet he could not change what he had become, a kind of Frankenstein's monster, moving, walking and talking, yet dead inside, save for the unrelenting anger.

Sybil Shanley was an Assistant Medical Examiner with the Coroner's Office. At first Ryne entered into the relationship with the most selfish of motives, with a mad rush of lustful, roller-coaster passion. Using Sybil, he was attempting to re-invigorate his dead emotions. Via the route of experimentation and rough sex, to some extent she did revive him, but it hadn't been fair to Sybil from the beginning. One night, being honest with her, telling her of the horrible cause of his numbness and intermittent impotence. She understood too well his confession, finding that what she took for love was something entirely different and not at all pretty. He'd hurt her badly. He didn't love her. He couldn't love anyone, ever again, he tried to explain.

He'd stopped short of telling her he was *afraid* to love anyone ever again.

Still, a bond was forged between them when he had unexpectedly broken down and bared his soul to her. They had remained close, supportive friends. His inability to commit himself to her fully had been explained away by the invisible scars of that terrible time.

He continued to use her, however, in another way; and quietly, pleasantly, she cooperated most of the time, not with sex or as a drinking partner any longer, but professionally, supplying him with information whenever he approached her. But Lanark strained the relationship to its limits with his last request.

He thought of it now, wondering if she'd come through for him or not. He had no way of knowing, not any longer.

He had hit her up for vital information on the autopsies in the "Glove" case. It was a sensitive case. It was being tightly monitored. In fact, both politicians and press alike were making hay over the case, everyone slamming the police department for its inability to put an end to the career of the murderer. Information leaks could cost people dearly. And Ryne had traded on their friendship beyond any right he had, placing unwanted, unneeded pressure on her.

"Absolutely not," she'd told him at first, before he began chipping away at the absolute. "It's strictly taboo for us to even be talking about it, Ryne. Hell, for all I know the phones could be bugged."

Pulling onto his street now, he wondered if she'd reconsidered, wondered if she had left word on his answering machine to call her.

When he pulled into his parking space behind the

bar, he began hefting the bags out of the back when Tebo loped out to him, shouting, "Not again with the garbage!"

"New case, new garbage."

"You must like this kinda' shit, Ryne."

"Call it job compensation."

"Perks, huh?" he asked, helping with the bags.

Ryne laughed, sweat glistening his face.

"Sybil's called a couple of times at the bar. Wants you to call back."

His eyes went wide, going directly for Tebo's with an enormous pleading.

"All right, I'll see to your bags!"

"Oh, and Jack, there's a bone on the driver's seat."

"Thanks for throwing me one."

Lanark laughed. Tebo was one of the few people who could make Lanark laugh. "It's not for you! Tell me if you have any idea what kind of bone it is. You were a butcher's apprentice once. What's it from? Check it out."

Before Ryne was in the door, Jack shouted, "Dog femur!"

"So, *Armand's* literally serves up real dog food! Interesting, if sick," Lanark called back, rushing for the phone. He was, after all, much more interested in learning more about the slasher of the North Shore from Sybil Shanley than he was Sorentino's predilection for dog meat. Or had she called simply to tell him she could not do it?

He dialed the number of the coroner's office, hoping Sybil'd still be there. His call was routed to her after a few minutes and she came on line. "It's me, Ryne . . . you called?" he asked.

"About developments in the case you're so interested in."

"It's important to me, Sybil."

"As well I know."

"Sybil?"

"Lanark, you can be a pain in the ass."

"I know all my short-comings far more than you do. Please?"

"This gets back to me and it could mean my job, you know that?"

"I do, and it won't."

"All right. Semen samples indicate more than one male attacker—if you can call it an attack."

"More than one?"

"Different semen samples, yes, different in the mouth than the uterus. Girl's like the others, too, in that there's no sign of having struggled against her attackers. Drug counts so high and varied, looks like she was punch-bowling it, you know, trying a variety of drugs at once."

"This true of the others?"

"They were all drugged, yes. Pentobarbitol's highest on the drug list. Anyway, hands and ankles do show signs of binding, particularly the ankles. Death came as a result of shock due to a lack of blood."

"Lack of blood? I thought . . . everybody's saying it was the throat wounds that caused—"

"No, the wounds were severe enough, but they appear to have been made *after* death, after a severe loss of blood, we currently surmise from the slit jugular vein."

"You're confusing me, Sybil."

"The blood was carefully drained from the victims.

The first cuts were small punctures for this purpose, the blood allowed to run carefully from the victims—"

"And *caught*, you mean? Like, like collected?"

"It seems so, since most of the blood found on the neck and other wounds was *smeared on* from the outside—"

"You can tell that?"

"—with some sort of brush, and Ryne . . ."

"Brush? Did you say *brush?*"

"This blood's not the victim's blood. It's someone else's. Smeared on by someone with a bloody brush, *artwork.*"

"Jesus, does it match blood left on the earlier victims?" Ryne had never heard of a killer purposefully leaving his own blood at the scene of a murder.

"No . . . it varies with each victim."

"Doesn't make sense."

"As much as the semen."

"Group sex . . . group murder?"

"Your guess is as good as mine."

"Anything else?"

"An interesting ring, gold, with an inscription."

"What insccription?"

"MS."

"That's all, just MS?"

"Afraid so."

"The others have such a ring?"

"One had a bracelet with the initials. Sorority, maybe?"

"I'll check around."

She indicated a few other incidental matters and they said a kindly good night to one another, after Sybil told him she'd finally found a man she might settle down with and he tried to sound pleased and heartened for her good fortune. "Remember," she'd said just before hanging up, "none of this information is known outside the lab except for Riordan's unit, my friend. It could really hurt me professionally if—"

"Not to worry."

Ryne instantly put in a call to a friend who was working on the "Glove" case, albeit in a peripheral capacity, in charge of filing, bookkeeping and secretarying for Riordan.

Peggy Morrisey was more fearful by far of involving herself with Ryne, even over the phone. Word was out he was *persona non grata* in Riordan's eyes and if she crossed Riordan, or should his waxy-eared snoop partner, Fabia, get wind of the fact Peggy even spoke with Lanark again, she'd be at Precinct 13 and lower on the scale of police totem than she already was.

He fielded her fears one by one, repeatedly saying, "What could it hurt . . . one name . . . one name. The girl had to have had a boyfriend, husband, lover? Some guy that ol' Riordan's pulled in and questioned, right? One name."

"Talk to the dead girl's parents, why don't you?"

"They don't need any more grief from cops. Please."

"Oh, Lanark . . . why should I risk my job for you?"

"All right . . . you're right, Peggy. I should never have put you on the spot."

"For all we know this damned phone is bugged."

"Is it?"

"It will be after today." She sighed and gave him a name. He wrote it down, along with a phone number and address she provided. Sounded all very upper-crust. *Burton Eaton-Heron, 2 Northshore Place, Winnetka, Illinois, 555-2121.* He was most eager to speak with Burton. Lanark threw Peggy a kiss through the wires and she said, "Why don't we try it for real sometime, Sugar?"

He laughed lightly into the phone, "Sometime we will."

Lanark hung up and thought about what he wanted to say to Burton Eaton-Heron. He concocted a story that he was on the investigating team that had already questioned him and that he must see him once again, tonight, to go over his testimony.

He placed the call and spoke to what sounded like a shaking chicken at the other end of the line. Burton told him he would be at a party tonight, and he gave the address.

"Partying?" asked Lanark. "Your girlfriend gets whacked the other night and you're partying?"

"She wasn't my girl . . . not anymore . . . not for a long time."

"Whose girl was she?"

"She . . . she slept around, man, I told you guys that!"

"All right, but I would like to talk to you."

"Be there then." The voice was annoyingly nasal, whiny. Rich bastard whiny, or druggie, Lanark wondered.

"Right, I'll be there."

It could be a routine visit, a questioning that gained him nothing, or it could lead to something. Lanark knew he must follow the slim lead. He rifled through his clothing for the appropriate attire for a high class party, coming up with a tuxedo. He quickly disrobed, showered and shaved. He'd be ready for Burton's party and on time. Admiring himself in the mirror, thinking he never looked so good, then pressing on the mustache he wished to don for the occasion, he suddenly remembered having left Tebo with all that trash out back. He grabbed a couple of beers from his fridge and raced out, finding the curious Tebo rummaging about the garbage himself. "Some weird stuff here, Ryne. Lots of sickie photos, child porn shots."

"Let me see those," he said, taking them in hand. They made Lanark's stomach turn.

"Oh, hey, by the way, Ryne, *they* called—"

"Who called?"

"Heard your code name over your radio, something to do with a stakeout tonight?"

"I got no stakeout duty tonight."

"Just telling you what I heard."

"Better check in with dispatch, clear it up."

"Ryne radioed in asking questions. . . ."

"Yes, immediately, get in touch with your captain," said dispatch in a reserved, professional voice.

"Wood?"

"No, laminated steel! Yeah, Wood. He's been trying to locate you. Something doing with your partner at the Logan Square stakeout tonight."

"Stakeout? Tonight? Keyes?"

He slammed the door and revved up the engine, tearing away, only seeing Tebo in the rear-view mirror for half a second. Tebo was tossing trash skyward and yelling at him to return. He felt a sudden fear rise in him like a mounting wave, a sensation like nothing he'd ever felt before, as if he knew *she* were in terrible trouble at this very minute but he was too far away to help, and when it was over news would travel brushfire-like throughout the Chicago Police Department that another partner of Ryne Lanark's was killed in action on the street, and Lanark was at fault. But most of all he simply feared for Shannon Keyes. He didn't want her hurt, maimed or dead. He wanted her safe and he wanted the time it would take to know her better, maybe well enough to understand the feelings he was showing himself now.

"God, don't let anything happen to her," he said through clenched teeth before getting on the radio to pick up a signal from Wood, Wiemer or someone else connected with the Logan Square rapist case.

"Lanark? That you?" It was Wood's distinctive growl.

"Where's your location, *exactly?* Where's Keyes?"

"I've got a whole bone to pick with you, detective!"

"Where's your location? Where the hell's Keyes? Give me her exact location, Captain, now!"

The briefcase was getting heavy. It was filled to bursting, and it was turning to lead in her hand. She'd had a few too many drinks, and it showed in the weave of her walk. She swayed a bit. Not so much to make it noticeable to any but those whose eyes might already be trained on her, but enough to be a tell-tale sign. She'd stayed late at the office party. Life was a drag if you couldn't party it away sometimes. Sure was dark here, dark and barren. The most alive thing on the street aside from her were discarded newspapers and bags animated by the wind.

The wind tore at her, dervish-like, revealing her legs beneath the coat. She tugged with her free hand to control the flap. Doing so, she heard faint footsteps, not behind but in front of her. She saw the dark figure of a hefty man coming straight toward her, his step sure and purposeful. He seemed to be coming right at her like a bull. Could it be him, the creep that had brutally raped two women in this very district over the past four months?

But he passed her without even a glance.

She'd been unable to find a taxi, and now she rushed toward the train station. As dingy as the station was, you could get a cup of coffee, and there were always some people about.

She stepped up her pace. The damned heels rocked uncontrollably until one snapped off, sending her to one knee. She picked up the heel and stared at it, cursing it.

"Can I help you, Miss?" The voice was mellow and calm, a foreign accent, Polish perhaps?

Looking up, it was a fright to see the same big man who'd passed by earlier. Hadn't he been going in the opposite direction?

"Let me give you a hand," he said. The eyes were shockingly dark, encircled with black rings and thick flesh. He was older than the chance appearance of before had indicated, older than any Jack the Ripper type had a right to be, perhaps. Perhaps he was harmless after all. Perhaps, but the sudden glint in his eye, and a smile of raw delight that spread apart his lips to reveal jagged teeth, told her otherwise: no man, in the dark, believing himself alone with a woman was safe. It could be the rapist. *It could be the Glove!*

She took the soft hand he offered, saying, "Oh, thank you, sir,' *remembering to slur her words drunkenly* but fear suddenly gripped her so tightly she thought it was his hands closed on her heart, squeezing. With a sudden scream she turned the briefcase and it came up like a projectile, slamming into the man's temple. When he fell back something metallic skittered across the bricks of the dark plaza. It was an enormous butcher knife.

He had a hold of her leg. She felt the pavement come up like a boulder to hit her. He clawed, moaning in pain, holding tight, tearing off the bug on her lapel. She snatched at the bug, calling into it for help, "He's got me! He's got a knife! Christ, he's big! I need help!" He tore off her wig, revealing her as a brunette. She tore free, desperate to get to her feet.

Shannon Keyes danced about the man, now on his knees, wondering what she'd do if the bastard got to his feet. He was a good head taller than her and was perhaps one-hundred and sixty pounds heavier. Little wonder the women this man had raped and beaten had been unable to escape him. Shannon instinctively kicked the knife farther from the killer's grasp, realizing he could have it. With another swift kick, she put her good heel in the man's cheek, stunning him further.

Where the hell's my backup? "Help! Damn it, now!" This part of being a decoy she wasn't having fun with. The ruse was up. She felt even more vulnerable than before. She knew self-defense, but it wasn't much good against a giant wielding a knife. As for the .38 in her purse, she'd never shot a real person before. She wanted to earn Lanark's respect, and Wood's as well, and she wanted to be the best decoy the precinct had ever seen. Now she stood over a groaning *night demon,* her service revolver trained on him, shaking with her tremble.

The killer was trying to get up again. Shannon's cheeks flushed with fear and adrenalin as she again approached, this time with her gun extended.

"You're busted, bastard! Don't even move!" *Make it ring tough and mean.* That much she was capable of, but if the man on the ground could hear the pounding inside her, he'd know Shannon was more afraid of him than he was of her.

"Why . . . why'd you do . . . do this to . . . to me?" pleaded the man on the ground.

She began reading him his rights.

"I am *Chef* Ramirelowski," he said. "I do nothing."

The accent was strong. The victims hadn't said a damned thing about an accent. Shannon's leaping heart skipped a boom as she pondered the possibility that she *could* have misread the signs. But even as she wondered this, Shannon knew that the man had spoken without a trace of an accent moments before, when he had asked his victim if she needed a hand with her heel.

"Shut up and listen!" she ordered him, clicking the hammer back on her .38, unsure if she could use it even if the man were to suddenly attack. She continued reading him his rights, and asked if he understood. At the same time that the now-accented man replied that he knew nothing of such things, Weimer, Wood and the others in three squad cars screeched into view.

"Keyes! Keyes, you okay?" It was Captain Wood, severely shaken. "Jesus, we lost voice contact and Wiemer was supposed to have you in his sights. Damn you, Milt!'' He grabbed Wiemer by the coat and pushed him hard against a brick wall. ''I should let Lanark have you for buzzard bait. That's your last mistake.''

''Hey, last communication was really garbled, and I just took my eyes off to light up. Max . . . Max'll tell you, it happened so fast.''

''None of your goddamn lame excuses. This could've turned out one dead officer, ass-wipe . . . *nothing.*'' Shannon wound up pulling the Captain from Wiemer.

''I come America, and I am chef at Petroff's. I buy you free meal, hokey-dokey?'' the suspect-attacker was saying to the Japanese-American Max. ''I love all thing in America.''

''You sure we got the right bird?'' Max asked.

''Ask him why he carries his carving knife over there,'' replied Shannon, pointing. ''You'll want to handle that with utmost care. It will prove to be the weapon that has injured the women he's raped.''

''Sure of that, are you?'' asked Wiemer, rubbing his own bruised neck. ''Are you?''

''Yes, damn it.''

As the other policemen put the man and his knife into separate cars, Ryne Lanark came barreling up. He was in evening wear, a black tuxedo, as if on his way to the theater, the tie torn loose and dangling. Lanark took in everything at a glance, and then said, ''So it's true. Captain, I don't believe this! Putting Shannon on the line like this so soon, and nobody but nobody's got the decency to contact me so I could've at least been here? No good, no good at all. Then I hear Wiemer's on backup!''

''Hey,'' Wiemer protested lamely.

"We tried contacting you, *mister,* and you tell me, just where the hell have you been?" shouted Wood.

"And I don't need your help, partner," said Shannon, still shaken.

"I'm sorry. I didn't get the word and I assumed—"

"Assumed what? That I'd spend all night curled up with the Chicago phone book?"

"You didn't answer my question, Detective," said Wood.

Lanark looked long into Shannon's eyes. They were radiant, energetic brown pools. Lately, they had been hypnotic and lingering. Lanark wondered why.

"This guy speaks fluent Russian," said Wiemer. "Says he wants to speak to the Russian Ambassador. You sure, Keyes, this guy was about to knife you? Seems too dumb to be a rapist."

"Yeah, I am sure of him," she repeated to the others.

"If my partner says it's him, it's him," Lanark said firmly. "It'll stick, Weimer, and you see the paperwork reads right. Took a lot of guts, doing what she did."

Wood stared at the two partners still gazing into one another's eyes. He backed off. His beef, he decided, could wait. He went to oversee the collection of evidence and to have a look at the big Russian himself.

Lanark said starkly, "I should've been here. I'm sorry. Just dumb luck I heard it on the police band."

"On your way to the opera?"

"Not exactly."

"All dressed up and nowhere to go?"

"I'm going to a party. How would you like to join me?"

"I'm hardly in the mood, or dressed for it."

"It's a cover, the tux, I mean."

Shannon stared hard again. "You're working?"

"I am."

"Sorentino case?"

"Glove case," he whispered.

"Are you kidding, after what Captain Wood said?"

"I need a date, you coming?"

She looked around. Lanark shouted, waving the brunette wig he took up from the pavement. "Captain, I'm taking Goldilocks home. All clear?"

"Go ahead, good idea," Wood called back.

"Coming?" Lanark asked as in a dare.

"I'm coming."

Then they got to the green machine he was driving and she examined it with a critical look of disgust. "You're going to a party in this thing?" The dark green paint and rust seemed all that was holding the car together.

"Just get in, will you?"

"Where's the party?"

She got in, glad to sit down, feeling so keyed up she could not control her hands which shook, and her mouth which hadn't stopped rattling on. "I . . . I grew up in St. Louis . . . just off the River, far from any shiny big buildings . . . filled with squalor and the stench of factories. Always had a dream at an early age to escape it . . . by maybe becoming the next P.D. James, writing murder mysteries, but the publishers weren't exactly being kind, and I . . . finally realized it might take twenty years apprenticing in the field before earning a dime. On my own, I looked through want ads and worked several jobs before taking the

87

exam for entrance into the academy. My parents gone, a sister in Buffalo, a brother in the Merchant Marine, what did I have to lose? Had no real ties, beyond—"

"Where'd you learn how to shoot, before the academy, I mean?" he asked, *just to slow her down perhaps? Truly curious perhaps?* She wondered.

"Girl's school," she jested. "No, actually, my father was an officer in the Army. Shooting and hunting was a hobby he loved. Anyway, he taught me, taught me early. You learn a thing early enough and it becomes, I don't know, second nature."

"So, you wanted to be a writer at one time?"

"Easier to want to be one than to be one . . . found that out."

"Imagination, good sense of possibilities is a big help on this job," he coached.

"Yeah, yeah, I guess that's right."

"Good observation, too."

"Yes, I know. Guess there's a lot that writers and detectives have in common."

"Who knows, maybe one day, after you've tired of being a cop, you can go back to it . . . writing."

The car was headed north on Sheridan Road, passing brick houses, corner taverns, shops, old hotels until it merged with the outer drive traffic and the roadside that was littered with high-rise apartments and hotels. "Where're we going, Ryne?"

"Winnetka, big bash up that way."

"Why? What's at this party?"

"The Glove, unless I miss my guess."

"You want to explain how and when and where you got a line on this killer?"

For the first time he laughed and it sounded like a

clear, faraway bell. "I like you . . . guess I like bravery."

"Is that what this is? You're turned on by a show of bravery, as you call it? So now I'm acceptable as a partner?"

"That and the fact I need an escort."

She laughed lightly now, easing down into the bucket seat, trying to figure everything out. "You mean to tell me you've spent all day working on the wrong case, the case Wood told you to back off of?"

"No, not at all, I did a lot of work on the Sorentino thing today."

"Oh? Anything I should know about."

"Lots you should know about." And he began to fill her in completely on what had occurred at *Armand's* earlier, about the girl, the boy named Tony Sorrel, the thug he'd left in Tony's rundown room, all of it, down to the porn photos.

"Why're you being so straight with me now?"

"It takes a certain kind of person to act as a decoy."

"Yeah, a wooden-headed odd duck. You still haven't explained about tonight, about this party we're going to."

"I have a good friend in the Medical Examiner's office and she—"

"She?"

"She, yes . . . she's told me in no uncertain terms that the last victim had a strange gold ring on her finger. She also had a card which proved she wasn't an AIDS carrier. Lot of good that did her, huh?"

"This day and age, Lanark? What's so strange about that? And what's that got to do with this party?"

"One other girl, too, had this same card. It's kind

89

of a yuppie fear, you know, getting AIDS and losing out on a life that's already been paid up, you know. Anyway, the girl had a boyfriend who was called in for questioning recently about the death. Maybe he, too, carries this AIDS-free card. Something of a badge in some circles. You know it's worthless, but if you don't have it, you lose out on some of the goodies, like free rough-and-tumble sex without fear of contracting the disease.''

"Whoa, partner, nobody in the M.E.'s department's given you that kind of information, about a suspect and his having been grilled about the card. Where'd you learn of this?''

"File room.''

"Are you nuts? Completely?''

"Anyway, the girl's boyfriend is a guy by the name of Burton Eaton-Heron, son of an Englishman and lady whose bloodline is undiluted and pure. A true noble family lineage, blood and money—old money, not your blue chip stock types, or IBM execs, or lottery winners.''

"Proving what?''

"Nothing . . . yet.''

"I don't understand, are we crashing Burton Eaton-Heron's party tonight? And if so, what are we looking for?''

"Not what, but who or whom?''

"You think the killer's a party-goer?''

"Party-goer, yeah, I think he is. My source tells me all the victims were into punchbowling drugs.''

"Playing Russian roulette with their brains.''

"Our party-going animal that likes white gloves, and blood, Shannon, who is he, what does he look like?''

"Sounds like a regular *Spuds McKenzie.*"

"Laps it up, does he?"

"Brilliant . . . we sound like brilliant detectives so far."

The car began a slow weave in and around, circling corners that shot down between canyon walls atop which sprawled grand houses. They'd gone well past the northern suburbs with well lit *7-Eleven* signs on every corner. Here the motif was blackness, broken only by the occasional street light, which only managed to make the darkness around it even darker. The wind swept trees and foliage about wildly, a timid rain hardly able to cover Lanark's windshield coming on, going away, coming on again, going away again, teasing. The stillness between them was suddenly broken when Lanark said, "Anything goes wrong inside there, you stick close by me, okay?"

"You expect trouble?"

"I invited myself, remember." Silence again as Ryne ran his hand through his hair, obviously tired and on edge. "Just do like I say . . . watch me close . . . at the same time mingle . . . see what you can find out."

"Sure."

He said, "Shannon."

"Uh huh?"

"There's another *oddity* about the deaths—"

"Other than the slash marks?"

"Yes."

She frowned when he hesitated. "Well?"

"Their blood . . . the victims' blood was drained."

"I know, throats cut, yes."

"No, not—maybe the reason for the throat slashing

91

was in order to drain these women of their blood, you follow? Drain as in empty, possibly *collect?*"

"Sounds like a damned mortician," she said in order to control the shiver his words had caused inside her.

"According to the pathology reports, they were doped up, bound, sexually molested. Marks on ankles and wrists indicate they were strapped or bound."

"Why are you telling me this, to frighten me?"

"To goddamn caution you. We're not dealing with a typical rapist, some loon like this guy you collared tonight. These women, don't you see, were trussed up like slaughter animals, slit at the jugular, their bodies drained of blood. The majority of their wounds were not inflicted until *after* they'd died, and the wounds . . . the wounds were smeared with blood to increase their ugly appearance after death, after the blood loss."

"Good Christ, why?"

"Bodies were later dumped like yesterday's trash."

She shivered now, unashamedly.

He saw the fear in her eyes. "You will be careful."

"After a bedtime story like that? What do you think?"

They drove on in quiet darkness, their headlights fighting a losing battle with the surrounding night.

"But why, Ryne?" she asked suddenly. "Just to see those girls bleed to death?"

"Why is hard to say, and honestly, I haven't the slightest notion . . . not yet."

"What do you know about this killer?"

"That it is likely more than one man."

"I see."

"All that's known for sure is that the killer, or killers, seem very sweet on blue blood. Very persnickity about the blood they're after.''

"Rich blood, you mean? Then I'm safe.''

"Top of the line is what they seem to be after. If courage counts for anything, Keyes, you're a would-be victim.''

"Should I say thanks?''

"Whatever, stick close . . . no wandering off.''

"Do you suspect this man, Burton Eaton-Heron?''

"I spoke to him on the phone, identified myself, and told him we had new evidence implicating him in the death of the latest victim—''

"Do we?''

"No, hell no—but she *was* his ex. So, we set up a meet. The party's it, a kind of neutral ground we both agreed on.''

"Is this party at Burton's house?''

"No, a neighbor's, some friend's place. Got the address. Stone mansion . . . should be coming up soon.''

"Mansion? Jesus, Lanark, I'm not dressed for a bloody mansion.''

"Don't sweat it, these kids are so out of it, nobody's likely to notice.''

"We'll be spotted before a leopard if I walk in in a business suit. If I'm not taken for a cop, they'll think I'm a lawyer.''

"All right, okay,'' he said, finding a secluded spot to pull over, far from any street lamps. Suburbia here was not ordinary suburbia, no rows of tract houses, only enormous homes several stories high, some a block long, many facing the beautiful vista over Lake Michigan. Houses here had servants' quarters and boat houses, magnificent hot houses, pools, and in some cases ancient stone burial sites, plots marked by an eighteenth-century crypt. Old money, Lanark had said, the generation of riches carved from nothing by antecedents. And what had become of it? Rich and powerful children now running amok? The blood-rich mixture so heady as to create such minds as those behind The Billion Dollar Boy's Club, and the recent spate of violent sex-related yuppie killings that rang out in the papers across the country almost daily? Or was this all too pat, too forced by Ryne Lanark's own blinders? She knew she'd do best to take a step back from any theories Lanark put forth, to hold back his as well as her own *prejudices*. Yes, that's exactly what they were laboring under, she decided, pathology reports and hearsay not withstanding.

"Why're you pulling over, Ryne, you're not dumping me here, are you?"

"Come round to the trunk."

"Bizarre behavior."

But she did as he asked and stared at what the light there rained down on, a great assortment of oddities, props, instruments, tools, makeup kits, and a suitcase with the lid missing, jammed with both men's and women's clothing. "Take your pick, but for evening wear, I like this one," he said, lifting out a royal blue, low cut dress which at first looked like chiffon, but it hadn't a single wrinkle in it.

"Specially made, and the fit's got to be right for you."

"Eleven?"

"Twelve."

"A bit large . . . but . . . beats this," she fingered the beige work suit.

"No time for returns."

"What about the yellow?"

"Thirteen, and let out . . . needed that one myself once."

"All right, maybe it's a small twelve."

"Try is all I ask."

She looked around, perterbed. "Where?"

They bordered a park-like area. "In there."

"Too dark," she complained.

"In the car then, unless you want me to hold your hand."

"All right, the car, but you stay here."

"Getting late, ol' Burt won't wait forever."

She made the change as best she could and found the dress fit well, too well. She complained of having put on some weight. He drove in the original direction, looking for any sign of the Stone place. When they came in view, Lanark knew it was well named, the fences, some eight-foot high, were solidly built of masonry, and the gate, too, had stone archways. At the gate they had to announce themselves and the fact that Burton Eaton-Heron had invited them.

"I can't believe you're actually driving this wreck into here," she said glumly.

"Sorry, but it's all I could get on short notice."

The party was in full swing, actually winding down, Shannon thought, seeing the lights inside were considerably dimmer than they needed to be. It was *mellow-out time,* the music, while loud, had slowed even as they cruised for a space somewhere on the crowded lawn-turned-lot. Nobody paid the least attention to them or their car, and for this Shannon was more than grateful.

"See, like I told you, a cinch," he said.

"It won't be if Wood learns about this."

"Will you stop worrying? There's no way."

She stopped at the stairs going in, looking skyward. The home was like some medieval church, story upon story, even with sculpted gargoyles and heiroglyph-like friezes telling forgotten tales on each balustrade. In a far window way up near the top she saw a curtain move and a pale, white face disappear ghost-like into the depths of the place, as if swallowed. Was it the face of a child or a child-like woman? She didn't know and looking again, she wondered if she'd seen anything at all. To their right, out on the dark lake, sailboats from the mansion grounds were still making their way ashore, leisurely, no rush, as if all time were one and nothing was worth hurrying after. At the boat house the water lapped at the boards like a hungry animal, partially asleep, licking at a dream.

"Lanark," she said, "the bones you found in the trash, what'd you say about them?"

"Sorentino's front is serving up dog on the hidden menu."

"Ughhhhhh." She had had a flash, the thought of an animal slaughtered, so vivid she could smell the still-warm blood, and now Lanark tells her of butchered dogs being sold at this *Armand's.*"

"Ready to step in it?" Lanark asked, looking her over. "By the way, you look stunning." She'd replaced the blond wig.

"Far from it," she replied, "but here goes."

Lanark knew the moment he walked through the threshold at the door which stood wide open that he'd overdone it with the tuxedo. An instant look told him that while everyone was dressed in what amounted to hundreds of thousands of dollars worth of originals, the originals were designer leisure wear, baggie trousers with pleats down the front, colorful suspenders and over-sized shirts Lanark would have used as sweats. Ryne instantly lost the tie, stuffing it into his coat pocket, for all the good it did. He knew the moment they walked in they were marked as not only untrendy new-comers to this scene, but definitely out of place. Shannon, too, appeared overly dressed in this crowd that got its notion of fashion from watching sit-coms, soap operas and *People* Magazine. The distictive few dressers in the group seemed to lean toward Boy George as a role model, while the others had routinely selected what was yuppie wear from *GQ*. There were no ties and no tuxedos and no evening gowns.

"Shit, Lanark," muttered an embarrassed Shannon, "I'm going to kill you."

"Wrong kind of party."

"Couldn't you have asked?"

"Sure, ask a suspected murderer what to wear to his party?"

"It's a social occasion, couldn't you find out, a detective?"

"Brave it out. Tell 'em we're from Nebraska. Here comes our host."

The welcoming party was a grim foursome who flashed eyes about the room to others who looked, for all the world, the picture of wholesomeness, even if one did have a hand up a drunken girl's skirt. Three of the young preppies came toward them from across the ballroom, as large an area as a normal-size house in itself.

Suddenly their combined smiles were flashed on like connected lightbulbs.

"Hi, name's Roy Lawrence, from Kiowa, Oklahoma," said Lanark, extending a hand, shaking each of theirs, his own smile like porcelain. "Me and my woman up here to see Chicago for the first time and I run into Burton with some tire trouble out on the highway and I fixed him right up, you know, and then he and me we got to talking, you know and come to find out we got a lot in common—like it was scary, you know. I mean he was a Scorpio, same as me, born under the same sign as me, and he likes the same drinks as me, and the more we talked the more it come that we got so much in common—'cept for the way we talk. Hell, we even got the same blood type and whataya call it, RH factor. Got a card to prove it in my wallet."

The committee didn't care for Roy. They simply stared at him, holding him at bay when a fourth, a good head taller than the others, and a most strikingly handsome youth with beautiful blond hair and stunning gold-to-hazel eyes, stepped in. "You were invited by Burton, were you?"

Lanark noticed another face in the near background, of a young man equally handsome, but his features were creased with worry, and he instantly judged him to be Burton.

"He tol' me there'd be a party and *if* we could, to come on over."

"Is that right?" said one.

"You're friends of Burton's?" one asked when Lanark mentioned his name again.

They were all tall and muscular and well-tanned, each with sharp, penetrating eyes, high cheek bones, luminous and smooth skin, handsome features and firm stances. They were singularly frightening in their joint perfection, like a line of robots.

Shannon stepped in, swaying her bare shoulders and throwing in a little Southern accent, "Is he here? Roy's told me so much about him, but didn't say what he looked like, or that he moved in such high circles, did you, Roy?"

"I only met him recently, sugar, I didn't know, did I, Burton? Burton! There you are! Honey, here's Burty-boy."

Lanark pushed past the welcoming crew and toward the one he prayed was Burton Eaton-Heron. Heron was supposed to spot him, not the other way around, but something seemed wrong in this picture. Were the others apprised of the fact Lanark was a cop?

Their actions seemed to indicate as much, except for the one who stepped past the others and now pulled Burton forward, saying he should introduce his friends to them all. Burton did so, a bit shakily, but suddenly calming, seeming to accept everything as all right, cool.

"R-r-roy Lawrence, Mrs. Lawrence, this is Matt Stone, Rodney Logan, Will Torrence, David Ridley, and of course you know me."

"Stone," said Lanark cagily, "now that wouldn't have to do with the name on the mailbox?"

"It would. My grandfather was Stephen Thomas Stone, my father Mark Stephen Stone, and now there's me, last hope for the line. Of course Mother, she believes there's no hope whatever for us. She's . . . well, she's gone a bit off the deep end and now she is Sister Stone, Evangelist, and if I hadn't come of age when I did, well, none of this—" he indicated the entire house with a majestic gesture—"not a single tile, would be ours any longer, the property of the church she's begun."

"Yeah," said Burton dumbly.

Stone gave him a cold stare and he fell silent. "Take Mrs. Lawrence to the dance floor, Burton. You dance, don't you, Mrs. Lawrence?"

"Yes, but—" Shannon began.

"Take her, Burton. Lawrence and I must chat."

Stone made small talk as Lanark watched Burton going off with Shannon. Stone spoke about his family, the long heritage of land ownership in the area, the fortune his grandfather had made out of the first investment he ever made, a big hole in the ground near Gary, Indiana, which still supplied most of the iron ore, copper and magnesium in the city. "Of course we've diversified. Everyone must, in order to continue to survive, grow, you realize. I have people that take care of the particulars, but I run the show now—mostly paper and computer exchanges nowadays, but you know my grandfather couldn't do it, nor my father for that mater. Family fortune was at a low ebb just before his death. Mother took the fear of poverty and his death as signs from God. She takes a great deal these days as signs from God. Have you seen her on the tube? I've turned over some funds for her to carry on with her show, do her evangelism. What can it hurt? Who can it harm? Perhaps it helps, in a world such as ours there is so little that does . . . help, I mean."

He offered Lanark a drink. "Anything, we have a full bar," he indicated the direction. They strolled on, out of Shannon's immediate sight. Lanark asked the bartender for a John Collins.

"You say, Tom Collins?"

It was a mistake nine out of ten bartenders made, and Lanark had learned to be forgiving about it. "No, I said John, John Collins."

"John . . . oh, oh, yeah."

Lanark found a wedge into Matthew Stone's conversation about himself. "This party's sure something." He pointed to the punchbowl on the table, filled with vials, some bottles recognizable as sleeping pills, others not so easily identified. From it, kids were taking large amounts of uppers, downers and in-betweens, punchbowling, as the victims of the Glove had done, according to Sybil Shanley. "Isn't that, you know, against the law?"

"Sure, Hank—"

"Roy, Roy Lawrence."

"Oh, yeah, Roy. But what else have these kids got, Roy? Figure it out. You ever wonder what it'd be like to live your life to twenty, and wake up one morning and realize you'd done it *all*, everything there was to do in life—*everything?* No more to learn, no more to want to learn, no more thrills, no more shocks, no more surprises? Add the apathy of their parents. Hell, I love my mother but she's out of it, in a world of her own. I know how these kids feel, and if they can get off for just one night safely, here, well . . . more power to them, huh, Roy?"

The bartender came up with the John Collins, but Lanark wasn't so sure he wanted to swallow it, not now, not with this guy beside him. "You ever meet a girl named Paige, Cynthia Paige, or Pullman, Karen Ann Pullman, Matt?"

"Maybe . . . lot of girls come to my parties."

"These two, and another one, were high on drugs like you got here, and they were gang-raped and gang-murdered."

"So, you *are* another fucking cop."

"I am."

"And what, you think there's some crazy killer—"

"*Killers,* Matt, plural." He watched for any sign of change in the young man's expression, but he was as good as his name, Stone.

"Okay, if you say so . . . killers. You think there's killers in my house, my guests?"

"They could be working your party, yes. Watch a girl all night here get herself into Nirvana, see to it she gets a ride, in this case a ride to her death."

"You really don't think Burton's got anything to do with these deaths, you can't. He's clean, man."

"Nobody's clean, Matt, not even you, not if you're supplying drugs to teens."

"I'm no supplier, man. This party's just like all the rest, it's strictly BYOB."

"Then I was right, everybody in the place contributed to those deaths. But tell me, Matthew, do you own many pairs of white theater gloves?"

"You better collect your broad and split, *Lanark.*" He knew Lanark by name. "Take your phony mustache with you."

"How'd you know my name?"

"My business to know."

"How?"

"Hey, you want Burton in your girl's pants, Lanark? Pay attention!" said Stone, laughing and pointing.

Lanark turned to see Shannon stumbling, near faint,

102

and Burton trying to get her up a flight of stairs. She appeared stewed and disoriented and terribly afraid. Lanark raced toward her but Stone snapped his fingers and four of the youths who'd looked like a party of surfers before now began pounding on Lanark repeatedly, knocking him off balance.

Lanark came up with a fist to one man's privates, eliminating him immediately. His only thought was to put these assholes away and get to Shannon.

One of them had Lanark suddenly by the neck, in an iron grip, trying to put a choke hold on him. A second sent a fist trailing lightning toward his left eye, but seeing it from delivery, Lanark yanked madly downward and it struck the creep on his back, sending him to the floor. The remaining two backed off enough to give Lanark time to send his own fist into the closest one's stomach—Ridley, he guessed. Ridley toppled to his knees and Lanark sent his own knee into his mouth, putting him out. The last one standing, waved his hands in a gesture of surrender and withdrawal. People all around stood with their mouths open, a few of the women had screamed, but most wanted no part of the "bad" scene.

Lanark took another step toward Shannon when the "surrendering" boy suddenly pulled an enormous knife that flicked open with a *swish*, jabbing it at Lanark as two others found their feet. The entire attack had been orchestrated by Stone who stood back, watching and assessing and laughing. Over the laughter and the shrieks of other guests, Lanark heard Shannon's voice, now shouting obscenities directed, he assumed, at Burton. He feared the punks might detain him too long for him to be of any help to her. He kicked out with a karate move that took the knife-wielder by surprise, sending his weapon skyward. A second kick sent him into a crowd of startled onlookers. But again, he was grabbed from behind. Again, he heard Shannon cry out.

Something inside Lanark, a dark and uncontrollable power rose up before his mind, blotting out everything that might stand in his way. With an energy born of hatred and adrenalin, he lifted the man who had him by the throat and sent him over his back and into the table where Matthew Stone stood sipping his drink and enjoying the fight. Stone side-stepped the flying thug who was unable to get up. Another raced at Lanark with a baseball bat, taking a swipe at his head. Lanark ducked. A second swipe at his legs made him jump and on the third swing Lanark grabbed the bat with both hands and yanked it free. With the bat in hand, he removed punch bowls filled with liquid and filled with pills, sending glass flying. He jabbed viciously at a third and a fourth kid who dared again come at him. Like a raging bull now, he went after Stone with the bat, saying, "Call 'em off, or so help me your skull's in Milwaukee, damnit! Now!"

"That's enough, let him go!" said Stone, his eyes only inches from the end of the Louisville slugger. Lanark saw the others back off instantly and he brought the bat down with a thunderous bang only inches from Stone's hand where it was on the table.

"You remember this, remember me, Mr. Stone, because I'm going to nail your bloody rich ass to the wall one way or another!"

Stone, shaken by the lusty, murderous hatred in

Lanark's eyes could only quake and say, "Get out of my house, pig."

Lanark, still holding tight to the bat, backed off to the center of the room and when he stood directly below a crystal chandelier, he exploded it into a thousand pieces with a single blow of his bat. Screams resulted and many of the couples in the room, realizing now he was a policeman, raced for the exits. Out of the corner of his eye, he saw Shannon, her dress torn, fighting her way towards him from a stairway. She looked as if she'd fallen, or was pushed down.

He went for her as the pack of jackals around him circulated like so many hungry animals, just waiting for a sign from their leader. But Stone only looked up at someone standing deep in the shadows at the second floor landing. He gave no sign to his bodyguards to resist Lanark.

Still, Lanark lashed out with the bat, clipping one punk on the chin, knocking him cold, when he dared get too close. He inched toward Shannon who was disoriented and confused and afraid, taking her by the arm and making his way with her to the door and safety.

Outside he breathed for the first time since taking up the bat, a kind of fear he hadn't expected coming over him as he realized he might well have murdered Stone or someone else inside, his mind had gone so dismally black with anger and rage. It was exactly the thing that Dr. Ames, the police shrink, had warned him of for so many months now; the kind of emotional blackout that was at root of hundreds of killings that occurred daily in the nation, crimes of passion. It was how he had felt about the faceless animals who had coldly and impassionately killed his family members. It was a passionate hatred. He vehemently wanted to destroy Stone here and now, not because he was convinced that Stone was a murderer himself, but because Stone and his goons, and his lifestyle had infuriated him, and because they dared attempt to block his way.

He expected he'd pay for his temper when next he saw Captain Wood, who, no doubt, would have a full report of the complaint sworn out against him. But for now, his first concern was Shannon who leaned heavily against him, moaning as if more asleep than awake.

He hurled the bat at the line of young blond-headed men who stood like the palace guard behind them, helping Shannon to the squad car. None of them took a step toward them, nor made another threatening gesture. Lanark wondered what had happened to his professional calm, and he wondered what might have happened had he reached for his gun instead of the ball bat.

Grim welcoming, her mind kept repeating in among the fog-bound mechanism of her brain. Faked, perfunctory greetings from people with their teeth capped, nails manicured. Well-groomed, pedigreed Burton Eaton-Heron. Shannon felt drawn to his image. Handsome beyond the right for any human flesh to be, well-built, young, firm muscles, rippling muscles. Works out regular, he told her. Makes love on a regular basis, he was saying now. Strong, firm hands, shining smile, beaming eyes, blond-headed Nordic look replete with salon tan. What more could a girl ask for?

Arm wrapped about hers, he had led her to . . . to

106

where? Dance floor? But where was everyone else? He'd fumbled for words at first, in a schoolboy-ish fashion, nervous and unsure with an "older woman."

They'd gone through a door somewhere, just off the dance floor, but she couldn't remember if it was a real door or a door in her mind. He boasted about his money, his ability to see she had all the comforts she could ever want. Meanwhile, Lanark was at the bar with their host, a man resembling Burton enough to be a brother or cousin. Burton had said of him that Matthew Stone had graduated Harvard with a degree in medicine, but that he was too bloody rich to actually practice it now. He makes more in his sleep one night than a cop makes in a year, she was told. She remembered that much for sure. God, she was foggy.

Something about a medical supply firm, one of the largest in the Midwest. Stone's parent company had bought it out. All the latest in med-tech, pharmaceuticals, you name it. Was that what was said? She tried desperately to hold to the thread of the conversation but it was as if it had become all a tangle, a loose and meaningless dream meandering through her consciousness.

Something engaging about Burton. He was such a gentleman, so different from Lanark, miles apart from the other men she'd known. Burton knew how to guide a woman, knew how to make her feel important . . . saw to her needs, always with that gentle touch. He treated her like a princess, speaking in whispers in her ear, kissing her hand, pressing it to . . . to his heart? No, what was that he pressed her hand against? He'd handed her a rose, lost now . . . somewhere below her feet, trampled on the dance floor.

Stairs. Weren't there some stairs involved? No, just a feeling of going up . . . flying but standing . . . an elevator?

No matter, she was in Burton's hands and his self-assuredness made everything all right, as if every word he uttered had been handed down by some greater god than even he. She no longer remembered his stumbling and bumbling and the fear that trembled its way through his frame when they first danced. She no longer remembered the too-high octave in his voice, or the beads of sweat just beginning about the thick neck and at the hairline. Whatever he was so afraid of didn't matter anymore, not since the punch.

"Like some punch, wouldn't you?" he'd asked. How long ago was that? Didn't matter.

She'd replied with a smile designed to calm him down, "Yes, yes, I'd love some."

While he had gone for the punch she did a cursory walkabout. There weren't too many couples in the place who weren't locked in embrace, sealed off from the crowd in their own little cocoons, most stoned to the gills. Another appropriate condition of being in the Stone mansion, she had mused at the time. She used the freedom from Burton to wander, mingle, as Lanark had suggested. She looked for the face of a killer in the crowd of innocents and post-teens. She looked for anyone who appeared out of the ordinary, other than herself and Lanark.

She stopped at the bottom of a spiraling staircase at the top of which stood a thin creature, pale and so frail-looking she might be made of linen, as if a strong wind would send her flurrying about like drapery. She was hauntingly fascinating in her quiet, deathly-looking state, her dress either a Grecian original or a shroud. Speaking not a word, she stared back at Shannon with eyes that spoke of mystery and serenity and sadness all at once, like a child molested and locked away just surfaced, too afraid to reveal a word to the very person freeing her. She gave the impression of vulnerability and susceptibility; easily shattered, like glass, and horribly white . . . skin as milky as cream.

It was the same woman Shannon had spied at the draperies in the window earlier. Had she come down to have a closer peek at Shannon? But why? She had taken her eyes off the woman for a second, seeing Burton pushing his way back toward her, and when she looked up again, the woman had vanished.

But she had seen the woman again, hadn't she? Moments later, upstairs . . . through the door . . . up the elevator . . . in the cold, clammy room where Burton had kissed her hand and nipped at her fingers? Or had that not happened at all? After all, they were still on the dance floor! He was warning her to go easy on the punch, that it was laced with bourbon, and she was saying she liked it that way.

"Careful, it has quite a kick to it," he cautioned.

"Thank you, I'm forewarned."

"Yes . . . yes, you are."

She sipped at it, then drank. It was heavily laced with bourbon, burned as it slipped down. The pace of the music picked up and the tempo began to get to her, Burton asking her if she'd like to dance after she finished her punch. "Oh, now, now," she insisted, wishing to make him feel at ease.

"Are you a cop, too, like him?" asked Burton, indicating Lanark with a thrust of his head in that general direction.''

"No," she lied, "just a cop's girlfriend. Got to see him whenever it's convenient for him. Like falling for a doctor, you know?''

"You ever, you know, see other guys?''

"Sometimes.''

"What about me? Like to see me sometime, you know, just the two of us?''

"Yes," she lied again, "I'd like that very much.''

"What about later, tonight? Lots of rooms upstairs. We could be alone.''

"I saw some people going up," she said, coyly when she noticed her vision was blurred a bit. She was feeling the weight of the eventful evening. "Do you know the older woman, quite beautiful, in the white dress that was at the top of the stairs?''

"No . . . no, can't say I do.''

"Very pale . . . no color at all.'' She was feeling very woozy now. The dancing making her head spin. The room was going round in slow, lazy archs, and she felt as if she were floating off the floor. As if from far away, she saw herself in two separate forms, the body dancing amid the others on the dance floor and another, flowing like a ghostly sheet in the wind, high above, looking down on the scene.

Loud music rocked her soul . . . a new group coming in, some from the boat house and grounds where, if one weren't a prude, sex could be had easily and lusciously beneath the junipers, at the greenhouse—*hot house,* her mind corrected, with Lanark, or maybe Burton, or maybe both . . .

Sex was suddenly and venomously biting at her from

110

every nerve ending, her body and mind alive with desire. Racing . . . racing naked, men chasing after her like she was a prized deer, she leaping gazelle-like and suddenly flying, a butterfly taking wing but suddenly caught, snatched within the confines of a brutal net that was being held by Lanark. He took hold of her wings and tore them in his rough hands and made her his slave.

The drink fell from her hands. She weaved and was caught before she fell, grasping at her own body just to touch it, to feel herself. "Lanark," she said, trying to get to him, feeling threatened and out of control. Burton was grasping at her, telling her to just relax. People around her were whirling in mass, an orgy of bodies writhing, all wanting to touch her, hold her, fondle her, strip her and look adoringly on her and she wanted them to. She got a fleeting image of the powerful Lanark knocking people aside to get to her.

"Get out of my way!" she heard Lanark's voice from far away. There was a commotion nearby and suddenly she felt pulled away in an iron vise, Lanark's grip or Burton's? She did not know, nor did she care.

Laughter followed her along with the images of snakes and naked women and young, well-tanned, blond-headed men like Burton and Stone.

Unknown to her, Lanark swept her from the party and out into the cool night air. She only felt the rock-hard smoothness of his muscled body against hers as she held fast to him, not knowing or caring if it were Lanark or Burton or some stranger. She didn't feel herself slapped once, twice and a third time, nor the roughness with which he snapped on her seat belt. She didn't hear the car whine into life and the wheels tear up grass as Lanark raced from the mansion. She only wanted one thing now and when she reached out and took hold of it, Lanark nearly jumped out of the moving car, causing the Javelin to swerve and just miss the gate as they exited the grounds.

"Jesus, Shannon, what were you drinking?"

"Don't know . . . but give it to me . . . more . . . more . . ." She giggled uncontrollably, tearing away her dress.

"Hey, damnit, Shannon, don't! Your . . . don't!"

She was trying now to get his shirt unbuttoned. "Stop it, now! Christ! They must've slipped you a controlled substance."

"Fly . . . fly," she said as she undid his.

"Jokes over, kid, no more!" He pushed her to the other side of the car, while guiltily enjoying the feel of the bulge that crept up from between his legs. "Shannon, just stay put . . . stay put."

"Got to . . . got to have you inside me . . . now . . . now . . ." she mumbled the words childlishly, pleadingly.

He stopped the car. "Get out," he told her and came around to the rear, finding a blanket. She went to her knees holding him about the middle. Lanark forced the blanket over her head and hugged her within it, creating a cocoon. It worked effectively with people on PCP, and while this wasn't "angel dust" or some other animal tranquilizer, he prayed the experiment would work. She slowed in her movements as if not getting enough oxygen or perhaps she'd simply calmed in the darkness of the artificial womb. He'd seen it work on druggies. He cursed himself for having let this happen to her, his partner. In a moment she was calm and still, and he laid her in the back seat, telling her gently to get some much deserved sleep.

This done, a car screeched up from nowhere, the headlights blinding Lanark who snatched out his .38, prepared to fire. "Cut the lights, Fabia!"

It was Riordan, shit, and his pimply-faced partner Fabia. How did they know he was here? They must've had the Stone place staked out the entire time, and now it would be Lanark's behind. If at all possible, he'd keep Shannon's name out of it.

"Thought you could pull a fast one, hey, Lanark? Who authorized this little excursion? Do you know you may've blown my whole operation? Burton Eaton-Heron is working for me. After your call, you asshole, I told him to let you come ahead, and we drew you in like the sucker you are. Meantime, Burton scored points with his chums, getting two cops fingered and tossed out on their cans. Thanks for making my job a lot easier, and our city a lot safer."

Fabia was laughing so hard he was in tears, saying, "Lanark, you dumb shit . . . Lanark . . ."

"Who's the girl? Your new partner, what's the name?"

"Not my partner, just an old friend who thought she was going to a party in Winnetka."

"Tell you what, Lanark, take your old friend and get back to the city streets where you can arm-wrestle with freaks like Sorentino. Leave the head games and high rise crime district to people who know what they're doing. And tomorrow, we have a talk with your superiors at the 13th who promised to keep you busy."

Lanark swallowed his pride and got into his car, just pleased that they hadn't marked Shannon. As he drove away, he heard Riordan add, "Got your old friend in the M.E.'s department too, hot shot! Going to bring her up on charges!"

He hoped Riordan was bluffing. It would take a lot to get somebody in the M.E.'s office canned, especially if they stuck to the facts, the known facts—that Lanark had been the one to hoodwink the information from the medical assistant. That he had lied to her. But Riordan was just jerk enough to take it the full mile.

He drove Shannon to his place and helped her up to his apartment over the bar, the green neon lights flashing off them as they made their way up the back stairs and to the door. It was a tidy old building, well cared for, renovated only a year before the death of his parents. It held untold memories for him, and he was comfortable here. Just below was the bar where, from a window, his Uncle Jack Tebo looked out at him and raised both hands grasped in a victory sign. It had been a long time since Ryne had brought a woman home with him. He hated to tell Tebo the truth, the disappointment he was in for might be too much for the burly, bearded man.

"I'm okay . . . okay," Shannon was saying. "Where are we?"

"My place."

She took his lips full in her mouth, her tongue caressing his. She smelled wonderful, her aroma filling his mind, weakening his resolve until he finally broke away. "Shannon, it's the drug they slipped you. You've got to sleep it off."

"Don't want to sleep . . . want to," she kissed him again madly, roughly, as if she wanted to crawl down his throat.

"Damn, damn," he said, getting really bothered now himself. "Bastards really got you."

"Ohhhh," she moaned, taking his hands and rubbing them into her breasts.

"Can't do this, Shannon . . . *Shannon!*"

He carried her to the bed, to which she gave an approving murmur, but then he again wrapped her in a blanket and added the pillow. He rushed out to the kitchen and put on some hot coffee, wondering if it would make a difference. The noise they'd made on entering must be driving Tebo up the wall, he thought as he put the coffee on.

But it was not necessary. When he returned to her, Shannon was fast asleep, twisted in the blanket, the pillowcase and the blue gown, now quite wrinkled. He drank the coffee and let her sleep, not daring to wake her.

He pondered a dark thought for much of the night, wondering if the victims of the Glove had died as happily and wantonly as Shannon had fallen off to sleep tonight.

FIVE

Thrum-thrum-thrum, thrum-thrum-thrum, the knoll beat with relentless pattern, never a false beat, never a miss, never a complication . . . *thrum,* beat, *thrum,* beat, *thrum,* beat. Beating on forever . . . beating like a heart in a chest . . . like blood racing through the ear . . . a wave in a conch shell . . . *thrum-thrum-thrum.* It filled him with a peace he'd never known, like a mantra.

But something like disinfectant odor assailed his senses, too, and this was annoying to the rhythm of the beat.

"Whaa . . . whrrrr . . . where . . . am . . . I?" he demanded through the haze of a blind insensitivity, believing himself as drunk as a kitten dipped in vodka.

"Easy honey . . . easy . . . you're just fine." Female voice.

"Going to take care of you." Male voice.

Both voices coming through the *thrum-thrum-thrum* that sounded like the bowels of God in his ear. The thrumming blended with the sound of his own blood pumping, the sound of his heartbeat. What was that sound again, he wondered, feeling too dizzy to truly care.

His limbs seemed immovable. Ankles burned, felt broken, as if the bones were sticking out. He tried desperately to touch himself, his face, chest, anything, but this was impossible. Arms wouldn't function. He tried also to focus his eyes, wanting most to see the cause of the thrum-thrum-thrum reverberating all around him and through him. It was everywhere, like a giant moth flapping wings over the top of him, while a worm ate its way through his bowels. The combined noise the creatures made was *thrum-thrum-thrum.*

He felt both sweaty and cold at once: feverish, fiery and burning as if his blood were boiling, afire with friction. Every artery and vein afire . . . but the skin clammy, creepily cold, beneath the thrum-thrum-thrum beating over him, under him, beside and around him.

What the hell was that noise?

He tried to ask aloud but only managed a gurgling sound. Had he too much to drink? Had he been doped up like one of the girls?

Burty . . . Burty . . . honey, it's me." Female, motherly voice.

"You're going to a better place, Burty." Male voice.

"You will live on, forever, through me." Female again.

This wasn't happening.

Not to him.

Couldn't be . . . real . . . only a *bad* nightmare.

But the *thrum-thrum-thrum* both mechanical and fluid and alive all at once, that noise of the bestial, sucking creature blotted out the hopeful wish that it was just a nightmare. *That thrumming in here is real!* He realized it now with a start, and he realized now what the sound meant; realized who the people talking to him were, an entire room full of them gaping down at his naked form. He realized it all just before the blackout that mercifully stopped the droning thrum in his ears. Dead, the *thrum-thrum-thrum* continued only until it sapped Burton Eaton-Heron of the last life-giving drop of his blood.

He didn't feel the jagged slit made across his jugular.

Nor the ritual cuts to the eyes, the nose, the chest, and finally the dismemberment of his manhood. Each member of the party had placed his or her mark on their fourth victim. This time, the girls in the group had enjoyed sex with the victim before he was hooked up to the death-dealing machine.

"You want to play, you got to pay," said the young woman who slit the penis shaft.

The others giggled, the sound of it ringing 'round the room. Then the doors were opened on a larger room, far more comfortable, filled with several beds, the lights dim and romantic. The girls fled into this harem room, still giggling, some falling, all of them high on drugs and the smell of blood.

"Didn't feel a thing," said the masculine voice in the room where a slab served as the bed and medical machinery the furniture, the room where Burton dreamed an endless sleep filled with endless pleasure that must soothe the lust and compulsion of his brain. "We'll dispose of the body."

Burton didn't hear the voices anymore. He didn't feel the pluck of the catheter as it was removed from his kidney, nor the light tinkle of the trays moved back with a big machine that had finally stopped in its constant chorus of *thrum-thrum-thrum*. He didn't feel the hard slab or the restraining ties, nor did he smell the

118

rich blood being packaged up in neat containers by the ghoulish boys who remained behind.

"Try this time to please dispose of the body properly." Female voice.

"It's more fun my way." Male voice.

"Do as I say!"

"I'll do as I damn please."

The other males watched the power play between their two leaders with interest, but did not stop in their preparations for disposal of the body.

"Take it to the cellar and burn it," she said. "Like you should have done with the others."

"No . . . no, I have plans for Burty."

"The police are getting much too close."

"They're going to get closer."

"Damn you."

"Aren't we all?"

Shannon slept till eleven, he until ten. First up, he telephoned Tebo downstairs and asked that two breakfasts be brought up. Tebo, an early riser despite the hours he kept, wanted instantly to know who she was and if Ryne had had a good time.

"It's not what you think, Uncle John."

"Never were much for talking about your conquests, boy. Be right up with those ham and eggs."

"Don't forget coffee."

"Maria's way ahead of you."

Marie was Tebo's second wife. Not much to look at but a fine cook, he'd always joked.

"Uncle John, she's the new partner I told you about."

"She is? Well, looks like you two are getting on much better, and from what I could see, she's quite a looker."

He looked across the room to where Shannon lay, now restlessly stirring. "Yeah, she is that."

"See you in a bit."

"Thanks, Tebo."

He tried to stir Shannon gently awake. He had slept on the couch and his neck ached from it. "Keyes, it's getting late," he told her. "Breakfast is on its way, then we've got only a little time before—" he remembered Riordan's threat and it made him wish last night hadn't happened. Riordan was sure to go to Wood, and Lanark would be busted to patrolman and returned to uniform duty. And for what? Burton Eaton-Heron, Matthew Stone and their lot had seen him coming, as much as laughed in his face and they'd disgraced Shannon along with him. It had been a nasty set-up, a two-way set-up. Not only did Heron bring in his buddies on the act, but he had called Riordan, complained of being hassled by another cop, and the result . . .

"Lanark? Where am I?" asked Shannon, coming round. "What happened?"

"Like some coffee? Breakfast?"

She glanced around, getting her bearings, her eyes blurry. "Ohhhh, feel like a ton of bricks fell on me."

"You were drugged, Shannon, the punch . . . at the party?"

"Oh, yeah . . . yeah. Where's the bath?"

"Behind you, help yourself."

She groggily made her way to the sink and threw water in her face.

"You okay?" he called out through the closed door after a time.

"Jesus, it's late."

"Breakfast is awaiting you."

When she emerged she looked a little better, but not much. The coffee helped to revive her. She studied his apartment as she worked on getting some toast down. It was manly, sparse, the decor thoughtful but failing a definite touch. She noticed his gun rack and asked him about the rifles and learned he was a collector. He told her he had gotten some from his father. "The bar downstairs was my father's. Now it's mine."

"What, your parents retire to Florida?"

"Dead . . . auto accident," he lied, "took my sister, too."

Casting her eyes downward she nodded sadly, "I'm so sorry."

"And you? Your parents, you said you were alone? Last night."

"Dad passed away of a heart attack. Mom . . . Mom just sort of . . . I don't know . . . followed? Is that the right word for it when someone decides they can't go on without their mate. Anyway, that's been quite a few years, and while it still hurts to think about them . . ." she choked, "I suppose it's also healthy to do so time and again."

Ryne nodded, "Yeah . . . I know."

"Anyway, Ryne, I'm sorry about last night."

"Sorry? Hey, it was hardly your fault."

"I know, but I should've been more careful. Stupid to take that drink and then actually drink any of it."

"How much did you drink?"

121

"So far as I can recall? Only a single gulp. After that—"

"Strong stuff."

"PCP? Cocaine, what?"

"A special blend, I think, laced with Spanish Fly, or some other aphrodisiac. Nasty bunch our Burton runs with."

"God, aphrodisiac? No wonder I had such lurid dreams all night. I . . . I didn't, you didn't—"

"We didn't, no . . . we definitely didn't."

She bit her lip in a pouting fashion. "Did I . . . was I? You know, bad?"

"Bad? No, you kiss terrifically."

"Naughty, nasty, bad?"

"Yes, you were but—"

"And you brought me here and put me to bed?"

"I swear," he said, pointing to the couch, "and you still have on your dress."

"It's your dress, and it was half off."

"Your dress, your doing, I . . . I didn't want to take advantage of you under the circumstances, and I didn't."

She relented, nodding and saying, "Gallantry survives."

"It did last night."

She straightened in her chair, took a deep breath and awkwardly changed the subject. "Did you . . . get any leads, anything on a suspect last night?"

"I was talking with the one Burton introduced us to, Matthew Stone, our host. He was so polite his teeth would have shattered if he'd smiled once more. All he talked about was the weight room upstairs, a full boxing ring he had had installed, really into body building and boxing. Bastard actually challenged me to a bout but—''

''Did you accept?''

''—you flipped out about then and when I looked over I knew I had to get you out of there, so—''

''Contact him again to accept this challenge. It might be a way back in.''

''Why bother at this point?'' he said glumly, almost to himself, thinking it'd be over as soon as Wood heard the news from Riordan.

''I don't know . . . something I felt about the place, something I saw . . . or someone.''

''What do you mean?''

''Can't put my finger on it, but there was a woman on the stairs and at the window, I'd like to speak to.''

''What woman was this?''

She tried to explain to him what she'd seen, what the woman's presence made her feel like at the time.

''Maybe the drug was working on you at that point?''

''No, no, I hadn't had a thing.''

''Are you sure? Drugs can do that, distort time, I mean.''

''I'm certain.''

''Not much time before our watch, Shannon. Listen, I'll drive you to your place, then I'll meet you there. How's that sound?''

''I would like a shower and a change,'' she said, agreeably. She sucked on her index finger, finding a cut there.

Ryne's thoughts were on Wood and what he'd make of Lanark's little sortie to the Stone place. Somehow he had to keep Shannon's name out of it, no matter what happened.

"Something troubling you, Lanark?" she asked, putting dishes under water, her finger stinging anew.

"No, no . . ."

"What? Even under the influence of a powerful aphrodisiac I didn't come onto you, right?" She laughed.

"Are you kidding? You were all over me."

"Now that's far-fetched."

"Not so far-fetched."

They continued the verbal joust on their way out, Tebo and his wife, Maria, peeking out from the downstairs apartment window as they left.

In the car, Shannon examined the nick on her finger once again. It was an annoying, deep little prick, the sort one gets from a rose thorn. The thought brought on a flood of images nipping at her mind, images related to the night before, at the party or in her dreams. She could not recall.

"What's the matter?" he asked her.

"Did you see me leave the dance floor last night, at any time, even for a moment?"

"I didn't have my eyes on you every moment, but I don't think so. Why?"

"Nothing . . . just *real* foggy about last night."

"You were out of it," he agreed. "Listen, if any flack should get back to Wood, you know, about our having gone out there—"

"How would anyone know?" she said as if it were a stupid suggestion.

He said, thinking of the fight and the subsequent run-in with Riordan and Fabia, "Yeah, how *would* anyone

124

know. In any event, *you* were not there. Just stick to that story, and you won't be sorry."

When they reached her apartment house, just off Rush Street, on a block of beautifully reconditioned brownstones, he said, "It's been a hell of a date, Keyes. One like I've not enjoyed in a long time, but please, don't forget your business suit in the back seat, and some time soon will you have the dress pressed and returned to me?"

She looked down at the well-worn blue gown. "Don't worry, it's not likely to get lost in my closet. It really isn't me."

"See you at the precinct."

"Cover for me."

"Not an easy request, Keyes . . . you'll be missed."

"I pulled double-shift last night. Wood won't mind if I'm a little late."

"No, guess not. See you then."

She went to her door and pulled her keys from her purse, slotting one into the keyhole, favoring the irritating cut on her right index finger. Maybe she should have told Lanark about her odd memories of the night before, but they were hardly what you could call vivid, and most likely dreams that would only lead the two of them farther afield.

As expected, Captain Paul L. Wood was upset on learning of Lanark's extracurricular activities, and the instant Lanark walked into the station, Wood's enormous index finger wagged out the door at Lanark. The other men were glad it wasn't them.

"Nice collar Shannon pulled in last night. They kick

the guy loose already?" asked Lanark as he came in and took a chair, before realizing Riordan was standing on the other side of the room and Fabia was sipping coffee from a styrofoam cup, glancing over the Captain's bookshelf.

"No way that guy walks, Lanark," said Wood, referring to the knife-carrying chef from Petroff's.

"His story failed the tests, huh?"

"Guy was a kitchen worker at Petroff's before they fired him. Picked up his accent from hanging around the place, mimickry. We got a positive ID on him as Louis Wellman, several priors, all sex offenses."

"All points to a good collar."

"Which brings us to you, and last night—the Stone place, Lanark, why'd you do it?"

"Captain, I was invited to a party and—"

"Invitation through coercion and then this, what's his name, Burton Heron turns up dead, just after you were seen pushing him around at this party."

"Dead? How, when?"

Riordan turned to face Lanark, his eyes a mass of dark concentric circles. He'd been up all night. This accounted for Fabia's subdued condition, Lanark thought. "Lanark, we figure somebody got jumpy, diced this boy up like a ripe watermelon, I mean pieces of him everywhere. But they got witnesses saying you threatened his life last night at this party. Now we had the boy wired, and we didn't catch any threats—a lot of howling on your leave-taking with Shannon Keyes—"

"Whoa, back up there, Shannon was nowhere near—"

"Cut the crap, Lanark, we know you were with your partner."

"Damn it, Captain, that's bull."

"She confirmed it, Lanark, to me, over the phone."

He groaned. "You tell her about Burton?"

"She is your partner, and she was there."

He nodded.

"Now, Lanark," began Riordan again, "we think we may be close to the Glove, and it has something to do with this crowd. Burton dated one of the dead girls. The other two were rich girls, one of the reasons I got the commissioner on my back and he's got the mayor on his. So, we're needing a decoy operation like nothing before. We need to infiltrate this bunch from the inside maybe, if we're going to get anything worthwhile. That's where you and your partner come in—"

"Whoa, they know we're cops."

"Yes, they do, but they won't, not after we're finished with you. You two are going to fit right in, trust me."

Lanark was confused. Last night Riordan was talking about destroying his career. Now he was talking about cooperation between them on a case Lanark was never before allowed entry to, not until he broke into it. "Why, why the sudden change of heart, Riordan?"

Riordan and Fabia exchanged a glance, Fabia displaying a frown of pure disgust before he said, "This Burton kid's ass was stuffed with white gloves."

"Down his throat, too."

"Throat cut like the women?"

"Right."

"Ankle bracelets?"

127

"Marks were there."

"Same m.o., same for the coroner?"

"Letter perfect, once the pieces were reassembled on the slab."

"Whoever hell it is, he isn't too bright," said Lanark. "Leaves a trail like . . . like bread crumbs. Now he does meat cleaver work on his one and only male victim—"

"Penis hasn't been found," said Fabia matter-of-factly.

Lanark swallowed painfully at this. "Where'd you find the body?"

"Trash bag," said Fabia.

"On the doorstep, here," added Wood.

"Like a return package," said Riordan, "for you, Lanark."

"Jesus, you really think so?" asked Lanark, his mind racing back to the three trash bags lying open in the courtyard behind his building.

"Dumped like trash," mumbled Fabia.

"On my doorstep," repeated Wood, gritting his teeth.

"So, what's our next move?" asked Lanark. "We working together, Al?" he asked Riordan.

"We are."

Fabia shook his head in light derision, obviously thinking what he'd like to say but knowing he could not.

"This brings the toll to four young people, all well off, all college graduates or soon to be, all in Burton's crowd. One male, three females," said Riordan.

Shannon entered, saying, "Got here as soon as I could, Captain." She exchanged pleasantries with

Riordan, was introduced to Fabia whose eyes lingered over her, and then she picked up the flow of the conversation, the impact of Burton's death settling in for both she and Lanark. They had been among the last people to see him alive.

"Does the coroner know what was used to cut Burton apart, Al?" asked Lanark.

"Captain, Lanark, it's Captain to you, and yes, he believes it was a power tool of some sort, very likely a rotary saw—"

"Industrial size, would you say?"

"Yes. Edges are jagged, however, and could indicate a less precise tool."

"Or an old blade."

"Or an old blade," he conceded.

Wood stood up and began to talk, taking control of the conversation now. "My people are working on other cases, Al, and so we need to know how much time you want these two detectives to put forth on this case."

"We'll leave that, and the details to you. We're providing the setup, no matter the cost, anything your people need in the way of cash, supplies, you name it. Comes straight from the top."

Lanark realized only now that somehow Captain Paul Wood had influenced higher-ups, and that this play was actually orchestrated by him, and not Riordan at all. To save face, Riordan was attempting to put a different light on the situation.

"Monies will then be routed through Division for the new Decoy Unit?" asked Lanark innocently. "Anything so long as we get results?"

"That's about the gist of it, yes," said Riordan.

"Manpower?"

"Within bounds."

"All right!" Lanark could control his excitement no longer. It seemed too good to be true. "But why, why so sudden, Captain Wood?"

Wood felt uneasy at the question and instantly waved Lanark down. "An idea whose time has come," he said simply.

"Besides which, Burton Eaton-Heron is the nephew of Councilman Edward Eaton-Heron."

"I thought that name was familiar," said Shannon.

"Isn't he the guy who owns almost every home for the elderly in the area, some clinics, too? Gets slapped with fines every year for not installing fire prevention—"

"Never mind the councilman's faults, Lanark, he's the victim here, not the perpetrator."

Lanark demured to Riordan's logic. "Oh, yes, of course, let's be certain the crooks we're after are not running our franchised old-folks homes."

"Enough talk," said Wood. "We'll start in on setting up operations right away. Special phone lines, separate quarters, everything right away. Now that this killer's delivering goods to you, Lanark, we'll make sure he knows how to contact you. As for infiltrating the rich and famous, you're going to have to delegate that to people placed under your command."

"My command?"

"It'll be your command, Lieutenant, for now, and if it works out, maybe it will stay that way . . . we'll see."

Responsibility, thought Lanark, Wood's thinking he can tie me down with responsibilities, put the ropes in my hands, give me what I want, and then . . . then things go bad, it's not his problem and there's a clear place to lay the blame, just like the killer knew where to lay Burton's remains. Lanark felt more than a wave of stomach-turning guilt over the fact the killer meant to send a clear and arrogant message to him via the butchered remains.

"The blood," he said aloud to Riordan, "Burton's blood, was it drained, like the others? Like the women?"

"No way to tell properly, there being so many cuts to the body, but the coroner suspects this was the case."

"Why? Why does he suspect so?"

"Amount of blood clotting at the wounds, or lack really of it, I was told."

"Like the women, then, the blood was taken . . . rich blood, from rich kids . . . by whom, for what reason?"

"And the marks to the face," said Shannon, "were they found on the . . . the last victim?"

"Yes, either the same killer or a convincing copycat."

"No copycat here, Riordan," said Lanark firmly.

Fabia's nasty tone returned with venom. "How the hell would you know that, Lanark?"

"Just a hunch . . . just a hunch."

"Come on, Fabia, it's time you and I got some rest."

"Oh, by the way, Riordan," said Lanark, stopping him at the door.

"Yes?"

"Maybe you can have your man, Fabia, here, bring us a copy of the file on the case thus far?"

"Why bother, Lanark, you've already seen it."

"Now how would I have ever managed a thing like that?" he replied incredulously. "Besides, my partner, Keyes, she needs to see it."

Fabia gritted his teeth, anger exuding from every pore. It was difficult for any cop to give up on a case, or to ask for additional help, or worse, to have it thrust upon him. Almost as if it destroyed his manhood. Lanark was enjoying every minute of it. "What, you want me to say please? Okay, please," he said, rubbing it in.

When the door shut Lanark's laughter rang out. Wood and Shannon stared at one another and shook heads.

"Why, why does a killer do that, send a message to a reporter, a lawyer, a shrink or, in this case, a cop?" asked Shannon when they returned to their desks. "Is it a plea for help? Does he want to be caught? Does one side of him go out of his way to get caught, because he wants to be punished, because he knows he's done these horrible things and deserves punishment and can't feel . . . feel redeemed, or just better, unless—"

"Bullshit, Shannon."

"Is that an answer, Lanark?"

"What you're supposing is that this guy has a conscience, a moral code, a god—"

"Maybe a part of him does!"

"No way . . . not this one."

"How do you know that?"

"The message wasn't sent to me personally, and it wasn't sent to convey a psycho-schizoid personality behind these brutal slayings. Shit, Shannon, can't you see?''

"No, I don't see."

"He's throwing it in our faces!"

"Just like that?"

"Yes, telling us he can kill at will, anytime, anyone, anywhere, any way he likes. He's better than us. Brighter, meaner, sharper, nastier, faster, brasher, all of it. That's what his body bag delivery is all about."

"Flimsy . . . you've got no proof of that."

"It'll come."

"You are so sure of yourself."

"Have to be in this business."

"I know, I know, it could be the difference between living and dying."

He leaned back in his chair, considering the sudden turn of events. In real life situations things twisted with shattering speed after days and weeks of nothing, very like his job. So much time spent in idle watching, waiting, expectation, then all hell suddenly breaks loose on what seems a routine call. Not like fiction or TV at all. Ninety percent of hurry up and wait. Now, with the speed of a train roaring in, Captain Wood had managed to make a real difference, to create within the dog-eared 13th Precinct something Lanark had long argued for, a full-fledged Decoy Department, unto itself, that recruited only the best, and Wood wanted Lanark to head it. He wondered if he were capable of such a task. He wondered if he wanted it.

"Isn't it great," Shannon said, as if reading his mind, "about the Decoy unit, I mean."

"Great . . . yeah."

"I mean no more working out of the back of your car."

"The real perk'll be having a complete wardrobe department."

"How long before we'll be in operation, do you think?"

"Can't say."

Her phone rang. It was the woman upstairs at the computer. "Got your list, Detective," she said. "Want it routed through the mail, or will you pick up?"

"Be right there." She told Lanark what she had, and asked him not to disappear, before she returned with the listing. "We can spend the afternoon making calls, see if we can get a lead on Tony, the girl you spoke about."

"Or something nasty on Sorentino? Maybe involve him in some fraud the FBI might like to hear about, put somebody on his behind."

"Boy, you sure think dirty. Any way to teach that?"

"Experience . . . with scum," he shouted as she disappeared.

"What, you like your coffee with scum in it?" asked Milt Wiemer from across the room.

Ryne waved a hand at him, not in a friendly way. Wiemer was packing a box now, clearing out his desk. Wood had made good on his threat of the evening before, and with the accumulated problems Wiemer had he was given a choice, back to patrolling a beat in a unit, or early retirement before pension. He took the patrol. And for the first time since Lanark had known him, he was stone cold sober. Maybe beat work was what he liked best, maybe that's where he belonged all along . . . maybe.

* * *

Tavalez Sorentino was somewhat new to the area, and this made the list of possible deputies to his network a lot harder to trace. While Wood worked on organizing the Decoy Unit, Lanark and Shannon concentrated on Tavalez.

"Where's a guy get a name like that, 'Tavalez'?" Lanark wondered aloud. They were driving a precinct car, unmarked, yet a distinctively police vehicle, some called it a "pastel" for its bland color, an off-white in this case.

"Need to dirty this car up some," Lanark complained. They were on Sorentino's ground now, dressed casually, in search of a man named Angelo Sorentino, a Tavalez cousin who might know where Tony and Karen might be. They learned this from an old woman Lanark had reached via the list Shannon had generated with her inquiry. They had split the list and spent most of three hours on the telephone getting nowhere. But they finally did, eliciting a remark from Ryne that he loved little kids and old people, who were guileless.

"Think I got one," Lanark had told Shannon when the old woman he spoke to said *sure, sure,* to his first question, after a preamble about his being an old Navy buddy of Tony's. Where could he find Tony?

"Sure . . . sure . . ." the woman repeated. "He live down on Hoyne . . . Hoyne, near the park?"

It was the place he'd busted. "He's moved from there, the landlady says." said Lanark. "I owe him a hundred dollars and want to pay him back. He's a good—"

135

"Ohhhh, then maybe you see his cousin, Angelo?"

"Where? Where can I see Angelo?"

"He work at that place, what's the name it is called?"

Shannon, listening in on the other line now shrugged.

"Oh, yeah, Carmellow's, on Wolcott, makes something, building tool? Yes?"

"Yes, I know where that is. Angelo Sorentino?"

"Yes, that's my sisterboy. He know Tony good."

So now they sat outside *Carmellow's*, a big sign saying it was an arcade. The machines here only made noise, whatever the old lady meant by building tools, they didn't know. In any event, they were here and cruising by for a second time, casing the place, sizing up the thugs surrounding the doors.

"Could be a drop point," said Lanark.

"Part of the Sorentino empire?"

"You got it."

"Do we go in?"

"Shake 'em up you mean?"

"Couldn't hurt, could it? Maybe we'll come away with a big bargaining chip."

He looked at her with a prideful grin. "I think you're gaining a little style, Keyes."

"So, how do we work the play?"

"Straightforward, we're cops looking to bust Angelo."

"Could lose his job at *Carmellow's*."

"Could, yes, if he's arrested."

"Could go bad on him if someone else got the idea maybe he's talking to cops, huh?"

"Okay, that's the ticket, but Shannon—"

"Yeah?"

"These guys can be like hair triggers, especially if they're *using* as well as selling, so be ready for anything."

"Gotcha."

Lanark swerved the car into the sidewalk and came within an inch of breaking the plate glass windows, the two lookouts racing for cover and safety in separate directions. He and Shannon rushed inside, guns pulled, the small crowd of young faces in the arcade parting for them but jeering at the same time, saying, "What's this, now you outlawing video games, man?"

The owner rushed up to them, pleading, asking what was wrong, his arms going up and down, a squat, square and broad-shouldered Italian. "We're here for Angelo! Angelo Sorentino. He works here?"

"No more . . . no more he don't," the man was lying. Shannon could even tell it by the way his eyes went toward the back room, covered with black drapes.

"He's in the back!" Lanark needlessly shouted.

"Careful!"

They made their way through a junkpile in the rear and came on a small room where two men were pretending to play a game of cards while a third, in the john, was flushing something down the toilet.

"Three guesses what's going on here, Keyes," Lanark said. "Which one of you bags of shit is Angelo Sorentino? We get him, the rest can go free."

"In there," said one of the card players, pointing.

"Thank you," said Lanark. "Cuff 'em, Keyes."

"But you said," protested the man.

"I lied . . . started lying a lot lately, dealing with your kind of gutter crap."

Shannon ordered the two men to turn around as she began to apply the cuffs, and Lanark ordered Angelo to open the john door, the toilet flushing again.

"This ain't right man," bitched one of the prisoners. "You ain't *s'pose* to bust this place. We pay our bills, man."

Lanark instantly turned and stared at this man. "What'd you say?"

"Shut up, Palo," said the other man. "Can't you see nothing?"

"Put these two in the unit, Shannon. I'm going to take care of Angelo myself."

Lanark kicked out at the john door twice, sending it crashing in. If there was anyone inside it might have crushed him. The room was a tiny cube that stunk of urine and feces, every surface brown with age and rust, the only light a window that had been Angelo's escape hatch. Floating in the backed-up toilet, two white packets.

"Damn," he moaned and raced out, catching Shannon at the car. "Get 'em in there, hurry. Angelo's got clean away!"

"How?" she asked, forcing the last head in and getting in beside Lanark half a second before he peeled out after Angelo. "Watch for him."

"We don't know what he looks like."

"Watch for anyone looking over his shoulder then."

It was going on dusk, the sun low in the sky, shadows long. Hard to see, dangerous time for small children on bikes, Shannon thought, seeing a playground full of them as they circled the block.

Then she saw him, and Lanark was right again, a thin, Italian man looking over his shoulder guiltily. He

138

got into a car and seeing them he revved up and tore out, barely missing a woman crossing the street with an armload of groceries.

"Hold on," shouted Lanark who let loose with the siren and placed the blue light overhead while sending the gas pedal to the floor, causing the two passengers in back to gasp.

"Get on the radio, call for support," said Lanark.

Shannon did so, calling the pursuit in and giving their position. They turned in tight, almost going completely around, on Ravenswood, following the El train as it sped alongside them. Just ahead Angelo's red Ferrari sped beneath the tracks, disappearing.

Lanark tried to follow without reducing speed. It sent them all to the other side of the car and when they straightened up again they faced a row of silent factory buildings, some abandoned. Angelo was nowhere in sight.

"Creep gave us the slip," she said.

"Not yet he hasn't."

Another unit joined them, then a third carrying Milt Wiemer and his new partner.

"Just what we need," said Shannon.

The guy behind Lanark said something in Spanish to his *compadre*. "You hear that, Shannon?"

"What?"

"Wiemer's been taking payoff money from these goons to look the other way and keep other cops off their backs."

"You understand Spanish?" she asked.

"Enough to get by. This guy just called Wiemer his connection. Told the other guy not to worry about it."

"Shhhhhheeeeeeet," said the man behind Shannon.

Lanark got out and went over to Wiemer. "Say, old buddy, you know which one of these shops here belongs to Sorentino?"

"What? Whataya mean, Lanark?" he asked.

"A car just doesn't disappear into thin air. It went into one of these doors," he said, pointing down the lane of factory doors facing the elevated tracks. One manufactured caps and gowns, another was a tool-and-die shop, a third had a sign with an enormous level on it. Lanark thought of what the old lady said about the boy working at a place that made tools. Could be the level place, but that seemed, to him at least, on the level . . . while the tool-and-die shop sign looked so faded as to say no one inside really gave a damn about the company.

"I think it's the tool-and-die shop, myself," said Lanark.

"Whoa down, there, Lanark," said Wiemer, "you don't want to go busting down doors without a warrant, do you? Could get you busted back to patrol like me and—"

Just seeing Wiemer's smug puss and jaunty walk from his unit to the enormous garage door, and recalling what the slime in the back seat of Lanark's car had said regarding Wiemer, Ryne felt the black hole of anger gape open deep inside his brain, growing and swelling and taking on a life of its own; he felt it swallow him up so completely he knew he was about to do something he'd regret.

Wiemer continued talking non-stop, booze on his breath—"Hell, you got no idea who's inside there. Could be some innocent person gets hurt. They'll call it reckless endangerment and you'll get your behind in

140

a meat grinder and Wood'll be doing the turning. No, my friend, listen up, you don't want to go busting in there without a warrant.''

"Yes, Milt, I do want to bust that door down, and maybe I'll use your bloody head—'' he grabbed Wiemer in a headlock and rammed his head against the unforgiving door—''as a battering ram!'' Lanark liked the feeling this gave him and so he did it again before he heard Shannon shouting for him to stop. He let Wiemer's limp form drop to the pavement.

Lanark knew that he didn't need a search warrant on probable cause while in pursuit of a man who has violated sixteen different laws and fled into a building. Milt knew that, too.

Wiemer's partner instantly jumped in, raising his night stick to Lanark, saying, "You had no call to do that!''

"Wiemer's a weasel," he said, "and he's on Sorentino's payroll. That's why—''

Wiemer had staggered to his feet and he rushed at Lanark, shouting, "Liar!''

Lanark's large fist sent Wiemer to the ground again where he remained on one knee, gasping and muttering and spitting blood. The guy with the night stick ordered Lanark away but Lanark said, "You cuff this creep and hold him and then I'll back away.'' With a foot to Wiemer's face, he sent the other man staggering over again.

"That's it!'' Milt's new partner came at Lanark with the stick. Lanark took him and his stick in stride, sending him toppling over when he grabbed the arm and twisted. A third cop on the scene caught Lanark by the

141

arm and shouted for him to cool down when Shannon took hold of him and he relented, backing off.

Milt's partner tried to help him up, but he snatched his arm away. Wiemer then suddenly unsnapped his holster, going for his gun.

"Lanark!" shouted Shannon, drawing her own gun, a bead on Wiemer.

Lanark wheeled and came around with his gun pointed. "Go on you miserable excuse for a cop! Give me a reason to turn your brains inside out! Come on!"

Wiemer's weapon was just coming up when his partner kicked it skyward, shouting, "This ends it, damn it! Lanark! Keyes! Put your weapons away, now!"

Weimer was staring down Lanark's barrel, shivering in his shoes, seeing the two weapons pointed at him. Keyes put her weapon away instantly. The other cops were trying to diffuse the situation, shouting for Lanark to put it down. He didn't do so until Shannon placed a hand on Ryne's gun and whispered into his ear, "He's not worth it, Ryne, not worth ruining your career over. Please, for me, for yourself . . . put it away."

When he did so, one of the other cops began to shout at him. "What's wrong with you people? You gone nuts?"

"Wiemer's been taking protection money from these creeps so they can keep their drug dealing business flowing smoothly," Lanark accused Wiemer and then stared at the other cops. "Any others of you into Sorentino for anything?"

"Can you prove that?" asked one of the other cops, a tidy, short man Lanark had seen around the station house, by the name of Gobel.

"In time, when we get our third suspect flushed out of there."

"You're sure he's in there?"

"Bet my badge on it."

"All right, Lieutenant, we'll give you backup. Tom, take Wiemer here back to the 13th, and on your way call for some real backup. Looks like a possible SWAT job."

"No, I want the kid alive, for questioning."

"All right, your play."

Shannon and Lanark moved in, trying doors. Everything was locked tight. "You sure he's in there?"

Windows on the large, industrial-size garage doors were painted over, no way to see in. Other units began to move in, effectively cutting off escape from any side. If Angelo was hiding inside, there was no way out for him.

Captain Wood came on the scene but he'd gone to work long before he got here, having Dispatch find out whose building it was, and a phone line into the main office. They could hear the phone ringing inside now, but if Angelo was inside, he wasn't interested in talking. "Curious to see what's inside, are you?" Lanark asked Wood.

"Any ideas?"

"You think the place belongs to Sorentino?"

"One of his investments, I assume."

"Funny, we just wanted to talk to this Angelo, and he panics, shows us drugs at the arcade and now this," said Shannon.

"I've suspected Wiemer of being on the take for a long time now, but haven't been able to nab him at it. Hope this sticks."

"It will," said Shannon in support of Lanark. "This is not a bright bunch we're dealing with here. They may even implicate Sorentino if we promise them enough."

"And it all began with Mother Sorentino whom you located in the phone book. Told you it takes being dogged."

"And clever."

"Still, we don't have enough to nail Sorentino," said Wood, bringing them back to reality. "What do you bet the arcade and this place are in someone else's name? A guy like Sorentino, he knows how to cover his backside, because he pays for legal advice, top dollar."

"Are we going in, or are we going to picnic out here all day?"

"Hold on, I've got an idea," said Wood, going back to his unit and getting on the radio. In a moment, he was back.

"What's the plan, Captain?"

"Seems we got a fire inside?"

"What?"

"I don't know about you, but I smell smoke, and where there's smoke—"

"Oh, yeah, I smell it *now,*" replied Lanark. "Head cold coming on, all stuffed up, didn't notice at first."

"When in imminent fear of fire," said Shannon, "call the professionals."

"I know the chief at the Damon Avenue firehouse. We'll get the door down."

A fire truck raced in, many of the firemen in confusion, wondering where the fire was. Wood talked briefly with the fire chief and without a moment's hesitation the garage door was being axed. In another moment an entire panel, large enough for a man to walk through, was opened and the firemen told to back off.

"I go first," said Lanark.

Wood stared at him and exchanged a look with Shannon. "You got a death wish or something, Lanark?"

"It's my case, my play—"

"Our case," said Shannon but Lanark was gone. The silence of the place was ominous and the fleeting thought he'd made a mistake, that perhaps the building next door held Angelo, went in and out of his mind. The large garage housed a mid-sized moving truck and a van but no red Ferrari. The machinery was all intact, drill presses, work tables, bundles and stacks of sheet metal and supplies all about, shelving to the ceiling. It all looked legit.

Behind him Lanark heard Wood groan the word shit. Shannon said, "Oh, no . . ."

The fire chief was telling Wood good-bye, turning to move his men out.

Lanark had been so certain; he couldn't let go the idea that somehow the punk had driven in here and perhaps out another door on the opposite side. He looked for the second door but there was none.

Shannon had gone to the shelves, picking about them, wondering what sort of tools were manufactured here. She found odd shaped, heavy metal plates, diecast items all around. Dust clouds lifted wherever she touched, making her sneeze. "This stuff's been on the shelf a long time, Lanark," she commented.

Her hands were dirty from the search. Lanark looked in every corner, found a stairwell, ignored it since the

Ferrari was nowhere in sight, deciding Angelo must also be elsewhere.

"Wonder what's upstairs," Wood pondered.

"Want me to check it out?" asked Shannon.

"We'll do it together. Better hurry, the owner's on his way, going to be hard enough explaining the door."

Wood and Shannon disappeared through an entryway and up the stairs. Lanark still could not let go of the conviction he was right, that this was the place. He moved about the perimeters and returned to the door where the van and the truck stood silently mocking him.

He stepped onto a metal loading ramp at his ankles, almost falling. Then he realized his error.

Going to the moving truck with the faded name of the company on its side, he saw that the bolt for the back was ajar. He took the handle in his hand and with a quick jerk sent the door flying upward, his gun pointing into the dark interior at the back end of the Ferrari, but no Angelo.

Upstairs! Lanark raced for the stairs, shouting a warning at the others when he heard the powerful burst of gunfire. "Shannon! Wood!"

The sound of shattered glass accompanied another volley of gunfire. Lanark got to the second floor just in time to see Angelo Sorentino's uncontrolled flight before he disappeared below to street level. Wood was bleeding badly from a wound in his leg and Shannon, near hysteria, had hold of Wood's leg and was tying off the artery pumping out his blood. She'd torn off her belt to do so.

Meanwhile, Lanark stared aghast at what they had uncovered in the warehouse, the true business working

146

out of this dump. In one corner was a mock bedroom, another a living room, and there were cameras and filming equipment, flood lights and backdrops—a regular theater. Tavalez Sorentino was in the movie business, porn, but pornography of the worst kind, Lanark could instantly see, for one wall was lined with ill-treated, poorly fed animals, ranging from goats and pit-bull terriers to chimps. In a small room, an add-on, noises of a different nature could be heard, low, near inaudible sniffling of a human kind.

The shots and the broken glass and the broken kid on the street below sent the backup cops in and they were helping with Wood while Lanark investigated the strange sounds behind the padlocked door. "Here," said Shannon, beside him now with a crowbar she'd found. "Open it."

Lanark put his weight against the bar and with a quick force the lock moorings pulled out of the door before the lock would snap. Good enough, Lanark pried off the whole metal piece and snatched open the door to find three completely naked bodies racked with bites, rips, tears, and festering sores, hardly capable of doing the simpering he'd heard. "The actors," Lanark said with a revulsion slithering through his spine. "Two girls, what twelve, thirteen? One boy, eleven?"

"Oh, God . . . Lanark," groaned Shannon, stepping past him and going to the one girl who managed to open an eye to her. Her other eye was bruised so badly she could not open it. "Get blankets up here!" she told Lanark. "You're going to be all right, you kids . . . now, nobody's ever going to hurt you again . . . ever . . . ever . . ."

Shannon held the one girl in her lap, rocking her

tenderly, putting a hand out to the others. Lanark grabbed blankets from the mock bedroom and they covered the kids who flinched, expecting to be beaten or bit or thrown into another *play* with a hungry bull-terrier or angry chimp.

"Now I really want this creep, Sorentino," said Lanark.

Paramedics arrived, one saying, "Jess, you see this? Christ, I never believed this kinda shit went on . . . look at this!"

"Get these kids to Children's Memorial," said Shannon. "They've got a trauma center for kids."

"Treat 'em like gold, too," cautioned Lanark. "Like they were related to the President, you got that?"

It was understood when Lanark added, "When I come to visit them, I want no complaints."

"Sure, sure."

"Go with them . . ." Shannon was telling the kids who couldn't have said no or resisted any treatment of any kind. They were like wounded dolphins, unable to move their own weight. "I'l be with you, I promise," she told them.

"You believe this?" Lanark asked her, and she saw for the first time Ryne Lanark shaken. "Can't stand this kind of thing."

"I know . . ."

"Angelo dead?"

"Took a .38 through the brain. If he isn't . . ."

"No interrogating him then, and these damned dogs can't talk."

"What're we going to do with the animals, Lanark?" asked Officer Gobel, himself sickened and pale.

"Animal cruelty, humane society . . . vet?"

148

"Police Division of Animal Control," said Shannon. "They'll want to get pictures. Look Lanark, Wood's on his way to the hospital, we got two guys to interrogate downstairs . . . come away . . . come on."

They started down together, single-file, as the stairway was shoulder-width. He was just back of her, speaking quietly in her ear amid all the commotion. "Found the Ferrari in the truck downstairs. Heard that first shot, and I thought . . . maybe . . ."

"I'm still here, partner."

Lanark wondered how he could have walked away from this if she'd been killed, and he began to understand why there was an unwritten code of conduct about two partners becoming romantically involved. He knew he must either resist his feelings for her, or somehow get Wood to rearrange things. The shock of that first fear of her having been hit still shook him along with all the other horrible sights Angelo Sorentino had provided. More now than ever he wanted to put Sorentino away in the one prison he could not buy his way from, talk his way from, or weasel his way from, the prison of the grave.

SIX

They had three set of suspects: Joe and Palo who'd been arrested behind the arcade for dealing drugs; Milton Wiemer for taking payoffs to protect the drop point. Enrico Carmellow, a dour businessman whose arcade had become the center of juvenile activity and drug activity at the same time. In charge of the interrogation, Lanark knew just what to do.

He first separated the suspects, placing them into tiny rooms with harsh lighting, grilling them with questions. Internal Affairs was called in to go over Wiemer. Shannon and Lanark worked on Palo and Joe separately. Blum and Max worked on Carmellow. Lanark's simple instructions to his interrogators were, "Use every shred of information you can wrench from one to intimidate the others. Create insecurity in them. Refer often to their allies, and what they're saying in the next room. Pretty soon they'll begin to think the only people they can trust are their new friends—the good guys. Tell them although you have a job to do, you'll try like hell to help them beat the rap."

Lanark took his own advice, at one point telling Palo, "We're not narcs, you know, and personally I don't give a shit about drugs. A person wants a good time, to abuse his body, that's his business, right? He wants to be stupid, let him. We got enough to do helping people who want help. Does a junky deserve help? I don't think so, do you? He gets what he deserves, right? Right?"

"Right, yeah, right," replied Palo.

"Good, then we understand each other. We don't care if the drug rap sticks, see . . . matter of fact, you go along with Joe, confirm what he's told us, and you two can walk away from this thing. We're after Sorentino for the pornography and child abuse charge, see? Look at those pictures again. A creep does that to kids, that's worse than any narcotics."

"I don't know nothing about shit like that, man," said Palo for the hundredth time.

"Guess we go back to Joe, tell him Palo don't want to help him. Come on, Officer Keyes."

Palo was left with a guard.

Wiemer didn't know anything about any pre-teen porn operation involving torture and animals. He only knew about *Carmellow's* and the drug trafficking there, and his confession of accepting payment for looking the other way only implicated the owner of the arcade, the man Lanark and Shannon had rousted earlier, the Italian whose name graced the arcade.

He, too, was brought in and shaken down, grilled in the hope he'd further implicate Sorentino, but he seemed to prefer the idea of going to prison himself to insulting Mr. Sorentino.

Wiemer was suspended pending a full investigation

from Internal Affairs. The word was he hadn't a chance of saving his badge.

Captain Wood was laid up for at least a week, and he placed the continuance of organizing the Decoy Unit into Lanark's hands, Shannon assisting. Now they truly had their hands full: three men to interrogate, plus the organization of a new unit.

Lanark asked for help from Max Yoshikani and Jeff Blum, putting them onto Carmellow. Now, watching Max work, Lanark realized the Japanese guy was—stereotype notwithstanding—an excellent interrogator. He moved with the mood of the prisoner, played him off against the others with precision timing, dropping bits of information perfectly, and then soaring to the point of dramatic anger and intolerance, to the point where Jeff would have to step in to calm him down and explain things "rationally" to Mr. Carmellow.

Because the prisoners had cooked up a phony story among themselves, Lanark reasoned that it would begin to unravel sooner or later. He'd like sooner, but he would also settle for later if need be. He didn't personally spend much time with Mr. Carmellow, much more now with the two henchmen. But now he watched from the observation room and when Shannon asked him what it was he was looking for, he told her simply, "Stress points, the little things that make 'em hesitate. Like now, Max's going in for the kill with Carmellow."

They watched as Max displayed pictures found at the warehouse, as he said, "You like the little girls, or the boy? You like to see them bleed? You like to see them play donkey with the—"

"I didn't have nothing to do with that!"

152

"Never? Not one time, ever?"

"No, never!"

"Who then?"

"Angelo!"

"Angelo's dead . . . you know he can't help you. Who put money up for studio? Who kidnap children? Tell me, Mr. Carmellow, tell me! Tell me! You *know,* and you must tell!"

"No! I don't know nothing!"

"You just drug runner, in business for yourself? Shit!" he kicked out at the man's chair viciously, almost toppling him. Blum rushed to Carmellow's aid, shouting at Max as if he were the criminal, telling him to cool down, leave the room, have a smoke.

Max came out shaking his head.

Blum offered the shaken Carmellow a cigarette, saying, "That Jap's a real yo-yo, nuts, you know? Here—" striking a match "—that better? Freakin' Japs, you know they think they won the war?" Blum worked the good guy routine, but this wasn't having much effect on Carmellow either.

"I didn't know about the kids, I swear . . . I swear. If I had—"

"You'd have told Sorentino to stick it?"

Carmellow shut up.

"He's afraid of Sorentino," said Lanark on the other side of the glass.

Lanark also watched closely whenever there was a reference made to one of the suspects about his accomplice. Whenever Tavalez Sorentino's name was mentioned, Carmellow shook. Blum and Yoshikani had shaken the other two by dropping hints that the other had decided to deal with them. They'd been kept apart the entire time. With the pornography warehouse evidence in hand, Sorentino wasn't rushing down to the precinct to bail out his people, and this, too, was being used as a lever against them. Carmellow had his own lawyer, but the man wasn't too smart and had been kept at bay by Lanark who had sent him to another precinct where Carmellow was not being held. In the meantime, they'd gotten Carmellow to believe it would go easier on him if he cooperated at least to the point of waiving rights carefully read to him in both English and Spanish.

He'd narrowed them into two camps, Carmellow, the shrewder, more calculating one, the two others simply hangers-on, part-time thugs, pushers that did business through the arcade. Angelo had been the real operator, the manager, Sorentino setting up Carmellow as the fall guy in the event something should happen, since his name was on the deed as well as the sign. Lanark, when he had gone into the tiny interrogation rooms in the basement, had always been friendly, asking if anyone had abused the prisoner, asking if they needed a cigarette, a sandwich, a drink, coffee? Now he re-entered the room where Blum was talking to Carmellow.

He proceeded to tell Carmellow his theory regarding Angelo as manager, information given him by the other two men in custody and a policeman on the force, an old friend of his, Milton Wiemer. "Look, you want to call your lawyer again? I don't know where he's been all this time . . . maybe Sorentino's got to him . . ."

"Don't be a fool, Carmellow," said Blum.

"All right, all right," he said, something snapping

in him. "So, you know everything, then why you asking me? Why? Just put me away then."

"We can put Sorentino away for this porn rap for sixty years, maybe more if we can prove he's also into drugs. What do you say, you going to prison for him?"

"I don't know about porn, nothing . . . only, only what Angelo told me to do."

"Do what, what Carmellow?"

"He used the arcade to bring in the kids, but I thought it was just, you know, regular smut . . . not . . . not animal stuff and . . . and suffering kids."

"What the hell kind of suffering you think goes on with kids on drugs, you stupid ass!" shouted Lanark, losing his cool. "You freaks making money by burning out kids' skulls with your garbage!" His anger was boiling, his wild temper on the verge of blowing.

Carmellow broke under the accusation, dropping his head to the table, tears welling up. "I was forced into the business! To stay alive! I'm either in business for them, or I'm dead!"

"For who, damnit, say it!"

"No . . . no, I . . . I didn't say nothing. I take it all back. I know my rights."

Lanark knew then it would take days, if they could keep custody of the creeps. Carmellow's lawyer was back, angry as hell at getting the runaround and threatening to bring Lanark up on charges. "Might have a problem with that, counselor," he sneered back at the man.

"We'll just see."

"Here, I'd like you to see just what your client's involved in," said Shannon, coming to Lanark's aid, shoving pictures in the man's face. "You want us to read him his Miranda's again?"

The lawyer's face bleached white as he took in the meaning of the pictures.

"I suggest you talk to your client, sir," said Max, "and if at all possible, we will be willing to work a deal."

"For Sorentino," said Lanark.

"You've got the wrong man, Mr. Carmellow—"

"Is in over his head, counselor. Save your advice for him," Lanark finished the discussion and opened the interrogation door, exiting and calling Blum and the guard outside. "Give 'em some privacy, fellows."

"I want another room, Lanark, without a camera and a one-way mirror."

Carmellow's face blanched. "They . . . you mean I'm . . . I'm on camera? Christ!"

"You didn't tell this man you were taping this interview?"

"Yes, we did," countered Blum. "Got it on tape."

Shannon, take Mr. Carmellow and his . . . *representation* upstairs to a conference room," asked Lanark. "Max, I'd like you to talk to Joe again."

"With pleasure, Lieutenant."

A uniformed patrolman came downstairs, calling for Lanark. "Something for you upstairs, Detective Lanark."

"What?"

"Crate, says fragile on it."

Equipment for the new unit, Lanark replied, had come sooner than he'd hoped. An entire wing of the top floor of the building had been turned over to them and he had been given a service elevator key. He had already had a duplicate made for Shannon, and like a newlywed couple, they were "decorating" their new environment upstairs, the *Stronghold,* they were calling it. He left orders with Blum to continue putting the screws to Joe and Palo, play one off the other, until something cracked. Meanwhile, he went up to see what had arrived for the Stronghold. Along the way he saw Shannon who'd gotten free, and together they saw to it that the crate, which turned out to be several crates, were delivered to the right place.

In their new quarters now, a room with old oaken desks and chairs, lots of windows and wall space, they began to look through some of the boxes, materials gathered from a list they had together made up for the Captain, of things they felt necessary above all else. Hollywood-style makeup and cosmetics and wigs, an assortment which rivaled that of a special effects man. "I could be the goddamned Werewolf, if I like," Lanark had told her, donning a man's wig that looked like Wolf Man Jack's wild head of hair.

"You look like a reject form of life from the '60s," she said with a laugh.

"It's great, isn't it?" he said, looking about the boxes like a child stolen into an attic, going through old trunks.

"You really enjoy dressing up, don't you?"

He quieted, giving a thought to something far away, she thought, then said cheerfully, "Just a kid at heart."

"Which reminds me . . . the hospital."

"Going to see the children?"

"Yeah, I called earlier. They're all a good deal better, their wounds are being looked after."

"You call the social services people?"

"They're over there now. Families have to be located—"

"If they've got family."

"—and someone'll have to give a positive ID on them. Meantime, I'd hoped to interrogate the kids, carefully, of course, see what I can learn from them."

"Take a picture of Sorentino."

"Got it. Also I'm wondering if these kids were runaways and we do find the families . . . well, suppose they had good reason to run away?"

"Child molestation?"

"Just a thought, but if it's something that sent them into Sorentino's clutches . . . well, just a vagrant thought."

"A good one. You're beginning to think like a detective."

"Like *one* detective," she countered. "See you later."

"Shannon—"

"Yes?"

He thought of the moment he'd feared she was shot. "Take special care. Sorentino knows by now one of his favorite shops has been busted. He may have someone watching the precinct. There's a guard on the kids at the hospital, but just be cautious, right?"

"Right, will do."

She stopped at the door, turned and started to say something, but instead, pushing back her hair, she asked a useless question. "What do you think happened to Tony Sorrel and the girl?"

"I have an idea, but we hardly have time now to follow up on it. Maybe tomorrow."

She was gone and he was left wondering what it was

she had started to say but held back. They were working well together, more surprise to him than her, he thought. For the first time since joining the force he had allowed himself to care about something other than the past.''

Lanark decided to take this time to play out his hunch about Tony Sorrel and his girl, Karen. He got on the newly installed phone and dialed Information, asking to be put in touch with the Great Lakes Naval Training Center in North Chicago.

Identifying himself, he was put through to an officer by the name of DeWitt. He told Dewitt that he wanted Tony Sorrel for: *questioning*. ''Is he at the Naval Base?''

''I'm not in the least surprised,'' said Dewitt, the noise of paper pushing coming over the line. ''From his record, I'm not surprised at all. Poor material . . . all we get these days, Lieutenant . . . runaways, hard cases, some hiding out from the law, a paternity suit . . . you name it.''

''Is he there? Can you detain him there for me?''

''No.''

''No, you won't detain him, or no, he isn't there?''

''He was let go.''

''Let go?''

''New Navy jargon for mutually agreed upon release of all parties to contractual agreements, you might say. He didn't find the Navy much to his liking, and the Navy certainly—''

''But he's getting checks from you people.''

''Not anymore.''

''Last check, can you tell me the address to which it was sent?''

''2314 West Hoyne, Chicago.''

"Damn."

"Sorry that we couldn't have been of more *service,*" DeWitt said with a chuckle for the pun. He was about to hang up when Lanark stopped him.

"What about a roommate, a buddy, anyone connected with Sorrel who could possible give me a line on him? It's most urgent."

"I can only look into it, ask around."

"Could you? And get back to me at this number?" Lanark gave him the unit number and they said goodbye.

Another dead end. Tony Sorrel seemed very much to want to disappear. Sorentino, no doubt, had a better fix on the young couple than Lanark at the moment, and he didn't care for being bested by such a sorry creep.

Sometimes police work could be maddeningly slow, providing the investigator with less than zero to show for it. He wondered if he dared dial Angelo's aunt again . . .

Shannon took to heart Lanark's cautious warning as she left the station in the unit they'd used to bust Sorentino's arcade and "film" industry, most of which was now being processed into law enforcement equipment, and would soon become a part of the property of the new Decoy unit which she was feeling proud to be associated with. The whole building seemed brighter as a result of the prospects for the unit.

On her way to Children's Memorial, Shannon stopped off for a quick check on Captain Wood, filling

him in on conditions at the station, the ongoing interrogations, and how the new unit was shaping up.

"Can't say for sure, but I think Lanark wants Blum
and Yoshikani in," she told the Captain on leaving.

"Already luring off my people!" Wood shouted
good-naturedly.

Shannon said back, "He's one hell of a good cop,
Captain. If he ever gets control of his temper, learns
to work within the system, and learns to trust people,"
she hesitated with the thought, pacing, "then he'll be
the best."

"Let me tell you something, Keyes, whether we like
it or not, we need guys like him on our side, passionate
men, angry men. Not sure I want to take the edge off
him completely."

"But by giving him responsibility for the unit, you
have, and believe me it hasn't hurt. He's still a loner
and a brooder, and after all's said and done he's likely
to go out and do it on his own, but I think, for the first
time in his police career, he's beginning to care about
other people in the department." She laughed lightly.
"He was proud of you the other day, Captain."

"For what, taking a bullet? That makes sense to
you?"

She smiled. "No, but it seems to to him. He even
thinks that maybe, just maybe, a female cop's not such
a bad idea, and that maybe he can give me credit for
caring almost as much as he does."

"I got Lanark out on a limb now," he said, "only
hope he doesn't saw it off with both hands."

She nodded. "You put yourself out on that limb with
him. We all know that, sir."

"What do you think? You think Lanark's going to

161

hang himself and me, too?'' A nervous edge was in the Captain's tone. ''Being stuck here, you imagine the worse.''

Shannon had sat back down beside him and had given Wood an unofficial and informal report; nonetheless she had been thorough, telling Wood how much she had learned from Lanark in so short a space of time. Not once since the night I bagged that rapist has Ryne treated me like a know-nothing, she thought, not since then had he lost his temper with me, either.

Leaving for to Children's Memorial, again it played in her mind. So much had occurred between them that it was difficult now to remember exactly when he'd begun to treat her like an equal. Things were going great between them.

Then she remembered Thom.

Thom Warren had left messages for her at the desk, and on her answering machine at home, and she hadn't had a moment's time to get back to him. He was going to be furious, she knew. But then, she did promise those poor children she'd be there at the hospital for them, and right now, that took precedence over her love life. Thom would just have to be put on hold a little longer.

She went to the underground lot where she'd parked at Northwestern Memorial, got into her car and now sped toward Children's Hospital some miles distant. Somewhere along the way she got the feeling someone was following her, but she couldn't be sure. She decided to throw them off, turning suddenly at an intersection, watching the cars behind to see if anyone followed.

Must be nerves, she told herself, but just the same she took a circuitous route to the hospital. God forbid those children ever come under Sorentino's power again, she thought as she parked and went inside. She identified herself at the main desk, asking after the children. A nurse gave her the room number and indicated the direction and soon she was standing outside their room, talking with a woman named Janie Moore from Social Services who had done some preliminary work with the boy, learning his name and the name of the two girls, none of them related.

The boy's name was José Mendez, of Mexican parentage. He'd run away from home, no reason given. He met a man at the arcade named Angelo who promised him lots of money, a place to stay and work, and he gave him drugs. That was all he could say.

"The girls?"

"One's mute, in a state of shock, *how could anyone?*, can't even look out of her eyes, *horrible!*, other one calls her Teresa, *the awfulness of it all*, her name's Yolanda Cana, left home to escape her father's advances, *poor things*, dehydrated, drugged, used, open sores left to fester . . . *How? to children—children!*"

Shannon tried to maintain her professional manner against all the horror chipping away at it. "Do you think you can locate José's and Yolanda's people?"

"I think so, but I'm not so sure we ought to return them to parents who mistreat them, or allow them to be mistreated."

"We don't really have proof of that," said Shannon.

"Yolanda said her father *sold* her to this man who put her in that warehouse."

"What?"

163

"Yes."

"My God." It was a terrible thing, and yet the cop in Shannon saw the positive side as well, for if they could get their hands on Yolanda's father, they'd have a stronger case against Sorentino, to whom he may well have made the transaction. Bartering in children for pornographic films. It could be the nail that closes the lid on Sorentino, if Cana could be located and made to talk. She thought of siccing Max on the bastard.

"You think Yolanda's well enough to talk with me?"

"She's doing the best of the lot. Has a scary, almost grown-up acceptance of the whole thing. In fact, she's doing better with it than I am."

"Thanks, Mrs. Moore. I'll have a talk with her."

It turned out to be Yolanda's stepfather who had sold her "to the movies" as he had put it to the little girl when in the course of doing business with an ugly man in a restaurant.

"Do you remember the name of the restaurant, honey?" asked Shannon.

"No, only that it smelled."

"Smelled how, sugar?"

"Are they going to send me back to my stepfather?"

"No, honey, never."

"My momma, will she leave him now?"

"I can't say, honey."

"Momma's sick . . . on drugs all the time, so she doesn't feel sick. He told her they would have a lot of money for me and I would have a job and be taken good care of."

"Where's your house, where your mother and step-father live, Yolanda?"

She gave Shannon an address. "You're sure now? No tricks?"

The little girl's eyes were the largest thing on her. "Are they going to arrest my momma, too?"

"You have any sisters, brothers?"

"Yes."

"How many?"

"Two, Laura and Charles, my step-sister and brother."

"Smaller than you?"

"Yes."

"You want them to be in the movies?"

She screamed at the thought, shaking violently and saying, "No, no, no!"

"All right, sweetheart, all right. We won't ever let that happen, not if maybe your mother does go to a place where she can get better—really get better—and you and your sister and brother will have to find a new home for a while. Do you understand? A home where you won't ever be hurt again."

"Like Janie said?"

"Yes, you like Janie, don't you?"

"Yes."

"You like me?" Shannon waited patiently for a reply from her. "You know that you can trust me?"

"You're . . . you're a policewoman like on *Cagney and Lacey*. I like you . . . I know you're a good person."

The girl's pale color turned suddenly paler and she looked tired beyond words. "You rest now, and don't for a moment ever believe any different. We're going

165

to find you and José and the other girl nice homes." Shannon only wished she could be certain of that. She knew that Cagney and Lacey would, but this wasn't TV.

At the door, Shannon spoke to the police guard, a huge, dark fellow in uniform. "Officer—" she read his tag "—Jenkins, things have changed in this situation we've got here."

"Lieutenant?"

"Those kids are eyewitnesses, and that means someone would very much like to see them dead. Frankly, I don't think we've got enough of a guard here."

"My relief's due any minute," said Jenkins, "but if you like, I'll stay a double-watch."

Funny, he neither sounded like nor looked like a Jenkins, she thought, and yet back at headquarters there was a Japanese man named Maxwell. Shannon looked carefully again at the man. Few cops liked guard duty, and to volunteer a double-watch was quite unusual. But then, cops were like any other group of people, as Wiemer so often proved, it took all kinds.

She started away, but halfway down the corridor, something nagging at her, made her turn and look back at the man. *His shoes* . . . like Ryne's that day when he was in the bum's clothing and his shoes were wrong. This guy had on a pair of Guccis's. No flatfoot she knew wore knife-pointed toes and high heels in the style loved by the Chicago Italian, even if Jenkins were part Italian, what cop would go all day in shoes so uncomfortable?

Jenkins, or the man pretending to be Jenkins, waved a brisk little salute to her stare. Then his fake smile eroded as she returned to stand before him. Janie

166

Moore and all others interested in the welfare of the children were at the end of the corridor, at the nurse's station.

"Can I help you, Lieutenant?"

"Just how long before your partner arrives?"

"Ummmm, ten, fifteen tops."

"Meantime, just so we understand each other, Jenkins, I'm going to wait inside with the kids. Humor me, okay?"

"Whatever you say, Lieutenant."

She was careful when going back through the door not to turn her back on him. Once she slipped inside, she got on the phone, dialed 911, identified herself and called for backup. Before she was finished, however, the Jenkins imposter pushed back the door on the darkened room and asked if all was well. "Everything all right in here?"

"Could use your help," she said, hanging up.

He stepped through the door.

"I've got a .38 trained right on you, Jenkins. Don't dare make a move."

"Funny, I got a Browning automatic trained on you, lady cop, and I'm telling you, not a move."

"I got others on the way."

"Nah, nah, you didn't complete the call."

The standoff was complete, except for a major weakness. He could threaten to harm one or more of the kids in the room, two of whom slept soundly. Yolanda was crying tearfully, trying to get to Shannon. "Stay where you're at, Yolanda," Shannon said.

"You want the kids hurt, lady? Nobody wants that, not you, not me . . . so, you just do as I say, and

167

nobody gets hurt. Throw the gun down, across the floor, let me hear it.''

Damn, Shannon thought. She'd allowed him the upper hand. No way would she risk the kids. ''What're your plans, for the children? Why should I listen to you, you're just going to kill them anyway.''

''No, you got me all wrong, lady. I don't kill kids, 'less you make it so I have no choice. The gun, now, or else!'' He cocked his weapon and pointed it straight for the sleeping head of the mute girl.

''All right, all right,'' she said, sending her gun skittering across the floor, paying close attention to where it settled.

''That's better, pretty lady, now we do business my way.''

''Sorentino's days are numbered, Peter,'' she said, stalling him, remembering his name from Lanark's recap of that day when he'd had a run-in with this same man. It worked to slow him down. Nobody liked to know that the cops were on a first-name basis with them. ''Your boss is in deep, not ankle-deep, up to his scalp with this prostitution ring with kids not yet in their teens, the filthy flicks, all of it—''

''Shut up, lady, just shut up!'' He was trying to think, to out-manuever her when Shannon lifted an IV bottle and threw it full force into him, followed by her lunging at him. But he was too big and strong, his grip on the gun powerful. The man peeled her away from himself, spinning her around and pushing her against the bed. José, seeing him, screamed and threw a food tray at him. He recognized him from elsewhere. Shannon fought with the arm about her throat, which in a moment would effectively cut off her air supply and knock her out, if the brute did not first break her neck. Her mind flashed to Lanark's description of the man he'd called Peter, one of Sorentino's thugs, supposedly a lout and a dunce, but he had caught her completely unaware and now poor Yolanda and the other two children were in danger.

Yolanda was ringing frantically for the nurse, and the thug, seeing this, reached out toward the girl, ripping out the alarm. While occupied in this, Shannon, with all her will and effort stomped as hard as she could on the man's Guccis, causing him to let go in reaction. She spun to face him, blocking one blow and catching a second that sent her to the floor. His gun raised to fire, he squeezed the trigger as she took up her weapon; the Browning's hammer went home with a click that rang in Shannon's ears, but it ended with a metallic click. The man's gun had jammed!

Shannon fired before he had a moment to squeeze again, her .38 sending him against the wall, grasping at the ceiling as if trying to scrape his way back to life. Peter *Whoever* was dead.

A nurse and two orderlies came bursting through the door to stare at the scene.

"I'm police," gasped Shannon, "he's a killer . . . tried to harm the children."

One of the orderlies called for a third man and a stretcher. The other went to the imposter and said, "This guy was standing guard almost an hour outside . . . If he wanted to harm these kids, why'd he wait?"

"I don't know," said Shannon, "but he tried to kill me."

The orderlies took the gunman out on a stretcher,

Yolanda and José clinging to Shannon, the mute girl glued to the nurse, Janie Moore trying to pry the two kids from Shannon, a look in her eye that marked her disapproval of gunplay in front of them, regardless of the reasons.

Shannon stopped the orderlies with a shout, "Make sure you hold this guy in your morgue for an ID, understood?" She hoped that Ryne Lanark would be able to prove her story beyond doubt. It might help, also, to locate the real Officer Jenkins.

The point the orderly made was a good one, and something the gunman had said, too, told her that Sorentino wanted the children alive if possible. The man must be mad to risk it, but it seemed so. Sorentino was making an attempt to regain stolen *property*, the children, not to kill them. She realized with a start that Sorentino knew they were worth more to him alive than dead.

Now she, as much as Lanark, wanted to put a hole through the man's heart.

SEVEN

Tavalez Sorentino, 36, 6'4"; 190 lbs., hair black, eyes brown, tenth-grade education, busted for armed robbery at age fourteen, in and out of juvenile homes, into drugs at fifteen, arrested for sex offenses that stuck at the age of eighteen, tried and found guilty, sent to Joliet State Prison having turned nineteen in the meantime and so treated as an adult criminal. Four years in Joliet, he learned from pros how to operate. On the street again at 22, he worked as a deputy in an organization, slowly moving up until now he was a man of means with his own organization and able to fill the needs and wants of not only himself, but others . . . a wide variety of others.

The big, gaunt Italian filled the small interrogation room, a look of utter disdain on his face, his hands held above the table, disgusted that he was made to sit on the chair, complaining of the filth, his well-tailored coat having cost him over two hundred dollars, he told Max Yoshikani and Jeff Blum. Beside him was his lawyer, now. He wouldn't utter a word without the man

171

present. He took full advantage of his rights. Now they couldn't get him to shut up.

"I am a provider of goods, a merchant, nothing more, a businessman in the country of free enterprise, how you can say I am anything less," continued Tavalez Sorentino, "with not a shred of proof! This is beyond my cognitive abilities, gentlemen! Me, a self-educated man who has raised himself and those dearest to him out of poverty, to make of my community a better place? Who is it that has donated money for the gangs to hold their dances in the gymnasium at the high school? Me, Tavalez Sorentino, the high school where I attended, as a boy. Who has given loans to businessmen in difficulties all along Milwaukee Avenue, and when one of these men goes bad, begins to deal in drugs, like Carmellow, instantly, you wish to lay it at my doorstep? *Why, why?* I am a simple businessman. I own *Armand's,* a simple buyout. I have nothing to do with the arcade, and as for this . . . *this* horrible notion of pornographic films involving minors, no! no! no! never!"

"You spent time in the Joliet pen," said Blum. "Learned a lot there as a kid, didn't you, Tavalez? Like how to operate in drugs?"

"No."

"Mr. Sorentino, I believe, has stated his position, Officer," said Sorentino's slick-haired lawyer. Both men wore three-piece suits, Sorentino's a pin-stripe, Navy blue. The lawyer wore an elegant gray. "Now, if you have no charges to make, we will be on our way."

"Just a few more questions, counselor, please," said Max, coming to his feet, drilling the lawyer with his pinched black eyes. "Like a little matter of your nephew, Angelo Sorentino. According to his mother and any number of others, he was in your employ! He worked for you!"

"He obviously set out on a few ventures of his own!" shouted the lawyer. "This is ridiculous! You men are wasting my client's time."

"God forbid," muttered Blum.

Sorentino was walking, his lawyer on his arm and all that Max and Jeff could do was frown and shake their heads. None of the so-called witnesses were talking. Carmellow was prepared to spend time on a drug rap, as were the pushers. More time might break them down, but to date Sorentino and his lawyer hadn't bought the veiled threats and innuendo about a handful of children who would in time implicate him.

"Oh, Mr. Sorentino," said Max, stopping him at the door. "Not a question, just a fact: you're soon to be finished one way or another."

"Theater, Officer!" the lawyer blew up, which Max had counted on. Lanark had asked them to keep Sorentino in custody as long as humanly possible.

"What, you going to sue a public servant for doing his duty, counselor?"

"Duty? When you harass and badger and coerce my client!"

"Coerce?"

"Try to subvert a member of the community, in good standing, a man who is a shining example of the rehabilitation efforts of this great State—"

"Come on, Carl!" Sorentino was now snatching the lawyer by the arm.

Blum and Max fell into a dead laugh when the door

173

closed, but it was tempered by the fact they couldn't hold onto the bastard long enough for Lanark to get from the hospital. Something to do with Shannon's having had a run-in there with someone on Sorentino's payroll.

"Think we should call Lanark?" Blum wondered aloud, pushing back his glasses.

"What for? Tell him what?"

"God, I want to nail that bastard Sorentino."

"No more so than the rest of us."

"His lawyer's greasy as a, a, an oil pit."

Carl Torrence did a lot of work for mob guys. "One day he's going to slip on his own grease."

"Look, Lanark wanted *Armand's* watched, you know, *deliveries.*"

Max shook his head, unsure, since he hadn't seen his wife and kids since the day before. "Doesn't that constitute harassment, Jeff?"

Jeff laughed. "Hell, yes!"

Max laughed. "Then let's do it."

"Who knows, maybe we can score back some points with Lt. Lanark . . ."

They began leaving as they talked. "We put in some extra time . . . who knows?"

"Place sure has changed since he arrived—"

"And her, that Shannon's something, too."

"Easy boy, you're a married man. Leave her to me," said Blum.

"That like Woody Allen trying on Brigitte Nielsen?"

"Fuck you."

"No, fuck yourself, Woody . . . it's all you're going to get."

Blum turned serious again. "And the Captain's changed, too, you know . . . going after that kid, getting shot. That's something."

"Kicking Wiemer out, that's something."

"Long time coming."

"We'll leave word with dispatch for Lanark. Come on."

"You got all those bad guys locked up tight?" Max asked the holding tank guard.

"They'll keep fine right here," he replied, "til you want another go at 'em."

"No requests, huh?"

"No sir."

"Come on," repeated Blum.

"Coming . . . coming Jew-baby."

"Nip Wonder."

"Gum-shoe Lips."

"Yellow Dog."

"Yellow?"

"Yes, yellow."

"I'll show you who's yellow . . ."

Ryne Lanark arranged for around-the-clock guard and surveillance units to protect the children at Memorial from any further attempts at kidnapping by Sorentino. The policeman, Jenkins, was found in a linen closet, a concussion from a blunt object to the head, Peter Gunnetti's gun no doubt. As for Shannon, she was holding up remarkably well, her shooting ruled a good one, and Ryne had indeed been able to identify the attacker as the same man he'd left tied to a chair in Tony Sorrel's boardinghouse room. Material in his wallet identified him further as Gunnetti, a known shooter for Sorentino. His attempt on Shannon's life and the attempt to take the children added one more link to Sorentino, and Lanark's veteran sense told him that Mr. Sorentino was shoveling it in over his own grave. A case was built against a man like him with care, each piece overlaying the other to form a complete and whole picture for a jury. So far, he was looking at mandatory sentencing for trafficking in illicit child pornography, a Federal offense, along with his drug action; attempted kidnapping, conspiring to commit murder, extortion and a half-dozen other counts of illegal activity. The pillar of his community, he was about to topple.

But to bring him down, even now, with all the accumulated "evidence" gathered on him, Lanark knew he needed more; he knew what he had wouldn't get past the D.A. and into court, because he had been that route before. So far Sorentino had done everything through intermediaries and so far none of his intermediaries—still alive—were willing to talk.

He knew he had to make good on his threats to Joe, Palo and Carmellow, to prosecute them to the letter of the law, and pray that one or more would crack once they saw that Sorentino expected them to go to jail for him where he would "take care of them" through contacts on the inside. There were several crucial moments ahead for Lanark's "witnesses." One or more might crack when faced with sentencing. One or more might crack *after* sentencing, begging for a deal to be made after the fact, begging then for re-location if they should testify against Sorentino. A final crucial time was the first few days incarcerated in a max prison where they learned quickly whether or not Sorentino had or had not any influence.

But either way, they were talking about a lot of time. The other alternative, prolong the suffering of the children who might or might not be credible witnesses against Sorentino, for now even Yolanda had identified Peter Gunnetti as the man who had purchased her. Another loop in Sorentino's concentric circles, layered on to protect him from prosecution.

Lanark had taken Shannon home after the hospital incident, calling in to headquarters to learn that Sorentino had walked, not surprisingly. He was more and more impressed with Shannon Keyes. She'd proven herself in several difficult situations now. There was much to admire about her.

"What's going to happen, now, I mean in the Sorentino case?" she asked, taking the first flight in a three and a half flight apartment building, refurbished and made into condos. Lanark ran his hand along the smoothly polished, gleaming bannister. The hallway was vividly lit.

Lanark explained to her his feelings regarding the case. She listened all the way to her door, and asking him inside for coffee and a bite to eat, she found her key and undid the door, opening it on a beautifully furnished room, glass and stainless steel modern lines everywhere, even framing several paintings of fish and coral and undersea life in a set over the plush, beige couch. The carpet was also beige.

"Where I hang my hat," she said, "come on in."

It was the opposite of Lanark's stark wood floors and wood furniture and brass bed. As modern and sleek

177

and Scandinavian as the furniture, Shannon's place was warm, inviting, casual and easy. He instantly liked it.

"Hungry?" she asked.

He hesitated, thinking he should perhaps leave.

"Well? Speak up, Lanark."

"Hungry, yeah . . . I could eat, but why not let me take you to dinner?" Some place neutral, he thought.

"Don't be silly. How about spaghetti? Sound good?"

"No, I mean, yes, but—"

"Settled. I'll cook, you relax."

"Let me help."

"No, you sit and watch TV, relax."

She took command here, and he knew this, allowing it, trying to do as she said. He sat back, flicked on the set and was instantly confronted with a newsman talking about the stepped-up attempt on the part of Chicago police to locate and put an end to the career of the mass murderer dumping bodies in alleyways and parks and now on the doorstep at the unlikely 13th precinct, "Where," continued the reporter, "a special task force to combat the killer is being put together."

Relaxing, Lanark began flicking channels, passing by various reruns, an aerobics channel, a gourmet cook cracking fowl jokes over the carcass of a duck. Almost settling for an old episode of *L.A. Law,* he tried one more number. This channel displayed a heavenly, cloud-studded set in front of which a white-robed woman was shouting at an enormous congregation. Behind the evangelical priestess, a choir came in on cue with a series of *amens* and hallelujahs! He was about to flip to the next channel when the woman began haranguing about how AIDS was going to level the world,

178

the Black Plague of our times, sent unto mankind to smite him for his evil just as Sodom and Gomorrah were leveled, so shall America and all the nations of the Earth to "purge" this Devil's Kingdom literally "in blood."

"Jesus," he moaned softly at the rhetoric.

In the kitchen, she was slicing bread. Hearing him and turning her eyes away for just a moment, she nicked her right hand index finger in the exact spot where she'd been cut before. "Damn," she cursed, staring at the blood when in it she saw something float across her mind's eye: a picture of her finger being pricked by a rose thorn held by the now dead Burton Heron, intentionally.

She shook with the memory that jumped out at her. It led to another, the memory of his having pressed her finger into something hard and cool on a surface like a table top—a glass table top?

"Great!" she heard Lanark shout at the TV evangelist. "Another one with a direct line to God . . . has all the answers."

Dazedly, Shannon rounded the corner and peered into the living room, saying, "What?"

Lanark looked over his shoulder at her from his sitting position on the couch and saw that she was staring fixedly at the set. "You okay, Shannon?"

"It's her," she said, pointing her blood dripping finger at the set. "That's *her,* Ryne."

"Her? What do you mean, her?"

"The woman I saw at the party, the Stone place. I didn't realize . . . she's so much larger on the screen . . . and they've got her made up. She's got eye shadow and rouge. She's not so pale."

179

"She gets any paler, she'll fade away," he said. "Are you sure it was her?"

Lanark snatched open the TV Guide and located the time and channel for *The Word In Stone,* Evangelical Church of Sister Sylvia Stone. Written, produced and created by Sister Stone, Evangelical Minister. "Her name is Stone."

"Matthew's mother, perhaps?"

"Yeah, that's right, he said she was into religion." He thought anew how Matt Stone had diverted Ryne while Burton laced Shannon's drink with drugs.

"And I didn't see her just the once, Ryne . . . but again, up close . . . in another room . . . a cold room."

"Another room? When?"

"Can't explain it. I can't remember the details."

"You're sure she's the same woman?"

"Absolutely . . . so white, so pale . . . like . . . like . . ."

"An angel of God?"

"Or a vampire."

"I don't believe in vampires, Shannon."

"I don't either, but I'm maybe willing to make an exception in this case.

He studied her eyes, and for the first time he saw fear in them. "What else do you remember?"

"Nothing . . . it's all, I don't know, mixed up."

Ryne studied the colorless, ashen face on the TV screen. "You were pretty well doped up. Your mind could be playing tricks."

"You believe that?"

"Don't know . . . just talking to hear myself think, I guess. Lot of rungs in this ladder, Shannon."

She nodded, coming closer, listening to the words of Sister Sylvia Stone:

"Our doomsday is at hand! God weeps that we have allowed the vilest, ugliest passions to prevail in our times! To taint the blood of our martyrs, our saints! The blood of Christ on the Cross! Lost purity His blood into ours! The blood of our Father! God, too, fears AIDS and rightly so, brothers!"

The congregation's *amens* were punctuated by the stark angel's repetitious, *"and rightly so . . . rightly so . . ."*

"We've got to talk to her," said Shannon.

Lanark clicked off the set. "What was she doing at a drug bash?"

"Looking for converts? Actually, she remained out of it, above it, as if it weren't there, studying it perhaps. She never came all the way down the stairs."

"Her son certainly was involved."

"You still think he had something to do with Burton's death?"

"I think so, yes."

"But proving it's another thing."

"Bears watching . . ."

"So does my dinner. Be right back."

But she didn't come back, and when she did call again, Lanark was in semi-doze. Shaken, he was told to stand and where to sit. She had dinner all ready.

They ate in silence for a time, except for his occasional remarks about the furnishings, the apartment and finally her meal. It was all to his liking.

"But I really should not impose on you any longer. Been a long day."

She laughed lightly. "Are you nervous, being here, like this?"

"No, no, nothing like that," he said, knowing it was true.

"What then?"

"Just that, well, being partners, it's . . . it is a little awkward, don't you agree?"

"Yes, yes, it is, but you know I haven't felt this *awkward* since . . . well, since I was in high school. In kind of—"

Her buzzer rang. Someone at her door. Her face instantly changed, and Lanark knew that she had a fair guess who it was. "Just a minute," she said, going to the intercom.

Lanark couldn't help but overhear from where he sat. It made him feel increasingly ill-at-ease. He began to fidget.

Shannon said, "Yes . . . well, I know . . . but . . . but Thom, it's just that . . . no! I never . . . okay . . . but . . . now? I'm exhausted, and it was . . . it has been hectic. We're setting up a new unit at the precinct and I'm up to my eyes in—Thom, Thom?"

She cut off the intercom and turned to Lanark, her eyes pleading.

"Boyfriend?"

She answered like a prisoner caught in a lie. "Yes."

"Wants to come up?"

"He does, and—"

"Shannon, we're just partners working on a case."

"You don't know Thom."

"Jealous sort, is he?"

She breathed deeply. "He can be an ass, yes."

"Tell you what, I was on my way out anyway. There a back door?"

"No, just the fire escape."

"Had enough of those for a while." He gulped down a final bit of coffee and got up to leave as she told Thom to come up, buzzing him through. "I'll see you in the morning," he told her at the door.

"Yes, sure . . . and I'm sorry for hustling you out."

"Understood . . . try to . . . forget it, good night."

"Night." Under her breath she cursed, "Damn."

On the stairs she heard the two men exchange a shaky greeting, Lanark merely grunting in response to Thom's good evening. She imagined Thom staring after Lanark, sizing him up. Thom was a stockbroker. He sized up everyone, imagining their net worth and then *deciding* on their net worth.

"Tonight," Shannon promised herself, she was going to make it clear to Thom that she was finished with him. Some of the things he'd said over the intercom had been both uncalled for and nasty. No man was worth taking shit for. Besides, he'd spoiled things between she and Lanark . . . or was that a notion she'd conjured up entirely out of the air, on her own, without the slightest real help from Ryne? She didn't know, and for now, she must deal with Thom Warner. She'd rather face Peter Gunnetti again. In his way, Thom could be as dangerous, in his manipulation of words and emotions.

A long-time friend and "business associate" of Ryne Lanark's was a Puerto Rican kid with a bad complexion and a lot of street smarts and savvy by the name of

Chicko Alverez. Alverez worked out of the Spanish community surrounding Eckhart Park, not too distant from the bar where Ryne's parents were killed. Lanark was very careful to meet with Chicko with utmost care, and they had a system that signaled to one another when they would meet. It was at St. Catherine's Church bulletin board where they signaled one another by placing up a notice for a ride to Havana, Montana and a bogus phone number, not that Lanark thought that anyone wanted a ride to Havana, Montana.

Whenever Chicko wanted him he left the message which Lanark checked for daily. Whenever he got such a message, he went to see Chicko. They met at St. Catherine's, not on the street, but inside.

Chicko was crossing himself now and kneeling before the altar when he saw a priest enter. The priest was a kindly looking man, a look of calm and peace in his eyes that made Chicko wonder how anyone deserved such pleasure. The black-robed figure acknowledged Chicko's presence with a perfunctory gesture and then continued on his way. Chicko nervously looked around, flashing his eyes to the door. Churches made him nervous, more nervous than anything else. He wondered why it had to be this way, why Lanark was so overly cautious; still, it was for his good as well as the cop's, and so long as the money kept coming, who was he to complain?

He saw the priest go into the confessional where he disappeared. He imagined the humble man suddenly stepping out with an Uzi, opening up on the place and splattering the old stone walls with Chicko Alverez's blood. Chicko watched a lot of movies, and his favorite hero was Rambo, but he knew the movies were one

184

thing, the street another. He knew that Rambo wouldn't last a night in Chicago, not if certain people wanted him dead. He knew that Lanark's caution was not unnecessary.

Chicko got up and calmly moved toward the confessional, a rosary bead in his hands that he had been grinding between his fingers and occasionally he caught himself twirling. He gave a last look to the doors at the back and on either side of the pulpit. Only a handful of people at this hour and nobody looked more dangerous than the old lady in the gray flannel coat with the babushka tied in a double knot at the chin. He stepped into the confessional.

The priest on the other side said, "Can I help you, my son?"

"Cut the shit, Lanark. I got a tip on your bad boys, the ones who diced your sister and momma? Killed your old man?"

Lanark instantly reacted. "This just another bull line, Chicko?"

"No, man, well, I don't think so. A guy was talking to another guy, and he talked to a girlfriend of mine and—"

"Hearsay, kid, damnit, I need something substantial. It's been years!"

"All I know is you should talk to a guy in Joliet by the name of Pinto—"

"What the hell kind of a name is that, Chicko?"

"Nickname, man, take it easy."

"What's this Pinto's real name, and what's he know?"

"According to what I hear, he knew these guys you're after. He claims to be a member of their gang."

"What's his real name and what's he busted for?"

"I don't know. All I know is—"

"Shit, Chicko, all you know is shit. This sounds like more crud. What, you think you can just string me along for bucks on garbage like this?"

"Hey, man, I'm sorry about the past, but that's done, this . . . this could be really—"

"Forget it, Chicko," he said sternly, although he knew *he* wasn't going to forget it, and that while it might take him some time he'd find out what he could about a guy with the handle of Pinto in Joliet, especially *when* this guy was to be released. "For now, I want you to concentrate on a guy by the name of Tavalez Sorentino."

"Never heard of him, man."

"He doesn't work this area." Lanark explained all he knew about Sorentino to the kid. "You think you can get me some information I don't already know? Anything that might tag this guy, Chicko, he's real scum."

"I'll see what I can do, ask a few questions."

Lanark warned him. "Not too many questions, and not too loud. This guy's a murderer. Just as soon turn you into turtle soup at this place he runs and feed you to his Vietnamese customers as look at you, understood?"

"Don't worry about Chicko, man."

The confessional box on Lanark's side opened and a startled priest said, "What is the meaning of this? Who are you?"

"Just borrowing it, Father," said Lanark.

"Just a minute, hold on! Stop," said the priest rushing after Lanark, but unable to catch him. "What parish are you with?"

Chicko snuck out the other door.

EIGHT

Time passed.

At first it seemed there'd be a break in the Sorentino case, then all would fall through.

The D.A. listened to the evidence mounted against the man. Listened to the arresting officers, the tale of Angelo, the discovery of the children; he listened intently to the children. He then summed up what they had in three succinct sentences which amounted to *no case.*

Meanwhile, the audacious killer who had upset Riordan and the commissioner by unloading his last victim on the steps of the 13th Precinct had become strangely silent. During the same time period the special Thirteenth Decoy Unit (TDU) had officially gotten underway. They were already being called Wood's "holes," in that brand of humor cops reserved for cops. Another name floating about the city for them was *F-Troupe,* and *Lanark Bait.* They called themselves *D Company,* and this seemed to be sticking. Meanwhile, *The*

Stronghold had held fast among them, remaining their special name for headquarters.

Aside from working the Tavalez Sorentino case from every conceivable angle, they were being asked in on other, sometimes sensitive operations. One was in conjunction with the FBI, a mail fraud scam extending from the U.S. to Canada and wishing to go overseas to Japan. Someone with Japanese "connections" to further the scam into Tokyo had been requested during a setup deal. Yoshikani was ripe for the deal. Over thirty-five law enforcement officials, state and local as well as Federal were involved. They had vans filled with detection equipment Lt. Ryne Lanark had never before seen in action.

He, too, wanted in, if for no other reason than to learn of the new technology being used at the Federal level, and to see what could work for the 13th. This was the reason he had sat in the back of a surveillance van for fifteen hours. He began to wonder if he weren't becoming more cop than he had planned on becoming, taking on such responsibilities, gaining a budget, supervising people, him, a loner and a hustler and a hot dog. But the unit idea was a good one, one that could in time bring his quest for the killers he sought to justice—all of them.

The Feds had their target tied into PATRIC, the *Pattern Recognition and Information Correlations* computer network system which did much of what Lanark, or any detective did, but infinitely faster. Jammed full of data on all criminal records, descriptions, crime reports, field interrogations, stolen vehicles, outstanding warrants, it even knew the modus operandi of known criminals. PATRIC instantly cross-referenced bits—or bytes—of information fed into it, quickly coming up with likely human suspects. The same suspect list it would take Lanark perhaps months of footwork to locate.

"Lots of police forces are installing computer terminals in their patrol cars," the agent who Lanark was riding with told him. "Connected by their own radio frequencies to central computers—"

"Which in turn could have access to other networks at the state, regional or national level," added a second agent.

"Anyway," continued the first man, "the terminals allow the patrolman, or in your case, detective, to bypass dispatch for certain kinds of information."

"License numbers on hot cars, outstanding warrants," said Lanark, following the man.

"Or rap sheets on suspects picked up in the field."

"Cop in the car asks the computer, using a keyboard and gets the answer in seconds," finished Lanark, "beats hell out of what we've got now." He saw the significance of this to increasing his ability to investigate and apprehend.

"Lot of your other precincts in the city have 'em," said the agent. "Cost money."

Lanark watched as the Federal operative, using a terminal in his van, ran a files search on a vehicle. The request bypassed dispatch and went directly to the main computer. Ryne knew himself that during peak crime hours in the city that officers in the field couldn't get through to the dispatcher 40% to 65% of the time. Ryne knew immediately how important that was to running down men like Sorentino, or even his nephew, the now dead Angelo. He wondered too about the effectiveness of PATRIC on serial killers, like the suddenly silent one they had here in Chicago.

Another fascinating gadget that Lanark took to instantly was the LLS-TV camera, or low-light surveillance camera, used after dark on city streets. It was sensitive enough to *see*, or film, in the night-washed semi-darkness of the city streets. Lanark knew he wanted one of these mounted in his patrol car with sound accessories.

The Feds even had a couple of helicopters waiting on the big bust that Max figured in so prominently, but Lanark knew better than to push his luck with his superiors, and so did not add these to his Christmas list.

"We got this new stuff, too," said the agent, "that's really weird, a bacteria actually, that glows whenever it's sprinkled around heroin or explosives."

This made Ryne wonder what was in heroin and explosives that made this shit glow in the dark.

"Only problem is," said the second agent, where he sat in the surveillance van, "sometimes the stuff glows anyway and anywhere. Give me a good dog anytime."

"We got a stress evaluator aboard, too," said the younger agent. "Can detect when a guy is lying through voice frequency."

The back of the van was rapped on in two quick successions, a third slow, and a fourth quick. "Open it," said the older agent, recognizing the code.

It was their leader, a man named Frank Boaz, a big man with Cossack features who looked more like the bad guys if this were *Crime Story*. "It's a no-show, guys . . . it's over. Somehow we got smelled."

"Trying again?"

"Not soon. Disbanding for now."

It happened more often than not. Nervous buyers and sellers in such high-stakes lawless games simply didn't show up, spoiling months of preparation and the time in which so many men had persisted in their efforts. Law enforcement was often anti-climactic.

It was that way now with Sorentino.

It was that way with the "Glove" slasher. But Ryne, going over the files of the slasher victims in much more detail than ever he had an opportunity to do before noticed something odd that had him questioning the coroner's report: *puncture marks*. What kind of puncture marks? Drug needles?

"Catheter," came the reply from his contact in the coroner's office, "we told Riordan that."

"Riordan played it down. Marked it as probably drug tracks."

"We've seen enough drug tracks to know the difference, Ryne," said Sybil Shanley, the Assistant Coroner. "Every victim of the slasher lost their blood first. At first, we assumed this was done via the nasty wound at the throat, but I don't think so, and Black confirms my findings, that someone took the blood through an IV catheter."

"Ghoulish . . ."

"More so than what, slitting the throat and hanging 'em upside down by their ankles? That was our wrong assumption."

"But what about the ankle marks?"

"Not mean enough to indicate the weight of the bodies were suspended by them, Ryne . . . much more likely marks from tight bindings."

"Thanks . . . thanks again, Sybil." Ryne passed on

this new information, for what it was worth, to the others who had also been briefed on the encounter Shannon and Ryne had had at the Stone mansion.

The connection was a tenuous one, but all things pointed back. A plan of infiltration was underway, but it would take time. Meanwhile, Ryne had his new contact with the Feds run the slasher m.o., complete with catheter marks into PATRIC, and was awaiting a response. Seemed PATRIC was experiencing what amounted to computer diarrhea. It might take a day and some pink medicine.

But Lanark was not a patient man, not like the Feds were patient men. He didn't wish to see another day go by with either of his two big problems nagging at him, and he feared that soon, both of the ruthless people he was investigating would strike again, perhaps worse than before.

Sorentino's restaurant, *Armand's,* remained under near constant surveillance. Sorentino seemed to know, or at least sense this. He was, it might be assumed, cooling it. He had, after all, come close to catching something he didn't want to catch.

Meanwhile, Carmellow was coming up for trial. Sorentino could sweat that out for a while. This would be followed by the other two men. Sorentino could sweat these, too.

This and more had been told to the men and women under Ryne. Some six people now made up the unit, all hand-picked by Wood and Lanark. All of them had had undercover experience, and where Ryne could find it, *acting experience* in the theater. He found two of his people, Wil Cassidy and Myra Lane moonlighting at the Bridge and other Chicago theaters. They often worked together in theater productions, an avocation they had shared for several years. They knew of Ryne's work in the Chicago theater and had been surprised he did not make it to the top years before. They also knew of his great loss, but Wil and Myra, one of the few married couples Ryne knew who were also lovers, had known his parents and his sister. They had frequented the Lucky 13th for years before the incident, and they had been married before they went into the police academy. Often times a decoy operation called for a couple, working in tandem, capable of appearing either married or wishing to be coupled in a less official way. The Cassidys had run the scam on any number of occasions, sometimes as out-of-towners, sometimes as suburbanites, sometimes as exactly what they were, products of the city.

Wil was both lanky and hefty at once, a Clint Eastwood build with a voice that rivaled that of Richard Burton. His ruddy complexion and shock of auburn hair commanded attention as well, along with a pair of penetrating gray eyes that seemed made of steel until his easy smile and rolling laugh were displayed. He'd spent time in the Marine's special services unit in Alaska where Americans routinely faced down Russian Spetsnaz or "snake-eaters" as they were called, a Russian unit comparable to the American Special Forces operating in and around St. Lawrence Island, U.S.A., Alaska, 150 miles below the Arctic Circle where "games" of a face-off nature and "bugging" operations between the two superpowers was a daily occurrence.

He enjoyed talking about the "snow soldiers" whenever he had had a few drinks at the bar.

Myra, by comparison, was small, beside him even petite but well-trained in hand-to-hand at the academy, and like Wil, she had had some military experience. Hers had been with the WAVES. She'd spent time with Naval Intelligence in Washington, D.C., attaché to a general who was indicted for accepting bribes to reveal information on Naval secrets, largely due to Myra's turning him in with evidence in hand. It was, she had said, a sobering experience, and a disillusioning one, since she had all but idolized the man. To look at the slim, green-eyed blonde, and hear her semi-shy voice, to watch her avert her eyes as she spoke, no one would guess she was a cop. Her silken hair was almost white, but there was nothing pale about the keen emerald eyes.

The two of them had, for four years, kept Lanark's secret. They had done so without his ever having to ask it. So had the sixth member of the team, big Mark Robeson, a former boxer and now a black cop patrolling a beat. He had been a long-time friend to Lanark. He had, like the Cassidys, been at the funeral of three Lanarks in one day. Since then, Robeson had come to Lanark's aid in many a desperate situation, sometimes without being called, sometimes just catching information on the police band, hearing that Ryne was in a tight spot, and racing to the scene. It was a cause of concern to Robeson's superiors, in fact, and a likely reason he had been passed over for a sergeant's position just a few months before.

Mark had been grousing about getting out of police work altogether, spilling his guts to Tebo at the bar, on and off for weeks now. He was understandably pissed, disgusted with the stagnation of beat work and his place in the department, and the prejudice that infested the department. He had gone to the For-Blacks-Only Police Union with his complaint, but it was filed away, lost, forgotten or purposely pigeonholed.

Robeson, like Wil and Myra, had encouraged Lanark to join the police academy, and he also knew of Lanark's burning reason to join, telling him it was better reason than ninety-nine percent of others who joined. "Why you think I joined the ranks?" he'd asked Lanark one night at the bar, punching him hard in the shoulder to get his attention. "So's I could blow away *just one*—just one of the mothers who deals on my street, where I grew up seeing *my* best friend at eleven die in a hospital all alone 'cause Momma and Daddy were too busy on drugs to visit their third child who was dying of sickle cell? Shit, people selling off their pork chops and hams for the stuff, selling off their furniture, rings, clothes, the children's things, and soon the *children,* selling 'em into prostitution."

Mark Robeson also worked out at the gym where Ryne kept in shape, and often they would spar in the ring together. The muscular Robeson kept in incredible shape.

Among the six members of the newly formed Decoy Unit were Jeff Blum, Max Yoshikani and Shannon Keyes. Shannon was, in fact, made second-in-command. Aside from these three, Lanark had never before actually worked a case, side-by-side with the members of his unit. But he had heard enough of their harrowing police tales, along with stories from their pasts to fill several volumes on policing and detection work.

Still, actually working with another cop, no matter

196

how you got on socially, was quite another thing. The only sure way to know if you could work together was to work together, experience being the teacher. But such lessons were lost on the dead.

In any event, as it shaped up the unit was manned with one major objective in mind, and Lanark, for the time being, felt that this objective was being made, his own preferences and prejudices notwithstanding. That objective, as he had told Captain Wood, was simply to lay the foundation for the best tactical decoy unit working in the city of Chicago, to build the best Lanark possibly could build. Wood and his superiors might balk at some of the choices, even flinch, and cry out for changes if they liked, but on the surface the spread of people by race, sex and capabilities spoke for itself. No one could argue with the fact Lt. Ryne Lanark had a well-rounded, balanced team of professionals. On paper, it read like the crew of a futuristic enterprise where mutual respect for professional ability counted more than the color of a man's skin, or the bustline on a woman.

Lanark now had two women, a black officer, a Japanese and Jewish-American, along with himself and Wil Cassidy, two dyed-in-the-wool Irishers. He'd requested rank of Detective Sergeant for Robeson and he had placed Shannon in the secondary administrative role. On paper it all shaped up well. Still, Lanark hadn't a clue as to how well the team would operate as a unit. Robeson, like Wil, Myra and himself had done a hitch in the service, in Mark's case it had been Viet Nam. His view of teamwork in the field was, like Lanark's, skewed by his experience in Nam, so that authority figures were seen as complete assholes. But working with Lanark as his boss, perhaps this would not be a problem. Blum and Yoshikani were two who had no military background. Both had come into police work through the study of criminology, one at Northwestern, the other at U of C. There was potential for personality problems between them and the others. Shannon, while not in the military herself, had grown up on military bases, and she seemed well-versed in the idea of the unit working as a whole and in concert. As for Ryne himself, the idea had its appeal for trade-off reasons. He had been, and still was to a certain extent, a loner cop in an intensive manhunt for the men who had killed his family. The reason he donned the priest's habit and met with sinners at the old church on Ashland near Chicago. One day, he'd get a tip that would prove valuable, and one day he'd see the devils that haunted his nightmares face to face and, one by one, blow them into another dimension. Being on the outs with authority had had its *privileges* and appeal, *and still did,* but what the unit offered now was more than simple physical and moral backup, it offered the tools required for the kind of policemanship they were all best at; offered the headquarters where a team of people of like-mindedness could come together and hopefully stop some of the horror playing daily on the corner streets; offered, finally, an outfit for those on the outs with higher-ups, a kind of unit unto itself, protected to a degree by Wood and the record of successes they would, Ryne knew, begin to build.

He'd slept on it night after night. He'd accepted it as a good turn in the twists that had brought him to this juncture in his life. He only wished it had come sooner, before he'd lost two partners.

198

But how would this new unit perform? Soon, all too soon, that would be learned in the field, possibly on two fronts.

Word on the street was that Sorentino was about to make a move on another dealer, a buyout or a shootout was the way Ryne's snitch had put it. Everyone in the Special Decoy Unit knew one fact about drug dealers never taken for granted, that they were easily freaked-out nuts. They all knew from past experiences, many of which were recounted in the squadroom, of dealers erupting in the middle of a buy like Mt. St. Helen's, gunfire everywhere, mowing down anything that moved, leaving a tenement or stairwell washed with the gory remains. Reasons for such eruptions could be as slight as one man's blinking, spitting, lighting up a smoke at the wrong instant. Dealers were spooked so easily because the narc squads in the city were every-where. Even if a dealer like Sorentino read the signs wrong and killed a legitimate buyer, he reasoned it was better business than taking unnecessary chances.

The smallest suspicion caused deals to end in death. The slightest ripple and a meeting was canceled before it began.

The exchange of money from Sorentino's hand for ''territory'' from a creep named Carl ''Slippery'' Fish—actually Gerald Morris Fishman, according to his rap sheet—was to take place tonight, at a ware-house near the tracks of the Milwaukee Road, facing the Chicago River. It was a good mile from any cover the cops could take. Ryne's unit had gathered, and the strategy session came up with a plan designed to bag all the principal players at the warehouse.

Swinging a lantern, whistling an old railroad ditty of such vintage none of the other track tenders knew it, Derwood Casselman went about the inspection of a stretch of track not too far out from the main station downtown. He liked working nights. Most of the men working for the road these days didn't like work day or night, most being bums and derelicts and down-and-outers the company hired for cheap labor. "Well," he told himself, his thick gray mustache bobbing with the words he recited to himself, "you get what you pay for, and the company's got mostly shit." He grumbled and talked incessantly to himself, sometimes answering himself.

"Only an occasional kid nowadays'll work on the road because, like Derwood T. Casselman when he was a boy, just because he loves trains with a passion, loves to hear 'em, see 'em move, smell the diesel." He took a great whiff. The diesel and the grease was everywhere here, layers of it in the matted grass, years of it staining the rocks and painting the ties. "But a man like me with my love of the train, say over cars or anything modern, well, that is an odd and rare bird, indeed. The exception nowadays! Nowadays, you got men defecating up and down the line, stoned or sober, they don't give a shit; well, no, that's wrong, they *do* give a shit, but that's all they give! They certainly don't give a full day's work for a full day's wage! No, sir. No, sir. Just don't give one cursed damn no matter how many times you tell 'em that lives—lives!—are riding on what they do, or fail to do."

Like line men, the tracks weren't what they used to be either. Not by a long shot.

Derwood paced nearer and nearer the checkpoint where two of his underlings were supposed to meet and confer with him, and holding up his lantern, he caught sight of someone ahead. He called out. "Jack, Sid! That you?"

The sound of cars and the city lights seemed like a Hollywood set from way down here. Two stories above him, on the bridges that crossed the Chicago River, the city's traffic moved about its arteries and veins. But down here, it was like another world, here in this grease-blackened domain of the train engine. Why'd he feel like he was being watched tonight? he wondered. Was it just some bats flitting about the lamp post?

Some two hundred yards away, through a night-vision pair of binoculars, Derwood was being watched by the anxious members of the Decoy Unit, wondering if he was going to stumble into the way of the bust or not. Two cars had come in, followed by a third. One car moved off rather prematurely and it was decided they would let it go. The two additional cars were inside the warehouse now, and the Decoy Unit was closing in. Still, all was strangely silent at the warehouse and the single light had shown no sign of movement at the grease-blackened windows.

Derwood ambled closer, snapping the suspenders that held his overalls up. Out of the side of his eyes he watched for anyone on the bridges, anyone who might see him. But there was no one watching, and there hadn't been one iota of interest in the warehouse where his two men had gotten themselves drunk on the job again and had begun a quarrel.

So when Derwood got to Jack and Sid, there was no fist fight as he'd come to expect and Jack pulled off his floppy railman's hat and threw it down and stomped on it, revealing himself as Mark Robeson. Sid frowned a frown that was easily recognizable, even in the dark, as Wil's frown.

"It's a bust, Derwood," said Mark Robeson to Ryne Lanark as he snatched off his glasses and began to clean them. "Damn sure looks it, boys," Lanark continued in the voice of Derwood Casselman. "Look, if it's all the same with you, I'm going to have a look at the warehouse."

"We're coming," said Wil.

Somewhere in the surrounding blackness the other members of the unit were watching them. Wil, Mark and Ryne were within fifteen feet of the building when it suddenly erupted in explosion and flame, sending the men to the ground, shards of glass and pieces of wood scarring them all where they lay, the blast knocking Wil unconscious.

Immediately, the other unit members raced in from all directions to give them aid. Shannon was the first to get to Ryne, pulling his head into her lap, frantic.

Wood took command, ordering the van brought about and seeing that the injured men were rushed to nearby Cook County Hospital.

Wood remained behind with Max and Blum who'd wanted the parts played by Robeson and Wil. They'd greet the firemen on arrival. Wood wanted, if at all possible, to know what sort of detonation device had caused the explosion. He knew a lot of explosives experts working the city. He'd make it his personal vendetta to learn who had set this up for Sorentino, if it were the last thing he ever did.

At the Emergency Room at Cook, under the harsh lights, the damage done the men was not as extensive as it might well have been. All of Lanark's wounds were to the left thigh and shoulder. Mark had a bad gash over his eye that made him look like he'd just stepped out of the ring with Mike Tyson. Wil had suffered a severe concussion and Myra planned to remain with him at the hospital.

"They set us up," Mark agreed with Lanark.

"They used Alverez, fed him dummy information through another party," said Lanark of his snitch. "We should have been ready for it, should've known."

"Hey, Derwood," said Shannon, scoldingly, "just be glad nobody was killed tonight. You, too, Mark! Thank your lucky stars."

"Lucky, huh? Meanwhile Sorentino's still at large and Chicko Alverez is very likely dead.

"We'll get him . . . we will," she said it as if it were a promise and a given. "We will get him."

Much later, a body was found in the warehouse that proved to be Chicko's. From an examination, it was determined he was alive before the explosion got to him."

"Okay," said Jeff Blum, "we got ourselves a real fancy boy, here, in Matthew Stone. Twenty-four years old, three years ago he managed to get all of his mother's assets signed over to him, owns everything, the mansion, the cars, the yacht, the stocks and bonds. Worth well over six hundred million and growing. He's got ins with brokerage firms all over Chicago and New York. Lot of them party with him on weekends, particularly the young turks."

Lanark listened intently, started to say something but instead merely nodded, allowing Blum to go on.

"Not quite the graduate of Harvard he led you to believe. He was dismissed over some scandalous affair in the dormitory, only vague details, involved females and sleeping arrangements. No military record. He's known as something of an Anglophile, favoring fine English tailored suits, and he has met the Queen and the Royal Family. He's also had a personal meeting with the President—"

"What the hell about?"

"AIDS. He started one of the first information centers in the state about the disease, how it's spread, where to go to get tested. One of his 'write-offs' he tells the press, but he seems genuinely interested in it, right, Max?"

Max agreed with a nod and a word, "Passionate."

"Some time before this he had once ventured into the sperm bank business but this failed to secure him any profits, but the AIDS testing does."

"We came across something odd, though," said Max.

Blum continued, after taking a sip of his coffee. "Something peculiar regarding him from a source."

"What's that?"

"One of his business associates, somewhat of a new business venture, having to do with manufacturing test tubes, vials, any number of things—"

"What about this guy?"

"He said the kid doesn't do business with anyone

204

without first seeing the results of a blood test, said Stone was morbid about it. Guy backed out."

"Lot of people doing screenings of one sort or another these days, for various reasons," said Lanark, thoughtfully. "Nothing condemning in that. What about a urine test? Wouldn't that be simpler, easier?"

"That's another thing, this guy said Stone insisted on a blood test, wanted to be thorough, said he wanted to test for a number of things."

"But the guy didn't give him the blood?"

"Stone wanted it on a slide, right there in his office . . . said it was even too weird for his usual business-is-business attitude, you know."

"What about politics?"

"Gives to *both* parties, a variety of candidates, no rhyme or reason to his political financing."

"And religious organizations?"

"Only one, strictly his mother's church."

"A real momma's boy, huh?"

Blum laughed. "You could say so."

"Lie detector test, does the guy insist on that, no," mused Lanark, "no, he wants a blood test, but why?"

"Basically, what we've got here, Lieutenant, is a typical, rising young lion, *elitist,* who, if we wanted to psychoanalyze, might prove to do business by means of bloodlines, you know, *only the best and the bluest.* He also has under his corporate umbrella any number of private clinics, ranging from here to London, England, one in every major city in the States. Hell, if he wants to do business with a guy in England, he can still insist on the blood test long-distance. I think it's like a phobia with him, you know, fear of AIDS contamination."

"His old lady looks sickly. You don't suppose the prophetess of doom is herself contaminated, do you?"

"Who knows . . . possibly a reason for his Howard Hughes syndrome about doing business with 'clean people' only."

"You say he never completed his work for his medical degree?"

"I said not at Harvard. He went overseas and finished up at Oxford. He was *no* brilliant student, however, and he didn't particularly care for medicine."

"A chink in the china," said Lanark.

Blum squinted and said, "What?"

Max, who'd helped compile the information on Stone, laughed. "He means, Jeff, that this guy's a little too perfect to be real."

NINE

A more than nasty rumor was going around and it involved Lt. Ryne Lanark. In sum, it said that Lanark was *behind* the up-scale slasher killings, and that the dumping of the last body on the doorstep at Precinct 13 was done by him.

This made sense to those who could not understand how Captain Wood, Riordan and others in the chain of command could possibly turn over the administrative workings of a newly formed Decoy Unit to a man who was, a few weeks before, on the outs with departmental brass. Lanark, the rumor said, had arranged for the "super case" so that he alone could solve it, a fall guy just waiting in the wings.

It made sick sense to some guys.

Lanark tried to ignore it as the grapevine crap it was, but the rumor persisted as if someone behind it were determined to see that it festered.

But Lanark had the real case to deal with, and he now gathered his people together to give it a brainstorm. Lanark knew from experience that even if they had an eyewitness account—or several such accounts to these killings—that eyewitnesses were notoriously wrong. Wrong about providing so-called clues, the color of the getaway car, the make, model, even the number of tires it had. Descriptions given by some fifteen people in a bank, all swearing to the fact there were five holdup men, and the leader, while wearing a mask, was at least forty years old, were proven wrong by the film cameras operating in the bank. There'd been four gunmen, and the leader was slightly over twenty. Witnesses were fallible. Most were impossible, changing their stories again and again, depending on who questioned them when.

Regardless of these facts, they still needed someone who had seen something on the night of the murders, the very least at the dumping sites where the killer was known to have been. For this reason, where the bodies were found, got special attention over and above what Riordan's men had given the sites. Lanark reasoned there must be some person in the city who had seen something on at least one of these occasions. It stood to reason.

Every neighborhood had its share of people with nothing to do but stare out their windows and into those of others. Streetwalkers who worked long hours into the night. Insomniacs who walked their pets, unable to sleep for the vibrations of the living city all around them. People who met for petty and larcenous reasons amid the trees in a park, below viaducts, at all-night movie theaters and stores to conduct nocturnal "business."

These were the ones Lanark wanted the heat turned up under. Through surveillance of the sites, learning the comings and goings of the habitual night people, there must a clue be found, an "eye" witness discovered.

Lanark tacked up a map of Chicago and placed pins into each location where the bodies had been found. The final pin was needlessly tacked over the tiny red square representing the precinct. The earlier three deaths were almost on a line along the parks strung along Chicago's North Shore, but the last one was far afield of the killer's usual stomping grounds. It was evident in the placement of the body that it had been a message to Lanark, a grim challenge.

"Photos," said Lanark, holding up a manila folder. "Taken at each crime scene." He routed these around, drawing some guttural sounds and curious remarks. Lanark then indicated the folding table from which he took the photos, scattered with files. "Every field report, coroner's report, autopsies, and file on the cases are at your disposal. See that you familiarize yourselves thoroughly, got that?"

He then detailed every salient point having to do with the killer's m.o., the distinctive cuts, missing parts, and finally the missing blood. The siphoned-off blood shook them up, a rumble going about the room. No one had known this vital, secret information, kept secret by Riordan and his investigative team for more good reason than simply to keep the public from panicking. It could be the vital link should some authenticated confession ever surface. As it was, hundreds of weirdos and homeless people, mental cases and emotionally disturbed had confessed to the killings. So far, no one had confessed to drinking blood, yet.

Mark Robeson heaved his heavy black shoulders in

reaction to this news. Robeson was an old friend of Lanark's, but he wasn't one-hundred percent sure they could work together. "Lieutenant Lanark, you saying there's a ritual, like cult aspect to this whole case?"

"It would seem so. Shannon? Anything?"

"Still checking," she replied, 'but to date we're coming up short on the computer with this one. Lots of other cult rituals in there, but nothing resembling this."

"Bloodletting goes back a long way," said Max.

"Don't you know it," agreed Jeff.

"We'll be checking with knowns anyway, as well as occult shop owners, bookstores, the fringe," added Shannon.

"Lot more of those shops than ever before," said Jeff, disheartened.

"We're checking into this angle with Matthew Stone as well," said Captain Wood. "Son of the evangelist, Stone, and heir to a fortune from the Stone riches." Captain Wood had already gotten heat from above, higher-ups breathing down his neck for a quick resolution to what the press was calling the Upscale Murders. Wood said he now understood why Riordan was more than glad to unload the entire mess.

Earlier Wood had said to Lanark, "Riordan's team has been embarrassed by the episode."

"Embarrassed, shit!" Ryne had exploded. "People—young kids—murdered, executed, drained of their life's blood, and Riordan's worried about embarrassing himself?"

"Get real, Lanark," said Wood. "What do you think the Commissioner and the Mayor are worried about?"

Wood had explained that when Lanark and Keyes had gone to the Stone mansion they had arrived at the same point in the investigation that it had taken Riordan several months to get to. It so happened that the Commissioner was impressed with the speed with which Lanark had arrived at the same location so surprisingly, working on the case on his own time, with precious little of the information available to Riordan's team. Then the Commissioner learned that Riordan had turned Lanark's request to be on the investigative team down, and he blew his top. This resulted in the investigation being opened up to Wood's people.

Riordan's people were still officially involved, but from experience, Lanark knew that this meant the other team was dispirited and most likely concentrating efforts elsewhere.

"So," said Lanark now, scanning the faces of his team, "What kind of killer—or killers—are we dealing with? A serial murderer, a pattern killer, yes, but a pattern of *technique*, ritual, m.o., if you will, and not simply a psychotic who randomly attacks his victims. Nothing *coherently* disturbed about this killer, folks."

"But you're interested in what was in the killer's mind?" asked Blum, "Aren't you?"

"If it leads to him, yes."

"So," piped in Shannon, "you wish to know if the strange marks left on the bodies are meant to convey a message?"

"Do they?" asked Ryne. "Or do they suggest to you random bloodlust? Compulsion murder, some irresistible need to kill and mark?"

"And maim . . ." added Shannon.

"Yes, maim. Missing parts in three of the four deaths."

"Sex is part of it," said Wood. "Autopsy on the women bear this out. More than one man's semen left in the women."

"The bloodlust is secondary to the sex, perhaps?" asked Max.

"Not necessarily," said Wil, standing and pacing the unit room. Beside them the computers could be heard through the wall, humming. "It could all be part of a single, complex ritual—sex and bloodlust together. Happens often with these cults."

"No known cult has taken it so far, except for the Hell's Angels in isolated cases," said Ryne, "but we're talking about a succession of victims here."

"Earlier investigators have so far applied every technique known to us to learn information about the deceased: detailed autopsies, checks for fibers, toothmarks, debris beneath the nails, and from what the coroner tells us, these people died without a struggle. But they were doped to the ceiling," continued Shannon.

"What we need to build on are possible eyewitness sightings at the dump sites, where the bodies were tossed like so much trash—even outside these doors," Lanark added. "There's got to be someone somewhere who has seen something."

"There often is," commented Myra.

Wil nodded but also said, "And often there's not."

"Getting someone to come forward's impossible at times," said Jeff Blum sullenly. "Can't believe people."

"I don't care how hard it is, or how many hours it

takes, we're going to scour each dumping site with the intention of turning up someone who saw something. I want those areas staked out night and day," said Lanark. "Learn the habits and comings and goings of everyone in the neighborhood. If somebody was walking a dog through Lincoln Park last night at midnight, chances are they do it often. I want that man's name."

"Got it," said Wil who had been assigned this field area along with Myra.

"Meanwhile," said Shannon, "we're working on the Stone angle, that somehow the deaths are related to the weekend-long parties that occur there. We're setting up a couple, either myself and Lanark, or you and Wil, Myra, in Winnetka. They'll have to join the jumping crowd and mix."

"That's down the road," said Lanark. "It'll take time. Meanwhile, we're checking into the victims' pasts. Looking for common denominators aside from the size of their pocketbooks."

"And wallet," added Wood.

"Max and Jeff are doing the footwork on that, retracing many of the steps already taken by Riordan and his team."

"Going to fill the gaps," said Max, making them all laugh.

"Two of the victims occupied condos in the Gold Coast area downtown, not too far from where we found the last female victim, actually, within an hour and a half walk."

"The third female victim lived in Evanston, attending Northwestern University, majoring in astronomy," added Shannon.

"Burton Eaton-Heron, the male, resided with his

parents in Winnetka where the cheapest house on the block is a measly two-hundred sixty Gs," said Wood. "All very upscale."

"Reason why the *Tribune*'s calling him the Upscale Slasher. Press doesn't know about the vampire aspect of the case," said Lanark, "so far."

"Leak is more likely now than ever on information regarding the case," said Wood, looking around the room. "Not simply because more of us are working on it, but because, human nature being the same as when Adam and Eve shared lullabye land, people are going to stab one another in the back if they can."

Robeson who hadn't said a word as yet jerked his large, dark pupils up at this. "You like to explain that one, Captain?"

"You've all heard the rumors floating around about Lanark here being a goddamned mass killer, haven't you?"

Everyone reluctantly said they had.

"Going to bust the mouth of the next sucker who—" Robeson began but Wood cut him off.

"So, imagine what the next step will be, people? If you want to throw a wrench into the works and you had information about the case which is going to get people shaking in their beds at night and screaming for more police action, put more and more heat on Lanark to see him fail before he has a chance?"

"Give it to the papers, sure," said Wil, the others seeing the point now.

"Any way we can pinpoint this snitch?" asked Robeson, visibly angry.

"I've got connections at the *Trib,* but that won't help elsewhere," said Wood. "Still, if someone approaches the *Tribune,* my friend there will let me know. I'll keep close on it."

"Your friend," said Shannon, "he influential enough to stomp on the information?"

"*She* will if she can. If it's possible. But few decisions are made over there without a committee."

"They'll run it," said Lanark. "Who wouldn't?"

"But nothing, ladies and gentleman," said Wood, "not word one of what is said in this unit goes out that door. Understood?"

Everyone nodded.

"Then off to your assigned tasks," said Lanark, dismissing his unit.

They would next see one another on the outside but they wouldn't "know" one another. Robeson and Will Cassidy were in railroad worker uniforms, as was Lanark. Blum was dressed casually. He'd be driving a hack, and in the rear seat would be his fare, Max. Shannon and Myra would enter as the backup, along with Wood who, despite the crutches, wanted in. They had worked out a farcical routine that would get them near the warehouse with Lanark shouting at the other two railmen for sleeping on the job and failing to complete the assigned task given them.

A brawl and a fight would ensue and then the cab would enter the picture, at which time Lanark would call a truce to the brawl in order to give the lost cabbie directions.

Seconds later the cab was to go through the front door of the old warehouse, guns blazing, the others following in behind it as if it were a tank. Risky but everyone agreed, given the logistics, they had little other choice than a frontal attack. Every person on the team was jumpy but ready.

The young unit spent an exasperating evening with the warehouse fully staked out and left with nothing to show for it.

The big Sorentino bust didn't go down. Somehow they were wise to it. "Slippery" Fish was greased too well. Sorentino had contacts everywhere. Too much chance for leaks. No one knew exactly why. Could simply be that Fish had contracted the flu and called it off, could be Sorentino learned of the bugs on the phones used at the restaurant and at his home. Could be a sudden disinterest in dealing with Fish . . . anything.

What it amounted to in the end was a black eye in the department's face, a score one against the new decoy unit that had men and women about the place, inside and out. What it finally meant was that Tavalez Sorentino was still at large, still a free, model citizen of his community, free to traffic in children and drugs.

It was a disheartening beginning for Lanark's unit, and the ripples were felt throughout the precinct and beyond.

But Lt. Ryne Lanark meant to fry Sorentino, one way or another, and he made this clear to his people. He also made it clear that there were other fish to fry as well.

Lanark had arranged for a large bulletin board, cork panels nailed to a frame and hung on a wall in the squadron. Photos of the victims pinned to the board were like so many eyes overlooking them. Nearby stood the map showing the locations of the dumping sites, anadditional mockery. For the next several days, weeks, and possibly months, he planned to surround himself with every possible piece of information, and no one would know the case files as well as he. Detectives came in, stared at the map and the photos, rifled the coroner's reports and field reports from officers who had taken in evidence at the scene. Everyone was put on "skeleton crew" hours, grueling duty, twelve on, twelve off.

Shannon worried about Ryne. She held a cup of coffee in her hand now as she approached him. Two days had gone by but nothing surfaced, and yet everyone had the sense that the homicides, stable now, would go on nonetheless. The killer they were dealing with was not likely to remain silent much longer.

Shannon handed her coffee to Ryne whose eyes had gone dark with concentric circles. He was laboring over, for the hundredth time, the reports on the various victims. He surprised her with a chuckle as he took the coffee. He hadn't been too communicative lately, and not at all much fun. Since the night Thom Warner broke them up, they hadn't seen each other beyond the work place.

"What's so funny?" she asked.

"Nothing . . . not a damned thing," he said sullenly.

She leaned over his desk at what he was reading, saying, "Come on, what gives?"

"See this?" he asked, pointing to a list of items found on the last victim. He indicated a purse, contents were not enumerated except for keys, cards and cash. "Says she was carrying in excess of eight hundred dollars that

night, enough for a ticket to Rio and back. Rich kids
. . . old money . . . *something* the killer wants from these
well-to-do kids.''

"Maybe he's got hatred of the rich?"

"Brought on by what, poverty? Viewing *Lifestyles of
the Rich and Famous?*"

"Something like that, perhaps, I've heard of crazier
notions in the minds of killers.''

"Let's take a walk, get out of here," he said.

"Sure thing.''

Lanark called to Samantha Curtis, the middle-aged
dispatch officer assigned to him to man the phones and
see to routine office matters. She was meticulous, a bit
heavyset, graying hair that would soon be white, a head
shorter than Shannon with a voice like marshmallows
melting over a fire. She had a lot of guys come on to
her over the phone, and it made her redden. She
couldn't look at the photos pinned over Lanark's desk,
but she managed office affairs, the phones and the coffee with all the extreme diligence of a North Shore
maid. She was perfect for the unit.

"We'll be at the 26th Precinct," he told Samantha,
who replied with a kindly nod.

"Oh, Lieutenant," said Miss Curtis, stopping them
at the door.

"Yes, Samantha?"

"It's the men, sir."

"The men? In the unit?"

She was embarrassed. "I'm sorry to trouble you with
such pettiness, but could you please ask the men not
to call me Sam?''

Shannon stepped through the door in order to hide
her smile while Lanark soothed Miss Curtis with a re-

mark about seeing to it. Outside, Shannon asked him why they were going over to Riordan's territory.

"They've still got the victims' valuables under lock and key there. I want to personally view the contents of that purse, among other things."

She wondered what he was looking for.

He wondered what he was looking for, but he also thought about the night he had fought with Skully, when the S.O.B. had attempted to make off with the dead girl's eight hundred dollars. Not only was it theft, it disrupted criminal evidence. Had the purse been listed as empty, a secondary cause for the murder might be robbery as well as rape. No telling what was lost on the ground when the purse had been torn into and spilled. He wondered, too, about the other victims, what had been in their pockets, their purses, Eaton's wallet, if indeed he'd had a wallet on him.

The impounded evidence could point to some clues overlooked, or thought useless by Al Riordan and Morris Fabia. Only one way to find out.

They arrived at the 26th at eleven A.M. and took up residence, sifting through labeled boxes brought to them by a very meticulous clerk-officer who acted as if they planned to make off with it all, until Lanark displayed the contents of the victims' purses. Clothing that had been found on and around the victims had gone to the crime lab. Monies were not here. Lanark asked about this, and the clerk told him that it was placed in a safe and the bills registered and would, in time, find its way back to the deceased's family.

Shannon went through one box while Lanark went through a second. She felt strange in doing so. It was the first time she'd done this sort of police sifting. Lanark told her how much he had learned about Sorentino by going through the garbage tossed from his restaurant, and that he wanted to do the same at the man's residence. But this, going over the effects of a dead woman, was morbid and ghoulish in a way that sent a chill along her spine.

Rouge, powder and monogrammed mirror, bracelet with initials that seemed familiar—*MS*. She thought of the various possible meanings. Initials of someone's name? A manuscript? A sailing vessel? Medical abbreviation? Important or unimportant? She made a note to ask the girl's parents who had already undergone a great deal of difficult days and nights and questionings from police officials. She started in on the girl's wallet. Pictures of friends and relatives jumped out at Shannon, spilling. It was brim full of photos and loose credit cards from Visa to the local posh restaurant for member's only, called *The Anvil*.

"Do you have any pins over there?" asked Lanark.

"Bobby pins, safety, yes . . . lots."

"Insignia pins, like this," he said, holding up a strange looking, solid gold pin on the order of a tiny brooch, the medical insignia of the cross with two snakes curled about it."

"Huh-uh, no . . . but—"

"According to everything I know about this girl she was not medical personnel, nor did she volunteer time as a candy striper, nor was she interested in pursuing a degree in medicine . . . so, what's this?"

"Something a boy gave her?"

"Stone said he was a medical man, although not practicing."

"Kind of a weak connection, Ryne . . . but what do

you make of this?'' She showed him the bracelet. *''MS* could stand for medicines. Or for Matthew Stone.''

''Could bes . . . all we have are goddamned *could bes.''*

''Didn't you say the coroner had some sort of pin they were testing for residues, something from one of the earlier victims?''

''Yeah, an ordinary ring like you can get at any mall these days. Had the cross and snakes on it.''

''Symbol maybe? Another message the killer's sending?''

Lanark thought of the possibilities for a moment. ''I've got to see Eaton's body.''

''Morgue, ugghh.''

''Could be . . . important.''

They returned the boxes to the officer in charge, telling him they wished to sign out the bracelet and the pin. After doing so, they drove for downtown, the Crime Lab and the City Morgue where Burton Eaton-Heron's body had found its way. The entire way, Shannon felt increasingly uneasy, itchy and ill-at-ease, as if she were doing something she'd been forced to do as a child and wished not to.

''You okay?'' he'd asked her, but she wasn't about to complain. Besides, she didn't know what it was that so bothered her.

''Feel a little jumpy.''

''Didn't have lunch,'' he commented.

''Don't want it now.''

''You can wait just outside, if you like. I just want a quick look at the marks on the face.''

Can't you get those from the pictures? she wondered but said nothing. ''I'm all right.''

''Somebody on our heels,'' said Lanark suddenly.

"Spotted him a-ways back. We'll see how curious he is."

"What're you going to do?"

"Hold on."

The car careened into an alleyway narrowly missing a couple in heated embrace amid trashcans behind a restaurant. The car following, not wishing to give himself completely away, went on past the alleyway as Lanark raced for the next street, barreled down it and returned to the original street, cutting off people in his way, drawing curses. Then they were suddenly right in behind the car that had been following them.

The car ahead suddenly swerved, the driver realizing with a start that Lanark was directly behind him. He sped away, dangerously cutting off others and weaving in and out in a desperate attempt to keep ahead of them, to keep from being ID'd. There were two men in the car.

Lanark remained on his tail tenaciously, tires squealing, the bottom of the car scraping off the pavement at bumps, horns blaring everywhere. Prescription drugstore signs, pawn shops, department stores and gas stations went by in a blur outside Shannon's side window where she held on.

The car ahead of them, she realized, was a police car. She informed Lanark of this, but he already knew. He also appeared to have a good idea who was inside and from the look in his eyes, he wanted to murder the occupant.

The other car cut across a median, flopping wildly and fish-tailing away. Lanark did the same, move for move, following the other car down a one-way street, cursing his prey repeatedly.

"What's going on, Lanark?" she demanded.

"It's Riordan, I can feel it! Bastard's dogging our steps. He's not going to get away without me have a few words with him, personal and up close!"

"Watch out!"

The car ahead almost ran into a bench where two women sat waiting for a bus to arrive.

"Jesus," he moaned.

"Who is it?"

"Riordan's partner, *Ferret Face* Fabia. Guy hates my guts."

"Why?"

"No reason, just does."

"That doesn't make sense."

Lanark nodded, never taking his eyes off the car in front of them. "Okay, so I made trouble for him once on a case, made him look bad. Some years back. Creep never forgot it."

"You'll have to tell me about it sometime."

"Hold on!" Lanark shouted, hitting the gas pedal.

"Ryne, slow down!"

But Lanark saw red, his temper flaring like an inferno. "Nobody's tailing me and getting away with it."

"Don't be foolish, and don't get me killed!"

But Lanark, without hesitation, rammed the rear of the other unmarked car. Seeing the two men ahead of them jump in reaction like bobbing toys, Lanark did it again until he drove them to a curbside stop. "We'll see what the slime wants now."

The near lipless, long-nosed and rather colorless, indistinctive man who got out of the car was cursing and pounding his fists on the car top when Lanark walked up to him with a nasty grin on his face. *Must be Fabia.* "Ryne," she called to him, trying to calm him down.

"Stay outa' this," he called over his shoulder.

Fabia suddenly took advantage and swung, missing Lanark only because he took a step backward the moment his head turned. "Hey, Ferret, you're arm's getting shorter!" he said when the other man missed.

"What the hell you doing, Lanark!" shouted Fabia.

"What're you guys doing following me all morning?"

"Following you? Bull! You ain't seen the day you could make me! If I wanted to keep you under surveillance—"

"Who's that in the car with you?"

"New partner, Ed Kiley."

"Where's Riordan?"

"None of your damned business."

"He somewhere nearby with a hidden camera?"

"Don't worry, we left the camera at your partner's bedroom window, asshole," said Fabia.

Lanark's lightning fist shot up and Fabia, too slow, only half ducked the blow that sent him against his squad car. The man inside jumped out at the same moment and flashed a picture. "You cocksucker, Fabia! This guy's a reporter."

Fabia grabbed Lanark who took a step toward the reporter, but Lanark sent a fist into Fabia's midsection that doubled the man over. He then made a threatening move toward the reporter but Shannon stepped between him and the reporter who continued taking shots.

"Get that damned thing out of my face," shouted Ryne.

"Will you get control of your goddamned self, Ryne! Ease down, damnit," she pulled at his shirt as she spoke. "These men aren't worth losing your temper over, save it for the job." She then turned to the reporter and said to him, "And you, don't you have anything better to do than harass an officer who's done more for this city *today* than your whole damned newspaper does in a year?"

It was like talking to the cement, however. The reporter, a half-smile on his sharp face said, "The man said you were violent."

"Violent, I'll show you violent."

Shannon tried to hold him. "Will you get out of here now!" she shouted to the photographer. Fabia was regaining his feet.

"One more shot," said the reporter from the safety of the other side of the car as the crowd that had gathered began to cheer and jeer, some taking bets as to who would next be on the pavement. Fabia made some threats about having Lanark's badge for what he'd done to him and his car. The crowd laughed and cheered and called for more violence. Lanark's anger had subsided enough to open his eyes to the spectacle they'd all become, and he began to listen to Shannon who pleaded he come away and they get out of there now.

"Just one thing," he said, going to the reporter who started to dash away.

"Stop that man!" Lanark shouted. Some teenagers in dark leather jackets and gloves with the fingers cut out of them obliged Lanark for some reason not even he understood, perhaps to see what would happen if they did. One or two punched the sport-coated reporter before Ryne could break them up. As he did so, he accidentally on purpose crushed the man's camera below his foot. Helping him up, he apologized about the camera and said, "I just wanted to know what paper you're with, so I'd know where to look for my mug shots. Guess now, I won't be appearing in the nightly news? Bad luck."

Fabia had raced to where the reporter had fallen, and he pushed Lanark off, cursing him and helping the other man back toward his car.

With Shannon calling for the crowd to disperse, Ryne returned to her and they were preparing to leave when she said like an angry wife, "I hope to hell you enjoyed yourself, Lanark. You made us all look like squabbling shit-licking pigs! Just does a hell of a lot for community relations, you know."

People still milling about cheered this, some of the gang members saying, "Right on, Mama!"

She frowned and said in a calmer voice, "I'd like to understand what happens in your brain to cause such things?"

"Hey, he started it."

"That makes it okay?

"He's the bastard been spreading lies about me," said Lanark loudly. "Your paper print lies, mister?" he shouted his remarks over to the reporter. "What're you, *Enquirer?*"

"*Tribune,* and *no,* we don't print unsubstantiated stories, but Lieutenant, you didn't help your case much."

"You, Fabia, keep yourself off my back. I don't like leeches."

Fabia gave him the finger and Ryne exploded again but could not reach the other man before he sped off, leaving Lanark to stare at their exhaust and the ugly dents he'd made to the rear of Fabia's car.

TEN

At City Morgue they looked down on the blue-white face of Burton Eaton-Heron, a singularly pleased smile on the dead mouth, brought about by the wide, arching lips painted in blood. There seemed a ghost of a laugh there, *the last laugh?* Not quite, reasoned Lanark as he looked closely at the marred flesh over the eyes and across the nose and the slashes to each cheek. He studied the torn flesh as he might parchment that had been signed by the killer. What is it saying to me? he asked himself.

"Seen enough?" asked the attendant.

"Give me a moment more."

Shannon exchanged a look of concern with the attendant, a mere boy in medical practice. Then she took hold of Lanark's arm firmly and said, "What is it, Ryne? What do you hope to find here?"

"The signature."

"They look like random marks."

"Come on," he said, leaving the wall of refrigerated flesh behind as the attendant placed Burton's pieces

228

back into the freezer. Ryne knew the building well and in a moment they were in a small room with a chalk board. "Here are the marks being made on these people's bodies," said Lanark, charged up now. He drew two eyes, a nose and a mouth then a circle to enclose them. Across each eye he made a cross. At the nose he made a cross. "The three points of the 'T', a cross." At each cheek he drew a squiggly line, saying, "At each cheek a snake. Signature."

"Cross and snakes, like the pin."

"The MS bracelet may mean more than we know as well."

"Got to determine from what source these kids got the jewelry."

"Exactly, and see that the coroner has detailed records on the slash marks to the body. Each one means something to the killer. This random butchery and madness does have to do with some sick kind of reasoning."

"It all points back to the Stone place, Burton and now the marks and the jewelry. Isn't it time we got a warrant and went in there?"

"The homicides have cooled, remember?"

"What's that got to do with it?"

"If there were anything incriminating in the Stone place, you can bet it's been removed since our visit. We go rushing in with nothing and we find nothing. That's what they want . . . I can feel it."

"This isn't a chess game."

"But it is . . . it is . . . and now we've got to play pawns until the King's safe and the Queen's prepped. We've got to build a strong foundation of evidence, so when we snare him it'll stick. Can't overlook anything, not so much as a speck."

"Can't see why Riordan and Fabia overlooked this." She pointed to the board.

"Takes imagination. Besides, anyone might've overlooked it. We got lucky, simple as that."

"You're sure?"

"Hey, if anyone should be getting paranoia . . ."

"Just trying on every idea, like you taught me."

"I taught you?"

"Last few weeks, yes . . . lots."

He looked deeply into her eyes, a pleasure he had been denying himself all this time. She seemed more beautiful each time he did so, and he wanted her more now than ever, and yet he was afraid. For the first time in his life since the horror of that night which had changed the course of his life, he was afraid, not of a gunman or an axe murderer but of a commitment with a woman. Wil and Myra had seen it, felt the electricity between them and had openly scoffed at him for not pursuing her. "Look at us," Myra had said, "we work together and play together and it hasn't hurt us any."

That had been at the bar the night before and Shannon had been on stakeout with Max at one of the crime scenes. The multiple stakeouts had netted only a sad few possible witnesses, hardly capable of recalling what they'd had for breakfast, all swearing they'd seen nothing unusual at the drop sites, save one who had seen a dark blue, possibly black van pull up at the park and drive across the grass and into the bush. No plates, no distinguishing marks or decals or bumper stickers, antennas or hubcaps that screamed. "Plain . . . plain as empty sky . . ." the drunk had said of the van. "Just a black thing."

"Let's get that late lunch," he told her. "Now."

She smiled at the sudden suggestion. "Great idea."

"Damned Riordan pisses me off," he said when they settled again into the car.

She was puzzled. "Riordan?"

"Fabia doesn't go to the john without Riordan's okay. He put Fabia onto me. Gives into pressure from above to open the case wider, bring in our unit, and then he has Fabia sniffing around for what we turn up."

"Wood wants us to share information, remember?"

"Sharing's one thing, stealing's another. If they'd come to me, ask politely, sure we'd give them what we know, and maybe a crumb or two about what we suspect, but not this Mike Hammer shit, sneaking around, tailing us, asking clerks and attendants what we asked, what we signed out. Maybe the newspaper thing isn't Riordan's doing; maybe Fabia's freelancing with his own idea there, trying to discredit me . . . but you can bet Riordan's behind the other crap."

Lanark radioed in and speaking to Samantha, he was patched through to Robeson. He told Robeson to drop what he was doing on the Sorentino case and start asking questions around at dealerships and shops in the North Shore area in an attempt to locate a black van recently sold cheap, or repainted.

"Loooooong shot," said Robeson over the radio. "Hell, man, where do I start? Must be hundreds of shops up that way."

"Use the Stone mansion as your center and work in semi-circles of one mile, two, and on until you locate

231

the closest ones. Could be worse, could be concentric circles if Lake Michigan weren't right there. Careful how you approach people. Somebody up there's got to know that van.''

''If there was a van.''

''Yeah, just do it, detective.''

''Tell me something, Lanark . . . *why?* Why would they wrap bodies in their own clothes, put 'em in a van, drive for hours to another location and dump them out for us to find like that when they got Lake Michigan right there?''

''Something to think about, Robeson. Between auto shops.''

''Roger, will do . . . out.''

''He's got a good question, Ryne . . .'' she said on his right. ''But you don't have an answer for that one, do you?''

''Yes, I do, but it's only a theory and it could send us going off in the wrong direction.''

''The Stone mansion, you mean?''

''I don't think the killer wants to be caught, Shannon.''

''I'm sure of it.''

''He wouldn't leave such a clear trail to his lair in that case.''

''Unless he thinks the rest of the world is filled with incompetent fools and morons, perhaps.''

''The lead to the Stone place could be a draw, to lead us in the wrong direction.''

''Could be. We're back to could be again. What's this theory you're hoarding? You can at least share it with me, can't you?''

''He's like Sorentino in a way, his thinking. Once

he has his victim captive, in this case dead, he *owns* them.''

She took this in.

''Want me to go on?''

''You've been talking to Ames, the shrink you told me about?''

''Off and on, yeah.'' He didn't tell her he saw Ames on a fairly regular schedule.

Richard Ames was the enormously tall black police psychiatrist at the 24th Precinct where Lanark had previously worked. Ames was not only a good friend but the only police shrink Lanark had ever found anything to admire in. Ames was not bound to his profession to the exclusion of all else, nor did he have a handful of placard-type replies, or subscribe to any single philosophy. Psychiatry was not his religion. He didn't take any pleasure in seeing a man broken physically, mentally or spiritually, nor did he consider men apt substitutes for mice. He had never pushed Ryne into any corners. Instead, he had been a friend, allowing Lanark all the room and time he wished during the sessions, and even after Ryne's relocation, Ames wanted to ''give'' Lanark time, he wanted to continue working with him, despite the Skully affair and the fact Lanark was actually no longer his responsibility. It was an unusual sort of dedication Lanark hadn't expected, and it came from the man's heart.

But Ames was no softy. No pushover, no bleeding heart, he felt all policemen were too damned easily swayed by the demons of lesser emotions that tended to crucify the more important emotions they rarely dealt with. Deep down, Lanark knew the truth of this, perhaps more than Ames himself, since he lived such a life.

Ames was also perceptive, and could be *deceptive,* and he was keen, often right on the money in his kaleidoscope assessment of a man. It was to him that Ryne continued to go for his own psychological support, and now to him that he had gone for a psychological portrait of the killer, giving Ames all the particulars.

"Ames hasn't finished his profile as yet," said Ryne. "After lunch, we'll go see him."

"Sounds good."

"Before they pulled into the lot of a diner called *Cloe's* for a quick bite, Lanark located Wil and Myra asking for an update on their search for information on Stone. It was building. They wanted to spend more time on the man's mother, the evangelist, history on her husband and son.

Blum and Max were working on locating leads at another dumping site, but they came on when the others went off. Everyone was to cross-meet at The Decoy unit at midnight. Wood had, with the help of FBI agents interested in the Sorentino affair, paved the way for a bust at *Armand's,* a direct hit now, since the first had gone down as a no-show. Lanark intended on being there and he wanted at least two others from his unit to volunteer. Wil and Myra seemed most to want it, along with Shannon. Lanark would make choices at the midnight meet, but not a word could be relayed over the police band about Sorentino. No chances were being taken.

Ames kept telling them he knew nothing about this phantom killer that might possibly be working out some bizarre disorder known only to himself. "What can I tell you from a stack of reports, information gotten over the phone, a quick suggestion here, a jotted note there about the inner workings of this man's mind, a man I have not so much as an iota of sure, hard evidence regarding, a man who leaves chicken marks on his victims long after they've expired due to a draining off of their blood? A man who selects only top, rich, ripe blood from sorority sisters and high-born boys of the Miracle Mile, Gold Coast folk? And why should I give a shit? You have any notion how many poor little black boys and girls are raped and murdered every day out there? You got four fucking thoroughbreds been taken out of the race by a maniac. Let me tell you both something, Officers," Ames looked at Shannon in the eye to intimidate her, "six times that number die of a slasher in the black community and there's not a sniffle or a hoot from the goddamned Commissioner, the Mayor, the newsmen, us! Got to take years-long deaths in the Black community, like that time in Atlanta, and there the investigation was so half-assed we still don't know if the right man's behind bars or not. So, *what it is you want me to tell you?*" He put on his black on black act.

Lanark had seen it all before. Ames could go from a Bishop Tutu lecturing voice to a ghetto punk in a matter of mid-sentence. He kept you listening, kept you guessing what was on his mind, and then he laid it out buffet style for your pleasure: *What it is you want?*

"Anything you can tell us, Dr. Ames," said Shannon, "Even if it's just conjecture."

"Conjecture can lead you in a false direction."

"As it is, we have a direction. What you have to add

235

could conceivably tell us if that direction is warm or cold."

Lanark watched Shannon with Ames, to see if she had any skill with handling the twists and turns he planned for them. Lanark knew Ames could not help but have made some preliminary, if sketchy deliberations on the killer's mental condition. Ames loved the very thing he was telling Shannon he detested, conjecture over the unknown.

"Come on, Ames," said Lanark, "let's have it. You've stalled enough. We do have cases waiting."

Ames laughed lightly, paced about his congested office and scratched a pencil over the side of his face and said thoughtfully, "All the marks are, as you have guessed, Lanark, a *signatori* of the killer—or killers. There is a ritual aspect to the murders, a pattern that is taken step by step, almost painstakingly."

"We've established as much."

"The killer signs in flesh his handiwork, an artist of the macabre sort, a Picasso of the underworld. Autopsies revealed the women were sexually molested, but I submit to you they were, in a sense, willing sacrifices to their god. Drug-induced sex, yes, but willingly they went to him. No sign whatsoever of struggle, not a hair or skin fragment in the nails, not even a fight against their bonds, leaving the wounds at ankle and wrists almost imperceptible, almost missed by the coroner. As to the catheter marks, these are odd indeed. When first you mentioned them, I had thought they were on the arms, but later I learn they are in the back, the area of the kidneys. First victim and second were checked again when the marks showed up on the third.

"But the killer has a genteel streak about him, making his slash marks and mutilations of parts of the body *after* the victim has ceased feeling any pain. Maybe the killer can't bear the sound of screams.''

Shannon exchanged a look with Lanark who shrugged, saying, ''Possibly a real gentleman on our hands.''

''A gentleman butcher, less a sadist than a man detached from life,'' said Ames.

''Perhaps he once worked in a slaughterhouse?'' suggested Shannon.

''No, more likely something closer to a hospital,'' said Ames.

''Field hospital maybe—Nam?'' suggested Lanark.

''You cops always want to bring Nam into this. We're both vets of that war, pal, and it's not necessarily a truism that everybody who served in Southeast Asia came home a looney-toons.''

''Touché . . . but the hospital, doctor idea has merit. Young Stone went to medical school, and it ties in with some physical evidence we just unearthed.''

''Tell me about it,'' said Ames.

Lanark willingly shared the most recent finds and told Ames what he had suggested to Shannon regarding the cheek tears, eye slits and nose slashes.''

''*Good . . . possibly . . . perhaps,*'' Ames repeated throughout Lanark's talk. ''But our killer could just as well be a *hunter* who enjoys skinning and cutting up his game, you know, wearing L.L. Bean wear as he does so.''

The handsome black doctor was sharp. ''It's the marks that interest me, quick cuts, slash-slash over the eyelids, as if to close them down after death, the jab to the nose, the more contoured, slow cut to each cheek.

237

Sometimes the lips. Sometimes the breasts. Sometimes other areas. The depth and diversity and speed of each cut indicates to me, at least, more than one hand in this."

"Agreed again," said Lanark.

"Marks could be of derision, to disgrace the body, the victim—"

"But after death?"

"Stigmata then."

"Stigmata?"

"A kind of ritual significance to the marks, as in cult stigmata, not at all to deride, but to demonstrate superiority, to say that this victim died a worthy death, for a worthy cause, to give life meaning."

"We haven't entirely overlooked the possible religious implications of the ritual, or cult murder here," said Shannon.

"Nor have we ruled out the killings as some form of ritual punishment."

"Especially in the last case, since we had made contact with the victim the night of his death."

"I keep seeing the executioner in all this as viewing himself as a *sacred* executioner, marking his victims so that those who found them would know that they had not offended God, but had in fact placated God," said Ames.

"This line of interpretation is stretching it a bit, isn't it, Ames?"

Ames gave Lanark an unusual look, somewhere between derision and anger. "You asked my opinion." It was a tone Lanark had never heard Ames take before. "It is only one line of interpretation; one could speculate endlessly. One thing we agree on: the message is in the marks. Perhaps the most telling message being the marks on the victims' backs.''

Shadows had grown long in the doctor's office, and his stern face had become like stone, his face half in shadow, half in brilliant light from the window. He hadn't bothered to turn on lights. The room became very still.

Ames said impassively, *''He* wants us to know him. He doesn't want his victims confused with anybody else.''

''But why?'' asked Shannon.

''Wants his work recognized, his purpose feared, perhaps understood as well.''

''Attention?''

''Fame?''

''Notoriety?'' the two cops asked successively.

''He is a kind of terrorist, a megalomaniac. Look at the contempt he shows you, dumping one of the bodies on your doorstep, amid rubble, in a ditch, in the bushes. It's very likely he stands by when you're inspecting a crime scene, to watch you and secretly laugh at you.''

''You think he will strike again?'' asked Shannon.

''He's shown himself to be compulsive, and if he commands others, they might even branch out on their own, depending on how much power he actually wields over them. In cults, that has been shown often to be the power over life and death.''

''But he could stop suddenly, *as he has,*'' said Lanark, ''to *disappear* like many another serial killer.''

''Possibly . . . equally possible he will strike again and go on indefinitely. We have no way of knowing if we cannot know *the purpose.*''

* * *

Later Lanark and Shannon went to her place. Very little was said as they shared the few hours they had between mealtime and midnight when they must be back at headquarters. She put together a meal with him insisting on assisting this time, and she learned he wasn't bad help between the stove and the fridge.

"Man's got to learn to fend for himself," he'd said when she made mention of this fact.

Ever more curious about Lanark, she had asked questions about him from the few friends he seemed to have, Wil and Myra, Mark Robeson, and once at his bar she had had a long conversation with Jack Tebo, who seemed more willing to talk about Lanark than anyone else.

"Ryne's a good man, like his father," Tebo had said.

"His parents died in an accident?"

"Ryne can tell you more about that than I."

"Sometimes he seems so distant, a million miles away."

"Oh, don't be bothered by that. He's a thinker, he is . . . that's all. Not much time goes by he isn't puzzling over one of his cases—sometimes two at once!"

"That why he's so . . . angry? He's angry a lot. Sometimes it doesn't seem directed at anyone in particular . . . but it's there, always."

"He's seen a lot. Makes some cops hard, flinty. Him, it's just made him angry."

She accepted this at the time, but the more time she spent with him, the more she felt an insulating mystery about him. Records and stories on his earlier exploits and failures within the police department didn't begin to penetrate this mystery. If she did not know him better, she would think him a dangerous man—and perhaps he was. Perhaps she had tried to paint him differently. Perhaps the anger was just an excuse to brutalize people, as seemed the case with many of his arrests in the past. The stories surrounding him, also, about being unlucky for his partners, at first lost on her, were daily becoming understandable. It was not so much that he intentionally placed a partner in danger, so much as it was he sought it out, and riding with him anyone was in harm's way. The incident with Morris Fabia was only the tip of the iceberg. The car chase and subsequent death of Angelo Sorentino, Wood's wounding, it all found its way back to action taken by Lanark. It hadn't been overlooked that Angelo Sorentino might well have been the prisoner who would have turned on his uncle for protection. It was obvious he had known more about the inner workings of the Sorentino operation than anyone else.

And yet someone might say exactly the same of her run-in with Peter Gunnetti and her shooting him. It increasingly seemed to her that Ryne Lanark's bad reputation within the Chicago Police Force was both deserved and undeserved at the same time. Yet he did nothing to dispel it, and perhaps he enjoyed it. Perhaps he knew it carried weight on the street.

They ate, talked of interests other than police work. Shannon enjoyed scuba diving when she could find time. Lanark was instantly curious and interested, saying it was something he had always wanted to learn but had never found the time.

"Take it," she said, "it's something you'll never regret."

"Maybe . . . with the right encouragement, and teacher."

"Oh, no! I'm no instructor, but I know a good man."

"I love to swim."

"We should do it sometime."

He nodded, sipped his wine and reached across the table, taking her hand in his. She stared down at the gesture, taken by surprise.

"Shannon," he whispered her name. "Maybe when this case is over . . . we could do something . . . you know, like rent a boat, swim in the lake, together."

"That would be wonderful," she said.

He tightened his hold about her hand and she felt the blood pumping through his arteries as if trying to penetrate her own skin and join with hers. The heat between their mutual grasp increased until he released his hold and raised his fingers to lips. He came around the table, still touching. Nearing his lips to hers he ever so slowly pressed his to hers and the gentleness melted her resolve, flushed her face. She reached round his neck and pulled him closer, the gentle kiss turning to passionate fire.

"I think we'd better slow down," said Lanark, pulling away.

"Why? No, Ryne . . . kiss me again."

He looked deeply into her eyes and then he kissed her more passionately than before, placing his arm about her shoulder and grasping her legs, lifting her from where she sat, carrying her into the bedroom.

Their lips never parted and Shannon felt herself hungrily and madly searching his mouth with her tongue.

They lay on the bed for a long time in this embrace, exploring one another through their clothing, taking one piece off at a time, never far from one another's mouths. His firm hands found her supple breasts, exploring in gentle excursion, fumbling with and finding the catch to her bra, her blouse undone but still about her shoulders, his shirt torn away now, their passion firing them onto new heights of dizzying lust, her mind racing with questions of *how long, when did he first want me, what had first attracted him to me? Why?* And with the internal and giddy passions welling up from her innermost core, she could barely suppress the question of the future, *for how long will he want me after?* Would she remain attractive to him? How long would this moment last? How long could he feel this way about her? Was it purely physical? Did they have a chance? Beyond this present which was suddenly out of time, as it was out of control? The questions bombarded her and as Lanark found her most private parts with his exploring touch, she felt the old fear that came over her without warning or reason, the fear he would hurt her, hurt her badly and meanly and with rage.

"No! Ryne! I can't! No!" she began to shout in his ear. "Stop, please . . . please."

He raised his eyes to hers and saw that she was terrified. "Shannon, it's all right . . . it's all right." He touched her cheek, finding tears had come. "I'm sorry. I hurt you?"

"It's . . . I . . . I just can't . . . nothing you've done . . . Please, just give me a moment."

He raised himself from her, his gleaming body a wall

243

of muscle before her, chest heaving, finding it difficult to calm the raging fires within him. "I'm sorry, coming on so strong like that. Been a long time since . . . since I've slept with a woman I . . . cared about."

"No, Ryne, you . . . you were wonderful. It's me, just me."

"Nothing wrong with you that I can see." She was only partially clad.

"I still have difficulty in sexual relations since . . . since—"

He suddenly understood.

"—since the rape."

He sat alongside her, put his arms out to enfold her, pulling her into his powerful chest, wrapping her there like a doll against himself, gently rocking as she sobbed. "I had no idea."

Through her sobs she told him a familiar tale. At seventeen she's been badly beaten and raped by two boys. It had been dark, and she'd been left for another girl by the boy she had gone on a date with at a party. "I was hardly a beauty and known as a drag since I wasn't sleeping around," she'd said. She was offered a ride by another boy at the party and when she got into his car, she realized there was another boy in the back. They took her to a deserted spot near a lake, told her what she really needed and wanted, and proceeded to give it to her. She was so ashamed afterward that it took several days for her to work up the nerve to talk about the incident with her mother. Proceedings against the two boys led to a dismissal on the grounds of insufficient evidence and from that moment on Shannon realized that justice was something you had to fight for and even then, you often lost. The incident changed

244

her entirely. Not just the rape and the fear and the feeling of being a completely helpless animal there on the ground, but the aftermath. It was the reason she decided to learn self-defense, and eventually to join the police academy.

The terrible life experience explained a lot about Detective Shannon Keyes, Ryne believed. Little wonder she felt so close to those exploited children. Little wonder she'd made it a personal crusade to see to it they were not lost in the system, that they got full protection and were now being relocated in foster homes, records carefully being kept not by Social Services but the FBI.

"Hey, hey, it's okay."

"It's the reason I've had so many Thom Warners in my life," she said enigmatically, but Lanark, not wishing to pry, let this pass with a simple OK. He continued to rock her gently. They remained this way for some time.

"Talking helps," she managed to say after a while. "Thom, I never could tell Thom about it. As far as making love with Thom, he seldom pushed it and when we did, he wasn't very passionate, and I always felt, you know, in control . . . in control. Thom's big love was talk . . . talk about his trade, the brokerage, the money he was amassing and how he was going to buy us this enormous house in the suburbs, two cars, a pool. But with you . . . it's . . . it's frightening."

He sat her up and looked deep into her eyes, the moist, soft browns of the pupils making him think of a picture of a helpless, hungry child on a poster for the impoverished he'd seen somewhere. "I would never wish to frighten you. I'll just wait in the other room.

You get yourself together, maybe shower—there's time—and I'll wait.''

He started to get up but she held tightly to him, not wanting him to go, afraid for him to stay, a bundle of conflicting emotions wracking her. "No, Ryne, I want passion in my life . . . I want you in my life . . . I want it all.''

"That include the house in the country, the two cars? Thom and me?''

"No, no! Thom . . . I broke it off with Thom that night you were here last, and I haven't seen him since.''

He was taken aback by this. "You did? You haven't?''

"Lay back down with me,'' she said sensually, her tears dried. "Just for a while.''

Ryne did so.

She kissed him tenderly. She touched him with trembling fingertips. "Maybe . . . maybe if you let me lead? Just until I feel safe . . . maybe?''

"I'm willing to try,'' he said with a groan of pleasure as she reached for his groin and slid her tongue across his chest at once. "Willing to try . . . if you are.''

"I am . . . I need you . . . want you . . . in doses though . . . easy, nice and easy . . .''

The abused oldest girl, Yolanda, had fingered her stepfather but it had taken time to locate the man since he had taken up roots with the money for Yolanda and had moved out of the city. With the help of FBI authorities Salvatore Guippi was located in Louisville, Kentucky, where he had lost all of his profit on the horse races. He was picked up there by local authorities and Jeff Blum was sent to escort him back.

246

Now he was in custody and no one but the unit knew of this new development. It quickly changed plans for the Sorentino bust since Guippi, anxious to lessen the charges for his cooperation, agreed to being wired and sitting across a table from Sorentino with the proposal of selling him more children for his film trade.

The warrant for the bugging was approved. Guippi, still maintained as secretively as possible in the lockup, was ready. Agents had to be deployed. Lanark gathered his troupe. Myra looked like a second-rate hooker in her garb, a frilly, too tight, low-cut, low-rate dress that showed every nook and cranny, garter belt, black stockings beneath, high heels and a red wig, lots of makeup that created a caricature from her otherwise sensuous features. Wil was in a workman's uniform with a Commonwealth Edison insignia, hard hat and all. He'd parked the Con Ed van—surveillance equipment and all—outside *Armand's*. He then proceeded into the restaurant for a casual lunch, and had taken his position in a booth not far from Sorentino's business booth, remaining as close to the buy as safely possible. Myra then came in bitching about a broken heel and Wil offered to help her and she joined him rather spontaneously for lunch, and maybe an afternoon drink at his place. They were loud about it but not unnecessarily so.

Meanwhile Robeson had secured a dishwashing job in the back. He'd seen to it earlier that the usual man was indisposed. Then he promptly showed up "wontin' de job." Since he'd been on the inside he had seen the hidden menu items. The place sold dog meat to people out the back door. These transactions were photographed with high-powered cameras by Max from a rooftop overlooking the alley. Max then made a purchase out the back himself one day. At the right moment, Max and Blum were to enter the back way, the entrance paved by Robeson who would secure all kitchen personnel. It was understood that Armand himself was going down as well as Sorentino tonight.

Shannon manned the control center in the van, monitoring Sal's every word and Wood, increasingly bold, had come to the party dressed as a street bum and had taken up residence in a doorway across the street. The entire operation had remained so secretive that no higher ranking official above Wood, other than the judge issuing the bugging warrant, had an iota of information on it. The FBI was intentionally kept out of this one.

Now, Salvatore Guippi, a shakiness to his walk, was released a block away by Jeff Blum who radioed this fact through code to the van.

Shannon watched the slow progress of the fat, greasy-haired man as he approached *Armand's*. "Come on, calm and easy," she said to the empty van and then over her radio to the others. "A-C, going to granny's to put a fork in her snake." The others were alerted, the clock was ticking. The men and Myra on the inside didn't know what time it was but they would, as soon as Sal entered.

At this time, Wil was sending back a dirty glass, complaining of the service. Myra saw Sal enter first, knowing his movements were being watched outside by the LLS-TV camera in the van. Shannon said to those wired to hear her, "He looks like he's going to bolt and run."

"No, he isn't," Max replied.

"Secure the talk," said Wood.

They'd both seen Captain Wood stumble up to Sal, ostensibly to beg money, but he put something into Salvatore's ear. It looked like a gun barrel.

"Door is closed," said Shannon, her voice heard now by every operative except Wil, Myra and Lanark. Robeson, in the kitchen, had his ears plugged into what looked like an ordinary headphone connected to a radio, but in fact this concealed his own two-way bug. His big hands were in scalding hot water, soap up to his elbows. He'd complained repeatedly about his hands becoming so dry the black skin was cracking and the white was showing through. Armand laughed at his jokes. Armand liked him.

"Door is closed," Shannon's words rang like a bell tolling. This was it.

Robeson dried his hand, poked a look out front, and heard Myra telling Wil that she really adored men in *uniform,* and him saying that they were just coveralls.

"A real uniform's hanging in the closet at home, my army uniform."

Tavalez Sorentino was eating something at his plate with great relish, laughing and talking with a woman at his table. On either side of the room stood bodyguards, replacements for Peter, just as tough looking and just as large. Each man watched everything in the place with great interest. At other tables people were about their own business, including Armand, who seemed to have a little racket of his own going as people came in to place numbers bets with him.

There was Salvatore, looking around like a nervous cat, spying the man and going to him with a plastic grin and an outstretched hand. Tavalez watched him with interest, took the extended hand, exchanged pleasantries and told the woman to make herself comfortable at another table for a time. She did so with a pout.

"You don't look so good, Sal," said Sorentino.

"Been down with the flu, you know."

Fidel, a waiter at Armand's, moved about the tables, looking over his shoulder only once toward the door where Mr. Armand had disappeared when the dishwasher had shouted there was a problem in the kitchen that needed his immediate attention. Fidel had notions of learning the business so well that one day he would take over for Mr. Armand, or become a maître d' in a much better place. He knew he had a lot to learn, that he could learn so much from Mr. Armand. But he hadn't been on the job long at *Armand's*, in fact, Armand didn't even know he was alive. He'd been hired by the number one chef, a brother-in-law. He was not Oriental, but neither was his sister, married to the Oriental chef. They were Cubans.

Fidel's throat was one mass of gold, chains so thick and intertwined it looked like spaghetti for the gods. He lived for gold jewelry. As he tried desperately to explain in his broken English to Mr. Sorentino at table number seven, it was what he did with his paychecks. Sorentino had roughly grabbed Fidel by the wrist to "check out" his gold bracelets and rings. The inspection went on for a while, Sorentino admiring Fidel's taste. Fidel's hand was still gripping the glass of water he'd placed in front of the other gentleman who had

just joined Mr. Sorentino, when Tavalez finished looking at and assessing the amount of gold on the waiter.

"You don't earn that much money here, so how do
you get your money, Fidel?"

"Mi madre, she die, my heart bleed . . . but she leave
me much."

"Maybe you should consider investing some cash?"

"I have . . . *si!"*

"Not with me, you haven't."

Fidel shook his head slowly. "No."

Sorentino stared up into the black eyes of the Cuban
and studied his dark skin and the greasy black hair that
looked painted on and he said, "Listen, grease ball,
we'll talk some more about it, later."

"Yes, Señor Sorentino."

"Hey, I like that, don't you, Sal, Señor Sorentino."

Fidel was glad to be going from the table but then
Sorentino stopped him again, calling him back, asking
him his name and pretending to like him. "Say something for me in Spanish, Fidel."

"Lo siento, lo siento?"

"What?"

"I . . . Fidel . . . am . . . sorry, am sorry," he said
in a halting English.

"Sorry? Yeah, just *say* something in Spanish."

"Cuál es el próximo autobús para la Habana?"

Sal laughed at this but not too much.

"What's he saying, Sal?" asked Sorentino.

"What is the next bus for Havana, he wants to
know."

"Tell the man what you want, Sal," said Sorentino,
"my treat, anything on the menu."

Sal pointed to items on the menu he wanted and

the Cuban waiter bowed and scraped his way away from Sorentino, just the way the man liked it. Fidel heard Sorentino say he liked the Cuban guy, if only he could speak better English.

"He'll learn, he'll learn," said Sal.

"So, Sal," Sorentino continued their talk. "I thought you'd left Chicago for good, was up in what? Ohio?"

"No, not Ohio, my friend, Louisville, Kentucky."

"Kentucky?"

"Kentucky . . . the Derby, remember?"

"Oh, yeah . . . then you didn't do so good there?"

"No . . . that's why I'm back. I need more money."

Sorentino nodded. "Business ain't so good, Sal. I can't do no business for a while. Got heat on me so bad I'm like one big rash, you know."

"Freakin' cops," agreed Sal. "But what about soon, soon maybe? I got two other—"

"Shhhhhh! Sal! Come on, what's the matter here? You bring it down, huh? Unless, what, you talking to a microphone up your ass?"

Sal laughed nervously at this and Sorentino watched him with expert eyes. He sensed Sal was having some difficulty just sitting. "Look, Sal, you ordered up your favorite on the menu, right? So, let's eat, enjoy some wine . . . and maybe we'll talk, in more private surroundings . . . later."

"Sure . . . sure, Mr. Sorentino."

"Sal, call me Tavalez. Waiter, over here." Fidel was asking people at another table if they'd like dessert, but the couple, giggling, said they already had dessert planned and just wanted the check. Fidel exchanged a quick greeting again with Mr. Sorentino and Sorentino said angrily, "Where's this man's shish kebab? What kinda place is it treats my friends this way, huh? Fast," ordered Sorentino. "And a whiskey sour . . . you still like whiskey sours, don't you, Sal?"

"Seven and Seven," he corrected Sorentino who seemed fishing for a crack.

"Right away, Mr. Sorentino."

Fidel scurried off to the kitchen mouse-like. Sorentino laughed. "I like people to follow orders, my orders, Sal."

"So, what's this about cops hounding you, Tavalez?"

"Little trouble. Time will take it away. Sal, you got something you got to do, somewhere you got to go?"

"What?"

"You, look at you, you're jumpy like a cat in heat."

"I got a woman waiting for me." Sal was getting into the game.

Sorentino laughed loudly, long. This seemed to encourage Salvatore who added, "Hell of a woman. Just got out of bed with her and she wants more, always more. I don't got time for a piss before she wants more."

"What, you got to go? You know where it is, go!"

His drink came and Sal took a long drink before he said, "Yeah, maybe I will."

Sal hadn't seen the eye contact between Sorentino and the bodyguard nearest the john. Wil and Myra were draped over one another. Even Sal didn't recognize them.

In the van, Shannon was joined by Wood who now cursed.

"What is it?"

"He's on to us."

"How can you tell?"

"Gut feeling, experience. Look, you maintain here. Tell Max and Blum to meet me at the kitchen entrance, and tell Robeson to pave the way. I think Salvatore's going to the john marks an end to our little game. Fool goes in there and Sorentino's men are going to work him over for sure."

"Bug's in his shorts, isn't it?"

"They'll find it."

Wood made a careful circle and came up on the kitchen from one side while Max and Blum arrived from another. The door stood open, signaling them Robeson had secured the kitchen staff. When he entered the kitchen Wood found Robeson had two waiters and the cook and his assistant at bay with his revolver and a flaming shish kebab. "The order, for Mr. Sorentino's friend. I . . . must take it to him . . . now," pleaded Fidel.

"I'll be at the front door with Blum," said Wood to Robeson. Robeson nodded. "What about Fidel, here, and the order for table number seven? Wait," said Mark Robeson, putting a hand to his ear, listening to Shannon, then repeating her words to them. "Sal's back at the table, everything's cool."

A glance through a cracked door and Paul Wood saw that this was indeed the fact, amazing as it was. Somehow Salvatore had returned to the table in good health, bitching that Sorentino's men had shaken him down for a bug in the bathroom. Wood wondered instantly just how Sal had managed to hide the bug from the experienced bodyguards.

At the table Sal was saying, "Sons-of-bitches even

went through my BVD's! Christ, Sorentino, your nerves must be shot. You know me!"

Sorentino apologized effusively, adding, "I can't be too careful these days."

Sal began to make faces, feeling uncomfortable with something behind his ear. "Earache," he complained, "hurts like hell."

"Two minutes, Robeson," Wood told Mark, "then send Fidel here out with the order and we carry on as before."

Fidel said, "The meat, it will be black!" His gold chains jangled with his nerves. He didn't want to be in the middle of any trouble. His eyes were wide with fear, his face hot from where the flaming shish kebab flared.

"Put it out and re-light the damned thing," said Wood. Jeff Blum by now had had a wagon silently backed to the door and Armand, along with the kitchen personnel, except for Fidel, were placed in storage by a couple of officers. Wood and Blum went for the front.

Shannon continued to monitor the talk at table seven. "So, Sal, my friend, you said you have two packages you would like me to inspect, but you did not bring them with you, why not?"

"I got 'em, in the car with my woman."

"I didn't see you drive up."

"Parked down the street. Couldn't find nothing closer. Anyway, I got 'em. You want to deal, or not?"

"These kids . . . they got family?"

"Shit, Sorentino, they're my two."

"Ahhh, I see. Your stepdaughter and now your own. What sex are we talking?"

"Boy and girl."

"Ahhhh, good. What condition are they in? I don't like fat kids for my movies. The girl, she got—?"

The bug on Sal suddenly overheated, scorching him so badly he could not withstand it, tears and a grimace coming to his face, along with the acrid smell of singed hair and scalp. Little curls of smoke were rising off his cranium.

"Damn it, he's bugged! The bastard's bugged!" shouted Sorentino who pulled out a gun and leveled it at Sal's brain, ripping his hairpiece away visciously to reveal a buzzing, miniature machine. "I'll kill you!"

At the same instant Fidel arrived with the flaming shish kebab, now burnt to a crisp, and he plunged the spearhead into Sorentino's arm, the pain and fire spreading through him, causing him to scream and drop his weapon. In the split second this took, Wil and Myra had the two bodyguards in their sights, shouting, "Police, drop it!"

Robeson and Max took up support positions at the kitchen exits. Wood and Blum crashed through the front. People everywhere lay on the floor. One of the bodyguards panicked and fired, the .357 ripping an enormous hole in Jeff Blum whose body pounded into the wall and slid to the floor amid blood as Max blew away the guard, a single .38 through the man's skull.

Sorentino did a hopscotch about the room, his arm ablaze, making him scream. He resembled a chicken that had only recently lost its head to the block. Fidel tripped him with a judo move and brought him down, grabbed his right arm and the flaming left and cuffed the wrists. It took Myra with a pitcher of water to extinguish the flaming arm. Fidel wasn't about to. Fidel was too busy banging the man's face into the floor repeatedly until Wil pulled him off. It was then that Ryne Lanark showed himself, tearing away Fidel's brown elastic features and hair as he unmasked himself. He wanted Sorentino to have a good look at who it was that had taken him down. Actually, he wanted to do much more to the man. Stepping onto his face with his heel, he read Sorentino his rights, unaware that Blum was on the floor and dying by the second.

Shannon had raced in as backup and it took her to calm Lanark enough to point out to him that one of his men was down. "It's Jeff, damn it, and he's hit bad, real bad!"

Wood was already over Blum's inert form, shaking his head repeatedly. Max was beside himself with grief, crying unashamedly before he yelled something in Japanese and then went for Sorentino who was being hauled up by Wil. Robeson latched onto the wild-eyed Max, holding onto him with an iron bear hug, trying to calm him down.

Shannon looked at her watch. It had all happened in a matter of twelve seconds from the moment Sorentino had discovered Sal had imaginatively removed the bug from his shorts and placed it instead beneath his hairpiece.

Shannon, as with Max, couldn't control her tears for young Jeff Blum. He was dead.

They found Sal cringing below a table. Ambulances and wagons were called for. Everyone connected with the restaurant in any way was arrested. Officers from Internal Affairs came in and re-enacted the shooting, something that Wood had had them on call for, to rule as quickly as possible on the shoots as good.

* * *

They had Sorentino on tape, admissible-in-a-court-of-law tape, since a warrant for the bug from a municipal judge had been obtained and due process followed. Ryne Lanark was learning to work within the system, with the laws instead of against them or around them to get what he wanted, but he'd had to pay a high price, the life of one of his men . . . not Wood's man, not Riordan's man, not the commissioner's man, but one of *his*. And it hurt deeply.

"Wish we could take back that last few seconds," Shannon said to him at the van where the damnable tape was now in their hands.

"Our job now is to see that Sorentino fries for Murder One."

"Right . . . right."

Wood came to them, still in costume, joined by Wil and Myra. In a moment Robeson escorted a shaken Max to the van. They stood about it in silence for a time before Wood said, "I'll see Blum gets a citation for bravery. You all did a remarkable job in there. Thought it was going to fall through more than once. Lanark, you did everything right . . . everything."

It was like telling a doctor he'd followed the proper surgical procedure to save a life but that the patient died despite this. "Then why do I feel like such a bastard, Captain?" he asked, walking to the front of the van, climbing into the driver's seat.

"Stick with him," Wood said to Shannon.

She nodded, "And, Captain, you did a fine job, too."

"Thanks, Keyes. Not often I hear that."

"We'll get the tapes entered in evidence."

"I'll see that our friend Sal gets what's coming to him," said Wood. No hard promises had been made to the lowlife, but he had helped apprehend Sorentino. Some kind of protection was called for, whether he were sentenced to time or not.

"Later," called the others as Shannon got in beside Lanark.

"Jeff's folks are in Skokie," said Lanark. "Think I'll go see them tonight . . . explain things person to person. Better than getting a call from the station."

"I'll go with you."

"Tempting."

"Why not?"

"Hardest duty you'll ever pull."

"I am your partner."

ELEVEN

Lanark was right. Informing a dead young policeman's family of the tragedy was the hardest duty she'd ever pulled. It left both she and Lanark in a numbed sense of depression, so much so she wondered if there were a state of depression so low that a person simply felt nothing.

That was how they passed the night, in one another's arms, just holding on to the sense of touch from the other's body to guarantee one another of that possibility, the possibility of feeling again in time.

Sometime in the night, Shannon woke with a chilling start and a scream. She'd had such a vivid nightmare it were as if it was actually happening all over again, the night at Stone's place. This time she recalled vividly and distinctly the door through which Burton had forced her, and the freezer. Yes, there was a freezer in the room, or they were standing in a freezer.

"The rose," she said several times as Lanark held her near him, unsure what else to do for her, realizing she was having a nightmare. Was it Blum's death troubling her, or the rape again? He did not know.

"Night of the party," she muttered. "I tell you, Ryne, something happened. Something I can't recall, hidden from me by my subconscious."

"Tell me what you can."

She told him the bits and pieces, the images, but none of it made sense.

"We've got to see Ames again. Maybe he can help."

"But how?"

"Hypnosis, if you're willing?"

She swallowed hard. "Anything's better than this."

Dr. Richard Ames had lowered the lights and closed the blinds to his office, and now he sat opposite Shannon who lay in a completely relaxed manner on the couch in semi-daze. "You are counting now . . . going back in time as you do so. Yesterday, the night before . . ."

"Seventy-nine, seventy-eight . . ."

Lanark watched in silence from across the room.

"To the night of the party. You are at the party at Stone's mansion, dancing with Burton. Stop at this moment in time, Shannon."

"Yes . . . dancing . . ."

"You enjoy dancing, don't you? Let yourself float with the dancing, the music."

"Out of control," she muttered, "can't think . . . see . . ."

"Burton gave you a potent drink. It's made you dizzy."

"Dizzy . . . dizzy and horny . . ."

261

Ames looked up at Lanark for a moment, then resumed. "And?"

"And angry . . . very angry."

"What else did Burton do to you, recall."

"Pulled me through a doorway."

"Into the dark?"

"Very dark, away from the others, onto . . . onto an elevator."

"You're sure?"

"Up to a cold room . . . cold."

"A freezer?"

"No, a . . . a doctor's room, a clinic . . . cold table."

"He put you on the table?"

"I wouldn't go. I screamed, pulled away because he . . . he cut me, cut my finger. Got up and he was pressing my finger into . . . into something."

"What sort of something, Shannon, can you see it?"

She saw a big windowpane. "Glass . . . glass."

"How large is the cut, Shannon?"

"Big cut . . ."

"How large? How many inches would you say?"

"Five, six."

Lanark exchanged a look with Ames. "She have any such cuts?"

"Just a prick on the right index finger."

"All right, Shannon, is there anything else you see that you want to tell us about?"

"Straps, on the table, a stainless steel table. Another door. I run to it but it's a freezer and she's inside it."

"She?"

"The woman, the white woman."

"What is she doing in the freezer?"

"Getting . . . getting blood."

Ames shook his head, trying to make sense of this. "Anything else?"

"She . . . she touched me, held my hand up and pressed her lips to my cut, sucked on it. I . . . I ran."

"Where are you now, Shannon?"

"In the crowd, searching . . . searching for Ryne."

She'd suddenly become distraught, her voice rising to a strident crescendo, her body lifting from the couch as Ryne rushed in and Ames placed his large, soothing hands on her shoulders and spoke calmly to her, "One-hundred, kid, one-hundred." It had been the word he used as a pre-hypnotic suggestion to bring her round. It worked but she'd broken into a sweat and was cringing and clawing for Lanark all at once before she realized where she was.

"Shannon," he said, "it's okay, it's me . . . Ryne."

"Shannon," said Ames. "do you recall what you've told us, any of it?"

She shook her head, "Nothing of detail . . . some fuzziness about being looped, frightened . . . what'd I say?"

"You're sure you want to hear this?" he asked moments before flicking on the tape, a recording of the session.

"Yes, I . . . I must," she said firmly, Lanark holding onto her.

After listening to the full recording Shannon was amazed. She'd hidden so much from herself.

"Don't forget the part the drugs played in that, my dear," said Ames. "Add just a dollop of the conscious mind consciously wishing it away, and *voila*, short-circuit. The brain's like any other instrument. Abuse it, you lose it.''

"Now I'm remembering all sorts of things," she said.

"Floodgates have swept back," said Ames.

"There was an EKG machine, some other sort of machine, big, cumbersome looking, all around the table. Place was like . . . an operating room."

"And Stone said he wasn't practicing medicine," Lanark said.

"That freezer . . . the woman . . . the blood, what could it all mean?"

"We were just kidding about vampires," said Ryne, "but now, I don't know. Something weird is definitely going on."

"They took a blood sample from you," said Ames, "or so it would seem."

"What?"

"The nick to the finger, Burton pressing it into glass—that would be a slide. You saw the cut as six inches across in your mental state. The big glass may've been an ordinary slide, and if that were the case—" he stopped himself, imagining the worst.

Lanark finished for him, "The freezer, the woman keeps a cache of blood and plasma on hand."

"Properly matched, free of disagreeable things like disease," continued Ames.

"Particularly AIDS, Richard."

"Yes, AIDS."

"The woman's evangelism comes back to the disease of our times like a catechism. Her son, the doctor who does not practice medicine, supplies her with AIDS-free blood for some disorder she's had for years—"

"And in return," said Shannon, following the sick thread of this logic, "in return she gives him control . . . control of the house, the funds . . ."

"So long as she can carry on with her ministry and gospel."

"Crazy . . . sounds absolutely crazy," said Ames. "Classic crazy."

"Of course it is crazy, it's brought about four deaths here, that we know of."

"Matthew Stone's the butcher, the slasher then."

"He's more than just a slasher. Like the night we met him, he was behind every move the others made, orchestrating." Lanark thought for a moment. "Nine-to-one odds he's running a sex for blood clinic for dear old Mom."

"Of course, the drugs, the partying, the sex," she said. "The victims suffered multiple sexual assault."

"And multiple cuts," added Lanark. "I don't think it just evolved overnight. I think it's come about slowly to the point of murder."

"The *MS* sign, the insignia, a club code, a badge," Shannon reasoned.

"Very likely."

"But why do a blood test on me, on a cop, with the idea of including me in their cult?"

"Why do you think Burton was murdered? He'd compounded one stupid mistake with another by first inviting *me* in the door, and secondly taking you up to the testing room."

"I remember telling him I was just a girlfriend when he asked if I were a cop like you."

"Got careless. Maybe he'd swallowed one pill too many."

"If this is all true," said Ames, "you've got to raid that place, tonight."

"Likely chance, getting a warrant to raid a prominent family's house like that on such short notice," replied Lanark. "Not without probable cause."

"What the hell do you call this tape?"

"Most judges I know would call it bull, toss us out. Give it to us, and we'll make it work for us, in connection with everything else we've got."

Ames popped the tape from the recorder. "It's yours. Stop these madmen before they strike again."

"Thanks for your help, Richard."

"Yes," agreed Shannon, "that goes double for me, Doctor."

"I just ask one favor in return, Lieutenant Lanark," said Ames, his eyes nearly dilating with the thought in his mind.

"Whatever you want, Doc."

"When you apprehend these people, I would dearly love to talk to them."

"You would."

"Is that a yes?"

"Promise, if at all possible. But first we have to arrest them."

"What're we going to do now, Ryne," Shannon asked as they were leaving the 26th Precinct, passing the squadroom.

"We go after their friends, relatives if they've got any, turn up the heat on people around them, throw a scare into them."

"Like with Sorentino, you mean."

266

"Exactly. Standard procedure."

"Standard procedure got a lot of people hurt, on both sides, and Sorentino's lousy lawyer's gonna get him fifteen with parole."

He stopped in his tracks. "You got any other ideas?"

"According to stakeout they're not at the house now. They've gone on some sort of trip, right? I say we get inside, get some physical evidence to link them with the corpses—some of the blood in that freezer's likely to be Burton's, or the Paige girl, or the Pullman girl, or—"

"My thoughts exactly, but if we go inside without a D.A.'s warrant or some comparable paper, Shannon, and even if we did find blood that Sybil Shanley could match to any one of the victims it would be automatically ruled out of order and thrown out of a court of law as evidence gained through illegal search and seizure. You understand that, don't you?"

"Standard operating procedure."

"So many goddamned laws tying our hands nowadays we have to carry the Illinois Criminal Code book in the trunk of the car."

"You'd think a match-up on blood from the murdered girls—"

"It's not the blood or the facts that count; it's how you *obtain* them."

"We've got to get that evidence somehow."

"Maybe the unit can come up with a solution. Suppose the pool man burglarizes the place and we arrest the pool man with the goods in his hands, and the goods just happen to be frozen blood plasma? Why would a burglar bother with such a thing? Got to really think this through."

Fabia suddenly stepped in front of them with a rolled up newspaper and slapped it into Lanark's hands. "Seen the papers, lately?"

Fabia moved away with a smirk on his tight face. Ryne and Shannon studied the photo and caption on the front page below a headline that read: *Heat Flares Up Over Upscale Murder Probe Direction.* Lanark's picture was awful, his face displaying a bloody rage at his "fellow officer" who disagreed with the direction the investigation was taking. The paper briefly touched on how the city police department had changed horses in mid-stream, taking Fabia and his boss off the case and placing Lanark's people on it. In a nutshell, it said the Chicago Police Department had gotten nowhere and the case had ground to a halt. Then it added the little touch of speculation about why the last body was dumped on Lanark's doorstep. It ended with a nod to Inspector Albert Riordan who had to step off the case due to failing illness, but said nothing about what that illness was.

"Bunch of crap," Lanark said, going in search of Riordan and learning from a sergeant who recognized Lanark from his duty in the 24th that Riordan was indeed ill and in hospital.

Lanark was taken aback by this. "How long's he been in?"

The sergeant whom Lanark called Corky, short for McCorkle, said glumly, "A week now. Don't sound good, Lieutenant."

Shannon did the same calculation in her head as Ryne, and decided Fabia's greasy moves of the past few days had been his own concoction.

"What's he got, Corky?"

"Nobody wants to say."

"What does everybody think?"

"The bad one, Lanark."

"Cancer?"

"AIDS."

"That's . . . that's . . ." it was too coincidental for Lanark's liking. "Sudden, isn't it?" He knew the question was stupid, but he was scratching for words.

"Lanark, word around here has him getting the disease because someone wanted him to get it. He ain't no fag, you know, and he hasn't had a transfusion, and he hasn't got a habit . . . so? I mean, the whole department's shook up about it."

"What about Morris Fabia, he shook up?"

"Was at first, you know Fabia," Corky said. "He's up for promotion, and if Riordan don't come back . . . who knows?"

"Then Fabia's running his unit."

"Right."

Lanark exchanged a look with Shannon. "Guy's really broken up about his partner. Wonder when was the last time he went to visit him in the hospital?"

"You see Al today, give him my best regards, will you, Lieutenant?" asked Corky, going back to his duties.

"Where's he at, Corky?" asked Lanark.

"Casements Institute, on Devon."

"I'll tell him you send your best."

"We're all pulling for him."

"What're you thinking, Ryne? Ryne?" Shannon asked, following him out to the unit. He turned at the car and leaned over the top, shaking his head.

"Don't know. Damned Fabia. Any other cop you

269

could talk to. I want to talk to Riordan. You can come with me, or I'll drop you at the station."

"What is it you want from Riordan?"

"See if he has any clues as to how he contracted the disease. It occurs to me that if the killers can supply themselves with AIDS-free blood, then they can also do the reverse, stock up on the deadly stuff."

"The additional blood, used to smear the victim's wounds, you don't suppose—"

"I suppose, yes, and if that's so, every precaution needs be taken with the victims."

As they drove for the Casements Institute, a clinic that specialized in AIDS-related cases, Ryne got on the radio and asked to be put through to the Division of Criminalistics where Sybil Shanley worked. Getting her on line, he told her of his suspicions.

"We reported this to Riordan's man, Fabia, some time ago. I thought you knew. It was in the report."

"Not the reports we got."

"Damn, that's dangerous."

"Riordan's got it, you know."

"The report?"

"No, the godawful disease," he told her.

Sybil's gasp was audible through the phone. "Oh, no, that's . . . awful. A lab assistant's come down with it, too."

"Dr. Shanley," said Shannon, taking the radio from Lanark, "this is Detective Keyes, Lanark's partner."

"Yes, I've heard you two are getting on well."

She wondered what the doctor had heard. "In all the cases, was the smeared blood on the wounds, was it disease-ridden?"

"Yes, but we didn't test for it until we suspected,

270

when Riordan suspected, actually. It was his notion to check for it. We'd run blood tests, naturally, for makeup in case we might make a match if a suspect were ever found, you know, type and Rh factor, but we don't routinely check for diseases in the blood unless we suspect it as a cause of death, and this blood—well, it wasn't even the victims' now, was it?''

"Understood, then Riordan, or anyone touching the body of a victim, could conceivably have contracted the disease through contact with the blood?''

"Possible, not probable, but then it would depend on how soon after the blood was touched from the point before complete coagulation."

Shannon thought of the white-skinned woman in the cold room licking at her bloody fingers, and it made her shiver.

Lanark said glumly, "Riordan hasn't looked good since that night in Lincoln Park."

As they drove on through the bustling Chicago traffic, past neon lights that littered their way along an avenue of fast food places, signs heralding nude dancers, a strip of bars and discos, Shannon reached a hand across to his, leaving it to rest there. Lanark felt a twinge in her hand turn into a tremble.

"You okay, Shannon?" he asked after a moment.

"Ever get scared, Lanark, I mean deep inside?"

9"Sure, sure . . . we all do."

"Not you. I haven't ever seen you really afraid."

He shook his head. "You don't know what you're talking about."

"I think I do. You invite danger, court it. I'm afraid for myself and for you, because you don't seem to know enough to be afraid."

271

"You are wrong, on all counts."

"Am I? Something makes you reckless, what is it?"

"I'm paid to be reckless. Every cop is. As far as fear, when it comes in waves so high they threaten to drown you, you've got to ride it out."

"Something about this case is real creepy."

They arrived at the Casements Institute, pulling into a no-parking zone and going for the door. A uniformed guard there halted them, telling them they'd have to move the car. But Lanark pushed past him while Shannon flashed her badge and announced that they were on police business.

"I hate the smell of hospitals," Lanark told her with a sneer, going for the desk and asking after Albert Riordan.

Albert Riordan had gone down fast and what they found at the Casements was a shell of the large man, emaciated, his skin gone slack and ashen-colored, losing weight daily, his face caved in at the cheeks, deep wells where his eyes had been. Lanark found it hard to look him in the face, but he seemed cheered by Ryne's visit, a weak smile turning into a larger one on their entry.

"Detective Lanark and partner," he muttered through a thick throat, the voice not Riordan's. For Lanark, it was like seeing an alien takeover of the man's body going not so well. "What brings you to see the leper? News on our . . . case?"

"Riordan, I'm sorry . . . for this, for the way this worked out . . . I mean."

"Bloody stupid way for me to go out, huh? Get my

note pad there on the table. Some ideas on the case I'd like you to have. Didn't know what to do with my mind, you know, all this time, been worrying over the case. You wouldn't care to locate my service revolver, put it at the bedside, would you? No, didn't think so . . . Morris'll be only too glad to oblige, forget I asked."

"We just learned this morning," said Shannon.

"I figure I got it from the body," he said matter-of-factly. "Son-of-a-bitch set me up like a chump."

"Stone, you mean?"

"Who else? The bodies were ticking away like bombs just waiting to go off. Bastard's spreading AIDS while his whacked-out mother's spreading the gospel. Make sense to anyone but me?"

"Any chance you'll beat this thing, Al?"

"Only hope I'll live to see Stone get his." The breathing was labored. "Got pneumonia. Felt it come on on stakeout. Came in for a routine check and next thing I know . . .'

Ryne told him that Fabia had pulled the coroner's report dealing with the AIDS-infested blood. Riordan's eyes went wide with anger.

"Fabia's been acting strange lately, stranger than usual. He and that guy you used to work with have become very chummy, too, what's his name, Skully."

"Skully, right."

"I know Fabia's not lost any sleep or tears over me. I also know he has his eye on moving up in the department, always has had more than his share of ambition."

Ryne told him briefly of the newspaper account, and how Fabia had had him under surveillance.

273

"A royal asshole, Lanark, or is there something more to it than meets the eye?" Riordan, even facing imminent death, was still questioning human motive, still a detective, unshockable when it came to the nature of the beast, man. "If I were in your place, I'd watch him and maybe Skully, too, put a bird on their trails."

"But that's absurd," said Shannon. "What would we gain? I don't follow you, Detective Riordan."

"Sweetheart, you stay in police work much longer and you're not going to be sweet any more than the rest of us, right, Lanark?" He coughed when he tried to laugh. "Trust me, Lanark, tail the bastards, see what it nets you."

"I'll put some eyes out."

"Cautiously."

"You got any other advice?"

"Advice from a dead man is what you want?"

"Advice from a good cop."

"Don't overlook the conspiracy angle here, kid, and don't take any free drinks from anybody."

"Conspiracy?"

"I got stonewalled when I requested a warrant to search the Stone place, night before you entered the picture. Was told a warrant was being taken under advisement. D.A. was no help. We didn't have much, just the scared word of the one kid—"

"Burton, and he winds up dead."

"Anyway, here we are, waiting for a warrant, then you muck up the play, and the next day the Commissioner's on my captain's ass about the whole affair, looking into allegations I was doing a shit job of it, talking to Fabia who thought he saw his chance to crawl up over my backside, when suddenly the decision comes down that we open up the case to the 13th. Your Captain Wood had put in a request to have the god-damned 13th involved. It was an addendum to a request he'd made a few months before for setting up a complete Decoy Unit to work out of your precinct. He requested you head the department. Someone on high jumped at the chance to remove me from the case. That line Wood was fed, about you're looking like the fair-haired boy was cooked up by the Commissioner.

"Smells all right, when you put it like that."

"You ever hear of a case being so quickly turned in mid-stream, damn it? Newspapers right about that one. Something smells, all right."

"Stone has more influence than I gave him credit for, if this is true. But where does Fabia fit in, and Skully of all people?"

"Neilson told me a week ago how it went down at the park that night, between you and Skully, I mean . . . conscience was bothering the kid. I must've been blind. Now Morris Fabia's got Skully doing his leg-work for him."

"Thanks, Riordan, thanks for it all. We've got to go, but thanks for the information."

"Just one favor, Lanark."

"Anything, name it."

"Next time you come visiting, come with the news you got the bastards nailed . . . *before* I die."

Lanark exchanged a look with Shannon, grit his teeth and nodded. "Will do, Al . . . count on it."

"Not much else I *can* count on."

Lanark walked briskly away from Riordan's death room, taking the length of the hallway as if it were a dungeon in a labyrinth, Shannon rushing after to keep up.

"Hey, remember the man's deathly ill, Cowboy, and what he says could be colored by his emotional—"

Lanark lifted the note pad with Riordan's thoughts jotted down to her eyes. "He's a good detective, has good instincts."

"All I'm saying is that a bit of cautious salt taken with what the man said back there is in order. I mean, you don't suspect Paul Wood had anything to do with—"

"I don't know what to believe anymore. But this information, Shannon, stays between you and me for the time being, understood?"

"What about the other unit members?"

"No, no one else. That way we control it, and if there is some sort of cover-up or conspiracy going on, we won't show our hand too soon, understood?"

"Understood, but who's going to tail Fabia and this guy, Skully?"

"We'll watch them ourselves."

"They'll spot us."

"Not if we disguise ourselves."

"Things are getting complicated."

"Yeah, so I noticed, but that's what happens when a conspiracy's involved. Circles within circles.

In the car, heading back for the 13th, Shannon began musing aloud. "What have we got, Lanark? We've got four bodies—"

"A fifth, if you count Riordan."

"Four," she persisted, "a woman who preaches holiness but has a freezer full of freeze-dried blood, a son who sells sex during blood drives from a clinic in his mansion, a judge stalling on issuing a warrant to Riordan to raid the place, two cops in Riordan's precinct who may or may not be looking the other way for some sort of payoff—"

"Sex, money," said Lanark, "either way for Skully."

"Maybe Fabia's payoff is bigger, like being bumped up, placed in control of your old precinct?"

"Riordan would've been in line for it, Captain Thompson retiring soon. Could be."

"And the commissioner?"

"Given a nudge by the judge?"

"Maybe."

"Maybe a frame in the works, too, all that garbage being tossed around like yesterday's salad about me being on the scene at all the Glove murders, like I was some kind of goddamned vulture come back to see my own handiwork. That trash about me hacking up Burton and dumping him at the 13th, just so I could make a big-name case for myself by setting up some poor slob, planting evidence on him."

"Fabia's got that much hate for you?"

"Fabia's that much of a prick, yeah."

"And this guy, Skully?"

"We get him somewhere quiet, maybe we can beat a confession out of him. I'm going to watch him personally."

"Yeah, but if he's watching you—"

"All the better. I'll just give him enough rope and yank him in. All in good time."

The radio crackled into life and a masked voice came over, speaking directly to them. *"You want to live a long life or die like Riordan? Back off the Stones, or you'll die slow and painful.''* Then the voice was gone.

"Who the hell was that, Skully, Fabia?" She got on the radio, calling Dispatch, asking if they could identify the source of that latest communication.

"What communication?" asked Dispatch.

She said, "Had to be Fabia, in a car nearby."

"Now you're willing to believe Riordan? No, I don't think it was Fabia, or Skully's voice. No, I don't think so. Didn't sound familiar."

"This is getting scary, Lanark."

"Sergeant Mark Robeson, for you, Lieutenant Lanark," said Samantha Curtis into the phone from just across the small room. Most people would have shouted, Lanark thought, but Sam never raised her voice. They were the only two remaining in the squad-room.

Robeson came on as Lanark glanced at his watch. Five-twenty in the early evening. "Got a lead on a van used by Stone's people, or so this guy tells me."

"You're remarkable, Mark! How'd you do it?"

"Followed your suggestion. Started canvassing from the mansion around. Came up with this body shop on Green Bay Road, not far from Ravinia Park . . . saw Lou Rawls perform there once, what a gas."

"Give me the address, I'll be right there."

"No van here now, man, what's the point."

"Already altered?"

"It's white now with a religious look."

"Religious look?"

"Guy wanted an enormous angel ascending skyward

out of smoke or something, shouldn't be hard to spot. Place here is called *Star Trux,* into galaxy and star stuff for your van. Place is also a gas station and Stone's got an account here. He owns an entire fleet of cars, vans, you name it. Anyway, I'm willing to bet he's retired this one from service, along with the tires.''

"The tires? You shittin' me? You got the tires?''

"In a manner of speaking.''

"Incredible . . . if they match the tire casts made by Riordan's investigative team, we've got strong physical evidence to link the bastard to the killings.'' Ryne had read of cases where the tire treads of a given vehicle were matched to such a cast, but he personally had never been involved in a case cracked in this manner. Over twelve match-points, minor and major characteristic flaws, pebble marks and distinctive wear marks had to be ID for a positive match. With all four tires, they *had* the guy. He just knew it. The excitement was almost too much to contain.

"That'd do it, all right. Only one problem.'' The calm statement from Robeson brought him down.

Lanark said, *"What* problem?''

"You ever hear of locating a needle in a haystack?''

"Mark!''

"I'm looking at a mountain of tires, maybe eight or—how much?'' he asked someone there with him suddenly. "Guy says it's more like fifteen hundred! Shitload of rubber, man. Owner says I can dig through them all I like, but he's got no idea which ones come off which cars, Ryne, so?''

"Mark, I'll get you some help. You've got some idea what you're looking for, I mean the guy's got records, bills of sale on the tires he sold, most likely the same size and number. Start there."

"Tonight?"

"Mark, they get wind of us snooping they'll torch the place and the tires'll go up in smoke."

"Right . . . okay, but you get me lots of help. Get me some men I can work with."

"Not to worry. The address."

Robeson gave him the street address. Lanark called Captain Wood for additional manpower, pointing out the importance of the find which so far was not exactly a find.

"I can't spare any more men for you, Lanark, as much as I'd like to do so," began Wood.

"But, Captain, this could nail the sonofabitchin' Glove to the wall! Those treads—"

Wood cut him off immediately. "*Especially* since there are *two* investigative teams working on this case as it is. Have you considered working out your differences with Riordan and Fabia, and asking them for help?"

"Sir, I believe someone on Riordan's team is *unsafe.*"

"Unsafe? Unsafe, like you mean can't be trusted? Lanark, do you honestly think you're the only cop in the city who'd like to nail this killer?" Wood sounded tired, unfriendly tired.

"No, sir, but there are stories floating around, makes me nervous, like somebody over at the 26th hasn't got his mouth screwed on right, and—"

"I've heard some of those *stories,* Lanark, and it's just sour grapes over what's happened, our being brought in, but I think Riordan's on the level. I know he can't control what his men say over a bar."

"I wish I could share your—"

"Work it out with them over there, Lanark, or get the job done with the men you've got! Hell, I have bled off as much as I can for the Decoy Unit. You're just going to have to live within budgetary means, Lieutenant."

"Thanks . . ."

"Understood?"

"Yes, sir."

"You don't like it, Lanark, better get used to it, we've all got constraints put on us. Part of being in command."

"Yes, sir."

He hung up and pounded a fist on the desk, making pencils jump and papers fly. Samantha Curtis gave him a look of such disapproval it reminded him of a fifth grade teacher with whom he was forever in trouble. "Call up my entire team, Samantha."

"But sir, some of them just left for—"

"Now!" he shouted, beginning to pace. "Inform them to meet me at this address as soon as possible."

"Yes, sir." She studied the note handed her.

"And thanks for staying over shift."

"Not at all, sir."

That night the Decoy Unit, dressed in their dirtiest clothes, found over forty tires that could have come from the van. Each one would have to be cross-checked with the casts which would have to be scheduled with the forensics. A match would tell them, and anyone looking at the evidence, that a van brought into this establishment, had come bearing the same tires as the van which had been identified by several people now as having been black. Records of the truck art shop and service station indicated that Stone had had a black truck which now was white with an enormous religious mural now affixed to it, and that these tires came off this same truck. Circumstantial to a point, since the exact tires were not still on the suspect vehicle, but strong circumstantial evidence nonetheless. Lanark believed that enough circumstantial evidence would ultimately hang Matthew Stone. The night had been well worth the effort, if forensics came through.

How long would that take, however? The dusk-til-dawn tire-stack search was simple compared to the difficulty of a microscopic search required now by the forensics, a search complicated by the fact some forty tires were suspect.

TWELVE

Captain Paul L. Wood saw to arrangements for Blum to have burial with full departmental honors. Everyone at the 13th kicked in for a special pension above and beyond. It seemed a pitiful gesture like laying a wreath of flowers over a coffin, useless in the end, but the money would go to help defray costs to his wife and children. His aged parents were crippled by the catastrophe, hunched over one another like two broken spirits, weeping. For the Decoy Unit, it was the first casualty. The thought on everyone's mind was a simple one. Who would go next in the war on crime?

The funeral was difficult for every member of the unit, but Max, above all, had a rough time. He and Jeff had been partnered for three years. He told Shannon it was like losing an arm.

Before the funeral was over, Sorentino's slick lawyer was screaming foul in the wiretapping of his client's phone, and trying to tell the judge the tape made at *Armand's* was entrapment and inadmissible as evidence. Failing any headway with the court, the lawyer was trying desperately to cut a deal with the D.A. and the FBI. He claimed his client had incriminating evidence against an entire drug ring, a ring that would make his operation look like a garage sale by comparison. Lanark had gone to Wood to block any such deals, and Wood assured him no such thing was going to happen, but the wires were burning for days between the precinct and Wood's superiors. Ryne wasn't so sure Wood could hold out against the D.A., the FBI and his own boss, Calvin Dewey, City Commissioner of Police. More and more, it was appearing shaky, shakier, shakiest.

Then Lanark got the word through a disgruntled Paul Wood who was throwing things about his office as he told Lanark the news. "They're sleeping with the bastard. Creep kills a cop, and they're getting into bed with him."

"Bastards," said Lanark through clenched teeth. "For what? What's he looking at, ten, five with good behavior? Damn!"

"He's looking to walk."

"What? That's . . . that's nuts, crazy! We've got him on murder—"

"Accessory to—"

"—bullshit, murder, and . . . and child molestation and—"

"I know all that, Lieutenant, damn it, I hate this as much as you!"

"What am I supposed to tell my unit?"

His eyes fell. "I'll speak to them."

"What do you tell Blum's wife and kid? His parents, Captain?"

"It's fuckin' out of my hands, Lanark."

284

"This sucks, Captain, and you know it."

"Feds suck," he agreed. "Know what they say? Want to hear the reasoning, Lanark? The bullshit I have to listen to? The crap the Commissioner swallows? They say now we got the man a long rap sheet, next bust, he's a goner. Said we could pick him up the day after—if and when we have another—"

"That's crap, all a pile of rotten—"

"That's what I've told the D.A. and—"

"D.A. told us we didn't have a case! Now we got a case!"

"Not anymore . . . Lanark, not anymore. This guy Encinado's big time and they want him bad, bad enough to put the screws on the State house, the Mayor's Office, and finally to us."

Lanark grit his teeth, paced, wanted to pound a door with his fist. "Stuck us good, didn't they."

"Sorentino's tricky, and his lawyer's grease."

"Maybe Sorentino won't think it's so lucky when he takes one through the head."

Wood came around his desk and stared hard into Ryne's eyes. "I didn't hear that, Lieutenant. Now, back on duty. You've still got other cases waiting."

"Yes, sir, but if you don't mind, sir, I would like to inform my people of this action."

"Full immunity, if the Feds go for it," was all Wood said, feeling cut from the misfit Decoy Unit by Lanark's decision to inform "his" people himself. As captain of the precinct, he still represented what most of them distrusted, and how rightly so to do so when such things as this happened.

* * *

285

"Times like this," Lanark began his explanation of how the Sorentino affair was progressing—or *regressing,* as Shannon had put it, "times like this, I hate being a cop."

The others took the news with quiet equanamity, all but Robeson who looked and sounded like a piston about to explode, "Man, I don't believe this!"

Max took it all *too* quietly, Shannon thought.

"They haven't cut a deal yet, and I can't see them giving the guy complete immunity, no way," she said.

"You're naive, then," said Wil, with Myra frowning in sad agreement.

Lanark told her they'd all seen it happen before. "Not with a guy as dirty as this, but it's quite within the realm of possibilities, believe me."

"Nothing we can say or do to stop it?" she asked.

"I've voiced my objections to Wood," said Lanark, "yours as well. I've objected on behalf of Blum's wife, his kids, his parents. Wood's objected right along to those above him, and no doubt will go on record as objecting. But I've got a bad feeling about this one, and the more info I've managed to dredge up, the stronger the bad feeling that this creep's going to be back on the street within a few weeks."

"What do you know about this . . . *deal?*" asked Max.

"For some guy named Encinado. Sorentino turns state's witness against a long-time gangster by the name of Hector Encinado, a man the FBI wants badly for his part in a growing Colombian drug ring working through Miami. They're saying it makes our bust look like a garage sale violation by comparison. D.A.'s still not talking. Riding the fence."

Max snarled under his breath, saying something in Japanese that was an obvious curse.

"We can only hope for the best," said Shannon after a silence.

Headquarters for the Decoy Unit thrummed with the sound of nearby machinery. Lanark called their attention to another matter, the slasher case.

"We got a report from the PATRIC matchup computer system in D.C. with a crime very similar to our uptown deaths here. Happened a few days ago in L.A. Similar superficial marks to the face and body, blood drained from the corpse, gloves in orifices, nothing about needle or catheter marks to the kidney region in the back, victim drugged to the hilt, however.

"We took this information and placed it beside the itinerary of Sylvia Stone, the evangelist we've spoken of. She was in L.A. during this time period, preaching at the Temple of the Holy City, a guest of the Western Ministry of God. Her son, Matthew Stone, traveled with her. They used a private jet. Stakeout—Robeson and Max—say crates were boarded with them."

"Are they in L.A. now?" asked Myra.

"Yes, and will be for a few more hours."

"Ideal conditions for getting into the Stone mansion," suggested Wil.

"An attempt to secure a court order to that end has met with opposition. Seems the judge knows the Stones personally and is violently opposed."

"Great, the old boy network sets in and they're very likely to already know we're interested in a search," said Mark Robeson.

"We've sent our request directly to the D.A."

"That asshole?"

"He's got people barking up his behind for some kind of break in this case as well."

"How soon before we get the papers?" asked Mark.

"Not soon enough, unfortunately. Both mother and son are due back—"

"Damn, damn," interrupted Mark, expressing everyone's frustration.

"But what's to stop us from getting Lenny the Lifter to do a little work for us?" asked Wil suddenly. "He's in holding now. We get him kicked for a small favor, say check out Shannon's secret room."

"For one thing, Wil, it's against the law," said Myra.

Lanark laughed lightly. "Against the law, but a guy like Sorentino goes free."

"He's not free, yet," countered Shannon.

"Soon to be at your neighborhood theater then."

"I say we go with Lenny," agreed Mark Robeson. "Max, what do you say?"

"Sure."

"Take a vote."

"Hold on," said Lanark, "this isn't the polls, no damned democracy here. Anything goes wrong, the unit's busted. No, I'm in charge here, and I say there's going to be *no* vote."

Moans followed this, except for Shannon who smiled approvingly and said, "Now you're showing some leadership smarts."

"It's *my* decision," he said, "that *I* use Lenny, my idea, and if anything backfires, it's my ass."

"Ryne!" Now Shannon moaned.

* * *

They fully informed the thin, wiry Lenny Lomax of his "rights." He had the right to go in, take a few photos from a camera given him, place anything remotely like blood stains in focus, snap these, search for the medical room, photo the machines there and the freezer if he found one, and anything *inside* the freezer. He was informed of the fact they were investigating a series of homicides, from which he deduced the "Glove" was the target. He was warned not to lift anything for himself, or it was straight back to jail. If he followed directions, he would simply be re-arrested with the *stolen* camera in his possession, an ordinary Polaroid, and the series of pictures, all taken from the stone mansion, which the sly burglar was casing, *hightechwise*.

But just before Lenny went over the wall for the Stone house, Ryne told him that if he saw any packets of blood, or slides with blood smears on them, to lift these as well.

"Will do, Captain."

Lenny the Lifter, using all the tools of his trade, with the blessing of the cops, was good, but he felt there was something vital missing, something he'd gotten into the business for in the first place. It took him a long time to decide what that was. He decided as he defused the alarm system, without cutting the electrical current in the place. What was missing was the element of danger. Since the cops had put him up to it, and since they told him the place would be empty, the gig just held no interest for him whatsoever. Not that he liked being surprised by the homeowner, or collared by the cops, but knowing such risks had been neutralized took all the heart-thumping fun out of the theft.

He'd just do what they wanted and collect on his deal. Carefully now he cut out a pane of glass at one of the rear doors. He was told to make the break-in at least look legit, and that was no problem since Lanark had personally driven him to the whereabouts of his best tools.

For a cop, Lanark was strange, a difficult man to figure. He seemed to like Lenny, to take in every word he told him about his profession and why he'd gotten into it, and how it differed from ordinary B&E's, the messy, everyday neighborhood break and enter job. Lenny had learned his "craft" from one of the masters, Cornelius Grosclose, dead of a heart attack now. Lenny wondered if it were because of the man's profession, or because he just held so much in. Quietest, calmest, most unshakable man Lenny had ever known. Knew everything about breaking and entering.

The pane popped, Lenny reached in the door which opened on a sun room off the main room and a place large enough for American Bandstand. Personally, Lenny didn't like doing places quite so large. Too easy to get comfortable and careless with so much space to cover. He liked better to forage in a house like those say in Barrington Hills, sure they were upper crust but they weren't goddamned royalty. When you knocked over a house in a place like this, they threw the book at you.

He tried to recall his directions from Lanark. Locate an elevator off the main room. Take it up to a medical lab of some sort. Snap pictures of the elevator, the lab, and anything "out of the ordinary," he'd said.

He found a door which indeed opened on an elevator. Using his flashlight, he took it upward. The door opened on a lab. "Jeeze," he thought, "if they know what's here, why're they going to so much trouble?"

He snapped shots of the room, when his eyes fell on a cabinet filled with slides, literally hundreds of slides. He snapped a picture, tried to open the cabinet to bring some of the samples to Lanark, but nothing doing, the cabinet was locked. He put the camera down and went to work on the tiny lock with a hair-thick tool that eased its way into the small tumblers. Shortly, the cabinet came open with a click. He reached in and grabbed the first box of slides, seeing each labeled.

He saw that while the room was some sort of clinic, it was bare, no machinery to photograph as Lanark had requested. As for the freezer, it, too, was empty, not so much as a Morton's Dinner.

Except for the slides, Lenny would be returning empty-handed. To carry through on the plan he'd have to return with Lanark, back to the lock-up, but without anything marketable to trade with, he could see that much. He wondered if he dared chance a run for it, but he knew Lanark had the place surrounded.

Instead, he'd go quietly and resignedly back to where he had cut the electrical, and kindly rewire it for the servants, or whoever else might be asleep in the house of a hundred rooms.

He got into the elevator, realizing there was a noise coming from somewhere nearby, a thrumming noise, mechanical and steady, like a milker in a dairy, he thought. But there hadn't been anything like a machine in the clinic. Then he realized the elevator doors opened both ways.

He found a closed panel inside the elevator, popped it open and pressed a button that sent the second door back. His eyes went wide with what he saw. A clinic with machines, one running, a dude and a broad on a stainless steel table getting it on, completely in the buff. He snapped a quick picture and jammed the close button as the incredibly well-built jock raced at him, his mouth twisted in anger, the machine nearby going at a steady clip, *thrum-thrum-thrum*, the girl in some sort of euphoric coma it seemed, the tubes leading from her back were dark with blood!

Lenny bounced in the elevator car in a futile attempt to get it to go faster. Once he was at ground level, he raced from the door, certain his life was in danger. "Damned cops," he cursed. "Why? Why'd they set me up? Nobody was supposed to be inside but the servants. Maybe this freak is a servant?"

He forgot any niceties and raced for the door he'd come through, silently making his getaway, his heart pounding. No surprises, huh, he thought, racing full out, falling, dropping the file box of goddamned slides, shoveling and scooping up as many as he could, when he saw them coming from behind. Lights had come on in several rooms of the mansion. People were chasing him.

Somebody tackled him. Powerful weight held him down. A sudden stab of pain, an injection of some sort to his buttocks. They had him . . . damn, they had him.

"Police! Let 'em up!"

Through a haze, Lenny saw Shannon and Lanark straddled above him, guns pointed. "We got a call about a burglar in the area. Guess you kids did our work for us. Cuff him, Keyes."

"Yes, sir," said Shannon.

"What'd he make off with?"

Lanark recognized one of the tall, blond-headed men in underwear, some without even this, as one whom he had fought with at the party. He prayed the darkness would keep both he and Shannon from being recognized. Mark and Max, both wearing blue uniforms, came racing over the manicured lawn, tearing up sod, the siren roaring, the spotlight sending the more modest of the young people back indoors.

"We'll have to fill out a complete report if you wish to press charges," said Lanark.

"Damned right we want to—".

Another one said, "Drop it."

"We'd just like our stuff back, the stuff he took."

"Hey!" said Mark Robeson, suddenly, as he approached. "This guy's Lenny the Lifter, bigtime B & E man! He's wanted on every kind of charge downtown, Lieutenant."

"Can we have the camera and the other stuff he's taken, Officer?" asked the big blonde.

"Afraid not. This is evidence. We're taking this guy in, and whatever's in his possession.

"But—"

"Sorry, but we've got to. No choice, not with a guy like this. I mean, it's not like one of your buddies raked you off. This is Lenny Lomax," said Lanark. "We'll need your name, Mr. ahhhh—for the report—so you can get these items back, after this scum has been booked and put away."

"Ahhhh, Jerry . . . Jerry Mazure."

293

"Okay, good, Mr. Mazure," Lanark said, writing the name on the official document. "We'll be in touch."

The dope made it impossible for Lenny to get up. "What'd you do to this guy?" Max asked. "What'd you hit him with?"

"Nothing."

"Bullshit, he's drugged. What'd you tag him with?"

"Just a knockout dose of straight alcohol, that's all."

"This guy dies, sonny, and we'll have to come back for you, for Murder One."

"What? He was stealing from the house."

"And you used a lethal weapon against an unarmed man. Better be right about that dose. You're sure it's alcohol? Or should we take this guy to a hospital quick?"

"Just alcohol."

"Booze, or rubbing alcohol?" asked Shannon.

"Pentobarbitol, lady, just booze."

"All right, take him and his treasure trove and put everything in back of the unit."

"How'd you guys get here so fast?" asked the big kid.

"Told you, we got a call about a prowler in the area. Then we heard the fracas here."

The kid watched dolefully as the camera and slides were taken into custody. Just outside the gate, with Lenny fast asleep, Lanark found the developed photos in the man's coat pocket. He was no great photographer, but the flash had illuminated enough to tell them that Shannon's "testimony" would now, most certainly, hold up in a court of law. In addition, they had the pornographic shot of Jerry Mazure and the girl who was hooked up to some sort of *machine*.

"How'd we do?" asked Shannon.

"What's this look like to you?"

"Weird. What're those snakey things."

Shannon was right. There were two lines stretching from the girl to some big machine nearby. They were in the act of love, or so it appeared, but what was really going on between the muscle-bound Jerry Mazure and the helpless young girl connected to the oven-sized machine by tubes?

"At the moment we need medical assistance for Lenny," he told her. "Then we'll puzzle this thing out."

"Perhaps someone at the hospital can tell us what kind of medical machine Stone's got in operation here."

"Possibly."

Shannon looked over her shoulder and down at the hapless face in the back seat. Lenny had reminded her of a character in an Elmore Leonard novel, just as if he'd stepped off the pages and into real life. She'd liked him, despite his profession, perhaps because his was much more of a victimless crime than that of anyone she'd dealt with since arriving at the 13th and joining the Decoy Unit. They'd transferred Lenny into Lanark's car when they had gotten clear of the mansion, Lanark telling the others it was a wrap for tonight, sending them all home.

"I know of a few people at Evanston Memorial who'll cut through red tape for me," said Lanark now. "We'll have Lenny on his feet by morning. Don't worry."

* * *

At Emergency, Lanark got straight through, as he'd promised, and in a matter of minutes a young doctor named Edward Dorfman took over. Dorfman was quick. Each step, each move a precision one. Hand and eye and brain were in tune as he looked over Lenny there in the ER room. Then he burst into commands for the nurse, setting Lenny up with a room off to one side.

Dorfman's small mustache bobbed when he spoke. "You have any idea at all what he was sedated with?"

"Pentobarbitol, straight," said Lanark. "That's what we were told."

"Depending on the dosage, he should be all right by eleven or so tomorrow. He's comfortable at the moment, no signs to indicate otherwise, just a very deep sleep. Barring any unforeseen complications, Detective Lanark, is it? He should be all right."

"Doctor?" began Shannon. "Would you be kind enough to do us one additional favor?"

"Of course, anything within reason. I've been up for forty hours." He wiped his eyes without removing his glasses, the thick lenses resting on the fingers' edge at his forehead, when Lanark noticed the ring on his pinky, a medical insignia with the letters *MS*.

"Yeah, yeah, Dr. Dorfman," said Lanark, grabbing his hand and pulling hard on it, turning the palm down and showing the ring to Shannon. "Maybe you can help us out. Maybe you can tell us something about Matthew Stone and his sex-for-blood club in Winnetka."

"What? Wait a minute, I . . . I'm not really a part of that scene, my—"

Lanark forced the doctor against the wall, choking him with his loosed tie. "Don't give us any shit, Dorfman, the ring means you're in, you are one of them, up to your eyeballs in conspiracy to commit murder."

"Murder? No, never! What murder?"

"The Glove, the Upscale Slasher, he's Stone and his inner circle."

"Not me, I swear! My roommate's Jerry Mazure's brother. Mazure's in thick with Stone, so's his brother, but I . . . I only went there once or twice, to party. Sure, I figured, why not . . . meet women, risk-free, for a donation of blood. That's all they asked of me. Hell, I give blood all the time, for nothing, so why not?"

"Take it easy, Dr. Dorfman. If that's true, then you can help us put an end to Stone before he kills again."

"I swear, I had no idea. I knew he was eccentric, even weird on certain subjects . . . but murder, I never . . ."

Lanark loosed his grip. "Did you know the Heron boy, Burton Eaton-Heron?"

"Only casually. I really didn't get on with the crowd there. I . . . I had to work my way through school. I just didn't fit in, and I'm married with a kid, in Tacoma, back home . . . just here to finish out my residency . . . and the . . . the bastards they had the room wired, cameras, you name it . . . had me hooked . . . still have me hooked, blackmail, for favors whenever they call, usually medical favors. Came in once with a girl with a perforated stomach wall out of nowhere.

297

Wanted her helped but didn't want any paper on it, you know.''

"Stone's a doctor himself, why'd he have to rely on you?''

"Stone's a quack, a bullshit artist, hardly a surgeon. Knows enough to be dangerous and that's about all.''

"So he's proved,'' said Lanark.

Shannon shoved the photos Lenny had taken between Lanark and Dorfman. "You can help your own case a great deal, Dr. Dorfman, by cooperating with us now. These photos were shot inside the Stone mansion. Will you identify the machinery in use here, particularly the machine attached to this young woman?'' She pulled the picture with Mazure clearly running a bizarre test on an unconscious young woman.

"Christ . . . yes, yes,'' said Dorfman.

Lanark let him go. Dorfman's index finger punched at the large machine in the photo that now lay on a small Formica table top. "This . . . this is an RBI-8000, older model.''

"Older model what?''

"Dialyzer.''

"Meaning?''

"Dialyzer machine, dialysis, for—''

"Purifying blood, isn't it?'' said Lanark.

"Yes, that's right.''

"My God,'' Shannon added. "We got would-be doctors playing God back there, Lanark.''

Lanark asked Dorfman, "Anybody ever likely to use this machine for anything other than purification of blood?''

"No, no, it's designed for one simple function, to purify blood in the event of kidney failure.''

"Autopsy on Burton showed no sign of illness before death, Doctor, so how do you figure—"

Dorfman began talking to himself, staring at the photo the entire time. "Archaic machine, really, method being used here, too, is gone out of practice. Notice the tubes to the back area, direct catheter to the kidney, quite painful after sedation wears off. Causes a lot of bruising . . . internal tissues are sensitive to the slightest touch, and this . . . well, it's brutal on . . . on internal walls . . . sometimes a perf happens, and you got instant contamination, you got troubles that could lead to death. Today's methods, hell, the whole thing's done with a single shunt to the arm, both outflow and in-flow, little irritation, nothing compared to puncturing the bowel."

"Do you have one of these machines in operation here?" asked Shannon, shaking him.

"Yes, of course."

"Show it to us."

They followed the stunned doctor to a room where a patient was hooked up to a dialysis machine which looked nothing like that in the picture. Dorfman was again in his element, explaining that dialysis is used extensively in studies of proteins and blood serums and in the diagnosis of blood diseases producing abnormalities of blood serum.

"Then it's used in diagnosing blood diseases?" asked Shannon.

"And the treatment of any poisonous condition."

"What about AIDS?" asked Lanark.

"No, you can't strain out a deficiency in the immune system through a blood analyzer and cleanser, no."

"Suppose you wanted to transfuse blood," said Shannon. "Would you give it a 'cleansing' through this thing first?"

"A novel idea, but the machine is not attached to every blood donor that comes into a hospital, no. A blood test is taken, and that is expensive enough. The machine's basic function is to purify that which the kidney no longer can."

"But supposing Stone has a phobia about unclean blood," suggested Lanark, "and he—or someone close to him—required a constant blood supply, transfusions, say a leukemia victim or even a . . . a—"

"Hemophiliac," said Dorfman, helping him along.

"Then would you recommend the machine in that picture?" Lanark held out the photo to him again.

"If I were selling medical equipment and some fool insisted on having one, for whatever reason—phobia or not—I'd take his money, wouldn't you?"

"How exactly does the damned thing work?" asked Lanark.

"Blood is siphoned out, run into an electrolysis bag, here," he pointed to the center of the machine. "Outside that bag is the dialysate—"

"The what?"

"Cleansing agent. A constant flow of blood passes on one side of this membrane, or bag, helped along by bombarding electrons. At the same time, on the other side of the membrane flows the cleansing agent. You can see the state of the art has greatly improved. This machine is faster, smoother, quieter. Why Stone is using stone-aged equipment, I don't understand, with his bucks."

"How exactly is the blood cleansed, the unwanted elements passed out?" Lanark asked.

"The dialysate attracts the waste products through the semi-permeable membrane. A liquid can't flow through, but will diffuse through slowly if there is liquid on the other side. Ever hear of osmosis?"

"All right, if this thing's anything like my fish aquarium at home," said Lanark, "then all kinds of modifications could be done at any point along the system of filtration, right?"

Dorfman nodded, "I suppose."

"An added tube spliced in anywhere along the passage line of blood, a bypass, to siphon off the now cleansed supply, take a pint here, a pint there, right?"

"Jesus, sure, but—"

"And if the operator so chooses, couldn't he simply siphon off all of the 'patient's' blood this way, by diversion, or simply pulling the plug on the return tube?"

"That'd be murder."

"That much we know."

"How *long*, Doctor?" asked Shannon. "How long does the procedure take on the old machine?"

"You thinking what I'm thinking?" Lanark asked Shannon.

"I'm afraid so."

"This girl in the picture could become our next victim, and that's probable cause."

"We raid the place, tonight?"

"We've got to call the unit together, and get backup."

"People," said the resident doctor.

"Right away," shouted Shannon as they rushed for the exit.

301

"People! Don't you want to hear about peritoneal dialysis?

"We'll be back for you, Doctor, later!" shouted Shannon over her shoulder.

"You're going to Stone's?" he asked as they raced out.

THIRTEEN

Lanark drove with mad abandon to get back to the Stone mansion as Shannon got on the radio, reporting in, asking for backup. At first the radio was filled with static, a reflection of the night sky which was now intermittently lit with a thunderbolt streaking corkscrew fashion amid the clouds. Yet there was no rain; only the hot, dry oven of this night.

"Unit 31, 31!" shouted Shannon into the static. "Call for backup, backup request, immediately." More static, and she repeated the message, adding, "Code-4, civilian in jeopardy, officers need assistance—" static was breaking up now as Shannon gave their location at Stone's address.

A dispatcher came on through the continuing static which abruptly lifted. "Have your location, 31," said the male voice at the other end, "assistance on the way, more information requested on suspect."

It was a standard dispatcher's question and Shannon described Jerry Mazure as they neared the Stone mansion.

"There's Stone, it's him and his mother!" said Lanark, shutting down his lights and pulling the car off the road, amid bushes and the wall, fifty or sixty feet before the gates. He was pointing ahead of them and Shannon looked up to see a light blue van with a milky white cloud picture along its side, out of which rose an ethereal, angelic presence. In the distance, the angel looked to be moving, rising on air currents, with the movement of the van.

"Bring the car round when I signal," said Lanark, getting out and fishing beneath his seat for something.

"Where—" but he was gone, racing toward the gate, something dangling in his right hand. He skipped amid the brush, edged along the wall, past shrubbery toward the gate.

Alone in the car, watching Lanark out there, her heart seemed to beat so loudly it was coming through her chest. On their drive back she noticed how many yacht clubs, golf courses and private beaches abounded here, how much these people had, and yet nothing was enough. She wondered what was becoming of the young, the new generation begging to be shocked, stunned, hurt. Was that the only way they could *feel* anything anymore? Was that the sick reasoning behind getting oneself ensnared by drugs and the likes of Stone?

Like Dr. Dorfman, just looking for a kick, a high, and all they needed was to take a blood test, then it was put up a pint, and finally, at least for some, it was put it all up.

Why'd they kill the three girls? she wondered. Did they want out? Did they know too much? Had they simply offended Stone, like Burton? And Stone's hypocritical mother, preaching her gospel against AIDS and disease-spreading practices wherever she went, victims of her son in her wake, as in L.A., and God knows where else. She was a kind of vampire after all, and him, finding some ghoulish gratification in making a mockery of his mother's gospel, maybe only a doctor like Richard Ames could explain that kind of behavior, maybe not even Ames was capable of explaining it.

"Christ," she said to herself, realizing anew that Stone's company had blood-testing clinics all over the States and overseas.

The limousine ahead of the white-blue van opened the gates automatically.

The gate opened from the center, each end retreating away from the other. Once the van had passed through, the gates on either side would move in toward one another and once met, would electronically bolt together at several junctures. Before this could happen, Lanark meant to stop it.

The van and limo ahead of them went through, and Lanark began a race with the gate. The noise of the gate sounded like a low-rumbling train in the far distance. It rolled on thick rubber wheels, robotically. It was returning now with speed born of a mechanical one-mindedness. Shannon saw that Lanark must lose the unfair race. There simply was no way he could get to it in time. But now she saw him throw a tire iron he'd grabbed from beneath his seat and it landed in the path of the two gates which suddenly and silently stopped and then reversed themselves, parting. Amazingly, like a garage door, the gate was sensitive to anything it closed down on. Then came Lanark's signal for her to bring the car through.

"We'll leave it for the backup."

"Neat trick," she said, picking him up and driving through, "smart move."

"Thank God it worked." He was panting. "We'll leave the iron here."

"They'll know we've gotten in."

"It'll keep them busy. Pull off to the side anywhere along here, there."

She pulled the car into some trees, the lights still out. Up at the mansion, Stone and the returning members of his group were just going inside. The disturbance of earlier hadn't quite died down, and lights were on all over the place, including where Lenny had entered the house, some men working on nailing shut the glass doors.

"What now?" she asked, taking a flashlight from the dashboard.

"We need to get upstairs to this hidden room, locate this girl before she's dead."

"How?" she wondered aloud.

"There," he said, pointing at a trellis that led up to a second-story balustrade, vines snaking their way in and out and up the old-style metal trellis-work. He started up first, helping her over the top. Once on the balcony, they went toward a pair of glass doors, behind them the quiet lull of Lake Michigan's waters lapping to shore. The doors were covered in thick, downy drapes on the inside, almost black by night, likely a burgundy by day. The door was locked.

"I hope they haven't had time to restore the alarm system," he whispered. "Here goes."

With the handle of his service revolver, Ryne Lanark broke the glass pane at the handle to the balustrade door. Reaching through, the heavy garment feel of the incredibly plush draperies like a bear pushing back, he cut himself on the glass when he involuntarily recoiled.

"Damn," he whispered, managing to get the door open nonetheless.

"You all right?"

"I'm fine."

Then they heard the mechanical drone from deep within, a *thrum-thrum-thrum,* constantly beating like an overloaded washing machine. The sound hung in the air like a groaning giant. Intermingled with this eerie sound were smaller, squeaking and moaning sounds.

"What's taking backup so long?" she whispered in his ear. "Something's not right."

"You go back, call again if you like . . . I'm going in."

"No way you're going in alone."

"Do as I say."

"We're in this together, Ryne."

He took a deep breath and nodded. "Come on, then."

He took the flashlight from her. They'd not dared to turn it on until this point, and Lanark was still unsure about how wise it would be to flick it on now. The place was pitch black, however, and he stumbled on something before he got a foot into the room. Shannon crashed into him when he came to a standstill. For a moment he felt like a cast member in a Keystone Cops silent.

Thrum-thrum-thrum, thrum-thrum-thrum, the unrelenting noise beckoned just beyond. Closer at hand they heard human sounds. Moaning, snoring, murmurs, whispers.

307

"This place smells," she said.

Lanark recognized most of the odors as human. Amid the smell of perspiration there was the strong, musk odor emitted by women during heated sex, and he also picked up the sure scent of semen.

"Careful of your step," he whispered to Shannon.

"Which way?" she returned the whisper.

"Trying to find the light. This way." He held the beam straight out and almost tripped over something bulky in his way. He regained control of himself and pointed the beam downward. The light sliced across several nude bodies, men and women, along with floor pillows, oversized comforters and mats. Sleeping like contented crocodiles, some writhing with their lurid dreams, stoned beyond caring whether or not someone of Lanark's weight was stepping on them, were Stone's invited guests.

Shannon gasped at the snakepit-like atmosphere of the place. Above the sound of sleep here could be heard the dull mechanical beat, a sound that seemed to have been designed to lull them all to bed like so many children.

These were the people Stone could take full advantage of, those who invited the Matthew Stones of the world to take and take again, to drink his fill of their bodily fluids and cast away what remained.

They moved onward, closer to the thrumming noise, the light casting an eerie laser through the blackened room, scanning the wall for any sign of a knob, a button, a lever, anything to open the next door in this maze designed by a madman.

"There," said Shannon, seeing the closed door like that of an elevator. The light fell on a circular button beside this. They made their way past sleeping figures to get to it. Standing now before the door, looking into one another's eyes, he asked her if she were ready.

"Maybe we should wait for backup."

"It may be too late for the girl."

She nodded, taking a deep breath. "Yeah, you're right."

His finger poised over the button, he asked, "Ready?"

"Ready, go."

The door parted from the center revealing a room with red light where a throbbing dialysis machine was pumping blood in and pushing it out of the girl in the photograph. She lay on her face in a most uncomfortable position, her bare body looking cold, flesh trembling, goose bumps everywhere. She didn't look quite real under the strange, red light.

They rushed to her but didn't at first know what to do. They couldn't simply snatch out the catheter. It could do irreparable damage, as Dr. Dorfman had said, and they didn't know if shutting down the machine too quickly could not also have a killing effect. They needed someone who knew.

Via a modification Stone had made in the monster machine, some of the cleansed blood was not being replaced, just as Lanark had suspected. They looked at one another, both realizing the dilemma at the same moment.

"What'll we do?" she asked as a door opened and into the clinic flushed a cloud of icy cold air from a freezer. Amid the cold smoke was Jerry Mazure, his hand in rubber gloves, naked to the waist, his muscles bulging, a look of shocked puzzlement on his handsome face.

Lanark's gun was pointed at Mazure's skull. "Take the girl off the machine, Mazure, now! Move!"

Mazure dropped some test tubes and vials he'd been carrying and hopped to where the machine stood, its noise almost deafening now.

"Hey, easy with that piece, huh? Easy," said Mazure making some adjustments in the machine.

"Get her off that damnable thing, now!" said Shannon.

"You can't just cut if off like a light switch, lady."

"Just get her off it," said Shannon, her voice edged razor sharp.

Jerry started the process of shutdown. "Can't do it too quickly. Danger of perforating the wall between—"

Suddenly another door opened, and another, and another, three additional doors, all opening on the operating clinic, one of them the freezer, again sending frosty air into the room. At each doorway stood several men with guns and at the freezer stood Stone, saying, "Electronics, Lieutenant Lanark, a wonderful thing, really. Ever hear of a silent alarm? Or cameras? Look overhead."

Lanark saw that they were indeed followed from the moment they had entered the house, possibly sooner.

"Drop your weapons, or you'll die, now!" ordered Stone.

"I don't give up my weapon," said Lanark, "to anybody."

"Ryne, do as they say," said Shannon, tossing her .38 down. She nudged him.

"She's right, you know . . . very smart, Lieutenant Keyes."

"You won't be so smug for long," she replied.

Lanark, seeing the hopelessness of the situation, let loose his gun, allowing it to fall at Stone's feet. For a half second when the creep bent to pick it up, he was tempted to kick his face in, but he held himself in check. Shannon was right. Backup was on the way. A whole damned SWAT team along with his own unit, cops from four or five suburbs all around the place.

Then Skully stepped out from the shadows and Lanark's mind was near to bursting with hatred. "Hello, Lieutenant Lanark. Your *backup*." He held up a scrambler. It had been him on the radio, not a dispatcher.

"You'd sell your soul for this, Skully?"

"My soul, hell, Lanark, you know a safer place than this for my soul? The streets, out there?" He laughed. "Mr. Stone and I have become quite good friends since he contacted me."

"And Fabia . . . him, too, right. Doesn't matter to you pricks that Riordan's dying because of this sicko, does it, does it?"

"Riordan chose his own course . . . I chose mine. You got no idea how big this thing is—"

"That's enough, Officer Skully." It was an order from Stone who now pushed his mother forward. The frail, shaking figure let out with a pathetic squeak. She's not well, you know," continued Stone, his handsome, tanned face, cold blue eyes and shining yellow hair belying the fact his heart was made of ice. "Rare disorder, requires a lot of attention, and who gives it to her but her dutiful son, so you can go on spreading the word, Mother, isn't that right, Mother? Tell the officers, Mother. They have a right to know." She was the opposite of the woman on the TV, so filled with fire and righteous indignation. Here, she stood before the group, Stone tormenting her along with Lanark and Shannon.

"Here's your greatest fear, Mother, Chicago's finest. One of them's got exactly what you need, Mother, the woman here. Now, you see I do have your best interest at heart, luring them here, allowing them to play out their little charade."

"You're a fool, Stone," said Lanark and the moment he did so Jerry Mazure's huge fist caught Lanark a powerful blow to the head, knocking him to his knees. A second young strongman picked their weapons from the floor.

"A fool, am I? Not me, Lanark, you."

"In a matter of minutes this entire place will be surrounded by cops, scramblers don't work so effectively as your blood-sucking machines."

"No, your people are gone for the night, my friend. It's just you, me, Momma dear, and *her.*" He indicated Shannon. "Last time you were here, sweetheart, Burtie got some blood from you. As it happens, you're a perfect match for—"

"Shut up! Shut up, Matthew!" said his mother, tears streaming down her emaciated face.

"Look at you, Mother, you can hardly stand it any longer. Look at *her,* young, vibrant, a perfect match. We take her blood, we make you better . . . all better . . ."

"For how long? I'm sick of it, sick of this life and what you've turned into."

"Now, now, Mother, don't forget the work of the Lord. He does work in mysterious ways, His reasons not to be questioned, His motives no human can comprehend, and for God's sake—for man's sake—don't forget the generations to come, Mother. Our work *is* important."

Stone moved toward Lanark, pulling his head up by the hair and speaking directly to him. "You've come close, Lieutenant Lanark, too close, to comprehending me."

"It's true, then," said Shannon.

"Building an AIDS-free club, an elitist group that can indulge itself any way it likes, so long as it can provide important and influential men in high places with sex when called for, with blood when called for. So you sign people up," continued Lanark, "and for a pint here, a pint there you give them insurance for the future, against an all-out time of plague? You selling policies as well as sex, a cult built around safe sex, Mr. Stone?"

"It's only a matter of time, Lanark, pick up the paper and read it! A million in this country alone infected, and these becoming more infectious daily."

His mother's shrunken eyes met Lanark's as she said, "The risk to uninfected people is . . . is growing."

"Look around you, Lieutenant, the brightest, the smartest shun the big-city lights, seeking refuge with me, here. Everyone here knows that by the year 2000 our society will be the only safe haven. The brightest

313

young doctors—some in this very room—the brightest people in every profession will work with us."

Jerry Mazure said caustically, "You don't have to go into the fucking future. Right now hospitals in Chicago, New York, San Francisco, everywhere are filled with AIDS patients. Nobody in his right mind's going to work there."

"Dr. Mazure knows of where he speaks. Did his residency at Evanston Memorial. Heard you were there tonight. Met a friend of ours who explained dialysis to you. Did he also explain how I am treating Mother for a rare form of leukemia? A lot of blood transfusion necessary to my treatment, as in all such cases, but we're not about to chance AIDS with hospital blood banks. Too many careless errors."

"You people are crazy," said Shannon.

"Look at the facts," countered Stone, pacing before her, looking her up and down. "The facts tell us that we face a future devastated, cities devastated, large populations devastated. Imagine the economic shock waves, the demographic losses alone to productivity. Tell me, do you read *Futurist* magazine? The time is coming when blood, rich and pure blood will rule, when it will be the highest currency. I have more stored away right now than all the blood banks in the Midwest combined."

"We could end AIDS tomorrow," said Mazure, "if people would change."

"No one expects people to change," said Stone smugly. "We're no different in that regard, are we, Jerry? We also believe in eat, drink and be merry, don't we? But we've eliminated the threat first. Meanwhile, I'm putting my money into disinfectants and rubber gloves and condoms, Miss Keyes. If you could be around to enjoy the finer things, I'd advise you to invest in my company. Fears fuel fortunes, you know. Imagine taking today's fear of AIDS and multiplying it by a simple number like five by 1991. People aren't going to want to go into the cities. Eventually, some areas devastated by the epidemic may be completely abandoned, like areas in Europe, you can still see from the air where overgrown villages were never reoccupied after the Black Plague. I know, I've seen them.''

''Every fourteen minutes,'' said Mazure, ''another AIDS case is reported.''

''Increasing all over Europe, too, as well as the rest of the world,'' said another member with a decidedly British accent.

Shannon kept shaking her head, unable to believe the basis for which these kids had conspired to commit murder. ''And you think murdering people is the answer?''

''He's only interested in one thing, Shannon,'' said Lanark, staring a hole through Stone. ''He means to build on a blood supply of private stock to create a master race, right, old boy?''

''Now that you know, you can die with the truth.''

''Meanwhile, your ailing mother attacks the problem in her own way,'' said Lanark. ''Charming family unit, Stone.''

''Brings in a lot of converts, all over the country, don't you, Mom?''

''It beats suburban 'electronic cottages' and air-tight mall life to avoid the soon to be AIDS-ravaged cities,'' said Mazure, the *litany* having been memorized by now.

''I don't want to see this!'' shouted Stone's mother,

running from the room amid Stone's berating laughter.

"But she'll gladly take your blood," he said to Shannon. "Yours too, Lanark, if it's a match. Stick him, Jerry."

"What?" said Shannon, but by the time she said it, Mazure had punctured Lanark's hand with an ice pick-like device that came out and went away like the sting of a bee. A second and third member of the elite club held Lanark while female members of the club, most stoned, giggled. Mazure then pressed a slide against the wound he'd inflicted, covered it and handed it to a fourth club member who went off with it, presumably to test it.

"We'll see if you're worth draining, Lanark," said Stone as Lanark's hands were being tied, "like Miss Keyes, here. Take him to the basement. Chain him there."

Then the others moved in on Shannon.

The helpless girl who'd been undergoing forced blood donation for the cause, was helped out, weak as a kitten, and dumped among the others in the harem room. Some of the sleepers were awakened and they groggily joined their leaders, asking what was happening, barely able to make their lips work. A few scrambled to their feet to watch at the doorway to the clinic as Stone began to work on Shannon Keyes.

One assistant was filling a hypodermic needle with some sort of drug. A second was flicking buttons on the dialyzer, the *thrum-thrum-thrum* sound now more like air going through pipes, a *siss-siss-siss* in her ears. A third young man who held Shannon in a powerful grip now ripped Shannon's sleeve completely away. Shannon knew she must stall for time.

"*Why*, why did you kill those three girls, Stone?" she asked him point blank.

"The first was an error, a common complication with the dialysis. She died on the table."

"And Burton?"

"Liability . . . talking too much to cops."

"The other two girls, members of your AIDS-free camp? What about them?"

"Does it matter? They wanted *out*, we obliged them."

"To hide the cause of death you *invented* the Glove, you decided to mar the body, to throw off the police. Then the others? You turned it into a party ritual, a cult game, for your amusement?"

"We sent them on to God, as Mother would say."

"She approved of your murdering people?"

"When she goes long enough with the pain and weakness that overcomes her, she'll be back for your blood, Shannon Keyes, make no mistake about it."

"The cuts to the face?"

"Makeup."

"Using infected blood on the corpses?"

"A little prize we cooked up for the cops. My idea."

"You're mad."

"But it is madness with method."

"You deliberately taunted us with the bodies. It wasn't just to throw us off, was it? Something you were trying to tell us, to tell the world, Stone? That you can do what you damn well please, that you're above—"

"I don't need you to tell me what I am."

"But you need all these other people around you to do exactly that, *King* Stone, you with your palace guard, holding court each night. *Who* gets hooked to that blood-sucking, bastardized machine of yours, *who* lives, *who* dies."

"You've a very quick mind, Shannon," he said, calling her by her first name with a queer smile. "Pity, you can't be trusted. Strip her," he ordered his assistants. The other young men his own age or younger took delight in doing as he ordered.

"But you can trust me!" she protested, "I *understand* what your reasons are now. I . . . I don't want to die."

"Die? No, you misunderstand, dear Shannon. You won't die, not if you work out. We'll keep you as a *constant,* one of our *major sources,* take out just enough, allow your body to replenish the supply for as long as . . . as I like."

"Can I have her, Dr. Stone?" asked the assistant who had her about the middle now.

"When I'm done with her, Oliver, if you're a good boy."

"Yes, sir."

"Let me go! Damn you, let me go!" she shouted, kicking, bringing her knee up into one man's crotch, doubling him over. The others got a tighter hold on her, continuing the process of dehumanizing her, tearing the blouse completely away, and next her bra.

"Give her the shot, Dr. Stone?" asked one of the assistants, holding up a hypodermic needle filled with a see-through fluid.

"Yes, now."

Shannon's lips was bloodied by the man she'd kicked when he dealt her a terrible blow, and the hypo was

318

plunged into her arm amid her cries of protests. "You bastards, you vile bastards," she shouted at them.

"Put a glove in her mouth," said Stone, throwing a white glove to his assistant who gagged her and forced her to the table where her skirt and panties were removed. Her ankles and wrists were secured to the cold steel table by straps. She lay on her stomach. She felt another needle injection in her back, a local anesthetic for the catheter insertion. Feeling a blackness come over her, she flinched with the insertion of the catheter which she either imagined, dreamed in a drug-induced sleep, or actually felt. It made no difference. All that made any difference now was the gentle lull of the seashore lapping unrelentingly against the rocks in a slumbering *thrum-thrum-thrum, thrum-thrum-thrum*.

FOURTEEN

Ryne Lanark assessed his situation as they led him to the chains Stone had spoken of. Once attached to a wall, without a weapon, he'd be completely helpless. He wasn't about to let that happen, not so long as there was a ghost of chance of getting free now, here, along the passageway leading to the final door to this dungeon Stone had created of his basement.

"You'll be just fine here, Lanark," said Jerry Mazure, the muscled-up neck heaving with laughter. "Get the door, Freddie," he told the other man with a gun.

The door was a thick, oak affair and Freddie had to concentrate on the lock and key, taking his mind away for a second. It was long enough for Lanark to strike out at Mazure, whirling and bringing up his foot to the man's testicles, causing him to double over. A split second later, Lanark rammed Freddie and together they flew through the now unlocked door to the bleak interior where Lanark's senses were attacked by the most horrendous odors imaginable, the smell of rotten flesh. Lanark dared not let Freddie go, holding on tightly, wallowing in some vile, gushy stuff as they did so. They struggled over Freddie's gun, Lanark pounding viciously at the kid's forearm again and again until he let go and it slid off into the muck and cavernous darkness surrounding them. Lanark had but one thing on his mind, Shannon and her well-being.

He brought his fist into Freddie's face twice with as much might as he could, knocking him cold. Then he heard Mazure at the door say, "You're a dead man, Lanark!" In the doorway, Mazure's silhouette was clearly visible, and had Ryne a gun, he could have ended Mazure's life without another thought. But he had no weapon whatsoever. He ran his hands along the floor, seeking the other gun, but he was coming up with what felt like cow shit and that was all. Bum luck when Mazure, unable to see him, was an obvious target. Suddenly, a blaze of fire roared where Mazure stood, as he abruptly lit up a torch he'd taken down from the wall.

The flame lit up a slime-floored dungeon, complete with chained inmates—several men and women decorating the walls, all in various stages of dehydration, malnutrition and slow death. But Lanark somehow kept his eyes directed at Mazure and raced at him as soon as the torch was lit, sending him into the wall. Lanark had the torch and the gun pinned when he suddenly yanked Mazure forward, rolling on his own back and sending him flying across the room. Mazure dropped the fiery torch, Lanark retrieveing it, and as Mazure rose up, Lanark rammed it into his face, catching his blond locks ablaze. Jerry Mazure screamed, blinded by the fire, his hands going to his face and hair, scram-

321

bling to put himself out. Lanark was no help, driving the man against the wall with the torch, burning his hand so badly he dropped the gun; he next rammed torch into Jerry's mid-section, catching his clothes afire. Ryne backed off to watch as Jerry Mazure went up in flames. The stench of the burning body added to the horrible odors that had first assailed Lanark's senses when he'd broken through the door. There was human excrement everywhere, and more than one of the bodies in chains here was putrid.

One woman on the wall, unable to lift her head, or speak above a whisper, begged help in an animal mew. Ryne looked around for some way to free these people, all the while fearful for Shannon upstairs in Stone's clinic.

He spied a set of keys hanging on the wall near the entryway. Lanark found the keys, opened the shackles, and he managed to get out the three people in the dungeon who were alive, finding a comfortable, temporary place for them. Then he set off for the second floor with the intention of murdering Matthew Stone if nothing else.

Sirens, in the distance, coming at top speed. Were they real or imagined? Lanark didn't dare hope, probably just racing by on Sheridan Road to some other destination.

He continued his upward climb along a stairwell he'd found that originated not far from the dungeon. He guessed it to be a secretive stairwell that could possibly lead to Stone's room, maybe the clinic. He didn't know.

He had retrieved his gun from Mazure. It was cocked and as ready as he. His guess was that Stone, held at gunpoint, was their ticket out of the mansion. Once out, he meant to blow Stone's brains away.

The steps were wooden, rickety and noisy. When he got to ground level, he saw there was a door leading out. Taking a glance through, he saw it was a direct route to the family plot and crypt, no doubt filled with Stone's handiwork these days, he thought. This door might be a way out for them. The sirens he thought he heard were closer. He wondered if he could get to his car, radio for help, but by then Shannon could be dead.

No doubt they'd gotten rid of his car by now, he told himself.

He marked the exit in his mind and moved on, taking one step at a time, cautious. Above he saw a single door, and he heard the now familiar sound of the dialyzer. He went toward the door, toward the thrumming sound, but this time it seemed quieter, subdued. He tried to account for this, but could not. Lanark then took the doorknob in hand and opened it, only to find himself inside a wardrobe, a closet filled with clothes. He opened the door on the other side of the closet and found himself in a bedroom with a large canopied bed and an enormous oaken desk to one end, the room large and expansive. Stone's room? he wondered. He wanted so much to rifle the desk, come up with the irrefutable evidence that would tell the world of this horror club of Stone's creation, but it would have to wait for another time, another chance. Shannon was worth more now to him than anything else.

The *thrum-thrum-thrum* sound wasn't at all like the big dialyzer in the clinic. Lanark went toward the muted drum sound now. It was coming from the room next to Stone's. There was an adjoining door, and Ryne opened it slowly and looked inside. It was Sylvia Stone hooked to a smaller unit, a shunt in her arm where the blood flow was making a path between her and the machine and back again. On the other side of her an IV was dripping plasma. She appeared, if not asleep, resting her eyes and mind.

Lanark wondered how much Stone cared about his mother. Would she make *bargaining* work? He was prepared to find out.

Going to the woman, he tried to determine how to shut down the dialyzer. After flicking a few buttons, he simply woke her with the gun at her eyes and yanked the shunt from her arm, drawing blood. "Get yourself unhooked here, Mrs. Stone, we have some business to attend to."

"It's not what I wanted . . . never," she began to wail.

"Shut up, and do as I say!" he ordered harshly. "Get yourself up."

"But I'm just so weak . . . too weak to fight Matthew."

"Come with me, and I'll show you how to fight Matthew."

"He's really a good boy, you know . . . he means well."

"Yes, Mrs. Stone, so I've seen, downstairs in his dungeon."

Her hands covered her mouth, "Oh, but those people meant to hurt us, he told me so . . ."

324

She was out of it. Stone had her on drugs like all the others.

"Move ahead of me," he told her.

But she was unable to walk, falling to the floor, blubbering.

"Damn," said Lanark, "wasting too much time." He lifted her and roughly placed her back on the bed, leaving her to her disease and drugs and machines. In the hallway, he carefully listened for the sound of the larger dialyzer once more. It seemed to be coming from his left at the end of the long corridor, going away from a large stairwell leading down to the main room. He saw that there were stairs leading up, and he marked these as another possible escape route.

He inched down the darkened corridor toward the sound of the blood-sucking machine Stone had created. As he did so he stepped onto some silverware and dishes outside one of these rooms, causing a shattering noise.

Inwardly cursing, he froze, leaning against the wall when suddenly the door opened. An older man, a towel wrapped about his middle, stepped out for a look when Lanark's fist hit him square in the mouth, knocking him senseless. Lanark pulled the door to quietly.

But a second door, across from this one, suddenly opened and someone grabbed him from behind. Lanark's elbow pounded into this man's stomach, and he wheeled to face his attacker, momentarily slowed by the fact it was Joe Skully. He brought up the gun and pounded Joe's face with it, once, twice, sending him veering back. He brought up his leg and caught the bad cop in his crotch, Lanark's hard-nosed shoe meeting the naked flesh with perfect result. Skully fell back through the doorway he'd come out of, holding onto himself, naked and squirming like a beached fish. Lanark brought his foot down at his face in quick succession until the other man was silent from a lack of consciousness.

Somewhere in the dark he heard a fear-filled squeal, barely audible. His eyes adjusting, he made out the figure of a girl tied to the bed, ankles and arms, spread-eagled for Skully's enjoyment, a down payment for his loyalty to Stone.

Lanark removed the ties to the girl's ankles while she dazedly, dopily asked, "Who're . . . who're you?" She asked the question in drugged repetitiveness.

"You'll be all right now," was his simple reply as he tied Joe Skully's hands behind his back, and next his ankles.

"What're you doing?" she asked repeatedly. "What're you going to do . . . to me?"

The last question rang clear, like a bell, a wistful wish in there somewhere that she would be victimized by Skully's attacker. Her hands were still tied and now, as he approached her nude form on the bed, she pulled herself against the ties seductively, wantonly, saying it again. "What're you going to do to me? What do you want me to do for you?"

"I want you to stay right there," he said, showing her the gun in his hand.

She struck snake-like out at the gun with her mouth, taking the barrel down her throat. When he pulled it away and started out, she said, "I'm not going anywhere." He closed the door on her giggling laughter.

Ahead of him he heard the machine sounds inter-mingled with human voices. Doors lined the hallway, any one of which might suddenly open with another attacker. Holding his gun ahead of him, he made his way to the door at the end of the hall where the *thrum-thrum-thrum* of the dialyzer was beginning to get on his nerves.

Not another moment could be lost. He slowly, si-lently tried the door and found it was not locked. The sound of the machine inside had hidden the noise of his scuffle with Skully and the dishes down the hall. With a deep breath he threw open the door, catching Stone hovering over Shannon's nude form vulture-like along with his assistants, as if mesmerized by the dark flow of liquid coming out of her. "Don't make a move!" shouted Lanark as one raised his gun, forcing Ryne to blow a hole through his face, sending him against the wall, his blood splattering Stone's clothes and Shannon's bare back. She lay on the cold, sleek table face down.

"One move toward her, or the machine, you're a dead man, Stone!" he shouted. "You, what's your name?" he asked one of the stunned henchmen.

"Gary . . . Gary Thorn."

"All right, Thorn, you see to it the machine is shut down properly. You're taking orders from me now, not him!" he indicated Stone.

Three others stood around Shannon's helpless form.

"So, you think you're holding all the cards, Lieu-tenant," Stone began casually as Thorn worked to turn off the machine.

He replied with a wave of the gun in Stone's face,

327

pushing the still moist barrel into his nostrils. "You want to eat this, you creep?"

Another of Stone's boys reached for his weapon and Lanark grabbed Stone, spinning him around and using him as a shield. The other man had his gun pointed but Stone was between him and Lanark. Lanark fired, sending the gunman to his reward. "I mean business, here! Shut that goddamned thing down! Do it right. Anything happens to my partner, you're all dead of gunshot wounds."

"Jesus."

"Easy . . . easy . . ."

"Doing what I can," pleaded Thorn.

Lanark twisted Stone's neck in the headlock he held him in, enjoying the sound of his discomfort.

"The rest of you toss your guns to the ground," he warned them.

"You'll never get yourself and the woman off the grounds alive, Lanark," Stone muttered through his teeth.

"You, Thorn, see that every ounce, every drop of her blood is replaced, you bloody bunch of vampires."

"You can't possibly hope to escape, Lanark," said Stone.

Lanark only tightened his grip in reply.

"You're surrounded, don't you know that?"

"Yeah, and I've got Sister Sylvia down the hall, prick."

Stone's face bleached white. "You're lying."

"Call my bluff if you like. I took your mother off her machine and put her in a place for safekeeping. As for your friend, Jerry, I may let you join him. He went up in flames, boys, burned to death on top of a pile of shit in your basement, Stone. Ever think of getting a maid for that place?''

But Lanark's bluff wasn't fooling anyone, not even himself, so long as the groundswell of noise coming from the outside and stairwell continued to grow. If he could get Shannon on her feet, get her moving, they might have a chance out another way, but not like this.

At his back, Lanark heard men shouting and running, doors slamming. Every member of the boys' club was awake and aware of the danger in their presence and coming for Lanark. His only hope lie with holding Stone hostage and in praying that was enough.

''You're coming with us,'' he told Stone, dragging him across the small room, forcing the others into the freezer and locking it behind them, all but Thorn, who, unarmed, seemed to pose no threat. ''How long, damn you?'' he shouted at Thorn.

''Just a few minutes now.''

Lanark didn't have a few minutes. He'd locked the door and they were pounding on it outside now. He forced Stone to his knees in front of him, telling him he was going to make a nice shield. ''Order them away from here, now, punk, or so help me I'm going to blow your—''

''Go ahead, kill me!''

Gunshots at the doorway ripped away the lock.

Lanark pulled back the hammer of his gun against Stone's skull now. ''You won't be around to see what they do to me, Stone.''

''Lanark! You in there! Lanark!'' It was Mark Robeson's voice!

Lanark, twisting viciously on Stone's neck, holding

329

the gun in his ear, shouted back, "Yes! Mark, inside! Hold your fire!"

Robeson and several uniformed cops burst into the room, along with Morris Fabia. They stopped short, seeing the killing in progress Lanark was about to perpetrate on the helpless Matthew Stone. Lanark's grimace stopped them cold in their tracks. Stone's face had become beet red from lack of oxygen due to the choke hold Lanark held him in.

"I'm going to kill the son of a bitch, Mark, now, so there's no mistaking justice will be served," he said firmly.

"He ain't worth your life, Lanark, your freedom."

"Put the gun down, Lanark," said Fabia. "It's over, man, it's over."

"Ryne, let it go."

On the table, reaching a hand out to him at the same moment, Shannon murmured, "Please, Lanark . . . please."

Lanark's grip on the gun softened and he removed his finger from the trigger, finally replacing the hammer. He let Stone slump to the floor, giving him a push with his knee. "Here's your garbage, Fabia."

"We'll take care of him, Lieutenant."

"Whole bitching place is filled with stoned people with guns. You tell your men to beware," he said, going through the adjoining door for a blanket and placing it over Shannon, trying to warm her.

"Ryne . . ." she managed a word. "I knew . . . you'd come."

He kissed the back of her neck. "You're going to be all right, isn't she, Thorn?"

"Yes, she'll be all right."

"Another of Stone's converts, cuff him," he told one of the uniformed cops. He then looked up at Fabia and asked, "Just how did you guys find us? Our communication was blocked."

"Got a call from a Dr. Dorfman, Evanston Memorial," said Fabia. "One of Stone's blackmail victims. Guy wanted to stick it to Stone, and he did."

"Something to be said for revenge," added Mark.

"Stone was good at blackmail, bribery and just plain, old extortion. Tried to get to me through my wife and kids. Like he could see to it they contracted AIDS, or so Skully hinted. Skully was keeping watch on me while I was supposed to be keeping watch on you. I let him think it worked. Part of the deal was to keep tabs on you and report back. I was giving him rope, like Riordan would've done. Anyway, Mark here picked up part of Keyes' scrambled message, then a call came in from Dorfman for me. Took some doing to piece it together but we did."

"Dorfman's downstairs," said Mark.

"Well, get him up here!" shouted Lanark. "Shannon needs attention."

Robeson rushed out to retrieve Dorfman.

"Sylvia Stone's in a bedroom down the hall. So's Skully, tied hand and foot. Downstairs, the basement, you'll find three people in dire need of hospitalization, barely alive, Fabia."

"Got it."

"And Fabia?"

"Yeah?"

"You'll find a number of bodies down there, too, regular dungeon. One fresh body, badly burned, tried to kill me, Jerry Mazure. Should be another strongarm

331

down there, too, knocked cold. Some creeps turning to popsicles in the freezer over there, too. Round 'em all up.''

Fabia began shouting orders, dispersing his men to these various locations. An occasional gunshot was fired. All about the hallways people were being cuffed and escorted out to waiting vans, some of the uniformed officers having to scuffle with biting, scratching, freaked-out kids of both sexes.

Dorfman came rushing in ahead of Robeson, looking over Shannon, asking Lanark to give him room. Lanark managed to grab hold of Mark before he disappeared again.

''Down the hall, beside Sylvia Stone's room where Fabia is now, there's an office, Stone's den, a desk and files. Likely be books, ledgers, all his records and dealings somewhere in that room. Rip out the goddamned walls if you have to.''

''Consider it done.''

''They got Stone cuffed to the handle of a squad car?''

''You bet they have.''

''Good.''

Robeson was gone. Lanark remained close to Shannon, holding her hand, when Max, Wil and Myra showed up at the doorway. He sent the men immediately to help Mark. He asked Myra to find Shannon's clothes and to see that she was taken safely out of this place as soon as Dorfman thought it advisable.

Ambulances arrived, paramedics now filing through the mansion, Fabia telling them where to go. Lanark grabbed hold of one of them, insisting he go with him to Sylvia Stone's room.

"She's dead, Lanark," Fabia informed him flatly.

"What?"

"Dead as in no life signs."

"But when I left her—"

"See for yourself, damnit."

Lanark rushed to her room, Dorfman coming up behind him. Sylvia Stone's white nightgown was stark against the pool of blood she lay in. The carpet was soaked with it at the bedside. It looked at first like the work of a madman, that she'd been hacked to death, but there was no sign of either a struggle, or terrible gashes or wounds.

"She was alive when I left her," said Lanark to Dorfman who went completely around her and shut off the small dialysis unit that was humming and sputtering.

"Hooked up wrong," Dorfman said, holding up the woman's arm where the shunt was only partially attached, allowing the return flow of blood to secrete onto the floor. "She bled to death. Unusual, for a person familiar with this equipment."

"She was on drugs."

"Might explain it . . ."

"What else?"

He raised his shoulders. "Woman like her, in the public eye, professed saver of souls . . . the humiliation of all this going public . . . you figure it out."

"Suicide?"

"Might explain it."

"She chose her own way in the end."

"I'll go back to your partner. Nothing I can do here."

He stopped Dorfman with a hand. "I haven't thanked you for putting in that call."

Dorfman just stared, got on his feet and said, "Whether you people believe me or not, I . . . I had no idea how far he had taken his phobias. After you left the hospital, they called me, Stone's man Mazure. He told me what had occurred there, told me if I didn't see to it that the burglar died of . . . of complications, they'd see to it I died of complications. I knew what I had to do. Crazy, I thought the parties, the fun, you know, it was just a safe place to have a good time."

He ambled out of the room looking very tired.

Lanark rushed to Stone's den to find Robeson and the others of his unit. They needed evidence now. Names, dates, records. They must be here, or at Stone's central clinic in the city. To confiscate records there might take too long.

When he saw Robeson's face beaming with a wide smile, he knew they had something.

"Membership records, Ryne. Found on the premises." He pointed to an oaken file cabinet with the lock pounded away by a hammer.

"God bless it, Lanark," shouted Fabia at the door suddenly, "Your crackers aren't being very smart about this! You don't be careful here, and this creep gets off like your man, Sorentino, only on goddamned technicalities. How'd you get this file, open, Robeson, Cassidy? Yoshikani?"

"It was open when we came in," said Wil.

Yoshikane gave him a military nod, agreeing.

"That's right," added Mark, hiding the hammer behind his back. "Lenny the Lifter *was* here earlier, you know."

"It don't matter," said Lanark. "With what we've got on Stone, we don't need any paper to search every inch of this place."

"Lenny's burglary attempt is on file," said Wil.

"All the paperwork anybody needs," added Robeson.

Fabia's frown turned into a half smile of knowing. "Gotcha, boys, gotcha. Okay with you, Lanark, my boys have a hand in the E.T. work from here on? For Al, you know?"

"For Al, huh? Sure . . ."

"May not believe it, Lanark, but that guy meant a lot to me. I didn't want no promotion that meant his death. Never wanted that. Riordan taught me a lot and when he—"

"You don't have to talk about the man as if he's dead."

"Didn't you hear?"

Lanark shook his head.

"Earlier tonight . . . 8:08."

"Damn . . . damn."

"Yeah, shit way for a guy like big Al to go."

"I had hoped to have the chance to tell him we got the slime."

"He knew you were close. He also knew at the end who was clean and who was dirty, and that some of the names on Stone's client list could get us all killed."

"Like Judge John Webster," said Robeson.

"Councilmen Ed Morris, Mort Kremluse, David Perol," said Wil.

"A couple of prominent lawyers, including one on the D.A.'s payroll," added Max.

"Sonofabitch, how far does this thing reach?"

"Far enough to scare the hair off your—"

Myra and Shannon were in the entryway, Shannon saying breathlessly, "We got 'em . . . didn't we?"

He went to her, held her up asking how she felt.

"I'll be okay."

"You did good work, Keyes," said Fabia as Myra helped her down to a waiting car.

"I'm right behind you," Lanark shouted after them before turning to Fabia who had a look of smug satisfaction on his face.

"Damned pretty that Keyes," Fabia said, "with or without her clothes, but then, I guess you know that, right?"

"Just what do you think you know?"

"You forget, I had you under surveillance, you know, to make my scam with Stone look good."

"Fabia, you surprise me."

"Why should that be the case? Sure I'm ambitious, and sure I'm moving up over Al's dead body, but that don't make me a ghoul, not like Skully."

"Thanks, in the future, I'll remember that."

"We'll work together again."

"What was the idea spreading rumors about me?"

"No, wrong again, I just talked to that guy with the *Trib* because he asked me to, and all I did was tell him the truth, Lanark, the unvarnished truth. As for stories about you being a killer . . . well, we know that you are, don't we?"

He said it as if he knew everything there was to know about Ryne Lanark, his reasons for joining the force, his desire to find and destroy the street scum that had done him so much unrelieved pain. Fabia had found someone who knew the whole story, but now seeing the wink in the other cop's eye, it was, for now, okay. Fabia understood Lanark more now than he had ever done so in the past. Perhaps it was good, his knowing. Still, Lanark knew, that at some time in the future, when it served Fabia's ends, he'd use the information as a wedge or lever.

"Better go see to your partner, Lanark. Get some rest and see that your unit gets some rest. We'll take care of the mop-up, no lie." Fabia went about shouting orders to his men. "And see that this scum-sucker Skully is cuffed, now! You got me?"

Lanark and Mark went downstairs where, out in the misty night air, they found Wil, Myra and Max surrounding Shannon who sat on a car seat. She was doing much better and when she saw Ryne she jumped into his arms. They held tight for some time as the others watched with smiles and encouragement.

Stone's prostitutes, male and female, were being boarded into wagons for lockup downtown. Stone was in the back seat of a cruiser, his eyes filled with indignation and anger, looking as if he were going to strike back at any moment.

"Anybody tell him about his mother?" asked Lanark.

"No, want me to?" asked Wil.

"No, no, this'll be my pleasure."

"Ryne?" asked Shannon, not understanding how he could be so cruel.

"You didn't see what he had hanging from the walls in the basement." He walked to the cruiser, indicated to the uniformed cop in front he wanted a word with his prisoner. The window went halfway down.

"Dr. Stone, your mother bled herself to death before we could stop her."

His eyes went wide, his mouth slack and he shook where he sat as if the news was trembling and slithering its way through his body and to his mind until he exploded in a banshee cry of denial.

"Afraid so, Stone. I do believe she couldn't stand you anymore."

Another cry of *noooooooo*, as Lanark left the cruiser with a word of caution to the uniformed officer in front. "Careful with this one, he's the Glove."

"The Glove!"

"Upscale Slasher, if you like. Murdered five that we know about, possibly more. Take every precaution and get him to Precinct 13. He'll be booked there, no place else, and don't take any shit from Morris Fabia, this sucker was collared by the Decoy Unit at the 13th."

"Yes, sir! Right away, Lieutenant."

"Careful," shouted someone coming out of the dark to stand before Lanark: Captain Wood, "careful, or our 13th'll be getting some respect."

"This one's going to stick!" said Lanark firmly. "And, if for some unforeseen, godforsaken reason not, I'll murder this guy on the street myself."

"Careful, Lanark, remarks like that can get back to haunt you. Don't repeat it, not to anyone."

Lanark was still keyed up, his nerves like exposed electrical wires spitting fire, but something about Wood's tone brought him down quick. "Sure, sure, Captain."

"You do everything by the book?"

"Yes, sir."

338

"You made sure Lenny was acquitted of charges before you let him run loose around here, tonight?"

"We saw to the paperwork, if that's what you mean, sir."

"Good, now just make sure he does his part from this point on. If it got 'round that the 13th put a burglar inside Stone's place, and that resulted in our probable cause, which in turn impacted on how we located damning evidence . . . well, a good lawyer—and Stone will buy the best—could shake this bust to its foundations. Some good work, so take care of the loose ends."

"Meaning Lenny?"

"Might be wise to have him disappear."

Lanark looked into Wood's eyes. "You don't mean . . ."

"No, I don't mean kill him. I mean see to it he's ready for retirement—anywhere but here."

"It'll be done. Seems our security on him at the hospital wasn't up to par."

"And Ryne?"

"Yes, sir?"

"A fine job . . . pass it along. Only wish I'd been involved."

"Next time, maybe?"

"Next time, sure. I'm sorry as hell about Sorentino."

"Then he walks?"

"Walked . . . past tense. Not quite released to the streets, however. He's due to testify against Encinado soon. Then he gets protective custody, a remake on his face, relocation, and then his freedom.

"Damn . . . a guy like that, witness for the prosecution."

"Look at it this way. One out of two scumbags, that ain't bad, Lanark."

"It's average, Captain, and when you're average you're as close to the bottom as to the top."

Lanark returned to Shannon and together they went home.

EPILOGUE

When Matthew Stone's private stock of plasma and blood was confiscated and thoroughly logged, it came to light that he'd classified the blood in order of lineage and genetics, European blue blood coming in just under blood tied to royalty. This in addition to blood labeled AIDS-free, AIDS-contaminated.

Furthermore, it seemed that Stone's own Harvard blood was linked with royalty. He was, or believed himself to be, a distant cousin to King Henry VI. This according to a report found in his private papers, put together by the same publishing concern as that which produced *Burke's Peerage*, the trusted Who's Who and Bible in royal bloodlines.

News of Stone's bizarre operations, the scandalous nature of Sylvia's evangelism masking her son's murderous bent, and the true nature of his world-wide clinics, touched off a conflagration in the press, radio and TV. News of Stone's blue blood clinic and his connections to every level of society and government made for a million questions and twice that many suppositions.

Even the vice president of the United States, said to have blue blood tied to royalty, was being pursued by the press for possible connections with Stone.

Matthew Stone infuriated and enraged the judge overseeing his hearing, with a sudden outburst of smug contempt for the proceedings. This, along with the true meaning of Stone clinics and Stone evangelism coming to light, got Stone held over without bail. Jury selection was still going on as more indictments against Stone's clients, cohorts, and people like Dr. Dorfman were forthcoming. The list read like a who's who of the Midwestern city, crossing all kinds of lines, from racketeers to judges. Al Riordan's captain, Thomas Duval, for one, two judges and a member of the D.A.'s staff were only the immediate indictments. The ripple effect threatened prosecution in every major city where Stone's clinics had been operating. Information went out to overseas authorities as well, and from every center records were subpoenaed. Captain Paul Wood and the police commissioner were not among the indicted, nor had they been involved in the conspiracy to protect Matthew Stone from earlier detection.

Records from the take at the mansion and Chicago clinics already revealed hundreds of "preferred" people willing to trade blood for sex in Stone's club. Just how many card-carrying members there were, and which of them knew the inner workings of the club, of the deaths and drug-induced transfusions was not entirely clear yet. Duval, like most club members, expressed shock, amazement and outrage on learning of the activities of the inner circle of the AIDS-free "dating service" they thought they were getting for their blood contribution to the "bank" once they tested free.

The case would have its effect for years, and some people who felt at safe distance now might, a year from now, be charged.

As for Stone himself, and his immediate circle, the "ritual" murder of four people certainly must condemn them to life terms, if not the death sentence, now reinstated in Illinois for serial murderers and unusually heinous crimes. This, so far as everyone was concerned, fit the bill.

Meanwhile, Tavalez Sorentino had done his part for the FBI, and for him it wasn't at all a bad deal. He escaped a prison term, he escaped justice of the sort Lanark would like to have administered. No one at the 13th Precinct knew where he was now, nor was anyone to ever know, as he had been relocated by the FBI for his part in the bargain struck between them for Encinado. He'd been given a new face, a new name and identity. Rumor had him in Hawaii, but given the FBI's recent budget cuts, logic placed him in California, Florida or Texas.

One member of the 13th was determined to find out just where, and he had some friends of long standing in the Federal service, friends not above taking a chance for the right price, and no matter what the cost, finding Sorentino was worth it to this man. It had taken a long time to set up, but information was waiting in a locker at O'Hare International Airport, his friend laughingly telling him on the park bench where they secretively met that he could jet right off after the bastard tonight if he liked, once he read the copied dossier.

The cop stood before the locker now, wondering if

he could go through with it after all, knowing that if he opened the locker he'd be on the next flight to wherever the information sent him. He'd have to make quick work of Sorentino. He knew from experience that now the Feds had what they wanted from the scum bucket, Sorentino was on his own. If he had any guards around him he'd have had to hire them, and on what the Feds allowance to an informant was, this seemed unlikely. No question but a shoot would be simple, quick and easy, once he knew of the bastard's location.

The dossier would provide that, down to the address. He had placed a thick dark mustache and beard on to cover his features, along with dark glasses. Now, in top coat and hat, he approached the locker, feeling like Peter Sellers. Maybe the caution was foolish, but if he meant to murder Sorentino, he certainly didn't want it getting back. His alibi arranged, his "double" jetting off to a well-deserved vacation in the Bahamas, he meant to take care of unfinished business.

Tavalez Sorentino had done his thing for the FBI, and now they'd dumped him like yesterday's laundry, completely on his own in a foreign place. He missed his Chicago. The bustling street noise, the activity, the place that was his territory. Something akin to animal instinct was luring him back.

This place was supposed to be heaven? He'd gladly trade the quarter acre of sand for one concrete apartment window in one brownstone any day. This place was for shit. Not for him.

They got him a house with what they had called ocean frontage. In fact he was some distance from the ocean in a backwater area where, for most of the day, he was surrounded with a weed bed when the tide went out. Also the view wasn't so good because of the overhanging cliff to his right, and another on the left.

It was an older house too, with some termite problems, and a toilet that kept backing up. One of those houses that stuck way out over the side of a cavernous drop in Southern California, and should there be a *serious* storm, Jesus, he wondered fearfully about what they called mud slides here, not to mention earthquakes. One had hit not too far away, jarring the place like an elevator snapping its cable.

Still, it wasn't such a bad trade for life in prison, or a death sentence.

He'd tried desperately to forget about his failed business, the seemingly endless trial, all those fearful days and nights in which he'd had nightmares about a man who stepped from nowhere and blew off the top of his head. He'd tried to forget, but the thought of it all was like a pair of walls coming closer and closer in on him, readying to crush him. Forget about Chicago, he tried to tell himself.

He had a monthly income from the government, his *benefactor*, and he should be happy with the sun, the sea, the sand, but he was bored.

His fantasy was to make a break from here. Wouldn't take too much. He had a new face, a new look, and he could ditch the new identity along with the Feds, create new paper and be whoever he chose to be, return to Chicago maybe, and start up where he left off—*after* blowing Lanark away.

Sure, it might take some doing. Sure, he would face difficulties, but that was life. This, by comparison, was a slow death, a prison. He was lonely for one thing, lonely for the touch of a young thing, a girl just into her teens maybe. It was one thing the Feds didn't provide.

Saturday nights he'd go into the honky-tonk nothing of a town in search of someone to bring home, but the place was bare. So now he was in San Francisco looking, just cruising, when he found a bar that looked good. There were broads outside, but they looked old, used, dirty. He parked and went inside for a look around.

He ordered at the bar and took in the great supply. Someone was doing a fine business in prostitution right here. Why go back to Chicago at all? he told himself. Why not start his new business right here?

He pulled his drink from his lips and cast his eyes over a girl at the end of the bar who seemed to be staring with interest at him. With his old flare, he indicated she should join him. She did, and they made small talk before he offered her money for her services.

She wasn't so young as he liked, but not too old either. Her red hair had been dyed and the makeup was too thick for his liking, but she could tell him about her pimp, lead him to the source, with the right persuasion. He liked persuading helpless women.

"You got a room nearby?" she asked him.

"Don't you?"

"It's not so nice, for a man like you," she said.

"A hole, huh? You maybe like a better place to stay? I got a house, you could stay the night."

"I gotta work, man."

"I'll pay you double what you make in a night."

"Really?"

"Really."

The deal was cinched. Outside he pointed out his car. "Get in," he told the woman.

"I want the green up front," she replied, a real pro.

Exasperated, he pulled out his wallet, looked her over and decided what was, to him, an equitable price for the night. It didn't matter, since he'd get it back anyway. He handed her three hundred dollars.

"All right!" She got in, giddy. "Hell of a night," she remarked.

"Since I give you a down payment, you can give me a down payment, sweetheart," he said, getting in and driving down the block. "A *down* payment, get it?" he loosened his fly as the car pulled into a deserted alleyway.

She raised her shoulders, "Sure, if that's what you want. You're the man in charge, sugar." She sidled over and put her hand about his manhood, dipping over it, teasing at first as Sorentino's clenched teeth let out a seething sound of contentment and expectation when suddenly the cold end of a gun barrel was plastered against his temple.

"What the hell's going on!"

The woman rushed from the car, saying, "He's all yours! Enjoy! I didn't!" She spat and hurried away.

It was a setup. The bitch was paid to set him up, and he'd paid her also.

"Get lost, honey!" shouted the gunman whose face could not be seen by Sorentino.

"Yeah, sure . . . sure," she said rushing to obey.

"And you never seen either of us!"

Sorentino pleaded. "What the hell's going on, man, what you got against me?"

347

"A kid named Jeff Blum."

Sorentino recognized the name as the dead cop in Lanark's division. "Wait . . . that wasn't my fault, man!"

"Go on, Sorentino, spill your brave guts all over the car. I'll do the same for your brains."

"Fuckin' Feds sent you, didn't they? Didn't they?"

"Eat this," he said, about to pull the trigger when Sorentino began blubbering, begging for his life and covering his face with his hands, when suddenly he went for a hidden gun holstered to his chest, insurance against such a thing as this. But before he could slide the weapon out, the contents of his skull exploded all over the dashboard and he was dead, the horn on the car a requiem to him.

The hole put through Sorentino was massive, the work of a large caliber Magnum at close range. The instant the cop got back to his motel room where he was registered under a false name, he'd wash thoroughly and destroy the clothes he wore. As for the gun, it could never be traced back to the cop from the 13th Precinct of Chicago, since it had belonged to one Tavalez Sorentino, confiscated during a raid and never catalogued. Nobody would be any the wiser, except maybe Jeff Blum, who might rest comfortably in his grave now that Tavalez Sorentino had gone to the Devil.

**CRITICALLY ACCLAIMED MYSTERIES
FROM ED MCBAIN AND PINNACLE BOOKS!**

BEAUTY AND THE BEAST   (17-134, $3.95)
When a voluptuous beauty is found dead, her body bound with
coat hangers and burned to a crisp, it is up to lawyer Matthew
Hope to wade through the morass of lies, corruption and sexual
perversion to get to the shocking truth! The world-renowned author of over fifty acclaimed mystery novels is back—with a
vengeance.

"A REAL CORKER . . . A DEFINITE PAGE-TURNER."
— *USA TODAY*
"HIS BEST YET."
— *THE DETROIT NEWS*
"A TIGHTLY STRUCTURED, ABSORBING MYSTERY"
— *THE NEW YORK TIMES*

JACK & THE BEANSTALK   (17-083, $3.95)
Jack McKinney is dead, stabbed fourteen times, and thirty-six
thousand dollars in cash is missing. West Florida attorney Matthew Hope's questions are unearthing some long-buried pasts, a
second dead body, and some gorgeous suspects. Florida's getting
hotter by deadly degrees—as Hope bets it all against a scared
killer with nothing left to lose!

"ED MCBAIN HAS ANOTHER WINNER."
— *THE SAN DIEGO UNION*
"A CRACKING GOOD READ . . . SOLID, SUSPENSEFUL,
SWIFTLY-PACED"
— *PITTSBURGH POST-GAZETTE*

*Available wherever paperbacks are sold, or order direct from the
Publisher. Send cover price plus 50¢ per copy for mailing and
handling to Pinnacle Books, Dept.17-239, 475 Park Avenue
South, New York, N.Y. 10016. Residents of New York, New Jer-
sey and Pennsylvania must include sales tax. DO NOT SEND
CASH.*

THE EXECUTIONER
by Don Pendleton

Available wherever paperbacks are sold, or order direct from the Publisher. Send cover price plus 50¢ per copy for mailing and handling to Pinnacle Books, Dept. 17-239, 475 Park Avenue South, New York, N.Y. 10016. Residents of New York, New Jersey and Pennsylvania must include sales tax. DO NOT SEND CASH.

THE DESTROYER
By Warren Murphy and Richard Sapir

Available wherever paperbacks are sold, or order direct from the Publisher. Send cover price plus 50¢ per copy for mailing and handling to Pinnacle Books, Dept. 17-239, 475 Park Avenue South, New York, N.Y. 10016. Residents of New York, New Jersey and Pennsylvania must include sales tax. DO NOT SEND CASH.